ack Strange is a writer fro
nd mystery, both with gay
s both a journalist during the week, and a bookseller
veekends, and somehow finds the time to fit in writing stories
vith representation, fun, and love at the forefront. With a degree
n English Literature and Creative Writing, Jack enjoys being
reative, whether it be hosting podcasts, writing articles, or
reating characters.

ack lived in Vancouver, Canada, before moving back home to
Vales. He lives with his boyfriend, and their three cats, Bali, Mrs
Moo, and Dolly. When he isn't writing, he's reading and sharing
is reads on Instagram, TikTok and YouTube. You might also find
im reading tarot cards online and at festivals.

instagram.com/JackStrangeAuthor

tiktok.com/@JackStrangeAuthor

x.com/JackStrangeBook

facebook.com/JackStrangeAuhthor

LOOK UP, HANDSOME

JACK STRANGE

One More Chapter
a division of HarperCollins*Publishers* Ltd
1 London Bridge Street
London SE1 9GF
www.harpercollins.co.uk
HarperCollins*Publishers*
Macken House, 39/40 Mayor Street Upper,
Dublin 1, D01 C9W8, Ireland

This paperback edition 2024
1
First published in Great Britain in ebook format
by HarperCollins*Publishers* 2024
Copyright © Jack Strange 2024
Jack Strange asserts the moral right to be identified
as the author of this work

A catalogue record of this book is available from the British Library

ISBN: 978-0-00-865958-5

Printed and bound in the UK using 100% Renewable Electricity
by CPI Group (UK) Ltd

To the Strange family. All my love.

Playlist

My Only Wish (This Year) - Britney Spears ♥
Santa Tell Me - Ariana Grande ♥
All I Want for Xmas is You - Mariah Carey ♥
Hey Sis, it's Christmas - RuPaul ♥
Not Tonight Santa - Girls Aloud ♥
Jingle Bell Rock - Lindsay Lohan ♥
One More Sleep - Leona Lewis ♥
Merry Christmas Everyone - Shakin' Stevens ♥
Mary's Boy Child - Boney M. ♥
Mistletoe - Justin Bieber ♥
Last Christmas - Wham! ♥
Love Story - Taylor Swift ♥
Old Flames - Kesha, Dolly Parton ♥
Talking Body - Tove Lo ♥
Back To You - Selena Gomez ♥
Gimmie! Gimmie! Gimmie! - Cher ♥
Unwritten - Natasha Bedingfield ♥
Everybody - Backstreet Boys ♥

Chapter One

Everything changed when he first saw Noah Sage. He loved those romantic tropes: your breath catches in your chest, your heart beats fast, you shake. He'd always laugh when he read those romance books with their cute moments. Only that was fiction. It didn't happen in real life.

But no, all of that happened. Every bit of it.

Standing in a crowd, lined up at the entrance to the Hay-on-Wye winter literature festival, were two women screaming like groupies at a rock show. They drew looks of disapproval from the uptight literature crowd who came to the festival to absorb 'culture, darling', and nothing more. Amongst all the literature highbrows were the avid book readers of Noah Sage's successful romantic book series, all of them wrapped in coats and woolly hats to shield them from the cold December weather. The die-hard romance fans outnumbered the 'culture, darling' fans, their introverted tendencies overpowered by their need to be seen and meet their literary idol.

Quinn Oxford had read every Noah Sage novel from cover to cover. As one of Hay's booksellers, he needed to know the new releases, especially when written by someone who was part of the queer community. He owned Kings & Queens, a bookshop selling queer literature, or anything written by queer authors, which, of course, meant Noah's books. Plus, he loved romance novels and carried no shame about it. What could he say? He was a sucker for happy endings.

Not the massage kind.

Kind of.

'All of this for a *romance* writer?' A passing voice said, as Noah Sage's black Bentley came driving down the path cleared of snow.

The screams gained volume as a window rolled down and the face of Noah Sage came into view.

That was when everything changed.

The screams disappeared and the surrounding crowd melted like the snow at their feet. Noah's car seemed to go by in slow motion, and then stop altogether when Noah's eyes met his.

Those green, green eyes. Lusciously green, like the Welsh hills. Oh, how they sparkled. They looked deep, inviting. They were hypnotising.

Did he admire my blue eyes and the way I stared at him, taking in every part of him I could?

Did the world stop for him, like getting lost in the perfect book?

Did he see me and only me, with my wavy black hair, my cosy jumper, my lightly freckled face? Could he even make out my features like I could his?

Somehow these thoughts came to Quinn as he stood there, feeling a connection between him and the romance writer. His heart beat so heavily in his chest that he thought the surrounding cage may break. He swallowed, his mouth dry. He panicked because he couldn't breathe.

He had last felt like this during an allergic reaction to penicillin. This was less frightening.

Never had he seen a man so perfect.

Quinn couldn't go there. Love wasn't on his mind right now. Not after... Well, it didn't matter.

And then Noah was gone, the two girls next to him feigning a faint.

'He looked right at me!'

'Me too!'

'Did you see those eyes?'

He deflated. So, everyone else experienced the same thing. The culture lovers and die-hard romance fans alike, star-struck, and all drawn in by the writer everyone loved and read.

The Bentley disappeared into the makeshift car park of the infamous festival. Every year, the Hay-on-Wye literary festival sprang up in the same field, white gazebos popping up along the Welsh landscape like wild mushrooms. The summer was the liveliest, when people flocked from all over, not only enjoying the literature that the world offered but also enjoying the rare, hot British summer. It was always sunny in Hay.

Except for when it snowed. Like now.

The winter festival was popular, and being so close to Christmas, people came to enjoy festive shopping. Down the road was the famous Hay town, full of bookshops and a book reader's heaven.

'Have you got tickets to his show?'

Quinn turned to see Ivy Heart standing next to him. He hadn't seen her arrive; such was the way with Ivy. She seemed to sprout and pop up when you least expected her.

'Of course.'

'Me too. Let's go together!'

Before Quinn could say anything, her hand, full of rings with glittering jewels, grasped his, and she escorted him across the field to the ticket entrance.

They scanned their tickets and entered the festival under the canvas canopy. Wooden walkways stretched away from them to different stages, all housed in similar gazebos. The atmosphere here was lively, with people browsing pop-up bookshops, buying from local makers, or drinking at the makeshift bars. The aroma of hot chocolate, gingerbread biscuits and sizzling food made Quinn's stomach rumble.

'Champagne?' a young waitress asked.

'I'll take two,' Ivy declared. Quinn held his hand out, expecting her to give him a glass. 'Oh, no. Both for me!'

The server smiled as Quinn took his own glass; the bubbles fizzed inside, and they strolled further into the festival.

'I can't wait for Stephen Fry's talk,' a passer-by said.

'And Margaret Atwood!' another said. 'I heard Dua Lipa is interviewing her!'

'Shame it clashed with the talk by André Aciman.'

'Ah, books,' Ivy said with a deep breath. 'Count ourselves lucky we live in this area of the world, Quinn. It's just magic, isn't it?'

'I love it,' Quinn agreed. 'One of my favourite times of the year.'

Magic was the right word. Enchanting fairy lights crisscrossed above the walkways from the top of the canvas tents, glittering a warm yellow. Decorated Christmas trees were on every corner, their tinsel and baubles hanging with precision.

'Christmas is your favourite time of the year?'

'I think so,' Quinn said. 'Who wouldn't love it?'

'Worn-out people spending too much money because they get pressured by society,' Ivy deadpanned. 'Me? I prefer Halloween.'

Quinn observed the rings on her fingers, the glittering amethyst necklace around her neck, and her hair tied up in a stylish bun. 'I wouldn't have thought you were big on your horror.'

'Not the horror side of things, Quinn.' Ivy laughed. 'No, the spiritual side. Samhain. The veil is thin between our world and theirs.'

Quinn paused. 'Theirs?'

'Theirs.' Ivy's eyes widened. 'The dearly departed.'

'Of course.'

4

'You don't believe?'

'No, I do,' Quinn said. 'I haven't thought much about it.'

'No, people seldom do. It offends them.'

Ivy Heart intrigued him from the moment her flyer arrived through the door of his shop, a business card with her name attached, a name sure to catch attention. She ran a cleaning company, and the locals loved her. She carried herself well; a confident woman with an answer for everything. People were mesmerised by her as she walked by, how she shook her head and her hair fanned out around her. She was tall, athletic, beautiful, stylish. She gave off the vibe of a woman who loved herself, but not in a conceited way. Quinn thought that if she were to write an autobiography, it would be titled *Confidence and Class*.

'How's your bookshop looking? Sparkling clean?'

'I keep on top of things.' Quinn sipped his drink.

'You know where I am if you need help.'

'You saying my shop doesn't pass the cleaning test?'

Ivy grinned. 'I'm saying, why waste time cleaning when you could focus on selling books?'

Quinn nodded, savouring the champagne.

'How is the shop going? Business booming as usual?'

'Always.' Quinn smiled, but he hoped Ivy didn't sense how he forced it.

'It baffles me how these bookshops survive when there are so many of them.'

Quinn lifted his glass. 'Thank the man responsible, Richard Booth.'

'He's pleased you toasted him.'

Quinn looked around them, as if he might see the flamboyant ghost of Richard Booth, Hay's pioneer, float through the crowd.

Outside the tent hosting the talk with Noah Sage, the line of people entering included the two women Quinn had been standing next to. 'Now, don't embarrass us this time, June,' one said. She clutched all three books from Noah's romance series. 'Don't do what you did last time.'

'I didn't do anything last time, Deb!'

'You stormed up on stage with him and demanded he sign your teapot,' Deb said. 'It was mortifying!'

'It was *not* a teapot,' June hissed, blushing. 'It was a tea *cosy*.'

'Same thing. Let the man speak and we'll get him to sign things afterwards.'

Quinn and Ivy followed June and Deb into the tent, where string lights created a warm glow over bustling bodies. Already the seating area was almost full, and they walked to the back row and sat at the end closest to the aisle. Two shimmering Christmas trees lit up the stage with wrapped presents underneath and a projected image of Noah on the black wall.

'Wow, good view,' Ivy said. 'We'll see him in all his glory.'

Quinn stopped, his thoughts drifting to something a little more inappropriate. He sipped his champagne just as Ivy made a start on her second. As the hum of chatter engulfed him like a warm bath, he looked at Noah's image, which definitely didn't need any airbrushing. Somehow, through photos, he still had that piercing stare, one that was welcoming, yet seemed to suggest something more. Kind of like he knew something you didn't. It kept Quinn frozen to the spot, like staring at his eyes was a competition he couldn't lose.

The image of Noah changed to a familiar face, that of television personality Blair Beckett. The audience swooned at the man on the screen with a well-trimmed beard and sleek black hair. It looked like he'd been caught unaware while adjusting a crisp white shirt, its three buttons undone, with just a glimpse of his chest hair. His eyes held less command than Noah's, but they were dark and crinkled at the side, a smize that rivalled Tyra Banks.

'Bloody Blair Beckett,' Quinn grumbled.

'You don't like him?'

'I think he brings bias to the news,' Quinn said. 'He can't help but slot his opinion into the report, and it becomes more about Blair Beckett than it does about, say, social injustices.'

'He's a well-respected news reader.'

'Well, good for him.' Quinn shrugged. 'I also don't like that he can just put his name on a children's book and *bam*, he's a children's author.'

'But he wrote it.'

'Did he?'

Ivy paused for a moment. 'The spirits say yes.'

'Well-read spirits.'

'I think he's quite handsome.'

'So does everyone in this room.' So did he, but he couldn't say that.

The lights dimmed, and people erupted in applause. Quinn joined in the applause as Bloody Blair Beckett came on the stage, not a hair out of place and a beaming smile on his flawless face, followed by Noah, who cast Blair's handsome features into shadow.

'Hello, hello!' Blair's voice rang out over the audience, and Quinn was almost certain the people in front of him might faint. They were screaming so much they hadn't caught their breath. 'Let's get the lights on you all. I want to see you!'

The audience got louder, and the house lights lit up the crowd. Ivy flailed her arms, lost in the excitement. The champagne in her flute came sloshing towards Quinn, landing straight in his lap, creating a damp patch.

'Ivy!' Quinn leapt to his feet, feeling the chill reach places chill should never be. 'I'm wet!'

The last words echoed around the room. The house lights seemed to act as a spotlight for the wet patch on his grey trousers. Quinn realised every eye was on him.

'Do you need help there?' Bloody Blair Beckett asked, a look of concern on that perfect face of his.

'No, it's okay, just an accident.' Quinn winced. An accident?

7

Now everyone thought he was incontinent! June clasped a hand to her mouth while Deb looked disgusted. Why did he choose today of all days to wear his heather grey trousers, the ones that felt so soft on his skin, and now clung to his crotch with a chill colder than the snow outside? He stumbled down the stairs, his footsteps louder than a crashing giant. Walking in front of the stage, the spotlight illuminating him, he heard an audible gasp from the audience.

'Good lord. The man *has* wet himself!'

Some people laughed; others made little muttering sounds. Quinn eyed the stage, his eyes finding Noah's.

Noah took all of him in, looking him up and down.

'I'll be right back,' Quinn heard himself say as he wished the ground would split and he would fall through the cracks. 'Carry on without me!'

He stumbled through the doors as the audience resumed their applause, just as Blair Beckett cracked a joke about excitement getting the better of people.

'Bloody Blair Beckett,' Quinn groaned.

Chapter Two

'Quinn, there you are!'

Ivy rushed to him, but he turned his attention to his Welsh brewed beer, staring into the glass with discontent. Fizzing beer had never been so interesting. 'Leave me alone.'

He wore a pair of tie-dye elasticated harem trousers, something that was being sold on a self-confessed hippie stall for an extortionate price. They clung to his ankles, almost cutting off the blood supply. His grey trousers, still wet with champagne, were in the cloakroom for him to collect later. He felt like a fool.

'These look very good on you,' Ivy spoke, admiring his new trousers. 'The colours suit your aura.'

'Ivy, not now.' He slurped his beer like he was at his lowest ebb, willing away the pain inside.

'Look, I'm sorry, I got excited.' She sighed. 'Besides, nobody talked about it after…'

'After Bloody Blair Beckett joked about it, yeah,' Quinn said. 'I missed the whole thing.'

'I wondered if you were going to come back.'

Quinn turned to her, fighting back tears. 'How could I? Everyone thought I'd wet myself!'

Those nearest at the bar looked at Quinn with concern. Ivy shook her head in a way that said, 'I'll deal with this', and they nodded with sympathy.

'I told them it was champagne. Besides, people forgot as soon as Noah started speaking. You would have *loved* it, honestly. It was *so* good, Quinn. He spoke about his romance novels, but he also spoke about queer stories. I asked him why he hadn't written one yet, and he said he was thinking about it.'

Quinn perked up, almost forgetting about his ordeal. 'He did?'

'Oh, yes.' Ivy smiled. 'And now he's doing his book signing at the bookshop tent, and I think you should come with me to meet him.'

'Ivy, no, I can't.'

The last thing he wanted was to meet a man he fancied who no doubt thought he had pissed himself.

'You absolutely can!' She touched his arm again, the rings cold on his skin. 'He won't remember. No one will. They will be too excited to see Noah!'

'Ivy, no.'

Ivy cocked an eyebrow. 'You always do this, Quinn. You shy away from moments that could change your life.'

Quinn wanted to tell Ivy that life-changing moments never happened to him. Average life, average person. The most average man to ever live.

'But these.'

They both looked at his trousers, garish and brash.

'They are perfect.' Ivy said, with no sense of irony. 'Now come. Bring your beer with you.'

She took his hand, and clutching his pint, he allowed her to usher him across the bar area. They swayed over to the pop-up bookshop. That was the thing about Ivy – she navigated the cramped festival like there was no one around. People moved for her, smiling as they did so, and she thanked every one of them with genuine enthusiasm. He supposed that if they were looking at her, they weren't looking at him and his trousers that felt like they might catch flight if a gust of wind came through. Quinn couldn't see through all the people, but when those nearest to them parted, he could see Noah. Despite the other authors signing away, Noah had the biggest line. At the corner of the room stood Deb and June, who both looked like they were arguing over a signed tea cosy.

'Well, Deb, you know I bought you that after all.'

'No, this belonged to my grandmother.'

'No, no, I remember buying it from Hay market.'

'Well, explain this bloodstain then!'

Ivy dragged Quinn away before anyone could question why a tea cosy had blood on it.

Quinn took a deep breath as he took in the crowd. He craved the sanctuary of his bookshop. A row of shelves on all sides of the tent were full of people reading blurbs, adding things to their baskets, and talking. Despite the cold weather outside, the chill didn't reach the tent. Electric heaters glowed Santa Claus red, and the same fairy lights from outside twinkled here in the tent, too. Christmas music played over the speaker, but it didn't feel gaudy. Instead, it added to the cosy atmosphere; warmth radiated from every passer-by.

'They're saying a white Christmas, you know,' Ivy said.

'That'll be surprising.'

'Will it?'

Quinn didn't answer. Anxiety twisted in his stomach, his legs feeling like that time he overexerted himself on a treadmill without eating and then never went back.

Maybe that was because of the cut-off blood supply.

'What are you going to say to him when you meet him?'

'Nothing, Ivy.'

'Nothing? Say *something*.'

Quinn was more than happy to say nothing at all. He didn't have to have a conversation with Noah Sage because staring at him for too long would turn him to stone. Not because he was Medusa or anything. His hair was too perfect to be compared to hissing snakes, but Noah's looks were enough to petrify him.

He struggled to speak his mind at the best of times. Telling Noah how much he loved his books and wanted to know everything he could about him was not an option.

'Come on, there he is.'

They joined the back of the queue, miles away from Noah. The pile of Noah Sage books on the nearby round table was dwindling. Quinn recognised other authors who were about to finish their signings early or were twiddling their thumbs, waiting for any last stragglers.

Quinn watched Noah as they got closer, and closer, and too close, no, this was too close. He was all smiles, ever the professional. His teeth were perfect: straight and a Hollywood white done by professionals and not with whitening strips ordered from Amazon like Quinn tried once. He bared a dazzling grin for photographs, asked every person about their day, signed with accuracy and speed, and wished them farewell.

Quinn's heart started beating faster as they got closer. He realised he didn't have any books with him. What would he ask Noah to sign? He thought about the blood-covered tea cosy and wondered if it was too late to go back and ask if he could borrow it.

His throat tightened. Was his tongue swelling?

'Your throat chakra's blocked,' Ivy said.

'My throat is very wide. Thank you very much.'

Ivy held her own copies, the covers crumpled at the edges, well read. She chatted away, telling him about something he couldn't focus on. With every step they took, it was like he couldn't remember how to walk. What if Noah asked about his accident? How would he explain it was champagne? That, yes, he was an adult, and yes, he had full control of when and how he peed. That no, he didn't sit there and release. Would he even be able to say one word, with that thumping heart of his, the dry throat and mouth, the shakes that made him question why he was getting so flustered over a man he only knew by name?

You're being silly. You're star-struck.

Yes, that was it. Star-struck. This was one of the most famous authors of the moment. That's all this was: overwhelming feelings of complete disbelief that he was in the presence of someone with so much media attention and exposure.

This must be what groupies feel like when they first meet their favourite rock star. Only the groupies end up joining the band on tour, and they get up to many devious and fascinating deeds, and then rush to the clinic for antibiotics two weeks later. This would simply be a 'hello, I didn't wet myself,' and that would be that. If he could even string a sentence together.

Quinn met many authors. You couldn't own Hay's very own—and only—bookshop dedicated to queer stories without meeting writers. People came from all over to browse his selections on everything from LGBTQ+ history to the latest gay novel. He created a staple piece on the scene here in Hay, which made the ordeal in the tent such an embarrassment. People who lived here knew him. He did not want that to be something that was brought up all the time.

Quinn tried to recall being star-struck over other authors he'd met in this small Welsh town that straddled the English border. He was no stranger to author signings, whether they be in his own shop or at someone else's. He'd spent many a night at a pub chatting away about writing and books with authors, with writers, and with those who devoured every page they could get their hands on.

So why was this feeling so intense? So scary?

A simple high school crush? Maybe.

Two people separated them now, with Noah's eyes fixed on the person in front of him. He didn't know that Quinn was about to arrive.

So, calm down, Quinn told himself. *He sees so many faces that he will not remember you. It was dark anyway. Those house lights weren't as bright as you think.*

But that stare. That moment when everything stood still. Had he imagined it?

And then it happened again. Next in line. Noah looked up. Quinn looked away, but not before his eyes met with those green eyes once more.

Such was the standstill moment of the situation that Quinn didn't see the man with the headset approach. He didn't see the pretty black-haired girl, who had been on the phone, head towards Noah.

'I'm sorry, ladies and gents, but he has to go,' said the man with the headset.

'Oh, dear,' Ivy said.

What was happening?

Noah got to his feet, the woman next to him telling him about something, the man with the headset looking tense but apologetic as he explained to Ivy, to Quinn, to the queue growing behind them that Noah had done his time, and that signed copies would be available on the bookstand.

'I'm very sorry,' Noah said, and for the first time, Quinn thought he looked tense. Up close, that carefree persona wasn't as convincing. Perhaps because he was moments away from meeting a man who people thought wet himself.

Quinn looked at Noah one last time, part of him wanting to savour ever being so close to a man of his stature, another part of him wanting to feed the curiosity that was gnawing away inside him. His heart squeezed, and it flipped, when he saw Noah watching him.

'Nice trousers,' Noah said, before turning away and

disappearing into the crowd with the girl and the man with the headset.

That *voice*, thick with the sing-song Welsh lilt, gentle yet firm.

'Oh. My. God,' Ivy gasped. 'I told you! They are *gorge* on you!'

With stinging cheeks, shaking and aching legs, and a thudding heart, Quinn threw back the pint he was holding until it was empty.

Chapter Three

'It was awful, Dad, awful. The man thought I'd wet myself.'

Quinn shivered in the graveyard underneath an ancient yew tree. Turns out, thin fabric hippie trousers were not the most practical thing to wear in the icy depths of winter. With a gloved hand, he brushed aside the snow from his father's gravestone. Despite the darkening sky, it felt light here, almost if the light came from the heavens.

He'd said goodbye to Ivy, promising to meet her at the local pub later in the evening. He held a bag with his wet trousers. After today's ordeal, he needed time to himself. Except he wasn't by himself. Not when he came here.

Quinn observed a fresh bouquet lying beneath his father's name: GERALD OXFORD. Even seeing his name made Quinn want to cry. He wondered if his mother left the flowers lying in the snow. He didn't even know for certain if Claire still visited the grave. They didn't talk about Gerald often, if at all, and his grave was definitely not something to bring up in conversation.

Quinn crouched so that Gerald's name was eye level.

'Did Mum leave you these? I wish you could tell me. I know what you're thinking – why don't I just ask her myself? In all honesty, Dad, I don't want to.' Quinn sighed, white mist floating before him. 'She's so... Well, I doubt you want to know about Harold. But ever since he came around, she's ... different.'

Talking about his mother out in the open felt strange. He glanced around the snow-covered graveyard, almost expecting that people would watch him like he was performing a soliloquy. But underneath the yew tree, everything felt so private. Gerald's plot felt secluded, even though it was in a long line of passed souls, some of whom no longer got visitors.

He couldn't recall how he'd started talking to his father like this. Since his death, Quinn needed someone to listen to him. He found it hard to talk to people when they were in front of him, as if they might judge him. His father's dead ear wouldn't judge. His father wouldn't judge full stop. Gerald always had time for Quinn and he never felt like a burden. He had been more to him than just a father – he was a friend and a trusted source of comfort.

Losing that ruined Quinn. When Gerald died, Quinn lost his confidence. The ability to talk to others seemed to die when his father did.

A red robin landed on Gerald's gravestone, holding a twig with a red berry in its petite beak. Quinn smiled.

'You're listening, Dad,' Quinn said.

When Gerald had been alive, a Reliant Robin was a staple piece in the town. Shining red, it would always be parked outside of Gerald's bookshop, drawing stares of admiration from locals and tourists. Quinn remembered as a child clambering in the odd-shaped car and feeling like he was in a spaceship.

Robins always reminded him of his dad.

'Anyway, back to that romantic novelist. I think you would have liked him. His books are fantastic. They sweep me up in ways other romance books can't do. Something about his writing speaks to me, you know?' The robin hopped. 'No, it has nothing to do with the fact that he's fit.'

The robin cocked its head, the twig shifting.

'What else is there to tell you?'

The robin fluttered its wings, and Quinn feared it would fly away, breaking the connection Quinn had, or at least thought he had, with the red-breasted bird.

Instead, the bird fixed him with a stare, the way it always seemed to do whenever Quinn visited the graveyard between Hay and the neighbouring valley of Cusop Dingle.

'Shop is going okay,' Quinn said, because telling the truth to his dead father was out of the question. 'I've got someone helping me out now. Always feel like I've made it if I have an extra pair of hands to help me. Like my business is growing, you know? His name is Daniel Craig.'

The bird hopped, and Quinn laughed.

'I know. Unfortunately, he looks nothing like Bond. He's straight, too, before you get any ideas. Not bad-looking, but you know. Straight. I had my apprehensions about bringing a straight guy into the fold. Not that there's anything wrong with straight guys, Dad.' Quinn cleared his throat. 'As far as I know, you were one yourself. No, it's just that the bookshop has this safe feeling to it. A place where people can speak openly if they want to, and without fear of any sort of judgement. Hard to do when someone is straight and you've been told you're wrong all your life by, well, straight people.'

The robin fluttered to the roses, inspecting them. Quinn fought back tears. This was a robin. Only a robin. But he couldn't help but let his imagination run away with him that this was a sign from his father, and that the robin would go back to wherever his father was and tell him all about the beautiful roses.

'I guess you can call him an ally. He's quite interested in reading about sexuality and the like.'

The robin flew up and away, disappearing into the murky grey landscape.

Quinn sighed, smiling.

'Maybe I'm boring you,' he said, getting back to his feet. 'I'll be back soon. Miss you. Love you.'

For a moment, he didn't want to go away. The world waited for him out there, and he didn't know that he could face it at this moment. But the trousers weren't protecting his legs, and his feet had turned to ice. He trudged away from the yew tree, from his dad and the roses, and walked back towards the village of Hay.

It was then that he saw someone standing in the otherwise deserted graveyard. Quinn could only make out the side profile of a man close to the only entrance. Quinn needed to bypass him to get out and get back to his shop before closing. He had little time, but there was no way he could go any further.

It was also impossible that the man stood staring at another grave was Noah Sage.

No, his eyes were playing tricks on him. A cruel trick of the winter light.

Quinn took the path, averting his eyes, hoping he wouldn't have to see the figure.

But as he got closer, his footsteps trudging through the snow, the person turned to see who approached.

It *was* Noah Sage.

Of all places, why would Noah Sage be here, in this graveyard? The only two people surrounded by departed souls. Or at least, the bodies that once housed them.

'Hippie guy,' Noah said, taking in his parachute trousers, and Quinn wanted to dig his own grave and get in it. 'Fancy seeing you here.'

Why was he speaking to him like that? Like they were friends? Familiar? This felt like he'd fallen and bumped his head, and now he was hallucinating.

'Cat got your tongue?'

Balls. 'You're Noah Sage.'

Great. That will do. State the obvious and wonder why Noah

stepped away from him. Because now he looked like one of those fans that wanted Noah desperately. Which he did, but not in the way those fans wanted him.

Well, maybe like Deb and June wanted him.

'That's right, I am.' A red blush crept up Noah's neck. 'And you are?'

'Going,' Quinn said. 'Have to dash.'

'Do you always hang around in graveyards?'

It was a warm question, a gorgeous smile on his rosy-cheeked face. God, he wanted to pinch those cheeks, but he couldn't because that is frowned upon. Pinching cheeks in graveyards was also a little weird.

Somewhere in the distance, he heard the tweet of a robin.

'Under the yew tree,' Quinn said, and then wanted to kick himself.

'I see.' Noah paused. 'You know, those trousers remind me of a parachute.'

Quinn wondered if he would ever be able to forget about this day and these trousers with their patchwork and their soft fabric. The way Noah stared at him, admiring the trousers like they were his own creation, would be seared on his mind like a tattoo.

'You're visiting someone.' Quinn nodded at the icy tombstone in front of Noah, so he would stop staring at him. He didn't want to catch the name, but couldn't help seeing the last name Sage. A relative of Noah's?

'I guess I am,' Noah said. 'Do you work here or something?'

'Me? Work at a graveyard? No,' Quinn said. 'Who works at graveyards?'

'Gravediggers, caretakers, cemetery workers,' Noah listed, and his gloved hand looked absolutely adorable and not at all like it would hold Quinn's hand perfectly.

'I'm not any of those,' Quinn said. 'Like I said, I'm going.'

And digging his own grave with every word he spoke.

'Alright, well, nice meeting you, hippie guy,' Noah said.

He would *not* be called hippie guy.

But alas, Quinn said nothing, because words evaded him. He squeaked and trudged away, wishing, hoping, praying that maybe he had fallen and bumped his head, and this was all some weird dream.

Chapter Four

How are you doing?

Dougie. Why did he always text at such inappropriate moments?

Every time the text came through, it knocked Quinn off his feet. Not because of those romantic clichés, but because every time he thought he was over this man, he came back to remind him of everything they once had.

Quinn stood outside his shop on Castle Street where foundation walls from the thirteenth century met the nineteenth. His shop, Kings & Queens, looked inviting with warm yellow lights, a perfect example of Victorian architecture.

'You okay? You look like you've seen a ghost.'

Daniel Craig, not the man who played Bond, exited the shop. He held his set of keys in his hand, ready to lock up.

'Oh, yeah, no, fine.' Quinn struggled to find his words. 'I'm just going to deal with something in the shop. You go home and have a nice evening.'

'You sure?'

'I'm sure,' Quinn said. 'How has today been?'

'Wonderful. Always wonderful.' Daniel's tote bag swung at his shoulder, full of books. 'Some reading materials.'

'That's good,' Quinn said, moving past Daniel to get to the shop entrance. 'Thanks for your help.'

'See you soon,' Daniel said, before stopping.

'What?'

'Those trousers look good on you.'

Quinn recalled his ordeal with Noah in the graveyard. The hippie trousers struck again.

'Go home, Daniel. You're tired.'

Daniel saluted, smirking, and headed to wherever it was he lived. Quinn looked at the converted church building and up to his apartment window above his shop, where a lot of nicer clothes waited for him.

The longer he stayed out on the street, the bigger the opportunity for people to see his hippie trousers. He headed into the shop and closed the door behind him, leaning against the wood and taking a deep breath.

The champagne. The spotlight. Noah.

He couldn't think any more about it.

Kings & Queens was his labour of love. Once falling apart, it was now perfect. Queer flags flitted from the ceiling, and across the bookshelves, from trans representation to asexual recognition. Lines of books stacked on oak shelves, reaching up to the ceiling. Good on Daniel Craig to align the books before leaving. Christmas table displays selling *A Christmas Carol* glittered under the twinkling lights strung between the aisles.

The floor, reinforced varnished wood, creaked under his feet. The place used to be Hay's very own church centuries ago. Now, it was a place of safety for a community Quinn felt needed serving in Hay.

He placed his wet trousers in a paper bag at the foot of his checkout counter.

His phone buzzed again, and the peace and serenity came crashing to the ground. Tense, he looked at the text message on the screen.

I miss you.

Dougie.

Dougie had broken up with Quinn almost six months ago. It had been hard because he left when things started getting tough for Quinn. He didn't share his concerns when Dougie announced he needed to leave. It also didn't help that Dougie left on their one-year anniversary.

Classy.

'I'm moving,' Dougie declared in this very shop. 'To Cardiff.'

He said it as though the city was the most foreign, faraway land in the world. Not an hour and twenty minutes away.

'And I think we should see other people,' Dougie finished.

Quinn couldn't even remember what happened after that. All he could think of was that above them, his apartment was decorated for their one-year anniversary. That night should have been special.

Until Dougie, Quinn had let no one in. Who needed love? He much preferred getting lost in the pages of romance novels. That way, he couldn't get hurt.

He also knew that Dougie had walked all over him.

Quinn was notorious for letting people do that to him. Only Dougie was the one with the heaviest feet.

A defence mechanism, maybe. But he never fought back. He hated confrontation to begin with. Then he doubted his own knowledge when making a point. Yes, it was much better to appease the other person by nodding along and giving them three bags full, sir. And those romance novels let him escape to a world where the men were perfect, and people like him owned their beliefs.

Quinn let Dougie, his first love, step over him on his way out. Six months later, he had moved on and fallen back into the rhythm of life before Dougie.

Now that rhythm was hit with the blues. His phone buzzed.

> Cardiff isn't the same without you.

When had he even been in Cardiff with him?

It wasn't like they had any memories there.

His phone buzzed again, and this time an image of Dougie's dick graced his screen.

He exited the text, as if a crowd of people surrounded him and might see him looking at something so inappropriate.

What a way to make an apology.

If that was even what it was.

Who said I miss you and then sent you a dick pic?

Guys like Dougie. Guys like Noah wouldn't do such a thing.

He considered typing back. Maybe saying don't text me again. An eye roll emoji, perhaps. Or just block his number.

These thoughts left his mind as quickly as they entered. He would say nothing, and hope that it would go away. It was something Quinn always did.

His eyes drifted to the counter at the window, lingering on a drawer.

Yes. Everything goes away if you just ignore it.

I'll ignore this.

But could he ignore his trousers? Quinn observed them, complimented by Noah, adored by Ivy. Perhaps they weren't so bad, after all. He'd keep them on. He considered himself calm enough to spend an evening with Ivy. He didn't want to be sitting with her flustered over Dougie and his texts. No, he would put this out of his mind and that would be that. Dougie was horny. He didn't miss him. That was all.

Another message.

Remember this in you?

Quinn ignored the text and left for the pub.

Chapter Five

It was a winter's evening, and Quinn and Ivy found themselves in the Rose & Crown on Broad Street. With flagstone floors, brown beams, and a fire crackling in the fireplace, it oozed traditional British pub. They sat in a window seat on a cushioned bench where they could feel the warmth of the fire. A waiter handed them their third gin and tonic each, garnished with blackberries and an orange peel, and a pint of lemonade to Ivy, before heading back to the busy bar to take more orders.

Quinn, still sitting in his tie-dye trousers, much to Ivy's appreciation, stirred his g&t, the ice clinking against the glass.

'Come on, smile for me,' Ivy pleaded. 'It's not fair to see you so low.'

Quinn forced a smile, but inside he wanted to cry. This morning, he had woken up excited about the day ahead. He couldn't wait to mingle with friends, enjoy the winter literary event, and then go back to work the next day as the festival entered its last weekend. He'd been looking forward to the rush that would happen at his shop, something that came every festival season.

Instead, he found himself as flat as Ivy's lemonade.

'I just keep replaying it in my mind.'

'Oh, stop,' Ivy said. 'It wasn't *that* bad!'

'But it was!'

Quinn hadn't told Ivy about the graveyard because it was too humiliating, and the more he thought about it, the more he was sure it never happened. Weird things transpired in graveyards, and being compared to a parachute by a romance novelist was apparently one of them.

'You know what I like to do in these situations? I like to break them down.' She stirred her gin and tonic. 'So, let's do that. Some champagne spilled on you. It looked like you wet yourself, I'll admit. But that was, what, a minute of your day?'

'And?'

'So, the day has twenty-four hours in it, and you're allowing yourself to feel low over one minute of it?' Ivy asked. 'Look around this room.'

Quinn did as he was told, memories of being in school and being told off by a teacher coming to him. His eyes drifted over the bar, where people gathered, waiting for orders. Every single table in the place was full, with people eating, drinking, socialising. He couldn't recall the last time he saw the Rose & Crown so busy. It was like summer in Hay again. Only a light snowfall had begun outside.

'Notice anything?'

'People.'

'And not one of them looking at you or those trousers!' Ivy smiled. 'See him? And her? And them? Well, they were in the talk. They saw what happened. Are they laughing about it? Are they talking about it? No, they're not. No one remembers it. So why do you?'

'Because *he* saw it.' Quinn sighed. 'Noah Sage!'

Ivy waved a hand, dismissing it straight away. 'No. No, no. He complimented your trousers.'

'Because he remembered what happened!'

'I don't believe in coincidences, Quinn, but this time I do!' Ivy said. 'He genuinely liked them, I can tell.'

'How?'

He hadn't laughed in the graveyard.

'Because you can tell when someone is genuine.' Ivy lifted her drink and took a sip. 'Now, I've had my fair share of embarrassing moments, but you have to learn not to give a damn. Time spent on negative energy is time wasted.'

Quinn drank his gin and tonic. He nodded, leaning back in the booth. He couldn't tell her that Dougie had taken up another five minutes of his day. Since being in the pub, he had received a frenzy of texts, each one getting more aggressive, because not responding to a dick picture was enough to fracture his masculinity. 'Fine. You're right. These gins are helping me forget.'

'You are a drama queen, Quinn!'

'Hey, you don't know that for certain.'

'I'm an expert judge of character, remember?'

Quinn laughed. He enjoyed Ivy's company despite the commotion she caused at the event. It hadn't been her fault. She got excited, like everyone else. The girl wasted champagne, for Christ's sake. That was worse than what had happened to him! If anyone was to blame, it was Bloody Blair Beckett calling for the house lights to come on.

'You're thinking about him, aren't you?'

For a moment, Quinn thought she meant Noah. But judging by the look of sympathy on her face, he knew she meant his father.

'Always.'

'I'm here whenever you need to talk.'

'I know.'

But he would never talk to her. Not about his father. Not even about his mother and how she'd moved on, leaving Quinn behind to find out who he was without his dad around. He looked outside, wishing he would see the robin again, so that he would know everything was going to be okay.

The pub wound down after a busy night, and as they were leaving, their conversation turned to business.

'I set up my cleaning company when I finished university,' Ivy explained as they walked away from the pub and tucked into fish and chips they got from the next-door takeaway. The snow was still falling, heavier now, and their footsteps left a trail behind them. 'We've been going pretty strong ever since.'

'What made you set it up?'

'I wanted to be an architect, and I'm sure I could have been. I qualified. But I tried it and realised why give all my time to someone else, when I could be bettering myself?' Ivy said. 'It hit me on a retreat I went to in Indonesia. I needed to look after myself, mentally, physically, emotionally, and energetically. So, I listened to my spirit, and I did something that I knew I could do but would allow me to live a balanced life.'

Quinn didn't know what type of retreat Ivy went on, and he didn't know how she could look after herself, but he nodded all the same, seeing how she lit up talking about her experience.

'Sounds similar to why I opened the bookshop,' Quinn said as they walked up Lion Street, soft snow compacting under their boots. He could tell, as they stepped gingerly, that tomorrow the pavements and roads would be lethal. In the homes that they walked by, Christmas trees glowed. The butter market, where local traders traded all day, was now deserted, with twinkling lights wrapped around the iron gates. It was cold, but the gin they had consumed numbed the feeling.

Ivy smiled. 'I'm so proud of my business, too. Even though people tell me I could do so much more. They seem to look down on me when I tell them I'm a cleaner.'

'You're not a cleaner,' Quinn said. 'You're an entrepreneur. A successful woman in a world dominated by men.'

'Slay.' Ivy clicked her fingers. 'I don't think I ever asked about why you opened your shop.'

'Well, I went to university and did English literature because I always loved books,' Quinn said. 'I wanted to be a writer. Still *want* to be a writer.'

'Do you write?'

'Yes.'

'Then you're a writer.'

Quinn, feeling a warmth of validation from Ivy's words, took in the looming castle towering on the hill. Lights were on in the downstairs window, the shadows flickering as those inside walked by. The once derelict castle was now being renovated. A poster advertised the grand reopening on Christmas Eve.

They walked along Castle Street, where supermarkets, clothes shops, bakeries and banks met with more bookshops. The town might have been cosy, but it had all they needed. They stopped outside Kings & Queens, turning their backs on the castle.

'And here it is.'

'My favourite shop in town.' Ivy smiled.

Quinn fumbled to find the key for the shop. He swayed, and Ivy steadied him. Both hooted with laughter, forgetting they were outside, forgetting that they might wake people. Finally, the key sliding into the lock, he opened the door to his bookshop, his pride and joy.

In the darkness, he walked to his desk, pushing past the till to switch on a lamp. The dull yellow light illuminated the shop.

Four rows of bookshelves had long since replaced church pews and stretched all the way back to where the original altar remained. Stained-glass windows depicted Christian imagery, which now looked down over glass cabinets of crystals, books, and LGBTQ+ flags.

'Just magic.' Ivy sighed, closing and locking the door behind her.

He let Ivy walk around the shop. Truth is, he needed something like tonight. He threw himself into his work so much that he neglected social life, and had been neglecting friendships and relationships with family. Maybe that was why his

31

relationship with Dougie had failed. Tonight had given him the opportunity to relax and reflect on what was in front of him.

He rearranged his desk, which he had left messy the day before. Daniel Craig hadn't tidied the desk since the time he, Daniel, had tampered with his organised chaos and Quinn went all quiet. Quinn hadn't even needed to say anything. Daniel knew and never did it again. He wasn't a mean boss, but he couldn't say what he wanted out of fear of offending Daniel. After all, he'd only tried to be helpful.

Quinn wrapped receipts together and placed them in the accounts box, then stacked books he needed to price and put on the shelves. He moved his mouse, waking the computer from its sleep mode, and checked his emails, making note of stock enquiries and shipping updates. Behind him, in the bay window, snow billowed in a strong wind.

He could hear Ivy near the back of the shop, humming a Christmas song to herself.

His eyes drifted to a letter he had put to the side. His heart sank. That happy joy inside him extinguished. The blissful numbness left by the gin turned toward a heavy hangover.

Just ignore it and it will go away.

Reaching for the letter and turning it over in his hand, the seal already ripped, he knew he shouldn't read it again. It was better to ignore it. Deal with it tomorrow. That's what he kept telling himself.

But the alcohol had other thoughts.

Despite all his protests, he took the letter out, looking up to make sure that Ivy was nowhere in sight. He unfolded the letter and stared at it, tears spilling onto the paper.

The words FINAL NOTICE OF EVICTION stared back at him, so cold and hollow.

He looked back at the shop in front of him which, even in the dim light, was still colourful and full of joy. He'd spent years crafting a space that could offer something more, something safe.

A shop full of books that were selected to retail, new and rare, for both the academic and the casual reader. The arches of the still beautiful chapel, renovated with thought and precision to honour its history and bring it into the modern times.

He turned and observed the castle from his perfect view at his window seat.

He opened a drawer in his desk and dropped the letter inside, where a pile of similar letters was stacked. He closed it, taking a deep breath. 'What the hell am I going to do?'

Chapter Six

When Quinn awoke the next morning, his head ached and his mouth was dry. Memories of the incident at the festival came rushing back to him. He closed his eyes, remembered what Ivy said, and tried to think positive thoughts.

Only there was nothing positive about this hangover.

Or the angry messages from Dougie, who seemed to regret thinking with his dick.

Quinn texted him back.

> Sorry about last night. I wasn't in the mood.

> Not very nice to ignore me, Quinn.

> Sorry.

> It's fine, babe.

Quinn grimaced. Babe? No, he was not his babe.

> You know we're not together anymore, don't you?

And whose fault is that?

Quinn gripped his phone, trying to decide if he should throw it at the wall or change the subject with Dougie. He knew he shouldn't be texting him. To entertain him was wrong. Keeping the connection open meant it wasn't closed, but blocking him and shouting at him that it was over felt callous and cruel. Instead, he left him on read, the kindest rejection he could think to do.

After popping two paracetamols, drinking what felt like two pints of water, and showering, he wrapped himself up and headed outside, feeling more human.

He looked at his shop, closed for now but opening before the festivalgoers came on by. Oh, how cruel a world it was to be having such a good book season, only for this to all go soon.

'Hot chocolate, Quinn?' Mr Andrews from the ice cream shop asked.

'Don't mind if I do!' Quinn smiled, forced to take his mind off the impending doom. 'How much?'

'Free, my boy! The snow! We're celebrating.'

'A white Christmas on the way?'

'Oh, definitely.'

Quinn sipped his drink as he trundled along the snow, his feet sinking and his socks becoming wet. So many merry faces, familiar faces, and Quinn could lose it all.

'Morning, Quinn!' Janet from the corner shop waved.

'How do you do?' Michael from Richard Booth's bookshop asked.

'Fancy a snowball fight?' one kid asked.

'Not today,' Quinn said. 'Tell your mum she has a book waiting for pickup.'

'Will do!' He threw a snowball straight at Quinn and ran away laughing.

Rude, Quinn thought, but smiled.

He thought about a morning coffee brewed at one of the local cafés. Maybe he'd get a bite of breakfast before joining Daniel on site. In the morning, only the locals were around. It was too early for tourists to venture into town. This was the slice of heaven that Quinn cherished. The community aspect of familiar faces, getting ready to start their days.

Other than the familiar faces heading into their respective businesses, the streets were quiet. As Quinn headed towards the Cosy Café on the corner of Castle Street and High Town, he spotted someone coming out of the shop.

'Ah.'

Ah? What was he, a child sounding out the alphabet?

Noah nodded, as if he expected to see Quinn here.

'Morning. Where are the parachute trousers?'

'Burned in a sacrifice.'

'Shame,' Noah said. 'They looked good on you.'

Quinn said nothing, instead looking past Noah into the quiet Cosy Café, which had yet to have the morning rush and the busy afternoon crowds.

'Busy day of caretaking ahead?'

Was that his idea of a joke? This wasn't how he expected an interaction with Noah to go. Whenever Quinn pictured it, at least the clean version of it, it was a couple of words exchanged and a signed book. Not a cheeky man who wound him up like they had their own inside jokes.

Noah's collar of his coat was turned up, and a scarf was wrapped around him, so thick it almost covered the bottom half of his face. It was cold, but not Antarctic cold.

'You look like you're hiding.'

'I am hiding.'

Quinn hadn't expected this response. 'Hiding from who?'

'Hay.'

'What?'

'What sane person comes to a café at seven something in the morning? I'll tell you who. Psychopaths.'

'I come here every morning.'

Noah shrugged. 'Point proven.'

'Hey. You're here at seven in the morning.'

'I'm not around for long. Wanted to pay Cosy Café a visit before leaving.'

Leaving? Oh, so he wasn't sticking around. Why would he? He didn't live here. Not anymore.

'What, got some attachment to Cosy Café, have you?'

'Actually, yes,' Noah said. 'Used to come here all the time. It's the setting I used for a café in one of my books.'

'The Morning Sunshine Café?'

Quinn hated himself for knowing what café Noah meant. So much for even pretending to play it cool.

Before Noah could say anything, Quinn spoke again, as if his next words would erase the confession he'd made about reading Noah's works.

'Anyway, why are you hiding from Hay?'

'I don't love coming into the town.'

'Then why come here?'

'A person should always face their fears,' Noah said.

'Well, if you're trying to hide, you could at least...' Quinn didn't finish the sentence, but instead reached for the collar of Noah's coat. Crooked, it allowed a glimpse of the person behind it. Taking the coat collar, he adjusted it so that it stood rigid, but as Quinn drew his hand away, he felt his fingers graze Noah's cheek.

Their eyes met. Noah smirked.

'Enjoy your coffee, hippie.'

He stepped away from the door onto the street and walked away like he hadn't just made Quinn's legs weak.

'I am not a hippie,' Quinn whispered, because speaking it loudly was too scary. He could still feel Noah under his fingertips. He wasn't a mirage. He was a physical being.

He ordered his coffee in a daze, then walked back towards his shop with his to-go cup. As he strolled towards his shop, he looked up at the castle. The final eviction notice came to mind, and he felt the fear grip him.

A person should always face their fears.

The castle made him fearful. At least the person behind the castle frightened him. And he was in there right now.

He'd ignored every other eviction notice, but something about this one had changed something inside him. He'd hoped that by ignoring his problems, they would go away. Whenever he faced something uncomfortable, he ran away from it. Quinn, the man who never stepped one inch out of his comfort zone. He had no intention of doing that. Not when it involved the man in the castle.

But Noah's words rang in his ears like tinnitus.

Emboldened, possessed by something he couldn't explain, he entered his shop and picked up the final eviction notice letter. Even looking at it made him shake. He took a deep breath. Could he do this?

Looking around at his shop, the sanctuary, his creation, told him what he needed to do.

He had to at least try.

After stumbling onto the pavement, he went through the castle walls' archway and onto the castle grounds. He paused to admire the bookshelves against the stone wall, which were unspoiled by the weather. He began his slow climb to the castle itself, trying his hardest not to crash to the ground with all the elegance of an ice-skating giraffe.

When he reached the castle doors, he pushed them open and headed into the hallway.

I can do this, I can do this, I can do this.

The castle had always been grand, but for years, it had survived by being propped up with scaffolding. The place needed serious work, and at one point it had seemed like all hope to restore it was lost. Richard Booth, a man who proclaimed himself as the King of Hay, took this castle to live in. It was because of him that the town became known as the town of books after he spotted an opportunity to make Hay stand out from the crowd.

Rest his soul, Quinn thought.

He remembered stories his father had told him about Richard Booth. Like the time he strutted down the high street wearing a crown, or how he once declared his horse the Prime Minister of Hay. His father had even been a member of C.I.Hay, the secret service agency. When Quinn asked his dad what they did, his dad replied, 'Get pissed a lot.'

Quinn looked at Hay Castle, destroyed in a fire in the seventies, and thought of the many parties Richard Booth had held there when he was alive. Bonkers and raving, according to his mother.

Development work had now almost restored the place to its authentic glory. The roof, once caved in and the place of multiple bird nests and cobwebs, was now rebuilt, towering tall above them. Old stone carvings had been saved, and any shred of historical evidence preserved. The old stairway had been replaced with a reinstated structure and reupholstered with a red carpet. But the work wasn't quite complete yet. From somewhere in the castle came the sound of drills.

'Look who it is.' Harold Morgan headed towards Quinn, a hard hat and a high-vis jacket on his burly frame. His wild beard was flecked with white paint, as were his arms. 'Come to see the place?'

'I've come about this.' Quinn held up the eviction notice letter.

'Finally acknowledging them, then?'

'I acknowledged the other ones.' Quinn hoped Harold wouldn't challenge him. He ignored the other ones by dropping them in his desk drawer and pretending they didn't exist. Technically, he registered their existence. It wasn't his fault if he ignored them.

Okay, so maybe it was. But what else was he supposed to do? Eviction notices for a shop he loved were not something he could face. How could he, when someone else was handling his fate like a chess piece? Until now, there had been survival on the board. Maybe Harold would make a wrong move or change his mind. But with this letter that he held in his hand, and the word 'final', it felt like checkmate.

'So why the fuss?'

'It's scaring me.'

Harold waved a dismissive hand, as if nothing happened. 'It's fine. Don't worry about it.'

'You're *evicting* me!'

'Now, it's not an eviction...'

'Looks like an eviction to me.'

'You knew the risks,' Harold said. 'Come on, come look around.'

'No.' Quinn shook his head. He wanted to shout, but he knew his voice would carry through this gorgeous echo chamber. 'This is my livelihood. My entire world. And you want it gone so you can build some crappy information centre?'

'I've offered you a new shop here.'

Quinn watched his stepdad cross his arms, a grim expression on his face. 'The shop you've offered me is a box. It's not a shop. There's no way I could sell what I sell now and still make a living. It's a huge downsize.'

His voice wavered, and he was stumbling over his words. Why was it so hard to say what he felt, to stand up for himself? That confidence that gripped him earlier was crumbling around him.

'You're making things more difficult than they should be,' Harold argued. 'That church is a development opportunity, and will be a fantastic resource for us. Business is business. You should know that, if that rainbow shop is a business.'

'I won't have a job.'

'You have options.'

'What options?'

'That job offer in London,' Harold said. 'Time is running out for a career.'

'I'm twenty-eight, not sixty-eight.'

'You can't be thirty and selling books,' Harold said. 'You've been here your whole life. Don't you think it's time for a change?'

Two men carrying a ladder went by, their eyes averted.

This was Quinn's whole life. He was comfortable here, safe. People born in Hay rarely left Hay. When they did, they changed. Quinn didn't want to change.

'So have you. You've never left.'

'Haven't had to.' Harold held out his arms. 'This is my empire.'

'The castle?'

'The development firm.' Harold winked.

'Quinn!'

Quinn turned around to find his stepcousin.

'Gordon,' Quinn said, turning away from him as quickly as possible. 'Please. Reconsider.'

'What's going on?'

Quinn closed his eyes. Out of all the people to arrive now, Gordon was the last person on his list. 'This is between us.'

'He's my business partner.' Harold put an arm around his nephew. 'He should be involved in all business discussions.'

Quinn forced the letter onto Harold's chest, summoning all the courage in the world. 'There is no discussion. You're not having my shop.'

He stormed away, gritting his teeth. The drumming in his chest seemed to echo in his ears.

'The deal is almost done, Quinn,' Gordon shouted. 'You've had your final notice. It's just business!'

The cold hit him hard, and he shivered. He winced, the day bright, and the street came alive with people slipping and sliding on their way to the festival. The snow remained undisturbed by cars and had only been touched by footprints. Quinn couldn't help but look at his shop, dreading the day ahead and having to pretend everything was alright. Quinn wanted to cry, but he couldn't. Crying wouldn't solve anything.

He could only blame himself for thinking the letters would go away. He'd hoped his stepdad would see sense. To get the final eviction notice was devastating. These weren't strangers from a faceless corporation; these were people that should look out for him. Corporate greed had tangled itself in family ties. This was just business to them.

Well, it wasn't just business to Quinn.

They couldn't have it.

If Quinn lost his shop, he would lose himself. He looked at his apartment, peeking above the castle walls, where his income kept a roof above his head. The locals, who all waved hello, who had known him since he was a kid, would become memories. Quinn would lose his community.

As the snow fell, and Quinn made the steep descent down to the castle walls, he thought of telling someone. What would his mum say? Maybe she already knew.

After Harold had entered her life, he couldn't deal with the fact that his mother had moved on. Then he'd ignored it so much that he had refused to tell anyone, even his mother.

Quinn took out his phone, and after failed attempts with a gloved hand, he called his mum.

'Quinn? How're you?'

'Not good,' Quinn said. 'He wants the shop.'

'I know.' His mother sighed. 'I've told him to leave it.'

'Is that all you've said?' Quinn's heart sank at the realisation that she'd known and said nothing.

He couldn't work out how they'd got to this point. Wasn't his mother supposed to know he was upset about this? Had she thought he'd be okay with the prospect of losing the one place that gave him something to get up for in the morning? If he held the phone any tighter, it would shatter into a million pieces.

Quinn's father had once owned a bookshop himself on the same street. It had been a success, endorsed by Richard Booth, and decreed the 'Hayses of Parliament'. His mother always resented the fact that his dad left behind a career as a pilot, dragging them away from their nice and rather large home in London to Hay-On-Wye to sell second-hand books. His father established himself over the years, gaining a solid reputation, and was adored by the locals who still lived here today. Quinn had been too young to remember London. To him, his life had always been Hay.

And then he'd died. The shop was sold, and that was that.

Not a day went by where Quinn didn't miss his father. Now he had Harold, a man who made Henry the Eighth look good. Except he didn't have six wives, and had never been married before, let alone beheaded anyone. So, maybe Henry was worse.

Anyway, Quinn knew his father would have defended him, and this would never have happened had he … well, not died.

'What can I say?' his mother asked. 'Harold doesn't listen. He does what he thinks is right. He's said it's—'

'Just business, yeah, I know,' Quinn said. 'But this isn't just business, is it? This is my life. I'm going to lose everything.'

'He's not kicking you out of the flat—'

'Oh, the flat that I own?' Quinn forced a laugh. 'No, he's not. Just forcing me out of the shop I've built and nurtured. Mum, it's not just a bookshop. It's a community. A safe place. Without it, Hay loses some of its character. You can't let him do this.'

His mother sighed, one of defeat. 'I can only say what I've already told him.'

'You think I should give up, don't you?'

'He's offered you an alternative.' Quinn could almost hear her choosing her words with careful precision. 'The shop in the castle. You seemed okay before this. And the job in London, Quinn. Why would you say no?'

Quinn leaned against the stone wall, feeling it dig into his back. An icy breeze made him shiver, but he was thankful to be sheltered from the snow. It seemed if his mother couldn't return to London, she wanted to live vicariously through her son.

'The shop in the castle is a box, Mum,' Quinn said. 'It would only fit a shelf. Nothing more. It's a huge downgrade. No author signings. No evenings with those who need someone to speak to. We sell more than just books, Mum. We help people know they're valued.'

There was a pause.

'I wish you could keep it,' his mother said.

'So, you won't help me?'

'I'll see what I can do.' She said nothing else. 'Quinn, I've missed you. Have I done something wrong?'

'It's fine, Mum.'

'I haven't seen you in a while.'

'The shop is right there. For now.'

This was why Quinn never called his mother. These conversations. When the silence stretched between them a little too long, Quinn said goodbye and stared up at the new refurbished castle. The jewel of Hay, adored by the locals and the tourists alike, but the crux of Quinn's turmoil. When news broke that the castle was being restored to its former glory, Quinn joined the community in celebrating. He celebrated when Harold got the contract, helping him out of a business slump. Another property firm had been absorbing Harold's work left, right and centre. To get the Hay contract was one big FU to the rival firm.

Never in his life did he expect family to screw him over so badly.

Quinn stood tall, snapping out of the wallowing pit of pity.

If it's just business, then they won't mind what I do next.

Chapter Seven

Okay, so he didn't have a what's next. He didn't have a plan. He
didn't have a Scooby, though he wished he could call on the gang
to unmask Harold and reveal his true character. But he knew he
needed to do something. Fear held him back from telling everyone
in the bookshop that the shop was facing closure, but a small idea
formed in his head.

Inside his shop, he fixed a smile on his face and served every
customer, including Deb and June who came by to pay their
respects to him after his 'festival ordeal', like he had died. He tried
his best not to think about the letters in his drawer.

'I'm looking for a book on gender,' a woman said, not quite
meeting his eye.

'Sure. We have a lot in stock. Can I ask what it is you're
looking for?'

The woman, who he didn't recognise, looked around the shop.
She'd chosen a moment of quietness, of serenity after a rush of
people. Quinn had spotted her earlier, lingering at the shelves,
waiting for the right time.

'It's my daughter. Well, son.' She winced, and Quinn wanted to
tell her it was okay. 'Um... sorry.'

'Don't apologise,' Quinn said. He encountered people like this often. Parents wanting the best for their child, even when they weren't sure what was happening themselves. 'Your son?'

'This will sound awful,' the woman said, stepping closer to Quinn. 'She's a teenager. *He's* a teenager. He's always felt like something was different. When he was a kid, he'd hate me putting him in dresses or feminine clothes. I thought it was just a phase, you know? Anyway, he's asked me to refer to him as he and him, and he thinks … he thinks he's trans.'

Her eyes met Quinn's, and he smiled, hoping he reassured her.

'I'm going to recommend a book targeted at teens, but it might be worth you reading it, too,' Quinn said, motioning for the mother to follow him. 'Do you mind me saying something?'

'No, of course not,' the mother said, though she sounded like she wished for anything but.

'Talk to him,' Quinn said. 'Don't tread around it like it is something secretive.'

'But I don't know what to say.'

'And that's absolutely fine,' Quinn said, coming to the section of his shelves labelled 'gender and identity'. 'The main thing is that you are there for him to speak to, and you help him figure things out. He'll need someone he can trust right now.'

The mother nodded, taking a deep breath. 'I feel like I'm doing everything wrong.'

'You're not,' Quinn said. 'What's important is you speak to him. Don't worry about making mistakes. Just make sure that when he corrects you, you learn from it. Don't see it as something to be angry about. Don't take his own anger, if there is any, personally. Instead, open, honest, healthy communication is needed right now.'

She looked at the shelves of books, her mouth dropping open at the vast array of titles.

'Here.' Quinn handed her a copy of *What's the T?* 'Juno Dawson. She's very knowledgeable about the subject. Then this

46

one, *Gender Euphoria*. Shared stories from trans, non-binary and other queer writers on their own experiences.'

The woman took the book, inspecting the covers with a mild sense of fascination.

'Often, we overlook how the parents might feel,' Quinn said. 'So, two things. We offer a support group on Wednesday evenings. It's not run by me, but it's run by an LGBTQ+ charity in the local community hub. If you want me to, I can put your name forward to join. Your son is, of course, more than welcome to join, too.'

'Yes, please.'

'And then this book.' Quinn reached for a book on the top shelf, hardbacked. He handed it over to her. 'Have a look. It's for parents and how they can help their children through this process.'

'I'll take them,' the woman said, glancing at the blurb. 'Anything you can recommend, I'll take.'

'Okay, if you're sure,' Quinn said. 'Also, if you or your son ever want to come in for a chat, or just somewhere to be, then please do so. We have a place where you can sit and chat, without fear of judgement. Like I say, I'm no medical professional. I'm not qualified to offer any sort of therapy or advice. But I am here to sell books on the topic, to be a place for people to come to, and a person you can talk to about anything.'

The woman looked like she wanted to cry as she handed the books over to Quinn at the till. As she took the bag, she placed a hand on his arm.

'Thank you,' she said. 'Honestly.'

As she left, Quinn sighed. It was moments like these when he feared the loss of his shop. Here in Hay, he was the only place people could come to without fearing what the person they were talking to might think. He wanted to help people, craved helping people. He might not be a doctor, a psychologist, or the owner of a charity with valuable resources, but if he could help in other ways, that was a purposeful day to Quinn.

Losing that ability to be there for others was a hard prospect to face.

As he re-ordered copies of the books he'd sold, he rested his head against the nearest bookshelf. Harold was not only taking this away from him, but from everyone else that wanted advice, education, and a good queer read.

'Busy day?' Ivy strolled into Kings & Queens wearing a bright pink raincoat and fluffy earmuffs. She took off her gloves, still wearing her plentiful rings, and leaned against the counter.

'I was just about to close,' Quinn said, checking the time. 'It's been busy, but I think most people are enjoying the snow or staying indoors.'

Ivy nodded, as if all-knowing. She seemed to float across the shop, looking up and down the shelves. The snow continued to fall, like it had all day, burying the festival hype underneath it.

He got to his feet and headed to the door, turning the open sign to closed.

'We need to talk.'

Ivy's eyebrows knitted together. 'What's the matter?'

An idea had formed in Quinn's head when he saw Ivy swan into the room. Propelled by the woman seeking advice, and his own chat with Harold, he knew he needed to do something. Time was running out.

Quinn pointed to the back of the shop, and they headed there together, coming to the church's old altar, which had kept its original features. To the side of the altar were two confessional booths. Quinn pulled one of the purple curtains back, revealing boxes of stock. He slid in and looked at Ivy.

'You want me to hear you confess your sins?'

'Just get in the other one,' Quinn pleaded.

'I love this.'

Ivy did as she was told, climbing into the second booth. 'There are so many boxes in here.'

'Got to keep the shop stocked.'

'I've never done this before. Forgive me, Father, for I have sinned.' Ivy giggled. 'Oh, this is wonderful.'

'Ivy, please, I need you to listen to me.'

Quinn leaned his head against the solid oak wall behind him. Drawing the curtain, he put himself in darkness.

'I am all ears, Father.'

'Wait, you're the father.'

'Oh, yes.' Ivy cleared her throat. 'I am all ears, child.'

Quinn rolled his eyes. 'Ivy, something is wrong and I don't know what to do.'

'Go on,' Ivy said. 'There is no judgement in the eyes of God.'

Quinn adjusted where he sat, shifting a box of books with his foot. 'I think I'm going to lose everything.'

Those words, spoken so openly, scared him. Speaking them aloud felt like it was a done deal. It felt real. He tasted them, so sharp, like citrus on an ulcer.

'I've had a letter. Multiple letters. I've ignored every single one of them. But I can't ignore them anymore.' Quinn closed his eyes as tears welled, letting them trickle down his freckled cheeks. He didn't bother to wipe them away, even when the salty taste brushed past his lips. 'Eviction notices, Ivy. I'm being evicted.'

The curtain ripped back, and Ivy stood before him.

'What the hell is going on?'

'No blasphemy in this church.'

'Enough.' Ivy shook her head. 'You're being *evicted*? How long have you known?'

'A couple of months.'

'A couple of… A couple of months?' Ivy's voice raised to a shriek, the necklaces she wore jangling together. 'What? Why?'

'It was easier to talk when I couldn't see you.'

Ivy drew the curtain, disappearing from view, and Quinn heard her stomp back into the second confessional booth.

Quinn sighed, feeling lighter now that some of the burden was unloaded.

'The castle wants this as an information centre. That's what I've been told,' Quinn said. 'Because it's right opposite. They want this to be a place where people can buy tickets, learn a bit about the history, and then cross the street to the castle.'

'Why this church?' Ivy asked.

'I don't know. Maybe because it used to belong to the castle. I know they want the church to be the hub.' Quinn saw Ivy's shadow move behind the slatted opening in the wall between them. 'They want me out.'

'Wait a minute...' Ivy said. 'Isn't your stepdad the one rebuilding that castle?'

'Did I tell you that?'

'God knows all.'

Quinn laughed, but it was hollow.

'You're being evicted by your own stepfather?'

'Yes. Well, his firm. He owns this church.'

'Your stepfather,' Ivy said. 'And what's the alternative?'

Quinn chuckled, remembering the offer Harold had given him. 'He told me I could instead have the shop in the castle. But the room is a box. I could only get one shelf of books there. There is no way I could live like that.'

'And what about another shop?'

'There aren't any.' Quinn groaned. Shops don't come up for rent in Hay, and when they did, they were beyond his budget. 'And also, *this* is my shop. I wouldn't want to be anywhere else.'

'No, I understand,' Ivy said. 'We can't have this.'

'There's nothing else I can do, Ivy,' Quinn said. 'Do you think it's too late to do something?'

Quinn heard a commotion next to him, and Ivy screamed. Stumbling out of his own booth, he saw Ivy had tripped over some stock and landed on the altar floor.

Quinn gasped. 'Please don't sue me.'

'Would it help you if I did?'

Quinn thought for a moment. 'No.'

'It is never too late,' Ivy said, dusting herself off. 'That is what I was rushing to tell you, but here we are. Who have you told about this?'

'No one.'

Ivy got to her feet. She crossed her arms like a teacher who didn't like a student's attitude. It was not the first time he felt like a student with her. 'No one?'

Quinn shook his head.

'Mum knew, but seems to think I didn't care about being evicted because I didn't say anything. I thought she might talk some sense into Harold, but it doesn't seem to be that way,' Quinn said. 'I haven't told anyone else because I didn't think Harold would go through with it. This is home. I can't lose this.'

'And you won't, my dear boy, you won't,' Ivy said. 'Now, do you know who I am?'

It was Quinn's turn to knit his eyebrows together. 'Sorry?'

'Do you know who I am?'

Quinn couldn't tell if she was joking or not. 'Um … Ivy Heart.'

'That's right.' Ivy smiled. 'And Ivy Heart knows everyone. And knowing everyone means I know everything about them. I know the ins and outs of this town, whether or not people want me to. I've often thought about setting up a blog, like Gossip Girl, only it's called—'

'Where is this going?'

The sound of people laughing outside broke the stillness of the shop. A thud on the windowpane followed by shrieks of delight told them a snowball fight had broken out. The sun, the brief glimmer of light through the thick clouds, gone. It was dark already – the height of winter.

'Knowing everyone means I have connections,' Ivy said. 'You know the Hay Herald, don't you?'

'Of course.'

The Hay Herald was a staple piece on Hay's culture. A local

newspaper, as old as time itself, it seemed, with offices just around the corner.

'We start there,' Ivy said. 'We get this story out there. You are not having your shop taken from you.'

'There isn't time.'

'Why isn't there?'

'They want me out by Christmas.'

Ivy's mouth dropped open. 'They're kicking you out over Christmas? Holy Mary. No, no, no, no, no. This won't happen. Not on my watch.'

'Ivy…'

'No,' Ivy said. 'I have connections everywhere, and I'm not letting this go without a fight. You can sit here and mope around, but I'm taking action.'

'I'm not moping—'

'Quinn, with all due respect, you're a moper. And mopers never get things done.'

Quinn couldn't help but smile. In the darkest time of his career, there was a shining light in front of him, like Rudolph guiding a sleigh. Quinn realised that all this time he'd needed a friend, but had let no one in. Ivy had come at the right time, a messiah or an angel, or something else Christmassy. Whatever. All Quinn knew was that he needed her.

'I don't want to be a moper anymore.'

'Progress.'

'What do I need to do?'

'We show why people need this place,' Ivy said.

'I've got some ideas on how we can do that.'

Ivy thought for a moment. 'We need someone to bring the crowd in. We need to show that this is the place to be. My god, it's a shame you didn't tell me sooner. I would have got Noah Sage in here.'

Quinn's eyes widened, an idea forming in his head. 'Can you get him in here?'

'No, I'm not that well connected.'

The bell over the door jingled.

'Oh, I must have forgotten to lock the door.' Quinn sighed.

They both headed to the front of the shop, Quinn fixing an apologetic look on his face.

'Jesus Christ,' Ivy said. She grabbed Quinn by the hand, a regular occurrence in their relationship.

There he was, all six feet of him. He wore a black jumper and grey joggers, something Quinn forced himself to not look down at. His messy blond hair tangled on his head, and he wore glasses.

I didn't know he wore glasses.

It gave him a professor look. If your professor was young and insanely attractive.

'Hi,' Noah Sage said, looking at the two people before him.

Quinn didn't say a word. He looked at Ivy, wishing the rush of stinging blood to his cheeks would stop giving him away.

'Talk of the devil.'

'Blasphemy,' Quinn whispered.

Noah blinked.

'Noah Sage?'

Of course it was Noah Sage. What was she playing at?

'Yes.'

Oh, no. He sounded annoyed.

'I'm Ivy. Ivy Heart. I'm here on behalf of my friend, Quinn.'

She pointed to him, and their eyes met. Once again, they stared at one another, Quinn rooted to the spot.

'Hi, Quinn,' Noah said. 'We meet again.'

Please God. Help me.

Ivy looked at him as if to say, 'Why am I only now finding out about this?'

'Yes, we do,' Quinn managed.

'Quinn owns this shop.'

'The gay shop,' Noah stated. 'I love that Hay has that.'

'Well, good,' Ivy said.

53

But Quinn had to fight to hear what she had to say next. *He loved it?* Noah Sage knew about his shop? *His shop?* And he loved it? What was going on here? Had the fall earlier knocked him unconscious? Was he dreaming? Of course he knew about it. He was in it. But he *knew about it?*

'Because we need your help with the shop.'

'I don't know what you mean,' Noah said.

'I'm being evicted,' Quinn blurted. There was silence, and Quinn realised he needed to say more. 'I'm being evicted from my shop by my stepdad and my cousin. I know what you might be thinking. It's not a big deal. But it is. Our shop is a community for the community. People flock from all over to support us. We not only stock the bestsellers, but we have a vast section of LGBTQ+ books and books by LGBTQ+ authors.' He knew he was rambling, but he couldn't help himself. 'We offer a safe space for those who need it, offering help for anyone that might need it. We are a lifeline here, something different in the town of books, and my stepdad wants me evicted so he can turn it into an information centre for the castle that he's redeveloping. It's just business, apparently. So...'

Quinn faltered. What was he asking? There was that familiar feeling of stumbling over his words, making no sense as his heart beat with anxiety.

'So, we're trying to make people aware that this is happening,' Ivy said, saving Quinn. 'That Hay is about to lose something very important. And we need as much help as possible to raise the publicity. We're talking newspapers, TV spots, radio spots, and we know we can get that with you involved. You'll be helping a cause.'

There was silence. Quinn looked at Noah, willing him to speak.

'It sounds dreadful,' Noah said with a careful tone. 'And I understand. But there isn't much I can do.'

'We want you to do a book signing,' Ivy said. 'You can bring in the crowds and we can get the press attention, and we can put the pressure on.'

'I can't,' Noah said.

'Excuse me?'

'I'm going tomorrow. I won't be here.'

'You're not going anywhere,' Ivy said. 'Have you seen the snow?'

'I...' Noah looked behind him, and Quinn thought he was trying to think of an excuse. 'I just... There's... I won't be available.'

'But you see...' Ivy began.

Noah stepped backwards, his hand finding the door handle. He was about to leave, but Ivy placed a hand on his arm. 'Please, Noah. You would be an immense help.'

For a moment, Quinn thought he would say yes, that the three of them could come together and with his influence, they could save his shop.

'I'm sorry,' Noah said. 'You can always try Blair Beckett. I hear he's still in town.'

He closed the door, leaving Quinn and Ivy stood feeling dumbfounded.

'Bloody Blair Beckett?' Quinn choked.

Chapter Eight

'I'll ask again; I don't care,' Ivy said as Quinn made them a coffee. 'He's nervous about getting involved in, like, politics or something. He will come round.'

'His answer was obvious, Ivy. He's not interested.'

But Quinn couldn't help wondering why Noah came to the shop at closing, almost as if he knew by coming then, he could avoid the crowds. The man had been elusive in the town centre in the early morning, like a vampire about to retire before the sun shone.

Was he a vampire? Quinn had yet to see him in direct sunlight. He supposed he would look wonderful, all strapping and glowing that wonderful glow...

Stop it.

Quinn's apartment was a modern one bedroom with hardwood flooring and a bright kitchen. The windows looked out to the rooftops of Hay behind his shop, so he could see down to Lion Street and glimpse the bridge across the frozen river. At the other end of the apartment, he could see the castle. It seemed to taunt him every time he looked at it. Minimalistic, the apartment gave the impression of being bigger than it was. As he handed Ivy the coffee, he thought about how lucky he was that he wasn't losing his home. Just his income. His bookshop. His livelihood.

Which would mean he couldn't afford his mortgage.

Debt collectors. More evictions.

'Stop being negative.' Ivy held the green coffee mug in her ringed hands, the steam rising past her face. 'I've met many people like Noah. They say no at first, but they always come around. It's disappointing, but we will get him involved.'

'I imagine he wants a fee.'

'Capitalism.' Ivy sighed. 'A horrible thing.'

'The source of all of my problems,' Quinn said. 'Literally.'

They sat in the kitchen opposite each other at Quinn's breakfast bar. Ivy reached for a banana in his fruit bowl.

'It's not the end, though.' Ivy unpeeled the banana. 'Oh, no. We're just beginning.'

She bit into the fruit, looking thoughtful. Quinn got lost in his own thoughts of what life might look like without his shop. He already knew rent rates were out of the question and he refused to move his shop out of Hay.

There was nowhere else.

His shop was home.

'I can't lose it, Ivy. Because I enjoy helping people and I love my job, and how many people can say that? Then there's Dad. I'm his son. Son of a bookseller. I feel like it's a reputation of mine and that by losing my shop, I've failed. Failed him, even.'

'You haven't failed him.'

Quinn looked at a small painting of a robin hung up on his wall. 'I hope not.'

'Okay, okay, think, think...' Ivy placed her fingers on her temples. She looked like a psychic trying to tell the future. 'We have snow, meaning we will have stranded authors and notable people in Hay. We get them on board.'

'Why do we even need those people?' Quinn asked. 'No, not to be offensive, but can't we just rally the community together?'

Ivy took her phone out of her pocket and began typing away.

'What are you doing?'

'Just bought a megaphone. It will arrive at my apartment tomorrow.'

'We might protest.'

'Something like that,' Ivy mused. 'Do you have Instagram?'

'I do, but I don't think now is the time to—'

'You need to do an appeal.'

'An appeal?'

Ivy got to her feet; her eyes were wide. 'Oh, this is going to be perfect. Right, where is the best lighting? Ah, here! Sit in this armchair, and this lamp, oh how *glorious.*'

Quinn looked at her standing by the chair. 'I don't get what you're doing.'

'Do you have a social media marketing team?'

'No.'

'I took a course once,' Ivy said. 'I like to learn things, and being a boss babe entrepreneur, I had to better myself, so I know what I'm doing. Now, sit here and let me film you. Do we want to do a live, a reel?'

'You did not just say boss babe.'

'Do we want to do a live or a reel?' Ivy repeated.

'I … don't know what any of this is.' Quinn admitted, heading to the chair.

He sat down, and she turned the lamp on, angling it towards him. He squinted, and she smiled. 'Get used to it, movie star. We need to get you doing as many of these as possible.'

'I don't know what I'm meant to say. Shouldn't I have a script?'

Ivy finished her banana and headed back to the kitchen, where she dropped the skin into the bin. She sipped her coffee as she walked towards him again. 'No, just be you. Natural. Maybe we can mention your dad? Can I use your phone? We can film it straight in Insta.'

'I don't think I can do this.'

He wanted to kick himself. There was an urge within him to say what he believed to be true, but whenever it got to actually speaking, he couldn't do it.

Ivy removed a ring.

'What are you doing?'

She handed him the ring with a polished violet stone. 'This is tanzanite. It will help with your throat chakra.'

'Ivy…'

'No, Quinn, it's yours.' Ivy held her hands away, as if the ring never fit her. 'It will help you open up about your truth. It will help with your self-expression.'

Quinn looked at the stone, the silver band. He slipped it over a finger, surprised it fit. Ivy let out a little gasp, as if he was Cinderella fitting into the lost slipper.

Quinn unlocked his phone and handed it to Ivy. 'Use the bookshop account rather than my own.'

'Yeah, 'course,' Ivy said. 'Okay, so just talk about what's happening and what people can do to help, and we can go from there.'

Quinn took a deep breath and looked into the camera as Ivy counted him down. When she nodded, signalling him to talk, he spoke. 'Hello. Um… I'm, uh, losing my … no, I work at Kings & Queens, and well, it's a great shop and I … my dad used to…'

He heard his own voice playback.

'We ran out of time,' Ivy said. 'It needs to be quicker. And, action.'

'Hello. I'm Quinn. I live here in Hay, and I'm the one that sells you your books here at Kings & Queens. Uh…'

His mind went blank. He stared at the camera, his mouth open, with no sound coming out.

'Okay, it's fine, actors have many takes. Take three!'

Ten takes later, and they still didn't have a cohesive video.

Quinn waffled and fumbled his way through the dialogue, trying to get all he wanted to say condensed into one tiny video.

After yet another failed attempt, he groaned.

'I can't do this.'

'Yes, you can,' Ivy encouraged.

'No, I can't. It's not working. What the hell am I meant to say?' He looked away, lost in thought. 'This bookshop means everything to me. It's my heart and soul. It's run by me, for the community, and it's a shop that people shouldn't be without. And I'm being evicted, so they can turn it into a soulless corporate info centre for the castle. We're about to lose my shop and I need people's help. Otherwise, Hay loses something special. And you want me to get *that* into a short video? I don't know how to do it.'

He looked back at Ivy to see her grinning.

'What?'

'Oh, I'm posting it. I got it.'

'I wasn't looking at the camera!' Quinn said.

'No, but you said what needed to be said.' Ivy tapped a few buttons and then handed his phone back to him. 'And now we wait.'

Chapter Nine

Quinn woke up to his mobile phone ringing, blasting the voice of Mariah Carey's famous Christmas song. He loved the song, but all he wanted for Christmas was to sleep.

And keep his shop. That was obvious.

'Hello?' His voice was thick with sleep.

'Have you been ignoring all the calls?'

Ivy sounded excited on the other end of the line. Quinn sat up, the blanket falling from his body. He felt the chill in his apartment from the outside snow and drew the blanket over him again.

'What calls?'

'Quinn, our video, it's gone viral!'

'What?'

He put Ivy on speaker and listened to her talking about how the video reached almost two million views and was still rising. He found the video and read comments from strangers all around the world, people wishing him luck, asking him questions. The homophobic hate comments he got meant nothing to him. Instead, he dropped his feet over the side of the bed and realised what this all meant.

'People know about me.'

'The press has been ringing you.'

'What?'

Quinn scrolled down the comments and saw the verified accounts.

Hi. Sammy from The Guardian…

We're from The Mirror and would love to interview you.

Sorry to hear about this. ITV News here…

'Oh my god.' Quinn gasped.

'Right?' Ivy said. 'Now get up. I've been replying to comments on your behalf.'

Quinn went to his window, almost expecting to see the press gathered outside. There was nothing but snow, undisturbed because of a fresh falling over night. Hay was still and calm.

The stillness didn't reflect his thoughts, though. His mind whirled in different directions. How could one video, capturing his off-the-cuff remarks, be reaching people all over the world? Why would someone care about him and his shop, when they had never even heard of Hay? It made no sense to him.

'So, I'm acting as your press officer. I've told them to email an address I set up, or they can call your shop. I'm assuming you've diverted the calls to your mobile?'

'What? No, of course not.'

'Then you've missed everyone's calls! We need to get them right now. Let me get interviews set up with you.'

'Interviews? Ivy, I don't know if I can do it.'

Speaking in front of people? Speaking about what mattered to him when he was certain people wouldn't care? He hated attention. Hated people looking at him. There was no way he could do this.

Unless…

His father always told him to do what's right. To fight for what he believed in.

He believed in his shop. Believed that if he couldn't do it for himself, he'd do it for the people who loved his shop. He couldn't let them and the memory of his father down. All he needed was a firm belief in keeping it alive.

'You can! And you will. I will be by your side through it all.'

'I don't even know how to get them to listen to me.'

'They'll listen. They want to know what's going on.'

'Should I reply?'

'Leave it all to me. I'll keep you posted. Ciao for now.'

She cut the call, leaving Quinn in his apartment feeling at odds. The world might know, but did Hay?

His phone rang again. This time, Dougie.

He knew he shouldn't, but he answered.

'Quinn, hi.' Dougie's voice sounded brisk. 'I saw your Instagram post. You're being evicted?'

'I … thought you knew.' Quinn gripped the phone. 'When that first letter arrived…'

Quinn hadn't told a soul about his eviction notice, but Dougie was with him when the first letter came through. He would have shared it, only he left soon after, meaning Quinn had no one to fall back on.

'Yes, yes,' Dougie said, though he apparently didn't care to remember. 'Shame that you're losing it. Maybe now you can join me in Cardiff. You would *love* it here, Quinn.'

'I've been to Cardiff before, you know.'

'Living here is very different,' Dougie said.

'It's just Cardiff.' Quinn was sure Cardiff was a lovely place to live, but it wasn't like it was an undiscovered metropolis.

'Look, I *hear* you about this shop,' Dougie said. 'But I think you should focus on us.'

'Us? Dougie, there is no us. You made sure of that.'

Silence. Quinn surprised himself, too. Perhaps it was the

63

tanzanite. Would he have said that had Dougie been in front of him? Right now, Quinn couldn't play whatever games Dougie wanted to play. It was exhausting, and he was exhausted.

'You want us to end?'

This is what Dougie did. Quinn had only realised it three months after their breakup. Whenever there was an issue, it was Quinn's fault. Never Dougie's. Now, clearer than the crystal quartz on his bedside table Ivy gave him last Christmas, Dougie was doing the same thing again.

'You broke up with me,' Quinn said. 'Remember?'

'I had a lot going on,' Dougie said. 'You know, my mental health. But I'm in a better place now.'

Quinn had always felt for Dougie and his mental health issues until realisation dawned on him that those issues only existed when he didn't get his own way. Such issues only ever cropped up as weapons, guilting Quinn into submission.

Not this time.

'Look, Cardiff seems like it has been good for you and your...' – Quinn paused – 'mental health. I love that for you. You've moved on.'

And I've moved on.

Go on, say it.

Saying it would be final.

But he had known for a long time that Dougie couldn't come back. Wouldn't come back. Shouldn't come back.

Quinn stared at the tanzanite ring.

'And I've moved on.' Quinn closed his eyes. Silence. It stretched out like a yoga pose. 'And I think...'

Too much silence.

Looking at his phone, Quinn realised the call had cut.

'Alright then,' Quinn said.

He looked around his apartment, the ghost of Dougie walking around buck naked, his wavy black hair falling to his shoulders. The first man Quinn met hadn't been good for him but he couldn't see it. Now, after the texts, and that phone call, he could.

With a deep breath, he blocked Dougie's number, seeing the ghost of him fade into nothingness. It was over. He was free.

So why did he feel like he'd done something illegal?

He stared at the ceiling, wondering if he'd made the right choice in cutting Dougie off. He had to make changes. For too long, he'd let people decide what he should do. Dictate how he should feel. Dougie always decided, and Quinn followed suit. His father's death left him craving a person who could tell him what was right, what would make him feel safe. But in doing that, he'd compromised everything.

Now, through reckless choices and the suppression of his own desires, he'd hit a wall. Found himself in trouble.

Quinn moved the ring on his hand as he thought of all the things that were wrong in his life. The threatened closure of his shop, an ex that he kept letting back in, cutting off his mother despite her attempts to keep communication alive between them. All because he'd feared what would happen if he did what he wanted to do and said what he wanted to say.

No more. He couldn't do it. Allowing others to decide resulted in him forgetting who he was.

He went to his wardrobe and got dressed in a knitted jumper and some jeans, and then booted up and threw a coat over his hoodie. Dougie would not disturb his thoughts anymore. The shop would always come first.

Seeming to float down the stairs as he thought of the viral comments and attention hitting his social media accounts, he headed out into the snow and almost expected people to swarm to him like he was one of the Kardashians. He expected to be asked his thoughts, how he felt, who he was wearing. Instead, the still silence of snow so close to Christmas welcomed him.

The real world still didn't know what was happening. The bubble of social media struck again, and while it was great to have such recognition, he couldn't help but wish that the community here knew.

If they didn't know, then he should tell them.

But what if they were on the side of Harold and Gordon? What if they agreed that the castle, with all its celebrated restoration, needed such a place to help tell the history of Hay? What if that was more important to them than a bookshop selling queer stories? The people of Hay loved his shop and saw its value – such was their accepting nature. But the castle was sentimental to them all.

They loved his father and by extension, they supported him, but that didn't mean they would fight for him.

The conflicted feeling hit Quinn hard. Was he being selfish? Was he refusing to budge out of his own desire to keep his haven? Maybe now was the time to move on from Hay and let this place go, even though that was the last thing he wanted.

He couldn't do it.

The idea of leaving frightened him more than Dougie's pert bum apparition. Who was he if he didn't have a role in Hay's community?

What else was there out there for him?

The publishing job. The offer given to him all those months ago to become an editor for a publishing house. He applied on a whim after leaving Dougie, thinking he needed to escape Hay. Almost immediately, he regretted the application. The interview request filled him with dread. The job offer paralyzed him.

London. A city job. A life away from Hay where there was so much noise and people barging past and never any time to sit, catch their breath, and smile at one another. That was the perception this small-town boy had of the big city of London.

They say everyone should have a city experience once in their life.

Don't they?

He didn't want that experience, though. He was happy with

his small town, thank you very much.

Quinn unlocked the door of his shop and turned the closed sign to open. He went to his window display, where Christmas books lined a Christmas scene he'd made by hand. Crocheted snowmen and reindeer sat on yuletide logs reading *A Christmas Carol*, and the book itself stacked with gorgeous foiled binding at one end of the window.

Scrooge. He looked at the castle. Scrooge!

This was the Dickens experience. He was living in *A Christmas Carol*. Except without the starvation and Tiny Tim and the spooky ghosts.

'If there are any Christmas ghosts willing to show Harold the error of his ways, be my guest.' Quinn spoke out loud, listening for even the faintest sign that one of the ethereal beings had listened to him.

'I don't know if that will happen.'

Quinn screamed, jumped, and turned around to see his mother standing at his counter.

'What the hell, Mum?' With shaking hands, Quinn pulled out the chair behind his desk and sat down. 'How did you get in without making a sound? You bloody dormouse.'

'Thanks.' Claire caught a strand of ginger hair and curled it behind her ear. Crossing her arms, she looked around at the church, her eyes wide. 'This is such a relaxing atmosphere when you come in.'

'I haven't put the music on yet,' Quinn said.

'I always loved the music. Relaxing.'

'That's what this place is. To what do I owe this visit?'

'I thought maybe we could get a coffee. We should talk about this.'

'I need to run the shop,' Quinn said, but he didn't move from where he sat. He felt lethargic. His mind, racing with the comments on his social media, distracting him. Besides, she didn't need to know that Daniel Craig would be here at any moment.

Claire reached into her handbag, an old leather thing that peeled at the edges, and unfolded a newspaper.

'What is this?'

She dropped it on the counter and turned to the sixth page where a small column about his shop stared back at him.

Quinn's eyes widened. He snatched the paper up, gripping it so tightly it almost ripped, and read the sentences.

It wasn't much, but it was enough to get the point across. The story of a developer at Christmas evicting a queer bookshop seller was clear to see. A small picture of the shop, old and taken from Google's Street view, accompanied the article.

'It's in the paper, too?'

'What do you mean, too?' Claire asked.

Quinn took out his phone, showing his mum the video. She clicked into the comments, her mouth dropping open as the strand of ginger hair fell down again.

'Oh, no, this isn't good.' Claire shook her head. 'You can't speak to journalists about this.'

'Why can't I?'

'Do you know how hard Harold has worked?' Claire handed Quinn the phone back. 'He brought us from the brink of bankruptcy with this contract. This makes him look terrible. Your dad left us with a lot of debt, Quinn, and Harold brought us back from that.'

Quinn couldn't believe what he was hearing. 'You don't think what he's doing is bad?'

Claire crossed her arms again, seeming to withdraw into herself. 'Look at this place. It's gorgeous. You've had a good run. Harold's been kind to you by letting you pay not nearly as much as what it's worth. But this building is part of Hay. This building is part of the castle. It's part of its history.'

Quinn remained silent.

Claire let the silence stretch out. 'Sometimes we have to let go,' she whispered. 'This shop has served you well, but it can't be forever.'

'This is my job. My career. Of course it can last forever.'

Claire sighed. 'You're so much better than…' She stopped.

Quinn crossed his arms. 'Than what?'

'Than this,' Claire said. 'Listen, I came here because I saw this article, and there was a quote from you in it. I thought you'd been contacting the press, but I see it comes from this video you posted. Please tell me you didn't do it to spite Harold.'

Quinn shook his head. 'I didn't think it would go viral. I didn't even know I was being filmed. My friend is helping me get this out there. We're going to fight before we let this get taken away from me.'

'Fight?'

'Fight. We have a megaphone and everything.'

Claire placed a hand on her forehead, heaving a vast sigh. 'You don't fight, Quinn. I didn't raise you like that.'

'No,' Quinn thought of his conversation with Dougie. 'No, and it's got me in a couple of not so ideal situations. I've been silent all my life. I'm not being walked on any longer.'

Claire looked as though she might cry, like she was seeing her son for the first time. Despite everything inside him screaming for him to turn back, to say what his mum probably wanted to hear, to overthink and worry about others rather than himself, he stood firm. So firm he crossed his arms, because that proved how firm he was.

'This could get nasty. Your shop isn't worth losing family over.'

Quinn hated to see his mum so torn. But if Quinn lost this shop now, he would be the one struggling. He would be the one close to bankruptcy. He would be a Cratchit.

He had to risk everything to get what he wanted.

Quinn took his mother's hands and looked her in the eye.

'In the words of Harold, it's just business.'

Chapter Ten

The phone rang. Quinn answered. 'Hello, Kings & Queens. Quinn speaking. How can I help?'

'Hello. Emma here from Hay Herald. I'm getting in touch about a viral video of you regarding your bookshop.'

It was the only call that came to the shop. After all the comments from the press, not one of them contacted him, despite Ivy helping him set up his email and replying to every one of them. It seemed his video was yesterday's hit, and today it had dropped off the algorithms and faded into the ether.

'Hi, Emma, thanks for calling.'

'It touched us when we heard the story, and we could see the emotion in the video from you. Would you be willing to talk to us about it?'

'Yes,' Quinn said. 'When?'

'I can stop by within the hour.'

Quinn was about to answer when the bell above the door tinged. He turned to see who was coming into the shop, and he almost dropped the phone.

That familiar stopping of time hit, where the snow no longer fell outside, and the voice of Emma on the other end of the phone disappeared. Noah stood in the doorway, his eyes locking with Quinn's. They were no longer in the shop, but in the universe, surrounded by beautiful lights of red, pink, green, and everything in between.

'Quinn? Hello?'

With a thud, time sped back into action, and Noah hadn't been standing at the door staring at him like he thought, but somehow, he was right at the counter, and stood looking at a nearby display of books. Quinn cleared his throat, looking away, feeling embarrassed.

'Sorry,' Quinn said to Emma. 'You were saying?'

'I'll arrive with a photographer, and he can take your photo either before or after the interview. He'll probably want to take a few photos of the shop, too. We'll aim to get this story out by the end of the week.'

'Yes, absolutely, of course.'

It was something. The Hay Herald wouldn't set the world on fire, but it was in circulation enough here in Hay for at least the locals in town to find out about it.

Emma said her goodbye, and when her voice cut, there was silence. Not even the familiar calming music that Quinn played over the speakers sank in. His own heart seemed to stop as he stood there, phone in his hand, at a loss for what to do.

'This is a gorgeous book cover.' Noah held *A Christmas Carol* in his hand. 'I've never seen it like this. The foil is such a stunning touch.'

Quinn nodded but said nothing. Damn it. Why couldn't he speak? Say something. 'Thank you.'

Thank you? What was he saying thank you for? It wasn't like he had handcrafted every book cover and foiled it himself.

Noah placed the book back on the display, which Quinn had painstakingly worked on. He grimaced, and Noah looked at him. 'What?'

'Nothing.'

'No, something's wrong,' Noah said, his hands slipping into his pockets, recoiling from the books.

'I did the display carefully. Every book is at just the right angle. It doesn't matter. I can sort it out.'

Noah looked at the display with a smirk, and that smirk alone was enough to make Quinn want to worship him. 'It looks perfect to me.'

Quinn came around the counter, surprised his wobbly legs would carry him. 'I took a marketing class, and they said that when you have a physical shop, you have to not only be mindful of how things look, but you need to take in the things we can't see, too. You know, like the feng shui of it.'

Noah didn't need to know that his feng shui marketing class came in the form of Ivy.

'The harmonising of energy and surroundings. What do you see when you look at these books?'

Noah placed a finger to his chin, his forehead creasing. Quinn could watch him for hours. And that was what he did. At least it felt like he did. He stared for a long time, uncomfortably so, but Noah didn't seem to notice or care.

Where were his academic sexy professor glasses? Never mind, they allowed Quinn to see every detail of his verdant eyes. That chin was so sharp. The jaw so defined, peppered with facial hair. His finger was thick, with creases at the knuckles and the joints. His fingernail had little white dots on them, manicured and looked after.

Quinn bit his own, a habit since childhood.

'I see a stylish display of Christmas books for the Christmas season,' Noah said. 'And like I say, the foil is gorgeous.'

Quinn nodded. 'Yes, but it is more than that. Walk around it.'

'What?'

'Walk around the display.'

Noah seemed hesitant, but did as he was told. He strolled like a casual observer at an art gallery, looking up and down. His eyebrows raised, and he looked impressed.

'What do you see?'

'I never lose sight of the title.'

'And what else do you see?'

'I can always see the cover.'

Quinn smiled. 'And how did you feel when you saw that cover?'

'Intrigued.' Noah nodded, his back to the snowy window. 'Like I was seeing something old for the first time again. Nostalgic, but also safe, familiar.'

Their eyes met. The words hung between them.

Quinn nodded, blushed. 'Everywhere you go in this shop, you will see the cover of this book. You will see the display from all angles unless you stand right against the bookshelf. Those feelings are what this display captures.'

'And there I was, thinking this was just a pretty display.'

'It is.' Quinn smiled. 'And more.'

They fell silent, both looking at the books. Quinn couldn't handle it anymore. Taking the book perched on the top of the display that Noah moved, he set about putting it back in its place.

'Here, let me.' Noah brushed up against him, his scent tantalising Quinn. Quinn slid the Dickens novel back where it came from, Noah holding the books next to it so that the whole display didn't crumble like Quinn's willpower. One book wobbled. Quinn's heart stopped. They were going to come crashing down.

Without thinking, he moved his hand at the same time as Noah. His palm landed on the back of Noah's warm hand, Noah's other arm gripping onto Quinn to steady him. Heart beating hard in the close proximity, he exhaled.

The book display was safe.

But his hand still caressed Noah's. Their hands really did fit together. He imagined it locked in his, entwined like they were glued together. He swallowed, realising that Noah's grip on his arm had slackened.

Quinn cleared his throat, moving away, but not before Noah met his eye with that same flirty smile on his face.

'You're still here.' Quinn had to say something, and the obvious felt like the safest bet.

'Still here.'

Noah looked at the snow, as if the winter scene outside explained it. London felt a long way away from here now.

'Your friend sent me the fundraiser.'

'Ah, yes.' Quinn recalled the email from Ivy that morning. Their fundraiser was live, and he'd seen how much they had raised: a measly five pounds.

'I tweeted it.'

'You did?'

'And Instagram-storied it.'

'Storied? That is good grammar.'

'I knows.' Noah smirked.

'Well, thank you.'

'Of course.' Noah crossed his arms. 'I hope you don't lose this shop.'

'Me too.'

'Do you think you will?'

Quinn left the display, and Noah's strong, warm hand, and headed back to his desk. 'Yes, I do.'

'You do?'

Quinn sat on the chair behind his desk. 'Maybe it's for the best. Nothing can last forever.'

Noah headed to the counter, placing his hands on the countertop. Quinn looked at them, taking in every wrinkle, every crease. He couldn't get enough of them.

'You sound like you've given up.'

The words hit Quinn hard. He gripped the table, more so to steady himself than anything else. 'You think so?'

'If this place is as special as you say it is—'

'Hey, it is,' Quinn said, almost shouting. 'It's special to me.'

'Then it isn't for the best, is it?'

Quinn hated that Noah was right. Hated that this man didn't know him as much as he wished he did. Yet somehow, he saw straight through him. Called him out, even if that isn't what he intended to do. Maybe Noah had tanzanite on, too.

'What will you do instead?' His hand crept ever closer to Quinn's.

'I can get work elsewhere,' Quinn said. He had to focus on Noah. But that was hard to do when he looked like *that*.

'But will it be as fulfilling as this place?'

'No,' Quinn admitted. 'Not one bit.'

'Can't you compromise with the developers?'

'My stepdad? No. He's headstrong. He will never listen.'

'He has it in his sights and won't see anything else?'

'Yeah.'

Noah nodded. 'Sounds like my mum.'

Quinn bit his tongue, knowing who Noah's mum was. He heard all the stories and was aware that he'd be on shaky ground if he acknowledged it. If Hay was a kingdom, Noah's mum had become the town fool.

'Does it?'

Pitiful. Was that all he could say?

'She's a typical Aries,' Noah said, and his hand definitely moved closer this time. Quinn bit his tongue and kept his hands firmly on the edge of his end of the table. 'Determined. Skilled. Acknowledged. A true leader. Everything good. But ruthless. She did what she had to do. Salute to her.'

'I haven't seen her in a while. How is she doing?'

He felt like he'd gone too far. Noah's hand slid away ever so slightly.

Noah shook his head. 'It doesn't matter. What matters is you, and what you want to do.'

A secret floated between them. Quinn let it disappear.

'I don't have a choice here.' Quinn recovered from trying to acknowledge Noah's mother. 'I thought the press would get on board. I thought more people would care. But…' Quinn's voice broke. His eyes welled up and tears rolled down his cheeks, beginning to burn out of embarrassment. He covered his face, not wanting Noah Sage, *the* Noah Sage, to see how pathetic he was.

Then he felt him. He smelled him. He experienced him.

First the cologne, just enough to be powerful, but not enough to overwhelm. It smelled of citrus and of something he couldn't quite put his finger on. Fresh and airy, despite the colder month and the season. Earlier it had been a hint. Now it was like showering in all its glory.

He felt Noah's warmth, like a radiator on the highest setting, and the brush of a comfortable knitted jumper against his neck, warm like it was fresh from the tumble drier. Closing the gap, wrapping an arm around him. He comforted him, letting him cry, soothing him with his hypnotic voice that should be on audiobooks.

Jesus, he was crying in Noah's arms.

Wiping the tears away, wishing he could stay pinned against Noah's shoulder longer, he moved away, trying to regain control of the situation. If Noah thought him weak or foolish, he didn't show it.

But Noah didn't let him go completely. His hand slid down Quinn's arm and his fingers linked with Quinn's. It was only a comforting hand hold, Quinn told himself. Nothing else.

'What sign are you?' The words left Quinn's mouth before he'd even thought them.

Noah looked amused; an eyebrow cocked. 'Aquarius. And you?'

'Pisces.' Quinn managed a small laugh, making a mental note to look up Aquarius and Pisces compatibility. 'Sorry. I don't know why I asked that. You said your mum was an Aries, and I guess…'

Stop talking, Quinn. You cried in his arms and then asked for his star sign. You're not doing yourself any favours here.

Noah stepped closer, his eyes roving over Quinn's flushed face. His hand dropped from Quinn's, and he wondered if he imagined his touch. But then Noah wrapped his thick arms around him once more, this time stronger, a reassuring squeeze.

'You should fight, Quinn. Fight for what you believe in.'

A shiver ran over Quinn's spine, but it wasn't because of the cold snap outside. It was his visceral reaction to Noah's words that carried a weighted truth.

'I need to be brave enough.' Quinn sighed.

Noah held him even tighter. 'Look, you're going through a lot right now. You need to take your mind off it. Why don't we…?'

The bell above the front door tinged. Noah's voice stopped. The sentence never finished, leaving Quinn in agony, wondering what he might have said.

He looked to see who had disrupted such a moment, then spotted the woman in a black wool coat shifting snow from her shoulders. A man carrying a large rucksack stood behind her, brushing snow out of his hair.

Quinn wiped his eyes as they took him in with Noah Sage's arm still around him.

'Blimey. It's Noah Sage,' the woman in the black coat said.

Chapter Eleven

How did this happen? Quinn watched Noah sitting at the altar of the church, the camera guy snapping photos of him as he held his book. Noah fixing a forced smile on his face. The black-coat reporter, Emma, a beautiful girl that was riding on the wave of luck she surfed in on, poised and ready to interview him.

Something inside Quinn sank as he saw his opportunity overshadowed by the author, who was born and bred in Hay.

'So, Noah Sage, back in Hay. How does it feel to be back home?'

'I got stuck here,' Noah said, his eyes darting around the shop, trying to find Quinn. 'The snow cut me off. I couldn't get back to London. It just won't stop, will it? The snow, I mean.'

'Some might call that fate. Do you believe in fate?'

'Sure. Maybe. I don't know.'

'I think the roads are clear now,' Emma said.

'Yeah, but they're pretty treacherous for a four-hour journey back to London.'

'But you're home now. You came for the festival. How did that go?'

'I always love coming to the festival.' The words sounded

rehearsed to Quinn. 'It's great to know that the festival continues to have fans that flock from around the world. And it's always great to get to know others.'

'And good to come home?'

'Not really.'

Emma looked baffled. 'Not really?'

'This isn't home.'

Quinn averted his eyes, biting his lip. It hurt to hear Noah talk about his distaste at being back here in Hay, like it was some sordid place that nobody should ever go to.

'I think the readers of Hay Herald would disagree.'

'Let them.'

Quinn tried to pretend he wasn't listening, but he wanted to turn and lock eyes with Noah, to see his expression. His words sounded angry, tense, like he resented coming back to this town.

Emma cleared her throat. Quinn knew this wouldn't make the article. It would put Hay in a poor light. Imagine churning out a bestselling novelist only to find that he didn't enjoy being back in the town he came from.

'Your new romance novel is blazing through the charts. Any more in the works?'

'I always have a lot of ideas, and I'm halfway through the next instalment. The reaction to this book has been so special.' Quinn rolled his eyes, realising how easily Noah became interview ready. 'I would have never imagined this book doing better than the others, as it was a little harder to write.'

'Why?'

A pause. 'Heartbreak.'

Quinn, his arm raised to put away a book, froze.

'I see,' Emma said. 'Would you like to tell us about that?'

'Heartbreak can inspire a lot of things. A lot of the art you see comes from intense feelings of dread, grief, anger, hatred, hurt. I think that's what fuelled me to write this book. It feels rawer than the others, I guess, and I guess people relate to that because of what happens in the world.'

'Right. There is a lot to be sad about.'

Quinn glanced behind him. He could see the top of Noah's head through the display. He stepped back into the shadows, cursing the creak of a floorboard.

'There are. Like this place. We might lose this bookshop, Hay's only queer space. Why would anyone want to lose that?'

Quinn gasped and covered his mouth.

'What does this bookshop mean to you?'

Quinn stepped forwards, and this time he saw Noah looking at him.

'This bookshop means everything to me.' Noah broke the gaze first. 'When I was a kid, growing up here on the border of England, I felt so lost. The world seemed so much bigger than this corner of Wales, with its bookshops and its history. It felt old to me. It felt rigid. And inside me was this feeling that I was trapped as someone else. That I needed to escape, not only the confines of this small town, but escape me. I had never heard the word gay. When I did, it hit me. I was gay. Could I have been gay in Hay? Of course I could. Did I want to be? No. I wanted to see the world.'

Their eyes met again. He smiled, and Noah smiled back.

'So, I ran from Hay. I left it behind. I didn't know if I would ever come back. All I knew was that I needed to escape me, escape Hay, and escape … some other things.'

Quinn wondered if Noah's words alluded to his mother.

'But would I have done that if this shop had been here? Would I have wanted to escape so much if someone had been here to listen to my demons, to talk to me? Would I have stayed in Hay if I had instead escaped to the multiple pages of gay literature, of real-life queer stories and experiences? Of queer history? My story may have been a lot different, and this interview may never have happened.'

There was a thud, and they turned to look at Quinn, standing like a rabbit paralyzed in headlights. He had dropped a stack of books.

The photographer excused himself and went to help Quinn, leaving Emma and Noah at the altar. Quinn thanked the photographer, but tried his best to listen to the interview a few feet away.

'There are people like me in Hay. People who may be afraid to come out. Who may be afraid to be themselves. Then there are people close to Hay who call this their only safe place. There are those who want to be educated, and those who want to get lost in a queer romance story. And I think that is beautiful.' Noah nodded at Quinn, who held all the books he'd dropped. 'The story isn't me being back in Hay, Emma. No one cares about that. The story is about this bookshop, and how if nothing is done, we will lose it. You should talk to Quinn.'

Emma turned to Quinn, standing there with his eyes wide, his mouth ajar, his hands propped on the books he'd dropped. The photographer raised his camera and took a photo of Quinn, a flash blinding him.

'Delete that right now.'

Noah crossed his arms, smiling at Emma as she got to her feet, her trainers echoing on the church floor. Quinn allowed her to guide him through the shelves towards the front of the shop. Noah sat alone in the middle of the church, lost in his own thoughts.

'Well, that is quite something,' Emma said to Quinn.

'I don't think I've been this flustered since a woman had her baby in here.'

'Excuse me?'

'She came in and she gave birth right there.' Quinn pointed to the glass cabinet against the wall. 'Said she wanted to use my phone to call the ambulance and then refused to leave because she was in so much pain. She named her child Charles, like Dickens.'

'Wow.'

'This place has so much history. Apparently, it was the site of a murder when the castle was functioning,' Quinn said. 'Oh, and Richard Booth used it. Rumour also has it that this place was a boudoir.'

Emma probed Quinn on his own thoughts about the closure. Quinn recited as much as he could, feeling like his words weren't communicating its importance enough. Which then made him talk too much. But Noah's words came back to him about needing to fight. This was the way Quinn could fight. With words, with stories, with examples of how special this place was.

'Well, thank you, Quinn, for your time. It's appreciated.'

'I appreciate you,' Quinn said, somewhat breathless. 'When will this go out?'

'End of the week,' Emma said. 'Let's say Friday.'

'Great!'

Noah joined them at the front of the shop, moving much too close to Quinn. He froze. Only recently, he'd been touching him, hugging him. Now he was back like he'd never left.

Emma turned to Noah. 'Thank you for your time.'

'Happy to.'

'One last photo?' Emma asked.

'Sure.' Quinn held his hand out to Noah. He'd be lying if he wasn't using it as an excuse to feel Noah again. 'Where do you want him?'

'Oh, the both of you, please,' Emma said.

Noah patted Quinn on the back.

'An author and his biggest fan,' Quinn said.

Noah laughed, and Quinn laughed too. The camera flashed, catching them mid-laugh. Emma smiled.

'We'll catch you soon.'

Chapter Twelve

Quinn popped the champagne, fizz bubbling over the neck and trickling down the curves like an M&S advertisement. Two glasses in his hands clinked together as he poured the liquid into the glass, handing one to Noah in an awkward movement.

'Thank you,' Noah said, his fingers grazing Quinn's. It almost made Quinn drop the champagne, causing another accident.

'I can't wait to see that interview.' The interview had thrilled Quinn with the idea of what might get published. For the first time in a while, he embraced optimism like an old friend. He couldn't help it, but with an encouraging pep talk via FaceTime with Ivy, his thoughts had run away from him, imagining the success the interview would have, the saving of the shop, and the materialisation of a nice hot man to make him feel better in the dark, cold winter nights.

'You okay?'

Quinn realised he'd been thinking a little too long about that hunky man, because Noah's voice called him back from his daydreaming. Cheeks blushing red, Quinn cleared his throat.

'A toast. To Kings & Queens. To Hay.'

'And to you.'

Quinn's flushing cheeks flushed harder, if that was even possible, and as they clinked glasses, his eyes met Noah's. They sipped their drinks with the snow falling outside the window. Night had fallen in Hay, lit only by the fairy lights in Quinn's shop.

'Tell me about you.'

'Me?'

'You,' Noah said. 'I want to know the man behind this shop.'

Quinn wished he had somewhere proper for them to sit. Instead, he sat behind his counter and Noah sat on a small chair that he found in the children's section. It was bright pink and offensively plastic.

'What do you want to know?'

'As much as you want me to.'

Quinn drank from his glass, his eyes darting around the shop. Thank god for the atmospheric lights. It made enough shadows in the place that he didn't have to see Noah clearly, and read too much into his expressions and hypnotising mannerisms.

'Well, born in Hay. Lived in Hay. Mum's a nurse. Dad's ... gone. Stepdad's a dick. I studied at university, came out of university, expected to have a career, but I opened this shop because I didn't like the sound of those boring nine-to-fives and hectic city jobs.' Quinn sighed. 'Disappointed Mum in doing so.'

'I'm sure that's not true.'

'Mum expected more from me. A proper job, is what she said to me. She wanted me to go into publishing – "at least put that degree to use" she said. When I said I'm putting it to use here, she shook her head. A gay bookshop is not what she envisioned.'

'Because she doesn't agree with it?'

'Oh god, no. Nothing like that. I think she wanted more from me than to follow in Dad's footsteps.'

'Where is your dad?'

'He died.' Quinn thought about his dad's wide smile, blue eyes, and always unkempt hair. 'Six years ago.'

Quinn's gaze fell to the floor as he tried to fight back the tears. It didn't matter, anyway. It was too dark in here to see the small tear that fell down his face. He waited, hoping time would move on, and that Noah would change the subject, but there was silence – the kind of silence that seems hollow, yet full of static energy. It felt charged with something unexplainable. His thoughts raced, yet not fast enough, because there wasn't enough to distract from how empty everything seemed.

Emotions could be a fickle thing. Three sips of champagne and already he was crying? Wow! That was a record for Quinn the Pisces. He'd always tended to live up to that slippery fish water sign. His father's voice swam back to him, passing the Piscean fish in the stream. *Your emotions will get the better of you, but that does not make you weak.* Those words, spoken to him in his father's North-Walian dialect, seemed as clear to him as if he was in this very shop.

Quinn sometimes wondered if that was why he let people walk over him, why he needed to appease others. He was so in tune with his own emotions that they overflowed to others.

'What happened to him?' Noah seemed to have the tendency to bring Quinn back to land. Hooked, lined, and gutted.

'Car crash,' Quinn managed and the tears fell now. He was a quiet crier, but his shoulders must have betrayed him, shaking like an earthquake, because then Noah was next to him, and his hand held tight to Quinn's. 'One day, he was a smiley, classic dad. Next, we're burying him.'

'I'm sorry.'

Quinn pulled away from Noah, overwhelmed by how close he was. That citrus smell was back, making him feel like he was on some Aegean fruit farm. He wiped his eyes with his free hand.

'Don't apologise. It's fine.' Quinn cleared his throat again, forcing back the tears that wanted to come, but damming them up as best as he could. 'I'll see him again someday, I'm sure. He would have been proud of this place. I know he would have been.'

'You said you followed in his footsteps. Was he a bookseller?'

'He was a pilot at first, lived in London, then he was a bookseller,' Quinn said. 'Knew everything there was about good first editions, limited editions, what would sell, what wouldn't. He owned the shop two doors down from here, and people loved him. People often speak fondly of him. They come in here to talk to me about him, and it's like he's still here, you know?' Quinn got to his feet and pointed to a photo of a man pinned on a notice board. 'That's him. My dad.'

Noah joined him at the board. His face broke out into a smile, and Quinn loved to see it. 'He looks kind.'

'He was kind.'

'And he looks like you.'

'Thanks.'

'Handsome.'

And Quinn made a noise that sounded like a whimper and a mouse's dying squeak.

Noah's hand was on the small of Quinn's back now, rubbing him, and a tender jolt rushed through Quinn.

'He'd be proud of you.'

Quinn choked, Noah's resting hand feeling like a paperweight. 'Thank you.'

'And so, this is why you wanted the shop?'

Quinn nodded. 'I guess in some ways, yeah, I wanted to follow in his footsteps. Wanted to be like him. Because I learned so much from him. I thought maybe it would be like the two of us owning bookshops in Hay – it would add to Hay's character and its history. And then he went and left us and here I am with a shop that is going to close.'

'It won't close down. I promise.'

'Nothing's promised,' Quinn said. 'We think we're in charge of our fates, but we're not. Something higher pulls us where we're needed, and we just ... go with it.'

Noah headed back to the plastic chair and sat down. It

crunched under him and he froze. Quinn couldn't help but smile, feeling the weight of his father's absence leave his chest and the cold where Noah's warm hand had been.

'I don't know if I agree with that,' Noah said as he steadied himself.

Outside, two huddled figures trudged past the shop, their faces shielded by the snow. Quinn watched them go, wondering why people were out in the cold so late. It reminded him that there were more people around, that it wasn't just him and Noah left alone on Earth – this wasn't their world and their world only.

'You don't agree?'

'I made a choice to be a writer. Nothing else would cut it until I could be. I was prepared to starve until then because I was not getting myself stuck in just anything for the sake of it.'

'Well, it paid off for you.'

'And it paid off for you. You made a choice that was similar to mine. You pursued your dream and made it happen. Many people don't, and won't, do that. So give yourself credit. It's the fight that makes us. When we want something, why let others stop us? Why let people get in our way and dictate what our lives should be like? We're dreamers, Quinn.'

Dreamers? That felt nice.

The pair finished their champagne, and poured another, and then another, until all that came out was a single drop into Quinn's parched glass. Time went fast, and the two of them were heavy-headed and giggling.

'I can't believe you're still here.'

Noah stared out at the dark street. 'I don't want to be here.' He paused, catching Quinn's eye. 'No offense.'

'Um … none taken.' *Loads taken.*

'I mean, I don't want to be in Hay.'

Noah's words in the interview came back to him. By the end of the week, they could be in print.

'Why not?'

Noah rolled his shoulders, as if they might be tight. Quinn thought about offering him a massage, but he wasn't drunk enough for that.

'Too many bad memories.' Noah cleared his throat. 'I never felt like this was home.'

'But it was home?'

'No,' Noah said with some force. 'It's too... I feel claustrophobic. Like I need to escape. Almost as if I needed to shed my skin again and run far, far away.'

'Is that why you're a vampire?'

Noah blinked. 'Sorry?'

Okay, so maybe Quinn *was* drunker than he thought. A vampire? Really?

'I mean, you don't come out in the day,' Quinn said, as if this made complete sense and was the evidence needed to call Noah a vampire.

'Not true,' Noah said. 'You saw me in the graveyard.'

'Yeah, about that...'

'Mum's sister,' Noah said, pre-empting Quinn's question. 'I visit her whenever I come to town, which isn't often.'

'You would never come back here to stay?'

'Never.'

His words felt so final; weighted words that couldn't budge. An opinion so immovable, Quinn wasn't sure what to say. So, he changed tact.

'I'm surprised we never met.'

Noah smirked. 'The town isn't as small as we thought it was.'

'I need to ask something,' Quinn said, drunk on adrenaline and too much bubbly.

'Ask away.'

'In that interview, you said heartbreak inspired you. You're heartbroken?'

Noah waved a hand, trying to dismiss the conversation. But

Quinn, giddy, wouldn't let it drop. He moved closer to Noah, but not too close, because too close was too dangerous.

'I only ask because I was heartbroken,' Quinn said, surprised at his own courage. 'Guy called Dougie. A little while ago now, but he's been hanging on.'

'Well, I would have known he would break your heart. Any guy called Dougie is going to be a heartbreaker.'

Quinn laughed, even though it wasn't all that funny. Maybe he had reached that stage where making fun of an ex felt good, like he could rebel against the mere memory of him.

'Yes, well,' Quinn said. 'I thought he had my best interests in mind, and then he moved to Cardiff and thought he was better than me.'

'Oh, don't you know, they convert those who live in Cardiff into dickheads?'

'Shh.' Quinn laughed, his eyes wide, looking around as if people from Cardiff were about to flock inside and attack. 'You can't say that.'

'I can. I live in London.'

'What has that got to do with anything?'

'I'm a dickhead.' Noah winked.

Actually winked.

And it looked good when he did it.

'What? Cities change you?'

'Yes, I believe they do,' Noah said. 'For the better. For the worse.'

'Has it changed you?'

Noah didn't even think. 'Of course.'

Quinn paused, observing his cheerful smile, the flushed cheeks. 'For better or for...'

What was this, their wedding?

Noah shook it off, running a hand through his messy hair. Quinn watched the strands fall into place with a bounce, and something stirred within. Like a feral animal, he wanted to reach out and explore him, but that was the champagne talking.

'Yes, heartbreak is a funny thing,' Noah said. 'Use that as a strength, if you can.'

Despite the settling haze, like fog over mountains, Quinn wondered who broke Noah's heart. Who would even want to do such a thing? Why would anyone lose him when they had him? He couldn't bear to think of Noah being hurt, of carrying something internal, something that rotted him from the inside. Quinn's own heartbreak had dragged him across hot coals, then threw him into the fire, then stuck knives into him, all while giving him an elixir of life, so he had no choice but to experience it all.

Heartbreak, to Quinn, felt like torture.

'Is Dougie still in the picture?'

'No. Is yours?'

Noah said nothing. Quinn winced, sure he'd gone too far.

'I want to go out in the snow.' Noah put his phone away, but not before Quinn saw a text message on his screen. He wondered who Noah talked to, and he realised he wanted to see more of Noah, experience his life, understand him better.

'It's too cold,' Quinn protested.

'Come on. Just to feel it.'

'No.'

'We've got to go out anyway, to go back home,' Noah said. 'Or did you forget where you live?'

'I'm not *that* drunk,' Quinn said.

'I can't sit on this any longer.'

'Not comfortable enough?'

Noah lifted from his pink seat. 'You try it!'

'Come on, it's not that bad.'

'I implore you to sit on it for a few hours and then come talk to me.' Noah laughed. 'Everything goes numb.'

'Everything?'

Noah met his dangerous gaze. '*Everything.*'

His breath hitched.

Quinn put his empty glass to the side, his hands fumbling and knocking the empty bottle across his desk, and skipped to the chair. He sat on it, and as he did so it creaked before snapping, crashing the short distance to the floor.

They both burst into raucous laughter, hunched over as tears rolled down their drunken faces, merry on the interview, on winter spirit, and on the cheap champagne.

Quinn was glad there were no tenants upstairs, otherwise they'd complain at the racket the two young men were causing.

'Come on. I think it's time to call it a night,' Noah said. 'You can clear that up in the morning.'

'Oh, yeah, sure,' Quinn said, as if this was the craziest suggestion anyone ever made. 'I can't leave it like this. Let me clear away the mess.'

'Hey, the booksellers got to do what the booksellers got to do.' His words slurred, making Quinn giggle.

They were outside now, their exit a blur to Quinn, who felt a lot more intoxicated than he'd thought, certain that he had cleaned the shop only a moment ago. He struggled to slot the key into the lock, and considered leaving the shop unlocked for the night, when Noah spoke.

'It's a gorgeous night.'

Quinn turned, stumbling, to see golden light twinkling from every shop window. The centrepiece Christmas tree stood tall and proud, its branches dusted with white. The castle windows were a warm yellow, and that familiar silence stretched around them. Only this silence was no longer vacant, but full of life.

The snow fell, dusting their hair and their jackets while the alcohol numbed them to the chill.

Noah leaned against the lamppost outside Quinn's shop, an eyebrow raised, his smooth gaze on Quinn.

'Hay in the winter,' Quinn said, his breath materialising before him. He needn't say anything else. He was too mesmerised by the way Noah leaned against the lamppost so effortlessly. He was jealous. Jealous of a bloody lamppost.

'My mother used to say something to me when I was growing up.' Noah's eyes were fixed on the sky. Quinn hadn't been brave enough to acknowledge Noah's mother – the famous woman, the scandal. It didn't feel right. He only let himself go in that shop, which seemed so small when it had been the two of them. He'd been too afraid to let loose, reminding himself that Noah Sage was talking to him. *Him.*

Noah strolled the short distance from lamppost to shop door as Quinn's hand rested on the doorknob.

'She would say to me, "Anything is possible. You are who you say you are. You already are what you're meant to be. The possibilities are endless, and they're bigger than you and me." She used to take her hand, like this...' Noah's fingertips touched Quinn's chin. They felt so soft and warm, and they delicately raised Quinn's head to face the dark sky. 'She would say to me, "Look up, handsome", and I would say to her, "Why am I looking up?" She would tell me, "The version of yourself you want already exists. Make your wish, tell them what you want, and what will be will be."'

Quinn didn't know if it was the drink, or the desperation to believe, or because Noah's fingers rested against his chin, but he looked up and whispered, 'My shop will forever be mine.'

Chapter Thirteen

Last night was a dream. It must have been. A teenage dream, a fantasy, but one hundred per cent a dream.

Except as Quinn arrived at his bookshop, carrying today's paper, realising that he had in fact not cleaned away their glasses and the champagne bottle like he thought, memories of his night with Noah came flooding back to him.

Oh, how wonderful it had been. Noah's blond hair, his cheeky smile, his personality. Spending one-on-one time with an author he admired was surreal, which accounted for how much he drank and how heavy his head felt today.

Quinn stared at the empty champagne bottle and the two glasses, seeing the faint imprint of Noah's lips on the rim.

Quinn felt like that time he got high: light-headed and paranoid as hell.

What words did he utter?

Did he say anything bad?

Did he tell Noah he liked his eyes?

That he liked his books?

That he would have liked to have been one of the characters in his romance novels that got screwed by the lead?

No. No, he couldn't have.

Then he saw the broken children's chair and laughed.

Quinn cleared away the mess from the night before, trying to reassure himself that everything was okay. Wandering into the aisles of books, all arranged alphabetically by the author's last name, he came to the shelf of Noah Sage books. Looking at the titles, with a few copies of each, he traced his finger over the spines, like he could almost touch the man himself.

He read many genres of books. He grew up reading everything from Dahl to Dickens. He knew his books, and of course, his dad told him about titles. Quinn had hosted many author signings and met many famous authors, but Noah was different.

One, they were the same age.

Two, Quinn loved a soppy romance.

And three, Quinn fancied the fuck out of him.

He recalled the first time he'd seen Noah Sage – it was kind of like he was a stalker, only not crazy.

Well...

No, not crazy.

He had been reading a trade magazine, looking at upcoming authors, trying to find out the buzz, and it had featured Noah for his debut. A romcom, Britain's next Jackie Collins, only less fabulous. They praised him for realism within the genre of romance, able to tell gritty stories while keeping his characters fresh, exciting, and likeable.

Then the film rights sold.

Noah Sage hit the mainstream.

Quinn felt proud, especially because he was from this town. Quinn always wondered how he never met Sage. He soon discovered Noah went to a school over the border in England, and had left Hay at sixteen. Quinn had kept himself to himself, avoiding any male because of his feelings, and disappearing between the pages of books. In some ways, Noah did the same.

94

Certainly, last night's admission of hating Hay had been interesting. Who could hate Hay? The people were friendly, the shops divine, and it was literally the town of books a.k.a. heaven on earth. No, Noah was wrong. Maybe he hated another town that rhymed with Hay-on-Wye. Though, of course, Quinn knew that wasn't the case. Noah's dislike for the place was clear in the way he spoke about it. The way he cleared his throat and hunched his shoulders.

But Quinn felt drawn to Noah, from every titbit in an interview to the always updating Wikipedia page.

Wow. Am I a stalker? Quinn wondered.

He stepped away from Noah's titles, as if being too close would get him a restraining order, and headed back to the front of the shop.

It was the last weekend of the winter festival. He knew there were illustrious names up there, and normally he would immerse himself in the crowds and listen to the words of the authors, wishing he could be one as well. Only his life had taken him down a different path, and that was okay. He didn't resent that. A life in London beckoned. Courtesy of a friend, a job still awaited him should he ever change his mind, but he wouldn't change his mind. He couldn't.

Flipping the closed sign to open, Quinn unlocked the door, and then drank a copious amount of water, willing away last night's hangover and the faint taste of champagne.

He took pride in the shop. He adjusted the titles, reorganised shelves, and said hello to those that walked in through the door – each time glancing up at the castle as if it might come charging at him and take this all away from him.

As he scanned books into the system, getting them ready to hit the shelves, he thought of what he could do to save the place. The fundraiser wasn't working out. He needed a bigger profile, or at least someone to come along and change everything for the better. Maybe he'd stand on the street and tell every passer-by that Hay's only gay bookshop was about to close its doors. And what did they think about that?

But then what if they thought it was a good thing? What if they didn't see a problem with the castle taking back a building that historically had been its own?

Well, history changed. This wasn't the castle's anymore. Besides, he suspected Harold's motives. No doubt this building would bring in some serious money if it were to sell. All conjecture, of course. Maybe Saint Harold wanted it for a ticket office. Although, didn't it make sense to house that in the castle reception? Who was going to come here first and then go to the castle opposite?

Maybe Quinn could take the castle. Yes, that would be plausible. He could gather an army of drag queens and queers and he could take back ownership of both his shop and Hay's landmark castle.

Army.

Now, that was an idea...

The snow stopped, if only for a moment, and cheery voices went by outside.

'Enjoying the festival?' Quinn asked two twenty-somethings as they approached the till.

'Love it,' one girl said. 'We come every year. Summer and winter.'

She held the hand of the girl next to her, and Quinn smiled.

'That's fantastic.'

'We always come here,' the other girl said. 'Whenever we can. Sometimes we order online. I was a little worried the snow would stop us, but we don't live too far away.'

'Ah, I might have seen your names then.'

'More than likely,' the first girl said. 'Past couple of times, though, we've been served by a guy who always tries to sell us books on allyship.'

'Daniel Craig.'

The girls both mirrored the same humoured expression, and Quinn giggled.

'Yep. Bond,' Quinn said. 'He's straight.' The girls gasped, and Quinn laughed. 'But, of course, an ally.'

'That explains the pushing of those books, then.'

'These straight people – always shoving it down our throats.'

They shared a laugh, and Quinn handed them their bag of books. At that moment, Daniel headed through the door, saying something to a delivery driver outside. He held two boxes and letters and looked over them at Quinn.

'More stock?' Quinn asked, as the two twenty-year-olds disappeared into the winter street.

'Seems like it.'

Daniel dropped them on the table, and Quinn organised it.

'Say, Quinn, how did you realise you were gay?'

The question hit him out of the blue. Quinn thought for a moment, then shrugged. 'I guess I kind of already knew. People around me would talk about members of the opposite sex and I wasn't all that interested.'

'Hmm. I see,' Daniel said before disappearing into the back of the shop to put away his coat and bag.

As Quinn leafed through the letters, his breath held, he was relieved that he hadn't received anymore eviction notices. He supposed final meant final. Thinking about the girls, he wondered if he should have let them know about his predicament.

He took his time reading the newspaper with a fresh mug of coffee on his oak table and incense burning in all corners of the shop, an aroma of cedar and sandalwood filling the air. A part of him worried Harold may walk by, see him like this, and use it as evidence that the shop needed to go. Yet, in all honesty, days like these were rare for him.

He turned the page, pushing away thoughts of Harold, when he saw a photograph of Hermione Sage, Noah's mother.

ACTRESS LOOKING FOR **GHOSTWRITER** the headline read.

Quinn leaned forwards in his wingback armchair, the springs squeaking, and read:

> *Disgraced actress Hermione Sage has announced her autobiography via her website, only it's yet to be written. Taking to her personal website, the actress has asked for a ghostwriter to write her life story, documenting her rise to fame and her life after the cameras stopped rolling.*
>
> *Sage, 70, has starred in many Christmas films with the Romance channel, as well as a string of Hollywood movies, but her career ended after a sex tape involving her and a married man was leaked. Sage has since disappeared from the public eye.*
>
> *It's not yet clear if Sage will refer to the sex tape, something she has never talked about in public.*
>
> *Ghostwriters are being asked to apply via a Google doc link created by Sage.*

Quinn went to his computer, found Hermione's website, and clicked on it. It took an age to load, almost like it hadn't updated since dial-up internet. He spotted her latest blog post entry asking for writers to pitch a sample of their work.

Hay-On-Wye was a small place, and gossip spread with speed. Especially when it involved Hermione Sage. Hermione had been a local, and when she starred in a *Romance* movie, she jetted off to the States, where a new life awaited her. The locals of Hay were thrilled, but rumours had already spread about affairs and strained family relationships. Then, of course, the tape leaked, and Hermione's career crumbled overnight. The studios didn't want to work with her anymore, and that was that.

Quinn had seen her since then, but only once. She had walked through town, everyone going quiet and staring at her as she went by. He knew she lived across the border, just a few minutes away from Hay, in a small village known as Cusop, a sleepy town in the shadow of Cusop Hill that belonged in a cosy murder mystery novel.

Now, the generations that didn't know Hermione as an actress referred to her as 'the witch of Cusop Dingle', whilst the adults either called her the recluse or the spinster of Cusop Dingle. Hermione became a joke, and it forced her to stay indoors.

As Quinn grew up, many spooky stories spread about Hermione and the house in the small village. Rumour was that she now lived on 'millionaire row' in the home once owned by Richard Booth, the King of Hay, prompting some to refer to her as 'the queen that never was'.

At the time, Quinn hadn't realised that Hermione was, of course, a victim. The man who leaked the tape went on with his life, never being referred to, and in fact, writing a book about his 'sordid affair' with the actress. Hermione had been the butt of many a joke, with her films pulled from air, and was never offered more work.

Quinn sometimes drove through the village of Cusop Dingle, and his mind would always drift to Hermione, wondering if she was being looked after, wondering what she thought about the whole situation.

He wondered if she had a publisher.

Before he knew what he was doing, he clicked on the link Hermione shared and read the submission guidelines.

She wanted three chapters.

She wanted the writer to explain why they wanted to write her story.

And she wanted to know she could trust the writer to support her.

Quinn stared at the submission, lost in thought.

There was no way he could write it.

Could he?

Chapter Fourteen

A fresh bouquet of roses lay on Gerald's grave, the previous flowers gone. Quinn, confused, took out his phone and called his mother.

'Quinn?'

The way she talked to him almost broke him. It was like it confused her to hear from him. God, why was he being so rude to her? He needed her now more than ever, yet he'd been cutting her off. Harold. His dad. Pitiful excuses for being a sorry excuse for a son.

'Hey, Mum,' Quinn said, forcing himself to sound friendly. He heard his mum make a small exhale on the other end of the line, as if she was relieved this wouldn't be a hard conversation. 'I'm at Dad's grave. Um… Have you been here?'

'I've been meaning to,' Claire said. Her wary tone told him she feared a rebuttal. 'I just haven't—'

'It's fine, Mum,' Quinn said. 'I appreciate it's hard for you.'

Claire sighed. 'Yes. Thank you.'

Quinn gripped his phone tighter, looking at Gerald's carved name. 'Um, it's just that red roses keep appearing on the grave. I thought it might be you.'

'Oh,' Claire said. 'No, not me. Although...'

'Yes?'

'Well, he was popular, wasn't he? He used to get red roses delivered to his shop. For ages, I thought he was having an affair, but he said they would just show up. Like a secret admirer.'

Quinn shook his head. His dad had a secret admirer? Was it possible he'd been having an affair? Could someone in Hay be grieving for his father, like Quinn was, but in secret?

'Red roses?'

'Yep. He always denied an affair, but they came almost every week. I thought they'd stopped after... Well, clearly, they haven't.'

Quinn swallowed. 'When was the last time you came here?'

'Wow. It must have been...' Claire paused. Quinn closed his eyes. 'Too long.'

'I understand.'

He said goodbye to his mum and instead crouched down to the grave. 'Well, Dad. Where do I begin? Harold's evicting me. Things are changing too fast. That guy I embarrassed myself in front of? Well, he got stuck in the town and now he's ... well, we've hung out. Nothing romantic, of course. No, that doesn't happen to boys like me. And, get this, he hates Hay. How can anyone hate Hay?'

He waited, as if his dad would answer. If that ever did happen, Quinn thought he might be frightened, rather than elated.

The ground was covered in snow, but this time, he was wearing suitable clothing. He stayed crouched, though, because sitting on the ground wasn't an option.

'Then there's his mum,' Quinn said, looking out at the other graves. 'You remember her, don't you? Hermione Sage. Apparently, her sister's buried at the entrance. Yeah, about that. I saw Noah, her son, the other day at her grave.'

Quinn imagined the ghost of his father nodding along, as if this thrilled him. It was all he had to hold on to.

'Well, she's put a call on her website about someone writing her autobiography. You always said I'd be a writer someday, Dad. Hold on, though, because I haven't signed a deal yet. Right now, she doesn't know I exist. But I'm thinking about it. Submitting, that is. I don't know if it's the right thing to do, but...'

At that moment, a red robin landed a few feet away. Quinn laughed, and the robin tilted its head.

'That your sign, Dad?'

The robin hopped above Gerald's carved name.

'I'll think about it.'

As Quinn got to his feet, he saw a figure retreating in the distance. The way they walked, with a hurried pace, made him pause. There weren't many other graves underneath the yew tree. Which suggested to Quinn that the person had been coming in this direction and hadn't seen him crouched down.

The red roses. What if...?

Quinn tore away from his father, the robin, and towards the scurrying figure. Were those roses in their hand?

'Excuse me?' Quinn called.

The figure picked up the pace, fleeing the graveyard. Winded with a stitch, Quinn bent over. 'Wow, I'm unfit.'

The robin fluttered by, tweeting as it did so.

'Alright, Dad, you don't have to make fun of me.'

Quinn stared at the three chapters in front of him from a manuscript long since abandoned.

They had been edited many times, and each time, Quinn spotted something else wrong with it, which is why it could never be published. He couldn't remember now why he hadn't kept writing alongside his job. Maybe a part of him had lost hope. But now, the cursor blinking at the end paragraph of chapter three, Quinn felt silly. He was proud of what he'd written, if he could say so himself. There was no reason this book *couldn't* be on the shelves.

Except there was a reason: he didn't believe in himself.

He sighed, taking a swig of wine from the glass he had poured. Outside, rain replaced the snow, prompting a lack of hope for a white Christmas. His lights dimmed, the Christmas tree twinkling in the corner of his apartment. Despite the atmosphere outside being more suited to Halloween, Quinn felt cosy and warm, refusing to let his Christmas spirit disappear.

Christmas miracles.

That's what he needed.

This could be his miracle.

He saved the chapters, went back to Hermione Sage's submission page, where he had already filled out all his details, and then attached his three chapters. He stared at the submission page, almost deciding to exit out of it and laugh about his delusion later, but before he knew it, he hit submit.

The page disappeared, replaced with another page reading 'Thank you for your submission.'

Quinn leaned back in his chair.

He'd done it.

He took his wineglass, lifting it to the air and the empty room. 'Cheers.'

A knock at the door. Quinn almost spilt his wine down his chin.

Who would that be? And how did they get up the stairs? Unless he'd left the downstairs door unlocked? Meaning there was a stranger in his building. What if it was the retreating figure? Surely, they knew he'd seen them. They ran from him, after all.

Quinn headed to the door, but not before arming himself with the first thing he could find: an apple from the fruit bowl. Well, if someone attacked, he could pelt them in the head with something quite solid.

Quinn reached for the handle, and with a deep breath, opened the door.

'Oh.'

It wasn't the retreating figure.

Unless Noah Sage was the man leaving red roses on his father's grave.

'Sorry. The downstairs door was open, and I wanted to check you were okay.'

'You … me?' What was this, a matchmaking moment? 'You wanted to check on me?'

'That's right,' Noah said. 'Not often you see a downstairs door open. Worried maybe someone had broken in.'

'No, just my absent mind,' Quinn said. 'Um… Do you want to come in?'

Noah held up his hands, looking panicked. 'I wasn't hinting or anything. No, I wanted to check everything was okay.'

'I believe you. Oh, you think I'm inviting you in to like murder you or something?'

Noah choked. 'Not at all.'

'Right.'

'But now…?'

'Oh, just come in.' Quinn stepped aside, and as Noah walked in carrying his wonderful scent with him, he thought of what he'd just done.

Would Noah be angry at him for submitting chapters to Hermione? Oh god, had he done something awful?

'It's evening,' Quinn said as he shut the door.

'What's that got to do with anything?' Noah said, taking in the apartment. His eyes rested on the half-drunk wine bottle.

Quinn stepped in front of it, hoping that Noah wouldn't judge him for drinking wine alone in the evening. Normal when others did it, but not him. 'You're adding to the vampire mystery, you know?'

Noah rolled his eyes. 'Please, if I was a vampire, I'd be sucking your blood right now.'

Sucking his blood? Oh god. No, he would *not* think of Noah sucking any part of him.

Well. Unless...

No.

'You could fight it,' Quinn said. 'Like Edward Cullen. Wine?'

'Oh, sure.' Noah nodded. 'Edward Cullen? *Twilight* fan?'

'Team Edward.'

'Team Jacob.'

How absurd to be standing in his apartment with Noah, pouring him a glass of rich-tasting wine like this was normal. He handed him the glass to and watched him drink, mesmerised by his neck and his Adam's apple.

Noah gave an awkward smile, standing in the middle of the room.

'Sit,' Quinn said, as if he were a dog.

They sat apart on the sofa, Quinn trailing his foot along the carpet. What to say to a romantic novelist? What if he noticed his own books on his shelves?

'You know, you're never meant to invite a vampire in.'

Quinn panicked. Like maybe he'd made a huge mistake and sealed his fate.

But then he remembered vampires didn't exist, and he relaxed.

'Well, you're here now.' Quinn held out his glass. 'Cheers.'

They clinked glasses, and Noah's eyes turned to the laptop.

'Writing?'

'Oh, that, um, yeah, sure.'

Noah cocked an eyebrow. 'Hiding something from me?'

He couldn't tell him. What if he got angry? He couldn't handle an angry vampire in his apartment. That was the last thing he needed.

'Just thinking about some stuff,' Quinn said. 'Anyway, how come you're out at night again? It must be freezing out there.'

'I can't stay at Mum's for too long,' Noah said. 'Sometimes I need a break from her.'

Quinn must have looked shocked because Noah seemed to sense he'd said something wrong.

'Sorry, that sounds harsh. Mum is hard to live with.' Noah glugged down more of his wine, as if it might stop him saying anything more. But Quinn's stare must have prompted him to speak. 'Mum fears the world. She has been ever since... Well, ever since her career ended. It makes living with her quite difficult because she keeps talking about the press.'

'The press?'

'She thinks the press are out there to get her.' Noah rolled his eyes. 'The press. People who dislike her. She almost expects villagers to walk up the driveway with pitchforks.'

'People won't do that,' Quinn said. 'Have you seen how long it takes to walk from here to Cusop Dingle?'

'Like, five minutes?'

'Yeah. We can't be arsed,' Quinn said. 'Besides, my pitchfork has got rust on it.'

Noah snorted, covering his mouth. Quinn swore it was the cutest thing he ever saw.

'Right now, she's fixated on her autobiography.' Noah said this with such distaste that Quinn almost forgot about his submission. 'She gets these ideas and runs with them, but they never happen.'

Quinn tried not to look disappointed, which was hard not to do when he thought of how much time he'd wasted going over those three chapters for no payoff. If Noah was telling the truth, did that mean Hermione wouldn't even get in touch with him?

Well, regardless of what happened, he'd tried. That was all that mattered right now.

'Is your mum okay?' He almost didn't want to ask, but he felt like he had to.

'What have you heard about her?'

'Not much,' Quinn said, but his lie was feeble.

'A lot then.' Noah swilled the wine in his glass. 'Whatever you've heard, I bet you it's not true. But it makes Mum seem ten times worse.'

'But she must be thrilled to see you when you come here.'

'She's part of the reason I avoid this place.'

'Oh?'

Quinn thought of his own mother, how he'd been avoiding her. That was something he didn't want to have in common with the guy before him.

'Mum can be heavy.' Noah sighed. 'She went through a lot, and I know she's struggling to process everything that happened to her. It sounds awful, but she put a lot of that on me, and I'm not equipped to deal with that.'

Noah finished his wine and nodded at the bottle. 'May I?'

'Please.'

Noah refilled his glass, leaning back in the chair. Quinn tried to relax, too, while putting aside thoughts that Noah looked like he was comfortable here, like he planned to stay.

'She refuses to speak to people. Professionals. Refuses to even combat her issues and the problems in her life. Expects me to come along and hold her hand and clean it all up for her.' Noah glanced at Quinn. 'I'm sorry. It sounds awful. Unless you've lived with someone like her, then you wouldn't understand.'

'I'm not judging,' Quinn said, telling the truth. He thought of his shop, the space he created. In some ways, this felt like an extension of that. 'I listen to people. I'll always listen.'

Noah looked Quinn up and down, and honestly, Quinn thought he might faint.

'I know it's not her fault,' Noah clarified. 'It's my own stupid issues and my ill-ease with anything that makes me feel uncomfortable. I've tried, Quinn. Many times, I've tried to help her out. To link her with help. But she refuses. Thinks the world is out to get her. It exhausts me.'

'Is that why you were so keen on leaving?'

'In some ways,' Noah said. 'But also because Hay holds too many memories for me. Ghosts everywhere. I didn't like who I was when I lived here, so I hate coming back.'

Quinn finished his own wine, but didn't feel the need to refill it. He wanted a clear head for tonight, for what was in front of him.

'What ghosts?'

'Everyone feels entitled to me,' Noah said. 'Because they don't see Mum, they think they can tell me how unfortunate she is, and then share their opinions on her life choices and how she deserved her downfall.'

'People do that?'

'They do. Especially those who knew of her before it all happened. Mum's a legend around these parts, and not in a good way. It makes me feel embarrassed.'

'I'm sorry, Noah.'

Noah finished his own wine, placing the glass on the table. He leaned forward, resting his elbows on his knees. 'They cross every single boundary. And you know what the weird thing is about it all? I'm not ashamed of her and I want to defend her. I feel like telling these people to sort themselves out. But I can't do that because then they'll turn me into a bad guy and I'll look like the dick. So, I try to avoid this town as much as I can.'

Quinn looked out at the night. 'But don't you hate that? You grew up here. Don't you miss seeing the place? Walking around the shops? Don't you feel inspired here? Don't you miss the people who have been here longer than us? The people who know us both for who we are.'

'But that's it, Quinn,' Noah said. 'We've lived different lives. People know you and like you because they've seen you grow. People *think* they know me, but they don't. They know an old version of me, and a version of me that doesn't exist. The author me. They think that because I'm some Z-list celebrity, they can say whatever they want because I don't feel things the way they feel things. Imagine people coming up to you and telling you your dad is a whore. How would that feel?'

The word made Quinn cringe. But it flared something else within him: anger. How dare people refer to Hermione in such crude, cruel ways? No one would dare refer to his father as anything along those lines. So why was it acceptable to do so for Hermione?

Before he had the chance to tell Noah that he would help Hermione, Noah's phone rang.

Noah stared at the screen, and his expression turned to thunder. 'I should go.'

It was almost like he came out of a trance and realised where he was. He stood up, heading towards the door. 'I'm glad you're okay,' Noah said, reaching for the handle.

'Noah.' Quinn half stood, unsure what to do.

Noah hovered at the door.

'I mean it,' Quinn said. 'You can talk to me whenever.'

Noah's phone rang again. He nodded, tense, and left the apartment.

'Have you heard the latest on Hermione Sage?'

'Does she think anyone would want to read that book?'

'Must be desperate.'

'That ship sailed a long time ago.'

'I don't know, Deb. I'm quite interested in reading her story.'

'Don't be silly, June. She wants to steal some limelight from her son.'

Quinn and Ivy stood in the town centre, the castle illuminated above them, their attention on a stage set up despite the snow. The Christmas light switch on was a yearly activity, and this year Miriam Margolyes would hit the switch, so excitement spread through the town like Christmas spirit.

Only the talk this Christmas was all about Hermione.

Quinn and Ivy found themselves huddled with some locals of the town, and somehow Deb and June were with them, because of course Quinn couldn't escape the pair.

'Hermione Sage isn't an author,' Deb hissed. 'Her son is the author. She is a … a … well, I don't wish to say it.'

'Say it, Deb.'

'No, I shan't.'

'Okay, don't.'

'She is a harlot!'

June gasped.

'Yes, you made me say that.'

'She is not,' June whispered, looking around at the surrounding people. Up on stage, a group of dancers were high kicking to a rendition of 'Rocking Around the Christmas Tree'. 'I still watch her movies.'

'They're classics.' The local butcher chimed in, surprising Quinn.

'They're predictable,' Ivy said.

'How are they predictable?' June asked.

'Woman meets man. Man and woman don't get along. Woman and man fall in love. The end.'

'And what is predictable about that?'

'It's the same story in every one of her films,' Ivy said.

'So what?'

'Exactly,' Ivy said. 'I love them too.'

June seemed confused, but looked back at Deb, as if Ivy's words were final.

Deb shook her head. 'A woman allowing herself to be *filmed…*'

'We don't know the situation,' Ivy said. 'For all we know, they could have filmed her without her consent. And if she agreed to the film, what's so wrong about that? We should instead question why we, as a society, let her lose all her work because of one decision relating to sex. To me, that says a lot more about us than it does about Hermione Sage.'

Deb looked like someone had slapped her.

'Careful,' Quinn whispered. 'You don't want to be making enemies.'

Ivy ignored him, instead addressing the group. 'I would like to hear Hermione's story. I hope she finds a ghostwriter and gets a publishing deal.'

'Do you think people even like her anymore?' Deb questioned.

'Are you kidding?' Ivy asked. 'We're obsessed with her here.'

'I wouldn't say obsessed…'

'Wouldn't you?' Ivy asked. 'Hermione hasn't had proper fame in years, yet we still talk about her. Some people will tell you they don't like her. Others will talk about her with fascination. We all feel for her, and care about her, whether we care to admit it or not.'

'I certainly do not care about her.' Deb looked affronted, but June looked pleased.

'You *do*, Deb.' She turned to Ivy. 'I've caught her a few times watching Hermione's movies.'

'Only because you left it on.'

'Not true.'

Quinn thought Ivy might be on to something. The talk of Hermione may have been damaging, but intrigue, fascination and even a desire for her to do well, to return to some form of glory, fuelled it. For Quinn, after last night's talk with Noah, he wanted her to find justice.

'No one will publish her,' a man from the nearby fish and chip shop said. 'She's left it too long. No one cares about her anymore. I bet if you ask anyone here, they couldn't tell you why she was famous.'

'Well, not here, John. Everyone knows about her here,' Deb said. 'But go out of Hay and her name would be as irrelevant as, say…'

'Same Difference,' Ivy said.

Everyone stared at her with blank expressions.

'Who are Same Difference?'

'Hello everyone, we are Same Difference!' A shout from the stage came, and they turned to see a man and a woman standing on the stage, beaming smiles on their faces. Behind them, X Factor branding told the audience why they should remember this duo before they launched into a rendition of a pop song.

'Good one,' Deb said.

'I quite like Same Difference,' June said, and she turned back to the stage and waved with excitement.

Deb rolled her eyes but turned her back on Quinn and Ivy.

The others in the group disappeared into the crowd, leaving Quinn and Ivy standing together alone, watching the rendition of the X Factor contestants on the stage.

'I submitted some chapters to Hermione,' Quinn said.

'You did?' Ivy gasped.

'I did.'

'Oh, but that's wonderful! You have the connections, too.'

'I don't know about that…'

'The job offer? The friend in London?' Ivy said. 'Come on, she *has* to go with you.'

'Depends on if she likes my chapters.'

'She will. I'm sure of it.'

'How are you sure?'

Ivy winked. 'I know all.'

Same Difference finished their performance, but not before telling the crowd they had a new album coming out, and then they went off the stage to cheers. Quinn groaned when they were replaced by…

'Bloody Blair Beckett.'

'Be nice.'

'He can't hear me.'

'Hello Hay!' Blair boomed over the microphone. Deb and June jumped in front of them. Quinn looked around for any stray champagne. 'Well, it's almost time to turn on the lights, and get this town feeling even more Christmassy than it already is. Even in the snow, you've all turned out to see this, and we could not be more thrilled!'

'Why is he even still here?' Quinn asked Ivy.

'I'm still here because I just love Hay, and I've decided I'm going to stay for Christmas,' Blair said to the crowd, and Ivy's eyes widened.

'You didn't tell me you had the gift.'

'The gift?'

'Psychic!'

'Ivy, please.'

'Now, please join me in welcoming to the stage Miriam Margolyes!'

The cheers were deafening, and the wonderful Miriam appeared, waving, smiling, making the audience laugh. After classic one liners and a lovely story of her time in Hay, Miriam hit the button and Hay brightened up with the decorations that adorned lampposts, as well as the castle and its grounds. Hay was decorated for Christmas, but this added to the magic.

Chapter Fifteen

'You're a star, Quinn!' Ivy came crashing into the bookshop, startling the customers inside. She threw the newspaper at him, which he dropped.

Bending to pick it up, he saw Emma's article published. Only he was on the front cover, caught in a laugh, with Noah at his side.

'What is this?'

AUTHOR CALLS FOR PROTECTION OF KINGS & QUEENS was the headline.

He read the article, expecting it to be dominated by Noah, but it quoted both of them like they were equals. The main story, that Quinn was about to lose his shop, was clear to see. Emma did his story justice.

'Ivy, this is amazing!'

'And we're getting emails again! From all the journalists that ignored us after that video you posted on Instagram? Yeah, they're getting back in touch.'

'What does this mean?'

'We're getting your story out there.'

'What's going on?' one customer standing closest to the counter asked.

Quinn looked at the customer, then at the shop. The newspaper in his hands rustled. This was his moment. The wheel was in motion and it was now or never.

'Do you love this shop?'

'I...'

'I know you do. And I bet the rest of you do, too?'

The other customers nodded, listening to what Quinn had to say.

'Well, this shop is being threatened with closure. I'm being evicted. And it's all because of the castle.'

'What?'

Now Quinn thought he saw genuine concern on the customers' faces.

'Is this Hay's only gay bookshop?'

'Gay, lesbian, queer, trans...' Quinn said. 'We have it all here. It's Hay's only shop for LGBTQ+ support.'

'And they want it closed, and you gone?'

'Yes.'

'Homophobia.'

'Transphobia.'

'It's got to be.'

'I hadn't thought of that,' Ivy said.

'No, wait.' Quinn felt panic rise in him. His stepdad may have been a greedy businessman, but he needed to make it clear the reason this shop was going. 'My stepdad has renovated the castle. They want this church to be part of the castle as a sort of information centre before people head into the fortress across the street. Possibly a ticket office, though that doesn't make sense to me. Part of me wonders if he realises just how much this place is worth and he knows he can get a lot of money for it should it sell, but he won't tell me otherwise. It's just business to him. He's not coming for the shop because of its content. He's none of those phobic things. It's because he's thinking of greed, of business, and nothing else. He offered me a shop in the castle, but it turned out that the shop front would be a box room, and nothing like this. I wouldn't be able to live if I opened up a shop there. I'd barely get a shelf full of books inside.'

'He can't do this,' a customer said. She lifted her phone and took photos. 'I'm an influencer. I'll make sure I help raise the word.'

'Oh, you will?' Ivy grinned as Quinn wondered what an influencer was.

'I have 250k followers,' she said and Quinn gasped. 'I'll make sure people fight back against this.'

'Fight back?'

'Aren't you fighting back?' a woman wearing a trans flag badge pinned to her bag asked. 'Are you letting him evict you and close this place down? I came all the way from Scotland for this shop.'

'You did?'

'And I've been here a few times,' a male customer said. 'You helped my daughter come out.'

'Hey guys, it's me, Jenny, and I'm here at Kings & Queens, Hay-on-Wye's only LGBTQ+ bookshop. And I've found out they're evicting the owner and closing it down!' The influencer had her phone in front of her, filming herself. 'We must fight back against oppression and capitalist greed. When do they want you out?'

Quinn was on her screen, being filmed. 'Uh … by Christmas.'

'What?' Every customer gasped.

'No, no, no,' Jenny the influencer raged. 'Did you hear that, guys? They want him out by Christmas. No, we have to stop this from happening. Please let Hay council and the castle know they cannot threaten this shop with closure.'

Jenny stopped recording and instead began snapping more photos. She asked a bemused man next to her to take photos of her in the aisles, which she posed for with no shame. 'I'm going to do a post, too. Don't worry, you don't have to pay me.'

'I...' Quinn didn't want to finish the sentence. He had no intention of paying her.

'Oh Quinn, this is wonderful!' Ivy exclaimed. 'Please, if you can, please get the word out there, everyone.'

The door opened, and a group of the town's locals came in, each of them holding a newspaper.

'Quinn, is this true?'

'Are you really about to lose your shop?'

'I've had my final eviction notice.'

The shop erupted in outrage, broken up by Deb and June rushing in.

'Noah Sage has tweeted the article! Noah Sage has called for this shop to be saved!'

Ivy squealed, wrapping her arms around Quinn, jumping up and down like Noah was the saviour. She broke away from him.

'Please, everyone...' But voices drowned him out. 'Can I get your attention?' Still, no one listened to him. He stood on his counter, towering above the crowd. 'Everyone, quiet!'

They all stopped talking. Jenny took a photo of him.

'I appreciate you all coming here and I appreciate the concern. I appreciate the effort. But they have given me my final eviction notice. They want me out by Christmas. Is there really much we can do?'

'Yes, there is,' a voice from the doorway said.

Was this a pantomime?

Quinn turned; his eyes widened.

'I've got the news coming here to do an interview with you for the six o'clock slot,' Bloody Blair Beckett said, a grin on his smug and handsome face.

Chapter Sixteen

By the afternoon, Hay had been set alight with the gossip of Kings & Queens. To Quinn's amazement, everyone seemed outraged on his behalf. Many stopped by with concerns, voiced their anger, or asked how they could help. It made Quinn realise, for the first time, how important his shop was to the community and the town.

Bloody Blair Beckett stayed in the shop all day, attracting admiring glances and excited conversation from many of the customers and locals alike. Jenny the influencer disappeared, but her impact resulted in people sending emails and messages to Quinn and his shop.

This must be what it's like to be famous.

'The six o'clock segment will be live,' Blair said as a camera crew arrived.

Quinn nodded, shocked he was about to be on BBC News.

'Do you want me to be there?' Ivy asked. She was being polite. He knew she worried he would fuck it up. 'I'll wait behind the scenes, ready to jump in,' she said, before he could say anything else.

All Quinn could think about was the interview, which was

creeping towards him. He felt like a drag queen standing before RuPaul at the deciding lip sync, waiting for the words 'good luck, and don't fuck it up.'

Only Ivy was RuPaul as she continued to fret about the appearance. The usually calm, centred, and grounded Ivy had been replaced with a woman he didn't recognise.

'Ivy, breathe,' Quinn said, after she knocked over a green tea and a stack of books. Thankfully, the books weren't damaged. 'You're making me nervous.'

'I'm sorry, it's just … this is the moment!'

Her phone rang and pinged all day. Emails, texts, calls from other news outlets, all of which wanted Quinn to speak to them first.

'BBC gets first rights in this case, my boy,' Bloody Blair Beckett said to Quinn.

Quinn let Ivy take over selling stock on what proved to be a very manic, busy day. As it turns out, when people think they're going to lose something, they buy, buy, buy, hoping an influx of sales will prove its importance to the town. Daniel Craig hadn't answered his calls and had texted an apology that he was 'at a friend's house'. Quinn didn't mind. It was his day off and he wouldn't be the type of boss that demanded staff come in on their day off.

Quinn had one of the busiest days he'd had in a while – people bought stacks of books, with some sales bringing in as much as £300. Ivy refused help, even when she was juggling sales and phone conversations with journalists at the same time.

Blair mingled around, under the pretence of getting ready for his live, but Quinn knew he basked in being Britain's hottest and most popular television presenter of the moment. Quinn got sick of the swooning from the customers, and sick of himself for swooning too.

As six o'clock approached, Quinn asked about having the

customers leave the shop, but Bloody Blair Beckett insisted they stay. 'Makes for an interesting live!'

Ivy acted as the doorman and stopped more customers from entering. Quinn hoped Noah might appear, but his heavenly body didn't walk through the door.

It was six o'clock. The moment of truth. Blair's live hit for the headlines went smoothly, mainly because it didn't require Quinn to be on camera. Nerves took hold of him as he watched Blair talk, and he felt sick.

'I can't do this.'

Blair wrapped a brawny arm around Quinn with a smile on his face, his lovely aftershave aroma engulfing them both. 'Yes, you can. Just follow my lead.'

Quinn got into place, Blair's face one of concentration. He was apparently 'in the zone', Ivy whispered from behind the lens. Quinn forced a smile.

The camera was on them, and in the background was the frosted glass window and a group of customers standing outside, with some of them holding signs of protest – protest that the shop faced closure, not that he was about to speak to the nation like a Prime Minister begging for votes. Quinn glanced behind him, and with dread, saw Harold forcing his way to the front of the shop.

'Ivy.' He gasped, moving away from Blair with the intention of stopping Harold.

'I'm on it.'

She tore to the front of the shop, heading to the window, as Blair spoke.

'That's right, well, as you know, I'm meant to be on holiday here in Hay-on-Wye and I believe fate has led me to Quinn and his bookshop, Kings & Queens, which is being threatened with closure just days before Christmas.' Blair strolled through the shop, walking past customers, and joined Quinn. Quinn glanced behind him, seeing Ivy panic, moving back and forth, unsure if she should stay on camera or disappear. Harold began knocking on the glass door, to which Ivy squealed.

'Quinn, tell us what's going on.'

Could he not hear the noise of Harold?

'They have given me a final eviction notice for my shop here in Hay,' Quinn began as Harold began pounding on the glass with two hands. 'Um, because of the castle. The castle is refurbishing and they want to close my shop here and turn it into an information booth.'

Blair nodded with enthusiasm. 'And why is this shop different from all the other bookshops here in Hay?'

'Well...' Quinn began.

'Quinn, stop talking!' Harold's muffled voice came from outside. He barged past the crowd towards the door. Ivy followed him, still on camera. She tripped over a box of books, letting out a yelp, before plummeting to the floor.

'Oh, my...'

Quinn made to turn, but Blair brought him back.

'Because isn't this like any other bookshop here in Hay?'

Quinn turned back to Bloody Blair Beckett and his bloody handheld microphone and felt a bloody rage rise inside him.

'No, this shop differs from the others. It's Hay's very own, and only, LGBTQ+ bookshop. We've been here for years now, and we have offered a safe place for LGBTQ+ individuals to have a place where they can feel like they can get support. We have many books from queer authors, some established, others not, and we also sell books that are educational. I have seen people find their voices here, and others find their favourite authors. People come from all over the country to visit this shop. For Hay, losing an LGBTQ+ establishment would feel like a step backwards.'

Wow. Ivy's gifted ring did wonders.

'And it's also putting you out of a job?'

'Quinn!' Harold boomed at the door, rattling it in its frame.

Blair nodded, encouraging Quinn to continue. Quinn thought he saw the camera zoom in on him.

'Yes, I would lose my livelihood. Without this shop, I will lose my income. I will lose everything.' It hit him how close he was to the brink of falling apart. 'But it's not about me. It's about the people who see Kings & Queens as a shop that is safe, welcoming, inclusive, and a home away from home. We're here to educate, support, entertain, and…' Oh god. Not the tears. Please, not the tears. But they came before he could stop them, and the camera was zooming in on him now. 'And to lose this place would be an awful shame.'

'Well, there you have it.' Blair had the dignity to draw the attention away from Quinn's ugly crying face, because he definitely had an ugly crying face, and instead drew it back to his own composed, handsome one. 'This shop means a lot to not only Quinn, but to the community at large. Back to you in the studio.'

A pause, then the camera turned off, and Blair cheered.

'Quinn, you were incredible!'

Quinn dabbed at his face, feeling awful. The customers were now shouting at Harold on the other side of the glass.

'Was it okay?'

'Okay? Better than okay!' Blair said. 'You handled that like a pro.'

'And I'm okay, by the way!' Ivy said. 'If you weren't losing this shop, Quinn, I'd be suing right now. That's going to get this story picked up everywhere.'

'Have you broken anything?'

'Just my pride.'

'Here.' Blair flashed a smile. 'Let me help you up.'

Ivy took his hand, looking flushed.

Chapter Seventeen

Ivy was right. After the BBC interview, articles appeared in other mainstream newspapers, lifting his quote from the live. Some articles focussed on the story, while others used the clip of Ivy falling over.

Quinn watched the report and realised that no one could hear Harold's shouting. Blair's microphone only picked up their interview. If Ivy hadn't run into the frame, then they would have got away without seeing Harold.

Quinn found himself at the back of the shop, away from the prying eyes of the public, who dispersed as night drew in and temperatures dropped. He hid away from Harold, who stood his ground until 8pm, disappearing when he received no attention. Quinn's phone kept ringing, but not with interview requests. His mother was ringing, no doubt to ask him what he had done, and why Harold was so angry.

Quinn now sat at the altar of the old church with Ivy and Blair.

'They want to do a sit-down interview with you for the online team,' Blair said, his eyes on his phone. 'Looks like they want something for their website. Gives you a chance to talk more in-depth about everything. Up for it?'

'I guess so.'

'Yes, he is,' Ivy said. She had her own requests for interviews because of her fall, which had gone viral.

'How do you feel?' Quinn asked her.

'Oh, it's all for the cause,' Ivy said. 'I knew what I was doing.'

'I don't think you did,' Blair said, looking at her with his intense piercing eyes.

'No, well,' Ivy dismissed. 'People are talking. That's the main thing. Do you know how long it might take for this interview tomorrow? Only I've got him lined up with The Guardian, Mirror...'

More interviews. Quinn wasn't sure he could handle it.

'It won't take too long. An hour or two at the most. We can get everything we need,' Blair assured her. 'Don't suppose you could get Noah in, could you?'

'Noah?'

'Well, an author endorsing it is pretty big news,' Blair said. 'These stories can disappear from the limelight. Adding another name to it helps get people talking.'

Through all the bother of the day, Quinn had thought very little of Noah, except for the fleeting and dying hope he would arrive to see the interview. Of course, why would he have turned up? They weren't friends. They had that drink and ... well, it meant nothing, didn't it? Quinn couldn't expect the world from him. He'd been with him to celebrate the interview, not knowing where it would lead, and that was that.

Quinn felt gratitude for Blair being in town. Without him, the BBC interview wouldn't have happened.

'I'm tired.' Quinn hoped Blair would drop the topic of Noah.

'I don't blame you,' Blair said. 'I can be here tomorrow around ten-ish.'

'For the interview?'

'The very one.'

'He'll be here,' Ivy said.

'You will be, too?'

'You want me here?'

'I'd quite like that.' Blair smiled.

Oh, my god.

Blair and Ivy?

No.

Quinn watched Ivy blush and giggle, and the two of them disappeared to the front of the shop, where Ivy saw Blair on his way. He heard the door close and lock, and Ivy was back, failing to hide a beaming smile.

'Oh, what a day.'

'Be careful with that one,' Quinn said.

'I'm a grown woman,' Ivy said. 'But I will. Charming men like him are too good to be true.'

'Charming men don't exist.'

'You do.'

'Oh, Ivy,' Quinn simpered. 'Straight men, then.'

'Oh, I don't think he's straight.'

'What?'

'Bisexuals exist, Quinn, you should know that.'

Quinn looked at the bisexual flag hanging from the roof above Ivy's head. 'I know that.'

'Everyone knows Blair is bi.'

'Do they?'

'Someone hasn't read his book.'

'Can't say I have,' Quinn said. 'He was flirting with you just now.'

'Hogwash,' Ivy dismissed. 'No, right now we have to stay focussed on this issue. You're not losing this shop, Quinn. There's anger here. People will fight.'

'Well, we'll see.'

'None of that attitude, please. The law of attraction always works.'

'What's the law of attraction?'

Ivy's eyes widened. 'Esther and Jerry Hicks?'

Quinn drew a blank.

'Oh my gosh, Quinn.' Ivy shook her head. 'You own a bookshop and don't know who they are?'

'Authors?'

'Gurus,' Ivy said. 'They share what an out-of-this-world being known as Abraham shares with them. The law of attraction that works around us. What we think, what we feel, we attract. It's all about being in the mindset that good things will happen, and they will. Manifestation. If you believe and feel like this is a lost cause, and your shop is gone, then it's gone. But if you believe it is safe, that it won't go, then it will stay.'

Quinn sighed, getting to his feet. 'If only it were that simple, Ivy.'

'It is. We humans complicate things. Is it so hard to believe there are forces out there that we can work with?'

Quinn, his head pounding, could think of nothing but a paracetamol and some water, and a night in front of the TV watching *Eastenders*.

He said goodbye to Ivy as he locked up the shop. The street was quiet now, with Christmas lights reflecting off the snow. He shivered in the cold and turned to his apartment door, heading inside, feeling the warmth and reflecting on the day.

All day the wheels had been in motion, rushing down the track, and now he was at a standstill. Not a crash, but not safe yet. If all of this didn't work, then nothing would. As he unlocked his apartment door, he was hoping he had sent a coherent message to Harold. If this was just business, then Quinn taking it national was just business, too. Businesses had to survive, and Quinn's interview was his attempt to survive. It had happened, and it had gone better than he could have expected.

Maybe Ivy was right. She wished for this so much, believed it would happen, and it did.

Either manifestation was at work, or the stars had aligned.

That, or Bloody Blair Beckett couldn't wait to be the saviour, the hero, the saint.

As Quinn shut the door, his phone rang again. His mother calling.

Sighing, he answered.

'Harold is fuming.'

'I don't care.'

'What did you say about him?'

'I didn't say a thing about him. Just that I was being evicted.'

'The press is saying his firm is evicting you, Quinn. You must have told them.'

'They're journalists, Mum. They're going to put two and two together.'

'Is that him?' Harold's voice came from somewhere in the background.

'Don't put him on, Mum.'

'Let me talk to him.'

'Leave it be, Harold.'

'Tell him he is ruining my life!'

Quinn laughed, out of delirium more so than humour. 'I'm ruining *his* life? He's the one taking away everything I live for.'

'The press is hounding him, Quinn.' His mother sighed. 'They're outside the house.'

'That's not my fault.' But guilt plagued his body.

'What are we to do?'

'Go on with your daily life,' Quinn said. 'And don't speak to the press. Mum, I promise you I won't mention him. But this is my business that is under threat. You best believe I'm going to do everything in my power to keep it alive.'

He hung up and ignored her when she called back.

If manifestation was real, then Quinn focussed on attracting his power. It was time to find his voice.

Chapter Eighteen

Knock. Knock. Knock.

'Whawathaa?'

Knock. Knock. Knock.

What time was it? 3am?

Quinn, in bed, looked at his phone, the light from his screen blinding him. It was close to 7am, the dark of winter still lingering outside.

Quinn groaned.

Knock. Knock. Knock.

'Who is it?'

'The ghost of Christmas past!' Noah's voice.

Noah again? Had he left the door unlocked downstairs once more?

Hold on a second. Noah?

Quinn shot to his feet and almost toppled over. Noah couldn't be here. There was no way this was happening.

Crashing across his bedroom and into his open plan apartment, he almost expected to see smashed glass, mess everywhere, and hooded burglars.

'Quinn?'

The apartment was untouched, clean, cosy. He had left the Christmas tree lights on the night before, and they faded in and out, slow, lazy, like they were willing him to curl back up and hibernate.

He opened the door and observed Noah in all his morning glory.

No, Quinn. Do not *think of morning glory right now.*

Quinn looked Noah up and down, his eyes travelling over him, taking every part of him in. The duster jacket, the scarf around his neck, the bulge of his Adam's apple. On his chin, blond hair gathered to create the start of a morning's shadow. It was rugged, tantalising, the hint of what could be a gorgeously crafted mane of beard. He'd shaved it since they'd been together in the bookshop, but it seemed like a constant battle on Noah's part, judging by the way it grew back so quickly.

'Did I leave my door open again?'

'I'm thinking you want me to come in.'

How could he say that was what he wanted and Noah was welcome here any time? Instead, he gripped the door like he might faint.

Noah headed to the kitchen and sat on the barstool at his kitchen counter. It was almost as if he expected breakfast from him. He headed to the kitchen and refilled the kettle, trying not to think about a domestic life with Noah where they did this every morning after waking up in each other's arms.

'Coffee?'

'Chai tea?'

'N–no.'

'Coffee is fine,' Noah said. 'Uh … listen. Have you heard?'

'Heard what?'

'Harold was on BBC breakfast.'

Quinn gasped. 'He was *what?*'

'He's been on the radio saying that you agreed to close the shop.'

Quinn flipped the kettle on, listening to it crackle to life. His mouth still hung open, like he was Edvard Munch's Scream, only less artistic.

'But I didn't.'

'That's the truth?'

'Yes, that's the truth. I don't lie, Noah.'

'Hey, don't shoot the messenger,' Noah said. 'But if Harold is saying that, what do you think everyone else is going to think? Sounds like he's taking control of the narrative a bit. Classic damage control.'

'What were you doing awake at 5am?'

'Can't sleep.' Noah shrugged. 'That doesn't matter right now. What matters is you exposing Harold for what he is.'

'I have an interview coming up with Bloody Blair Beckett.'

Noah stifled a small laugh. '*Bloody* Blair Beckett?'

Quinn covered his mouth. 'Oh, god, did I say that out loud?'

'Hey, it's fine. Although I'm not sure what he did to deserve that name.'

'No, me neither, he's lovely.'

Noah nodded his affirmation. 'The one good thing was Harold was on BBC Wales radio at 5am. Maybe fewer listeners because of people sleeping? We have some time.'

Quinn picked up his phone. 'An Instagram post.'

'Yes! Let me take a photo of you!'

Quinn held up a hand, realising how bad he looked. Oh god. Noah was seeing the morning him. The side of him he hid from people who looked like Noah. Drool still sticking to his face and his hair at all these angles? No, no. 'I'll post an older photo of the shop with a statement.'

'Yes. You're a PR pro.'

The kettle boiled, and Quinn poured coffee while his other hand typed out a statement on Instagram. Noah watched him, and he tried not to feel the intense stare coming from him. He hoped his shaking hand didn't betray him. Hoped that he looked casual as he tried to focus on the words he wrote. He wondered how damaging Harold's comments were. He supposed having Harold adding to the story would mean his shop could stay in the headlines a little longer. If not the BBC, then he knew the other outlets would pick up on the story. Family dynamics always made the headlines. Hey, maybe he could get a spread in *Take A Break* magazine.

He hit the post button and locked his phone, wondering if his update would make any difference.

'It will be okay,' Noah said. 'What's on your mind?'

Quinn held his coffee, the warmth tingling in his hands. His eyes focussed on the red, green, and white lights, his focus sliding until the colours blurred. 'Harold has to do what he has to do. I guess he thought I was going to damage him and his business, but that wasn't my intention at all.'

'What was your intention?'

Quinn leaned forward, wiping his mouth in case he really did still have drool stuck to his chin. Thankfully, he didn't. Smooth. 'I've been thinking a lot about how I ended up in this mess. I let it happen and I can only blame myself. Since Dad died, I've ignored things. I guess you could say I always had this fear of taking responsibility for anything, but also when I took responsibility, I had Dad there to ask advice. Mum, too. But when Dad died, things changed. I felt alone. Truly alone. Ever since, I've let myself get lost in the emotions of things. Get overwhelmed easily. I hid all these letters and avoided Harold because I thought I could ignore it and it would all go away. I guess Harold didn't feel so bad taking this away from me because I hadn't really formed a good bond with him.'

Noah moved closer, and Quinn's breath hitched in his chest. 'Don't blame yourself.'

'Oh, but I have to.'

'Why?'

'Because it's my fault. I've been so pathetic and let things happen to me for too long. Forgetting I could make a change. Forgetting that if I didn't like something, I could speak up and change things. I've sat on the fence for too long.'

Noah's hand reached for Quinn, then he paused, seeming to think better of it. He let out a small, wistful sigh, giving Quinn a pitying look. 'It's family, too, isn't it? That can't be easy.'

'I always worry about what others think and never think about myself.' Quinn glanced at Noah's hand, wishing it went all the way.

'Time to be a little selfish, I think.'

'It didn't have to be this way,' Quinn said as Noah sipped his coffee. The large pink mug he held suited him. 'I told him so many times how my shop wasn't in the way. Told him not to get rid of me. Let him know I needed this. He ignored it. There was every intention of keeping him and his business out of this. He's panicked because an article put two and two together, and now he feels like he has to say something?'

'I know, it's crazy.'

'What did he say?'

'He said you had agreed to go, that you had a job offer in London and you were planning to move. That the shop could have moved into the castle, but you refused.'

'Yeah, forgetting to mention the size of the so-called shop.'

Noah met Quinn's eyes. 'Are you considering London?'

Quinn shook his head. 'Not at all.'

'Shame.'

Quinn tried not to over think what he meant by that. Why was it a shame that he wasn't considering London?

'It wouldn't suit me,' Quinn said. 'Besides, that job offer is one of those things where people say they'll be waiting, but I bet if I went back to her now, she wouldn't give me a job.'

'Did they fill the position?'

'I guess so.'

Quinn checked his own phone. Another missed call from his

mum, and a text explaining that Harold was just 'clearing his name'.

'Any reaction yet to your statement?'

Quinn scrolled through the comments, stunned that so many people seemed to be willing to help. 'I met an influencer the other day. She's shared it and has clarified that Harold lied. Bloody hell, more followers, too. People don't want this shop to go.'

'Because it's a special shop,' Noah said.

'You think so?'

'Quinn, Hay needs a gay bookshop,' Noah said.

Quinn diverted his attention back to his phone, to hide his own elation at Noah's enthusiasm for his pride and joy.

A journalist from another newspaper messaged him, asking if he would be free for an interview. Quinn replied he might not be, but he sent the vital information to her: that he had a final notice, that he was losing his shop before Christmas, and there was no other option but to close the business if he got evicted. He thought about asking Ivy about a press pack similar to the ones sent to him by publishers for their authors and their latest releases. Maybe he could have it distributed to any journalist that got in touch, so that he wasn't going back and forth with interviews like a desperate celebrity.

His phone buzzed again, and he expected to see another comment, but instead he saw an email from Hermione Sage.

Quinn did yet another impression of The Scream, only this time one of his hands came to his face. The other also would have done so if he wasn't holding his phone.

Why was she emailing now when her son was across the table from him? Noah hadn't seemed to notice that anything was different, so Quinn turned his back on him again and opened Hermione's email with shaking hands.

He scanned the email, expecting to see 'unfortunately' and 'you were very close', but he didn't see that. Instead, he saw a very direct, almost personal response.

Quinn,

Thank you so much for your submission to write my autobiography. I appreciate it. I knew your dad, you know. He was a wonderful man. I was sad to hear of his passing.

I have read your chapters, and I am in love with the world you have created. It is fiction, I know, but I can see your passion and your talent come through. I need someone to listen to me, to take down my words, and tell my story. I would love it if we could meet.

Doing a quick search of your name last night, I saw that your shop is under threat. Please tell me this isn't so. I don't venture into town much anymore, but I have been an avid follower of your shop since I heard it opened. I would like to discuss the options you have when I see you.

Quinn, please confirm if you are still interested in writing my story, and if you will meet up with me soon. We can meet at my home. I am sure you know where my home is.

P.S. Please take a copy of this email and then delete. I cannot afford for the press to hack my emails and leak that you are my ghostwriter.

He couldn't believe his eyes. Hermione Sage wanted to meet with *him*? He re-read the email once, twice, three more times. Was she confirming she'd hired him? Was this an interview? Was she more interested in finding out about his shop? Did she like his writing?

'Quinn. Everything alright?'

He must have tensed his shoulders. Maybe he made a sound. Noah might have a sixth sense, and if he did, he would need to introduce him to Ivy so that she could understand him better than he ever could.

'Um. I don't know how to say this...'

Noah stayed silent. Instead, he fixed him with a look that made Quinn feel like he needed to confess his entire life story, including all his sins. Not that he had many.

'Remember your mum's autobiography?'

'How could I forget?'

'Well…'

Quinn handed over his phone, showing Noah the email.

He held his breath as Noah clasped the phone, *his* phone, and seemed to take the whole morning to read the brief email.

'Oh, wow, Quinn. You applied?'

'I did.'

'To write Mum's autobiography?'

'That's right.'

Noah handed the phone back to Quinn. He stood, walking around the table until he was in front of Quinn. Placing two hands on Quinn's shoulders, he grinned.

'Come on.'

Chapter Nineteen

'Noah, where are we going?'

Quinn's feet, chilled even through two pairs of socks and a thermal skin-tight suit, trudged through the deep snow. The roads were empty, but lethal with ice, and Noah discarded his car to the side of the road and insisted on walking a country lane that looked like it hadn't seen life walk through it since the 1800s. The dead branches were taut and overgrown even in the middle of winter, their skeletons twisted at odd angles, as if they were full of pain and broken.

'It's not too far now. Do you need a hand?'

All he wanted was for Noah to hold him, to guide him through this snow, but he had pride. Plus, he was certain if he slipped, he would bring Noah crashing to the ground with him. Quinn looked through the dead trees, glimpsing a house covered in snow. A puff of smoke rose from the brick-breasted chimney, the shade of grey blending with the sky that threatened more heavy snowfall. He could make that, couldn't he?

The chill on Quinn's face pinched him, and he tugged his coat and scarf closer, wishing for the warmth in Noah's car. Or maybe the warmth of Noah himself. As his foot was hit with a fresh dosing of undisturbed snow, he groaned.

'Come on, hippie boy,' Noah said, flashing his sexy smile. He tugged at Quinn's coat, adjusting it as if it would make him warmer. 'It's just a bit of snow.'

'I could fall and break my neck.'

'At least that would solve the bookshop problem.'

'Noah!'

'Joke. I'm joking,' Noah said, nudging Quinn on the shoulder. 'I don't want you to die.'

Quinn glanced at the house. It didn't take much to deduce the route they were on.

'Why are we going there now?'

The house, imposing, regal, and set within acres of land, was the house Quinn knew to be Hermione Sage's home. Once belonging to Richard Booth, it was now the home of the faded movie star, and the setting of many ridiculous stories about 'Hermione the hermit'.

'Because she's asked you to write her book.'

'But she said to arrange a meeting. We can't just show up.'

'We're not showing up,' Noah said. 'I live here.'

Fair point.

'Come on, if you're that cold, let me warm you up.'

'How do you expect to do that?'

'Body heat,' Noah said with a shrug.

Body heat? Noah's *body heat.*

He could stand here in the cold and trudge through it and pretend that Noah's offer wasn't inviting, or he could leap at the opportunity to be close to Noah again. Body heat. That's all it was. Survival.

Quinn chose the latter. 'Fine.'

Noah wrapped an arm around him like he was a friend, a brother, and Quinn slipped his arm around Noah's waist with some uncertainty.

'You'll have to hold me closer if you don't want to break your neck,' Noah said, an eyebrow raised.

Quinn said nothing, but did as he was told, feeling Noah's toned back underneath him. The warmth was enough to convince him that this was a good idea, and he prayed that he wouldn't slip and take them both out. The last thing he wanted was to be responsible for injuring Noah Sage.

They continued to walk, Quinn no longer angry with the weather, but warm and curious. He couldn't believe he was about to come face to face with Hermione. The once Hollywood legend.

And then the scandal.

A scandal that was not a scandal, but just human need.

A source of gossip.

That was the image of Hermione that Quinn was more accustomed to: a faded Oscar statue. That golden glint, tarnished, chipped away at, and left to rot, not cared for and irrelevant. The press loved to speculate on where she was, forever reminding the public of her 'disgrace' and her 'scandal'. If only they knew that a woman who'd been the victim of misogynistic press now lived in the English countryside atop a hill that had Quinn panting harder than the last time he'd been with a man.

Noah hadn't even broken a sweat and didn't sound out of breath. He held Quinn like he was a delicate vase that needed protecting.

They stopped at iron-black gates with green ivy growing over the bars, twisting like a beanstalk that could one day take them up to the snowy clouds.

'We made it,' Noah said, and he gave Quinn a little squeeze.

'Thank you.'

Noah grinned, letting Quinn go. He feigned falling, and they laughed.

'Ready?'

'Ready,' Quinn said, before taking a deep breath.

Noah pressed the buzzer, looking into the camera. Quinn crossed his arms, observing the deserted landscape.

'You don't just walk in?'

'This is Mum we're talking about,' Noah said, and when Quinn looked confused, he sighed. 'You'll see.'

Quinn turned his attention back to the door.

'Hello?' Her voice was quiet, almost tired.

'It's me.'

'Come, quickly. Don't let them in.'

Noah exchanged a glance with Quinn that said not to ask, and the gate doors opened, which was a miracle considering the drive was covered in untouched snow. A Rolls Royce sat on the driveway, dwarfed by the mansion of the house that was from the Tudor period. Quinn thought it was a black car, but it was hard to be certain with the snow that lay on top of it.

They climbed two small stairs to get to the front door where Noah rang the bell and they waited.

And they waited.

And they waited some more.

Then the door creaked open half an inch, and one blue eye peered at them.

'Are they with you?'

'No,' Noah said.

The door opened, but there was no one there. Quinn thought a ghost answered until he saw who was behind it.

Hermione Sage was mesmerising. She blinked bright blue eyes through thick eyelashes, like they were a fan used to cool down a Greek god. Her blonde hair bobbed, curly and natural, and reminded Quinn of Marilyn Monroe. She wore a floral shawl with patterns of yellow daffodils and pink lilies stretching down to a hemmed line. It was a transparent mesh, revealing casual white shirt and cotton trousers.

'They're always out there, never giving me any privacy.'

He was struck by the hallway. Well, a foyer. He felt incredibly poor. The tiled floor had marble arches holding up a wide balcony that led to the west and east. Two spiral staircases led up to the next floor, which was dressed in a pristine red carpet. Paintings hung on the wall that looked like they'd come straight from the collection of Hans Holbein, and an antique cabinet near a closed door was full of books.

Hermione saw Quinn staring and crossed her arms.

'Who is this?'

Quinn felt somewhat affronted.

'Mum, this is Quinn. The man you emailed,' Noah said. 'He owns...'

'Kings & Queens,' Hermione said, a smile revealing straight white Hollywood-dazzling teeth. 'I like that shop. Oh, Quinn, I only sent that email this morning.'

'Noah was with me,' Quinn said, then panicked. She might want to know why her son was in his apartment. Perhaps she would speculate on their relationship, and then Quinn would have to admit that there was nothing to it, no matter how much he wanted there to be, because *look* at him.

Hermione looked Quinn up and down. He faltered under her gaze.

'I love your shop.'

'Have you ever been?' He felt bold asking.

'I've tried,' Hermione said, 'but the press.'

She said it as if it explained everything, as if that was final, but Quinn wasn't sure what she meant.

'The press is always outside,' Hermione said, twitching a curtain at the side of the door and peering through the window. They looked original to the house, which was Grade II listed. 'They always want the best shot. Not on my watch. I get seen when they need to see me. I'm fed up with the constant hassle.'

Quinn looked at Noah, trying to gauge his reaction. The landscape they'd trudged through had been deserted. It was them and only them in the lane, and Cusop Dingle hadn't seen excitement in years.

Noah's lips pursed. He stared at Hermione's back, refusing to meet Quinn's own quizzical look.

'They want an exclusive. Always want to know what I'm doing.' She bit her nails, the shawl falling away from her shoulders. 'They'll know when I'm ready to let them know. Noah, I thought you were in your room.'

'We popped out,' Noah said.

We?

'I see. Shall we get a cup of tea in the kitchen?'

'Yes, we would love that.'

Hermione led the way, and Noah linked his arm with Quinn. 'My sir.'

'Thank you.'

Noah escorted him to the kitchen. As Quinn felt Noah's arm under his, he tried to steady his racing thoughts. He'd offered his hand as a joke, like he was a butler in a stately home. But being this close to him, touching him, was a whole other experience.

'The press?' he whispered.

Noah cleared his throat, as if this was enough of an answer.

The kitchen was a stainless-steel cold place with wooden floors and a wooden dining table. It was large, but dark, because Hermione drew the blinds over the sliding doors and the kitchen window. Candles flickering in holders on the steel counter were the only light in the room. It was the only cosy feeling in such a clinical space.

'A clean kitchen is a cheery kitchen,' Hermione said, spraying disinfectant on the immaculate counter. She wiped it with what looked like a brand-new cloth and then wiped the kettle before turning it on. 'I get one of the townspeople to clean here.'

'Oh, Ivy?'

'You know her?'

'Who doesn't know Ivy?' Quinn laughed.

'I don't,' Noah said. 'Not personally, at least.'

'Shame. You're missing out on a lot from her,' Hermione said.

'Why are the blinds closed?' Quinn asked.

'Photographers.' Hermione took mugs out of a cabinet. She paused. 'Want a hot chocolate instead?'

'Oh, yes, please!'

'I have marshmallows too.' Hermione showed a door at the back of the room. She looked at Quinn. 'Mind fetching them?'

'Of course.' He curtseyed and then looked at the mother and son.

Noah burst out in laughter. 'What the hell was that?'

'I...'

A curtsey?

'I met the Queen once.' Hermione had a wry smile on her face. 'Curtsied on a broken leg. I think even then I did it more gracefully than whatever that was.'

She didn't say it unkindly. They shared the joke, and Quinn, cheeks burning, headed to the pantry.

He gasped when he saw inside. It reminded him of *Sleeping with the Enemy*. Or Khloe Kardashian's organised pantry. Same thing. Every tin stacked upon the other labels facing out. There were glass jars hosting stacked biscuits, assorted in colour coordination. Not one thing was out of place, and as Quinn stepped into the pantry, he noticed that not even a light coating of dust clung to the steel shelves.

Shivering, feeling like he was being watched, he almost forgot what he went in for. Looking past the biscuits, he saw bags of marshmallows in front of one another as if they were straight from the supermarket shelf. He took a bag, the one behind it flopping over, and felt the need to adjust it to keep it perfectly positioned.

This pantry was tidier than his shop!

He closed the pantry door in time to see Hermione carrying a tray with three mugs of steaming hot chocolate to the kitchen table. He followed her, noticing how the wooden floor was spotless, and he wondered why she employed Ivy to clean this house.

The hot chocolate made his stomach rumble. The sweet aroma and the floating pink and white marshmallows were the perfect sickly treat he needed. He shivered from the cold, his feet still damp, and berated having to walk back to Noah's discarded car. If Noah would even take him back to the town.

'Kings & Queens, what a shop.' Hermione stirred her marshmallows into the dark liquid. 'I always thought Hay needed some diversity. When I heard you were opening, well, I was so pleased. I knew your dad, you know.'

Quinn knew. His dad had always been proud to talk about his memories with Hermione Sage, the famous movie star.

'It was sad when he...' Quinn prayed she wouldn't say it. 'Well, you know. How's your mum?'

'Moving on,' Quinn said. 'But always grieving.'

'Yes, yes.' Hermione sipped her drink. Quinn watched her, drawn in by her. 'My husband was a wonderful man. When I lost him, I felt like the world fell apart. But women don't need a man to feel valued. I was at the top of my game and my career went from strength to strength.'

'You still are top of the game,' Quinn said. 'Everyone loves you.'

It was the first time Quinn had seen Hermione look vulnerable. 'I don't think that's true. The press won't leave me alone because all they want to do is remind everyone about how much of a slut I am.'

Quinn avoided both of their eyes, but the room was silent, and he knew Noah was avoiding eye contact, too. Was this difficult for him? To hear his mother recall something so traumatic in her life? The elephant in the room paraded around them with tassels and trumpets, impossible to ignore. Quinn bit his tongue, waiting for the elephant to finish the show and move on.

'We can talk about it, you know,' Hermione said. 'I want to talk about it.'

'You do?'

'Nobody has ever wanted to hear my side of the story. I have bottled it up inside me for years.'

'That's why you want someone to write the book?'

Hermione placed her mug on the wooden table. It made a dull thud, echoing in the steel room. 'Why don't you write it for me?'

Quinn almost choked on the warm drink. Noah raised an eyebrow, his smile spreading.

'Are you sure?'

'Your father said you always wanted to be a writer,' Hermione said. 'I've been waiting to tell my story for years, but I've not trusted anyone to do so. But you – I can tell you're a safe soul. I want to tell my story, and I want you to write it.'

Chapter Twenty

'I'm going to give you two some space,' Noah said, getting to his feet.

'You don't have to go,' Quinn said before he could stop himself.

The truth was, he didn't want Noah to leave. With their hot chocolates and the flickering candles, everything felt safe. Comfortable. The snow outside, the chill in the air – it all felt secondary with Noah nearby.

'It's alright,' Noah said, heading away from the table. 'I don't think I can hear this yet.'

'Noah…' Hermione began.

'Mum, it's fine,' Noah said. He placed a strong hand on Quinn's shoulder. 'You speak to Quinn. I've got some writing to do, anyway.'

And with a pat of Quinn's shoulder, he was gone, leaving Quinn feeling lonely, but also curious.

Being with Hermione was like a fever dream. He watched her, aware that she was probably feeling his gaze, but he couldn't take his eyes off her. She possessed something, no doubt what the producers and the directors saw in her all those years ago. He compared her to the photos he had seen of her, and, of course, her appearances in films. She still looked the same, ever so slightly older, though of course many years had passed. Either she'd aged well or knew an excellent surgeon, and if it was a surgeon, he wanted the number.

She looked like Noah. The same strong nose, the same eye shape, the same shaded hair.

Noah's footsteps faded away. Not surprising, considering this house was however many square feet with twisting hallways and god knew how many rooms.

'Why now?'

'Oh, plenty of reasons,' Hermione said. 'We'll get to that. I'm just ready for the world to know what happened all those years ago, amongst other things.'

'Do you want me to record this?'

'Do what you wish,' Hermione said. 'I have to admit, when I saw your name come through, I was relieved.'

'Relieved?'

Hermione stood up and headed to a nearby cabinet. She crouched down, reaching for something he couldn't see. Quinn watched, fascinated. As she turned around, she held a bouquet of red roses.

The red roses.

Quinn's gasp was louder than he thought possible. 'Hermione. Dad. You?'

Hermione returned to her seat and handed Quinn the roses. The aroma greeted him, almost transporting him back to his father's grave. The sweet, earthy tone felt familiar, yet strange, in this setting. 'I loved your father.'

Quinn didn't want to hear it. Couldn't hear it. He would forever regret signing up for this and finding out his dad had been having an affair with Hermione.

'Not romantically,' Hermione said, as if she suspected where his thoughts were going.

'But the roses. Your love?'

Hermione nodded. 'Your father was the kindest man to me. When everyone else hated me, made fun of me, laughed about me, your dad didn't. Your dad always had time for me, Quinn. He would write to me. Come visit me. He'd recommend books. Talk to me like I was a normal person. One time, I asked him if he was playing a trick on me. He said he didn't care about any of that stuff, but if I ever wanted to talk to him, I could. And you know what? I did. I felt safe with your father.'

The times his mum thought Gerald had been having an affair. All the evenings he would come home late. Roses being delivered to the shop, then to the graveyard. The fleeing figure. All of it had been Hermione?

'Why did you run from me?'

'I thought you might be the press,' Hermione said. 'I try to avoid people. I hate their stares. Hate what they're thinking about me. Like I say, your dad was my only friend here in Hay. He never judged me.'

Quinn leaned back in his chair, dumbfounded.

'Wow, Hermione.'

'Drink your hot chocolate.'

The drink helped him process everything he was thinking and the way Hermione's admission made him feel. She watched him the whole time as he thought of his father and the secret life he'd led with the Hollywood actress. As soon as Quinn got out of here, he would go straight to the graveyard and wait until the robin hopped on by and he would question everything. This time, he would make sure the robin responded.

'If you're going to write for me, Quinn, then we can't dance around the subject.'

Quinn cleared his throat, feeling that familiar sting of embarrassment in his cheeks. 'You're ready to talk about the sex tape.'

'The sex tape,' Hermione said. 'Yes, that, but more.'

'More?'

'People seem to only remember me as the actress who got filmed doing the deed,' Hermione said. 'Well, is that so shameful? There are people out there who will want to know what I did after that. What happened when everyone dropped me. Yes, I want to get it all out. From beginning to end. To now.'

'When do you want to start?'

Quinn sipped his hot chocolate, thinking maybe she would start in the New Year.

'Now?'

'Oh,' Quinn said. 'Well, I can…'

'Yes, you're busy, I suppose,' Hermione said. 'But we have to get this written fast. If you don't have the time…'

'No, no, I have the time.' He didn't, but he would not lose this writing opportunity. Besides, how could he when he'd found out that Hermione loved his father so much that she visited his grave almost every week? 'But the shop. There's a lot of press attention at the minute. I'm going to fight until—'

'You won't lose it.'

'It looks likely that I will.'

'No, you won't.' Hermione got to her feet and walked to the end of the kitchen, where she took something out of a drawer. 'I'll write you a cheque.'

'Sorry?'

'Think of it as an advance.'

'Shouldn't the publisher pay you that? Then deal with me later?'

'I don't have a publisher yet.'

'You don't have … oh.'

He tried to hide his deflated look, but he knew he had failed. He hoped Hermione would at least have some contract, some definite lead that she would have this published. Otherwise, would he just be wasting time? After all, Hermione Sage wasn't a desirable name anymore, through no fault of her own. It would be a risk to write a story that people may not be interested in hearing.

'That's okay. We'll get one. I'm sure of it. But let me pay you an advance. Something to get the developers off your back.'

'Um… look, we can sort out payment at a later stage. I appreciate what you're offering, but they won't be paid off. He's my stepdad, and he's adamant that he will get the shop. He already owns the place.'

'Then buy him out.'

Quinn forced a smile. 'It's not that simple.'

Hermione returned to her seat, the cheque book in front of her. 'I have money, you know.'

'I know.'

'And I can help.'

'I'm here to write your story. I'm here to help you.'

'Then let me help you.'

He reached out a hand, not sure why. It kept going. Oh, god, stop it. But he couldn't. His hand was getting closer to Hermione's, oh so close, and then he was holding her hand, like she was a dying patient in a hospital bed. Only this was Hermione Sage, Noah's *mother*, and he did *not* have her consent to be holding her hand.

'I appreciate it. But I'm going to fight this.'

Hermione didn't break away. Instead, she placed a rather warm hand over his and gave it a little squeeze.

'You know where I am if you need me to help.'

'I do, and I appreciate that.'

'I would come to the shop and speak out, you know, but…'

She gestured to the outdoors, and Quinn nodded. 'The press?'

'The press.' Hermione blinked. 'And there are too many memories.'

The only press around Hay right now was for him, not for Hermione.

Huh. That was an odd thought.

He pushed it away, feeling like he was throwing shade at the woman that was going to trust him to write her whole life down in a book.

Not to mention she had a hot son.

A hot son who felt the same way as she did: that Hay held too many dire memories.

Focus, Quinn.

'Are we going to talk about the press in the book?'

'Nothing is out of bounds.' Hermione smiled. 'So, you want a contract?'

'If you don't mind.'

'Yes, okay,' Hermione said. 'I'll have my team send something over.'

'You still have a team?'

Fuck.

If this annoyed Hermione, she didn't show it.

'An agent, yes,' she said. 'A lovely agent. Actually, she's my son's agent, too.'

'He's a lovely boy,' Quinn said. Hermione's face was one of unhidden pride.

'He's talked about you quite a lot.'

Quinn, still drinking his hot chocolate, almost dropped the mug. It hit the table harder than he intended, spilling chocolate goodness onto the surface. Hermione looked scared. The smallest drop seemed like the biggest mark in this cold, clean kitchen.

'I'll clean it up!' he gasped, getting to his feet, and rushing to a kitchen roll dispenser on the nearby counter. Hoping to change the subject, Quinn spoke in a high-pitched voice, and then blushed again. 'He's spoken about me?'

'Yeah, a few times. It's lovely to have him here for a little while. I don't see him often. Lives the luxury life down in London. I'm always asking him to come stay with me, but he never seems bothered.'

Quinn tried to focus on that change of subject, but he could barely focus on cleaning the hot chocolate. Noah spoke about him? This was almost as shocking as finding out about his dad's relationship with Hermione.

'Noah has been quite supportive of the shop,' Quinn said. 'He's showing me support in his own way. Did you see his talk with the Hay newspaper? I think that helped get the rest of the press interested. That and blood— um, Blair Beckett.'

'Oh, isn't he so handsome?'

'Yes, he is.' Quinn definitely meant Blair. Not Noah.

Yes, Noah.

Noah, who now entered the room looking like he didn't know that Quinn was hyperventilating about him.

'Everything alright?'

'Oh, dandy.'

He'd never said that in his life.

'What happened to needing to write?' Hermione asked her son.

'Well, I remembered something. Don't you have your interview with the BBC today, Quinn?'

'I do.'

'Shouldn't we go?'

'I ... should.'

'The BBC,' Hermione said. 'Please don't tell them about me. About this. Not yet.'

'No, of course not,' Quinn said, though he was sure they wouldn't ask. Or care.

'We'll see you later, Mum,' Noah said, giving her a soft kiss on the top of her head.

As they left, Quinn wondered if it was appropriate to be jealous of Noah's mother.

Chapter Twenty-One

Quinn wanted to dance. He was soaring, flying high, higher than Santa on his sleigh. Like Rudolph, when he found his purpose and led the fleet in the sky. He felt like singing from the rooftops, announcing to the world that he was going to be writing Hermione's autobiography.

Of course, they needed a publisher.

And he needed to save his shop.

The fear and the anxiety started creeping towards him, like the frost that crept across surfaces in the dead of night. It threatened to tighten around him, choke him, and make him struggle to survive. He wasn't high anymore. He was no longer Rudolph.

He was your bog-standard reindeer reject.

Noah got his car moving again, the tyres slipping on the black ice of the road until they found their grip.

Quinn's mind was buzzing. Why could he only fear the impending dread, like Krampus was about to come and snatch everything away from him? Why couldn't he allow himself this small sliver of happiness?

'Publishing can be fickle, and there's no guarantee her book will see the light of day,' Noah said, not realising that this was not what Quinn needed to hear right now.

He could write. Couldn't he? A degree told him he could. The chapters that Hermione liked meant he did something right. A job offer in publishing told him he knew something about writing.

He could write Hermione's story.

'Did you know your mum knew my dad?'

'I didn't,' Noah said. 'Did she know him well?'

'Very well, by the sounds of it. Sounds like Dad treated her kindly when nobody else did.'

'Hm,' Noah said, his hands tightening on the wheel.

'What?'

'Nothing.'

'No, something,' Quinn said. 'Your knuckles have turned white.'

'Have not,' Noah said before loosening his grip. He glanced at Quinn, meeting his probing stare. 'Oh, fine. It's just … that's hard to hear.'

'What is?'

'That someone was nice to Mum when everyone else wasn't. It reminds me I wasn't nice to her. Still not nice to her.'

Quinn winced, worried he'd offended Noah. He looked at the snowy landscape around them as they approached Hay, his eyes looking toward the graveyard. It wasn't that far from Hermione's home. No wonder she'd found solace in visiting his father.

'You're nice to her.'

'I could do better,' Noah said. 'But I'm glad she had someone in the form of your dad. That must make you proud.'

All the stories he'd heard of Hermione, and the way others spoke of her, came to Quinn. He wished he'd known all that time that his father hadn't been like them. That he'd been kind.

Outside the shop, Noah cut the engine.

'Do you want to come in?' Quinn asked, looking at Daniel Craig through the window.

'Best not,' Noah said. 'Got to do something.'

'Writing?'

'Something like that.'

Quinn watched Noah drive away before heading into the shop. Daniel dropped the book he was reading, the title catching Noah's eye. '*The Curious Man*?'

'I was … curious,' Daniel said, his cheeks blushing.

Quinn stepped a little closer to Daniel, noticing that the shop had a flurry of browsing customers. 'Daniel. If you wanted to talk to me about anything…'

'Coffee?' Daniel asked, snatching his book up from the counter. He hugged it to his chest as he disappeared to the back of the shop before Quinn could answer. Message received.

The bell above the door tingled, and Blair Beckett sleeked back his hair. 'Interview ready?'

His interview with BBC News for their online website went off without a hitch. Quinn, still thinking of Hermione, somehow said all the right things to Blair. After the interview, they filmed him doing things around his shop, such as taking orders from a customer in the form of Daniel and stacking the shelves. Blair explained that a digital segment, along with an article, would appear online in the morning.

The rest of the day went by in a blur, with racing thoughts of Hermione and her book, how the BBC coverage might look, and Noah's wonderful hair. Now, if he could figure out a way for Noah's hair to save his shop then he'd be grand.

Ten minutes to closing, Quinn decided to step outside and bring in a board advertising his Christmas reads. Dazed from the day, he barely paid attention as he left the warmth of his shop, crashing straight into the chest of a man.

He skidded, gracelessly crashing to the ground. A hand gripped his arm, steadying him mid-fall and pulling him back upright, back to earth, and into the proximity of a god.

'You alright?'

Am I alright?

Noah's eyes glinted at Quinn, freezing him in time again.

'Why do you keep running into me?' Quinn laughed. 'We have to stop meeting like this.'

Flirting.

How bold he was!

It was because of the feeling inside him, now rushing back: that elated high, gathering momentum now that Noah stood before him. His hand, hair growing on the back, clutched a disposable cup of coffee, and Quinn wondered why Noah wasn't wearing gloves. His hands would freeze in this weather. He imagined their icy touch on his skin, remembering how his touch felt. But in another circumstance, with different meaning, would they be rough? Gentle?

Stop it.

He was beaming so bright that if Icarus flew by, he would melt. Noah watched him, intrigued.

'Have they saved your bookshop?'

'What?'

'You seem happy.'

And then he crashed. The smile faded and disappeared. His broad shoulders shrugged. Icarus floated by with glee, surviving another day.

'No, it's been a weird day. A good day.'

'Well, I'm glad you've had a good day since I saw you.' Noah's voice dripped with sarcasm, before he paused and caught himself. 'Sorry. I'm going stir crazy here.'

'Why?'

'I thought I'd have a drive around. Maybe brave it and explore Hay a little. All it did was make me realise why I want to go back home.'

'What is home like for you?'

Noah moved aside as someone stepped out of the shop behind him. He reached out for Quinn, pulling him with him. They were pressed against a window, a Christmas display of shining, twinkling red and green lights, which lit them both up. Green looked good on Noah's skin. He wished a stampede of customers would go by so he could stay like this with Noah for longer than a moment.

'I live in a two-bedroom apartment,' Noah said, and even though the customer had gone, they remained at the window. 'I own it. Thank the lord for my book sales.'

If anyone else had mentioned owning in London, Quinn would have rolled his eyes. He might see them as bragging, trying to impress. But Noah admitted his owning of his home like it was shameful, like it was not to be shared. It was humble, acknowledging his privilege. Quinn couldn't help but smile.

'Where is it?'

'Um...'

'Come on, I promise I won't stalk you. It's not like I'm a stalker. I wouldn't be asking if I was a stalker. Stalkers just kind of follow, don't they?' *Stop saying stalker.* 'I'd hope you wouldn't think I'm a stalker anyway. No, you don't have to tell me. It's okay.'

Noah was smirking now, and Quinn liked it, but he didn't like it. That smirk was curious, humorous, and at his expense.

And it's driving me crazy.

'Chelsea.'

'Chels— *Chelsea!*'

Those passing by looked at this outburst like Quinn was a nuisance. He cleared his throat, feeling somewhat silly, the red colouring of his cheeks caused not by the bitter cold weather but by his embarrassment. 'Sorry. But that's, like, desirable.'

'Desirable?'

'Houses. Price wise!'

Noah, still smirking, nodded. 'Why I bought a place there.'

'Is it nice?'

'Yes, it's nice. But now I'm going to have to peep out the

window when I get back. Might not feel safe there. Seeing as I might have a stalker.'

'Why are you so paranoid? You're like your—' Quinn stopped. Not his mother. Never bring the mother into things. 'Characters in your books. Suspicious of the motives of others.'

'You should always suspect others. I mean, you just said you're not a stalker. Isn't that what a stalker would say?'

'You don't have proof of that.'

Noah looked Quinn up and down, placing a hand against the window, leaning towards him.

'Being at my talk at Hay. Locking me in your shop. Saying, "why do you keep running into me" and "we have to stop meeting like this" like you're following me.'

Quinn swallowed, so close to Noah that he could see all the finer details of his face. 'And who has come upstairs and knocked on my door twice? When there's a whole other door outside you have to get through first that always seems to be left unlocked?'

'Isn't it your responsibility to lock it?' Noah was grinning now. Warm, friendly, so bloody sexy.

Hearing his words recited back to him, like it was poetry, made Quinn feel like he might faint. Only he might faint because here was Noah thinking he was a stalker. 'I think you have a key.'

'Yeah, I got one cut.'

'Please tell me you're joking.'

'Depends,' Noah said.

'On what?'

'On what kind of stalker you'll be,' Noah said.

Was he flirting? No.

Flirting with me?

'Well, you might have to find out what kind of stalker I am, then.'

'A fun drunk one,' Noah said, his breath dancing over Quinn's skin.

157

Quinn laughed, recalling their evening together. How long ago it seemed. 'Did I embarrass myself?'

'I don't remember.' Then he paused. 'Did I?'

'Oh, you told me how to find your house, enter it, and your daily routine so that I know your every waking moment.'

'Bingo.' Noah moved back, sipped his coffee, and Quinn never felt so jealous of coffee before.

'Listen, this may seem like what a stalker might say, but fancy doing something?'

Did I just ask that?

'Doing something?' Noah asked. 'Like what?'

Like kiss. Taste each other. Fuuuu…

'Like, something fun.'

'I want fun.'

Where had Quinn heard that before? Grindr?

'What about your shop?'

'Closed.'

Before Noah could say anything, Quinn darted around Noah and inside his shop. Daniel, leaning against the counter, covered the book with his hand.

'Hiya, Quinn.'

'You'll be alright to lock up?'

'Course I will,' Daniel said. 'Speaking to Noah about your shop, is it?'

'Something like that.'

Quinn stepped back out into the cold.

'All good?' Noah asked.

'Brilliant.' Then, pausing, he turned back to the shop. 'Daniel?'

'Mm?'

'Can you bring the sign in?'

'Sure.'

Outside, Noah raised an eyebrow, arms crossed. 'Ready?'

'Definitely.'

So, throwing caution to the wind, they headed out onto the

snowy street, trudging into the layers of snow that wouldn't budge. As they exhaled, their breath formed misted shapes in front of them, which they could interpret if they paused. The winter dark took hold of Hay, and despite the cold, the place felt warm. Shops stayed open later, aromas of fresh baked confectionery and steaming caffeine drifting throughout the night.

'I smell something fruity,' Quinn said, and before Noah could object, Quinn took Noah's hand and dragged him down the slippery street. They went past the butter market, which was built to be cold, so god knows how cold it was in there now, and around the corner, where a woman in a large puffer jacket stood in the doorway, her face visible through the top like a mare ready to race. The two men laughed, jostling each other like it was only them in the street.

'Mulled wine, gents?' She smiled, taking them in. Her eyes settled on Noah touching Quinn's forearm. 'Oh, I heard you were in town.'

'You did?' Noah asked, dropping his hand and stepping away from Quinn. Quinn fixed the faltering smile on his face, convincing himself he was overthinking.

'Gossip spreads fast here, Mr Sage. You should know that.'

Quinn looked at Noah to gauge his reaction. He smiled, but he wondered if Noah felt a little awkward. His eyes glanced at Quinn and darted away.

Hay didn't change. Everyone knew everyone. And everyone loved everyone. Which meant that everyone gossiped about everyone. But it was a kind place, a joyful place, a place where neighbours looked out for one another.

The woman turned away from the door and went into the kitchen of a café that wasn't allowing people to sit inside during the dark night. She came back carrying two disposable mugs, steam rising from the top. Inside was dark red wine, scented with spices and citrus – a spicy scent that made Quinn already feel warm. Quinn made to pay, but Noah shook his head.

'I'll get them.'

'Oh, no, you bring enough to Hay as it is.' She winked at Noah. 'Have these on me, boys.'

'Thank you,' they both said.

'Will we see you at the wassail tomorrow?'

'The ... what, sorry?'

Quinn smirked, seeing Noah for what he had become. 'City boy here doesn't know what that is.'

Noah turned to him, grinning. 'Oh, so now I'm "city boy"?'

'The wassail happens every year, Noah,' Quinn said. 'I guess cities don't have any fun.'

'I can assure you cities are a lot of fun, hippie boy.' Noah turned back to the woman, who grinned at their exchange. 'What's the wassail?'

She showed a poster pinned on a board next to her. A colourful image of a horse's skull, decorated with tassels and baubles for eyes, was the focus.

'We gather and sing, going from house to house,' she said. 'It's tomorrow night.'

'What the hell is that horse thing?' Noah asked.

Quinn gasped. 'Do *not* disrespect our Mari like that.'

'Mari?'

'You *are* from Hay, aren't you?' The coffee seller jested.

'He left when he was sixteen,' Quinn said. 'City boy now.'

Noah nudged him, and Quinn wondered if he discovered the way to get more physical contact from him. Wind him up. The breaking away of a few moments ago had been forgotten.

'There was no Mari when I was here,' Noah said.

'No, she's had a resurgence,' Quinn admitted. 'It has to be seen to be believed.'

'There's a free drink to get you started,' the woman said.

'We'll be there,' Quinn said.

'We will?' Noah asked.

'Free drinks, Noah.'

'Great!' The woman beamed. She bade them farewell and waited at her door for another passer-by. They strolled down High Town Road, the snow slipping off the butter market gates as they trod on by. At the bottom of the street, all souls had disappeared.

It was just Quinn and Noah.

'Have you tasted yours yet?'

'Not yet,' Quinn said.

'Go on. Warms you up!'

Quinn did as he was told. He sipped, feeling the warmth on his lips and the sweet taste pinching his taste buds with a hint of spice. Swallowing, he felt like he had drunk ginger. It tingled as it went down, warming his chest. He drank some more, clutching the mug tight, savouring the warmth.

Warm lights from inside homes on the street spilled out onto the snow.

'Hay in the winter. Beautiful,' Quinn said.

'Hay any time of the year is beautiful.'

'Ah.' Quinn's eyebrows raised. 'So, you don't hate it completely, then?'

'I don't hate it here. I could never hate it here.'

'Don't you ever think of coming back?'

Noah pondered it, his eyes drifting to the stone homes, sandstone walls, and crooked windows. He smirked. 'No, I don't.'

'Shame.'

If Noah sensed the same words being used on him, he didn't show it. Quinn wanted to ask so much more. How could anyone dislike Hay? The thought of not being here made no sense to him. Quinn loved his life here. Saw his future here. The London job had been rejected because Quinn couldn't bear to leave this place behind. And now, with its snow and the glimmering lights, it reminded him why he fell in love with Hay.

They walked down St John's Place, neither of them saying anything, instead listening to the stillness of the night. No cars, no birds, no people. Just silence.

Imagine if Noah came back. What might happen then? Quinn could be his friend. Who was he kidding? He'd be his *boyfriend*. There wasn't any possibility that he could be only friends with Noah. But he refused to come back. He didn't see his life in this small town.

'When I was a kid, I always wanted to be a vet,' Quinn said, filling the silence that he could no longer stand. They stood outside a tapas bar, where laughter punctuated the still night. Quinn's voice, so docile, gave permission for the raucous noises of the restaurant's inhabitants to speak again. 'I thought that would be the career I would have. I always loved to read, of course, but I loved animals. Then, when I was eight or nine, I had an English lesson and the teacher was telling us about the story structure. Then I wanted to be a writer.'

'You did?'

'I did,' Quinn said. 'So, I wrote. And I submitted. I got nowhere. I studied English literature and realised that if I can't be a writer, I can be a champion of it. I can support authors, support writing, sell the beautiful art of crafting stories from words. And I have never been happier.'

They continued down Brook Street, lit only by a lone lamppost. Noah was closer to him now, and between the warmth of the drink and him, Quinn felt secure. He wondered if he was a lightweight, and if the wine was stronger than it seemed. He would blame the funny feeling in his stomach on that.

'I'm like that farmer boy who never leaves home,' Quinn said. 'Hypothetically, of course. I can't handle the muck of a farm. But you know the type. The ones born into the farm, and their dads teach them the trade, and they do that. My dad got his bookshop. I spent so much time there, and it just reinforced what I knew I wanted to do.'

Quinn was smiling despite the bitter, frigid chill. They were heading towards the bridge, huddled against the night, clutching their drinks tightly.

'I bet his shop had a huge impact on you.'

'Oh, definitely.' Quinn sighed. 'It was so perfect.'

'You love it, don't you?'

'Yes, I do,' Quinn said. 'It's a small patch on the earth, but it's my patch. I fit in here. This is my place.'

'London is mine.'

The words felt as cold as the snow.

'Ah, London,' Quinn said. 'If I lose my shop, I may have to follow you down there.'

They stopped at the edge of the bridge, and Noah turned to Quinn. 'Why don't you?'

Quinn's smile, so wide, so content, faded. He turned his upturned head away from the sky and found Noah's face, like he was cautious to look at him. 'Sorry?'

Noah moved closer. 'Why don't you come with me?'

What was he doing? Why was he asking me this? Maybe he was drunk. Bloody wine. Bloody Blair Beckett. Bloody Hay.

'Come with you ... to London?'

'You said you might have a job down there. An offer still standing?' Noah asked, and Quinn nodded. 'You may lose your prized possession, and I get it. It's hard. But think of the opportunity down in the city.'

'I don't know if I want to start again,' Quinn said. 'Maybe in my early twenties I would have. But now I've left it too late.'

'It's never too late,' Noah said. 'You can do anything you want at any moment in your life.'

'What's in London for you? Why don't you move back here?'

'My life. My friends. And my partner.'

Wham. There it was. He thought he'd doubled over, as if being punched, but he knew it was only a feeling inside. That warmth turned cold, like the snow was falling straight onto his heart. His smile faded until he stared at the icy water.

His partner.

The conversation in Hermione's kitchen. The plural we.

'Oh, I didn't know you had a partner,' Quinn said, hoping his high-pitched voice didn't give away the pain he felt inside.

'His name is Matthew,' Noah said. 'Matty.'

Of course, it is.

'He sounds nice.'

'Yeah.'

Silence. Stiffness. Cold.

Quinn had to say something, anything.

'Is he staying with you, too?' He knew the answer, but needed to hear it.

'At Mum's house,' Noah said. 'Spending Christmas with her. I haven't done that in a while.'

'Why not?'

'I spend it in London with…'

A patch of silence nipped in the bud by Quinn.

'Matty.'

'Matty, yeah,' Noah said. 'I invite her every year, but she always says no.'

'Why?'

Though Quinn knew the answer.

'The press.'

'Right.'

'They don't exist, by the way.'

'What?'

'Mum thinks she is still being hounded by the press,' Noah said. 'She is paranoid to leave the house for fear of them harassing her, but the only times she has appeared in the press is when she calls them herself. The true reason she won't go out is because of the people here.'

On this bridge, alone, feeling small and like a blip on the landscape, the words between them seemed to pour out. Quinn felt safe, and he thought Noah felt safe, too. Trust stretched between them like the bridge, linking them to each other.

'Everyone knows, don't they? They all know about Hermione

and her author son. Everyone thinks it's so simple, but they don't get it. I bet you all gossip about it and have a right old laugh.'

'Actually, Noah, no one cares,' Quinn said. Noah stepped back, defensive, his arms crossed, his warm drink held in his hand. 'Hermione is someone we wish came here more than she does. We miss her. What happened to her is a sad story. And you. You're one of us. You're both one of us. But neither of you wants to be here because neither of you seems to care. You don't remember the support available to you. You're both just hung up in your own little world, and that world isn't a real one.'

'How dare you?'

'It's true.'

'You don't know me.'

'No, I don't,' Quinn said. 'But I'd like to.' He cleared his throat, his eyes drifting over the bridge. 'I'm going to tell her story.' He dared not look at Noah. He dared not read too much into his expression.

'I couldn't think of anyone better.'

Had he said that?

Quinn looked at Noah, seeing him smile, but this time he didn't let their eyes meet. 'You mean it?'

'Of course,' Noah said. 'I haven't been able to talk to someone like this in a long time. You have a way about you, Quinn, that makes people feel like they can trust you. There's something about you that makes me feel safe.'

OH MY GOD.

Soaring, flying, fleeting high in the clouds, shining bright like Rudolph. It was back, and this time it wouldn't freeze and die in the crisp grip of winter.

'You don't think it will be weird?'

'No, I don't think so,' Noah said. 'I guess you'll be at the house, then?'

'Yeah, I think so.'

Noah met his eyes. That familiar feeling gripped them. Quinn was suspended in mid-air and a light illuminated them like the beam of God's light rather than headlights from a Jeep Wrangler crossing the bridge.

'I'll like that,' Noah said. 'A lot.'

Dare he move closer? Close enough to smell that aftershave that Noah wore, that Quinn had smelled on him the night in his shop? If he moved closer, what might happen?

But before he could even take one step, Noah checked his watch, and Quinn fell from the sky and landed in a heap on the bridge.

'I should head back home now,' he said, unaware that he had shot Quinn out of the sky. 'I might be a big boy now, but Mum still worries about me.'

'Mothers,' Quinn said, wondering just how much of a big boy Noah really was.

Chapter Twenty-Two

The morning came, and with it, memories of his night with Noah. Like every waking moment of his life, Quinn could only think 'if only' and 'what if', wishing he said something more profound, or at least something bold and clever.

Yet last night felt like he had cemented a friendship with the author. They spoke openly, talking like they had known each other for more than just a few days. It almost felt like they were old souls, together again, reunited after a past life.

He was sure Ivy would know something about past lives. He texted her last night, filling her in on Hermione and her book.

As he showered, he couldn't help but think of the faceless Matty. Who was he? Why did *he* get Noah? How long had they been together? What did he look like?

These open-ended questions left Quinn imagining the worst. The worst being that Matty was as desirable as a film star. That he had the media-approved body of muscles and a perfect symmetrical face, meaning that whenever he went outside, a scouting agent would stop him and say, 'Matty, you *must* be in our fashion campaign for Calvin Klein!' And then Matty would say yes, and he would pose in those wonderful tight boxer briefs, not needing any Photoshop on what was inside those boxer briefs, and Noah would be on the other side of the camera, a smile on his face as he swooned over his conventionally attractive boyfriend.

Yes, Matty was a Greek god, a perfect match to Noah's glorious features. Matty was no Quinn. Matty's better.

Feeling like the stalker he so desperately tried to assure Noah he wasn't, Quinn searched the internet for Matty no face. He typed in 'Matty Noah Sage', for which nothing came up, and then typed 'Matty model'. Being greeted with the men Quinn thought Matty would be didn't help. Any of them could be him. He found Noah's Instagram, trailing back in time to see if there were any posts of Noah with another man. There were none.

Quinn, however, did click on a photograph of a topless Noah taken on a beach somewhere tropical.

He had a V-line.

A V-line!

That classic V that seemed to point down between his legs, disappearing into red swim shorts. His blond hair was windswept, damp with salt water. Alone, the beautiful scenery paled in comparison. But someone had taken that photo of him. No doubt Matty.

A tattoo of a book was visible on the top of his arm. Quinn tried to zoom in by double tapping the image, and with horror, he saw he liked the photo. A red love heart appeared on the screen, fading away, betraying him so disastrously.

'No, no,' Quinn groaned, triple tapping, unliking and liking the photo again.

In dismay Quinn exited the app, swiping it off his screen, his heart thumping heavily in his chest. What could he say? What could he do?

That's it. I'm moving to Ecuador.

Yes, that is what he would do. Delete all the socials, change his name, and disappear to Ecuador. He would have a lovely life there; he was sure of that. He would live in solitude, in a home that didn't have internet, and he would forever think of how he had liked a topless thirst photo of Noah Sage by accident.

And then Matty would find him. His face would be one of beauty. Only it would be angry, contorted into hatred, because by him liking the photo of Noah, which was a year old, by the way, he had come between the couple, who were about to get engaged and get married, of course. The community would then oust Quinn in Ecuador, and he would have to be a nomad, on the run from Noah, Matty no face, and an army of haters.

Tired, with not nearly enough coffee, Quinn stumbled out of his apartment building, feeling the cold winter chill, and trudged the few steps to his shop's front door, underneath his apartment. Only he walked straight into a burly back, almost falling to the slippery floor. He looked up and saw a small crowd of people, all of whom he knew by their faces, some of whom he knew by name. They were outside the shop. His shop. They were clutching newspapers in their hands. When they saw him, their voices erupted.

'Is it true?'

'You can't sell. You just can't do it.'

'My daughter would never have told me she was gay if you hadn't been here to help her.'

'This shop is Hay's heart. You can't go.'

'Screw that developer. We won't have it.'

'And that video on the BBC was fantastic!'

'Woah, guys.' Quinn held up his hands, trying to calm the crowd. 'It's not even eight in the morning. I'm tired. What's going on?'

A woman at the front of the crowd unfolded the red top newspaper she was holding. A tabloid paper. He'd gone national. On the front cover was that same photo of him from Hay's paper: mid-laugh, Noah standing next to him, his eyes bright and his laugh as big as Quinn's. The headline read QUEER TODAY. GONE TOMORROW.

Quinn took the paper and looked at the photo, pretending as though he were seeing it for the first time. He looked happy. In that moment, when the camera snapped, Quinn had forgotten all his worries. It was almost like looking at someone he remembered from childhood, but their name and face evaded him. Only it was himself, of course, and he didn't recognise him.

This article used quotes from the BBC interview, and a few quotes from his interview in Hay's paper. The article even mentioned his dad, and for one moment Quinn thought he was going to have frozen tears on his face as the story recounted his father's own bookshop, and the way the community had loved him. But despite everything, the newspaper had captured the heart of Kings & Queens.

If his first published piece had been a whirlwind, this was even more so. With the BBC and now national newspapers publishing the story, and even ignoring Harold, he almost thought there was a chance to keep his shop alive.

'What can we do to stop this from happening?'

'They want you out by Christmas?'

'Well, that's next week!'

'Excuse me, excuse me!' Ivy's voice was like Gabriel floating down to greet the shepherds. The sea of people parted, like that dude in the Bible did once, only it was the actual sea and not a small crowd of middle-aged locals in Hay-on-Wye. 'Now, what can I do for you all?'

Some people smiled; others looked annoyed at Ivy's arrival. Her eyes darted to the newspaper, but judging by the copy she held in her hand, she already knew the story.

'Ah, yes.' Ivy nodded with vigour. 'Look. Kings & Queens is falling victim to capitalism. By his own stepfather, can you believe? Anyway, we love that the castle has been restored. We do not love that the castle wants to close the bookshop and instead open something for the castle here behind these gay rainbow doors. We will not be silent. There will be a group meeting tomorrow at Hay's community hall. Be there so we can plan our protest.'

People nodded, muttering that they would spread the word, and dispersed. Only two women remained: Deb and June.

'What was he like?'

'Did you smell him?'

'I bet he smells wonderful.'

'I hear he likes bourbon biscuits.'

'Did you eat bourbons?'

'Anyway, we just want to say that if Noah is behind this, then we are too.'

'Not that we wouldn't be anyway, Deb.'

'No, that's right, June.'

June rolled her eyes.

'But we will not let this shop close. You can count on us to be there.'

'Great,' Quinn said, already exhausted.

'Tomorrow at 7pm, ladies,' Ivy said. 'Spread the word.'

'And yes, he smelt wonderful,' Quinn said, and they erupted in excited squeals.

They headed into the bookshop, leaving Deb and June peering over their shoulders in case they saw Noah. Because of course Quinn must be keeping him tucked away to roll out for publicity.

The excitement that his story hadn't faded into obscurity almost made Quinn forget about his experience with Noah last night.

Almost.

But he needed to focus. The newspaper lying on his desk, his radiant smile looking back at him.

'What the actual hell has happened?'

'We got the attention we needed,' Ivy said. She shed her pink coat and hung it up on the coatrack. 'Now, I'm going to call the town hall and make sure that we *can* host a meeting there tomorrow. In the meantime, you will make me tea.'

'Oh, right?' Quinn had a few choice words to say about being bossed around in his own shop, but he bit his tongue. Without Ivy, things wouldn't be happening. 'I didn't know about the talk tomorrow at the community centre.'

'Neither did I until I said it.' Ivy smiled. 'Shame, because I had plans to eat my weight in gingerbread biscuits. Never mind. There's always the day after.'

Ivy stood at the counter, looking out the window at the towering castle.

'Just bad energy.'

'Hmm?'

'I sense terrible energy from that place.'

'Ah, okay.'

Ivy nodded as if she had said something profound, and Quinn watched her with fascination, wondering what was going on in her head. He was learning she was always five steps ahead, somewhere else in her brain, working something out.

Before he could ask her, the door dinged, and in walked...

'Bloody Blair Beckett,' Quinn muttered.

'I'm sorry?' Blair asked, a grin on his face. He was so pretty he hadn't heard a word Quinn said.

'Nothing. Hi, Blair.'

'Online article went down well, boys.'

'I'm a woman.'

'Yes.' Blair looked at her. 'Yes, getting lots of hits on the website and the socials.'

'We thank you for your time,' Ivy said.

Blair strode around the shop, taking it all in. His hands slipped into his trouser pockets, and Quinn tore his eyes away from the perfect peach bum toned in the gym. Bloody Blair Beckett. He would not be attracted to Bloody Blair Beckett.

'Is this an original church pew?' Blair shouted from the back of the shop.

'Yeah, we kept one back. You can even see some carvings in there left behind by some anxious people confessing their sins.'

'It says "Quinn was here 2k9",' Blair called.

'Yeah, wonder who that was.'

Ivy laughed.

Blair came back into view, holding a copy of his own book.

'You sell these?'

'Obviously.'

'I'm surprised,' Blair said, and Quinn hated to admit that he seemed surprised. 'It was a shameless cash grab for Christmas. Didn't think people would still care about this Llanelli boy now broadcasting the news.'

Quinn shrugged. 'Seems like people care. Unfortunately, I don't sell your children's books.'

Blair nodded and put his book on the nearest shelf, something that annoyed Quinn and his need for order.

'Let's do a book signing.'

'Are you serious?'

'If you'll have me do one.'

Did he want to be advertising an evening with Blair Beckett?

'Yes, we do,' Ivy answered. 'Tomorrow at 7, Blair. The community centre. Meet us there and we'll flesh out all the details.'

'Yes, ma'am.' Blair smoothed his hair into place before stepping closer to Ivy. 'Are you going to the wassail tonight?'

'I am.' Ivy twirled her hair in her fingers. 'Are you?'

'Yes,' Blair said. 'Shall we go together?'

'Okay,' Ivy said.

As Ivy and Blair arranged their date for the evening, Quinn couldn't help but wish that it could be that simple for him and Noah.

Wassailing in Hay was almost as exciting as Christmas itself. The small town came alive with people gathering on the streets, clutching hot drinks and alcohol. Starting at the top of Castle Street, a group waited for Mari Lwyd and her companions to lead the way.

'I've never seen anything like it,' Noah said.

Floating like an ethereal spectre in front of them was a pale white horse's skull, snapping its boned jaws together. Ribbons of red and green flowed from a white cloak, which trailed down to the snow-covered floor. The head turned left and right, staring at those gathered with green bauble eyes. A woman wearing a red scarf held Mari by a lead, guiding her around like a horse to its stable. Mari Lwyd approached Noah and Quinn and pretended to drink from Quinn's coffee cup before snapping her jaws at Noah's hands.

'Woah,' Noah gasped, looking alarmed.

His reaction only led to the Mari chasing him until she spotted another group and went to terrorise them instead.

'There's someone under there, isn't there?' Noah looked at the horse like it was a hard mathematical problem.

'Her jaws are operated by someone with a pole under the cloak, yeah,' Quinn said. 'But that ruins the illusion.'

'And what is the point in her?'

She wasn't the only Mari. Two others joined the group, their handlers handing out sheets of paper.

Quinn took one from the nearest handler, but not before Mari bit into it and tried to run off with it. When Quinn got it back, Mari snapping, he showed Noah the Christmas carols on the paper.

'She's a winter thing,' Quinn said. 'An old tradition. Hay does it a little earlier. We sing these carols with her leading the way. Her point is that she demands entry to homes, and the person at the door sings back, and then we gain access to the homes.'

'What happens when she gets inside?' Noah asked, his eyes shifting to each Mari as if he were afraid of an attack.

'She steals all the food and drink, chases the children. They all sing some more,' Quinn said. 'The usual.'

'I can't believe I've never heard of her.'

'She comes alive this time of year,' Quinn said. 'Yule. She helps represent the Welsh New Year. Lately, a lot of towns like Hay have welcomed the tradition back. It's beautiful to see.'

'Where did she disappear to?'

Quinn thought for a moment. 'I guess it comes from how the English tried to stamp us out. A lot of Welsh folk customs disappeared. She survived, though, and she's making her comeback like that time Britney did Womanizer on The X Factor.'

'Now *that* was a comeback.'

'She never left.'

The woman in the red scarf called to the audience that it was time to parade, and a nervous hush fell over the audience. They began their descent down Castle Street; the group singing Christmas carols, and the three Maris weaving through the crowd before scurrying off to nearby homes.

'I can't believe people are going with it,' Noah said as they watched one Mari dance through someone's hallway before running back out into the street.

'People get on board with it,' Quinn said.

'And people are singing in Welsh,' Noah said.

'That's right! Now, come on. Sing with me.'

It was apparent that Noah didn't speak Welsh, let alone sing it, but he tried. Quinn helped guide him, tracing his finger across the lyric page that they shared. Their hands were close, and Quinn wanted to let his little finger brush Noah's, but he couldn't.

As they went to the next street, Blair and Ivy joined the group, giving a wave to Quinn. He smiled at them, wondering if they would join them. But as Blair placed an arm over Ivy's shoulders, he thought they would rather have their own time together.

Quinn caught Noah's eye, and he smiled. Noah smiled too, but he looked a little too long at Quinn. Faltering, Quinn sang the wrong words, throwing Noah off.

'You did that!' Noah said.

'I'm sorry. You have a lovely voice, too.'

It wasn't a lie. Despite Noah leaving Hay all these years ago, he had kept that Welsh accent twang, and it was even more apparent in his singing voice, which kept the pitch and its soothing tone.

'Oh, stop it,' Noah said. 'If I could sing, I wouldn't be a writer.'

'What would you be?'

'A popstar.'

A nearby Mari, hearing this, turned to face them with those wild eyes, and snapped her jaws together. Noah, now getting used to the tricks, sang the next Christmas carol to the Mari, making the woman guiding her laugh.

The trickster spirit of Mari rubbed off on the crowd, with people helping to play tricks on others. As they came to the Rose and Crown pub, their final destination, people took over guiding the Mari to unsuspecting customers, her boned jaw nipping at their clothes. Inside the pub, the lights dimmed, and the Welsh carols continued. The Maris each performed a dance, which was more of a sway from side to side, but the big skull glittering with tinsel made the audience laugh.

Noah bought them drinks, and after two whisky's, they joined the crowd, dancing along with the Maris and the rest. Quinn had to admit that Noah could move. He sang along to Wham's 'Last Christmas', giving a very dramatic rendition and acting out the words with one of the Maris, who somehow showed emotion with her expressionless face.

Quinn laughed each time Noah committed to the lyrics, watching him give his best Backstreet Boys impression. Then he joined in and it felt like they were on stage together. During a Taylor Swift bridge, they found themselves close to one another, so close that Quinn could do divination on the light wrinkles in Noah's skin.

The crowd seemed to melt around them. Even Taylor's voice faded away.

Noah seemed to X-ray him, a hunger in his eyes like a vampire seeing his next meal.

It was sexy as hell.

Quinn placed a hand on Noah's shoulder, trying his best to muster up the energy not to move closer.

Noah's hand found Quinn's, looking at his fingers, that familiar expression of lost thought knitting across his brow.

What was he thinking?

Noah patted Quinn's shoulder, the sort of pat you do when two men want to show affection without showing affection. It was the pat he'd given him before, as if establishing a brotherly bond and nothing more. Quinn felt as though it'd stung him.

'I should leave,' Noah said, clearing his throat.

'Stay for one more?' Quinn asked.

'I told Matty I'd only be gone an hour.'

This time, the sting was more than a sore spot. He was deathly allergic and it was making it hard to breathe. 'Better get back, then.'

He hoped Noah sensed the shift, but he seemed to be a master at controlling his emotions. Noah finished the rest of his drink and then zipped up his coat. 'Let's do this again.'

An antidote to his swelling stings.

Chapter Twenty-Three

Quinn found himself in the bright community centre that Ivy had booked, still high on last night's activities. The building was full of familiar faces, all of whom were here to see what they could do to save Quinn and his shop. Blair Beckett, in all his television glory, seemed to strike the locals as royalty. He shook their hands, asked them questions, and seemed to care what they had to say.

It warmed Quinn's heart to see these people here, for him and his shop. Friends of his dad, customers of his shop, and Deb and June. He suspected they might be here more so for the chance of seeing Noah Sage, but he had yet to arrive. Quinn suspected he would not appear.

'I have invited him,' Ivy said.

'Who?'

Ivy gave Quinn a look. 'Noah. I know you're thinking of him. He's invited.'

'Oh, it doesn't matter,' Quinn dismissed, but he wondered if Ivy genuinely was psychic.

'You two seemed to have a delightful time last night.'

Quinn tried to fight away the memory of dancing with Noah – so close, yet so far. If Ivy noticed, how many others had?

'And what about you and Blair?'

'That is not on the agenda this evening,' Ivy said as she consulted her imaginary list.

Quinn headed to pour a mug of coffee, something that the local café owner had provided, and changed his thoughts to his mother. Would she come tonight? Hay was small, and she'd heard this was going ahead. She had texted him, even tried to call, after seeing the newspaper and BBC article. But she was more concerned about how Harold might be feeling, rather than how Quinn was feeling.

Quinn imagined what he would say if she arrived. *I know you're in a tricky situation, Mum, but for god's sake, stop him from selling my shop!*

He added a splash, and then a dash, of milk to his black coffee, stirred with a flimsy stirrer, and then brought it to his lips, feeling calmer now that he had something in his hands and something to distract himself from the eyes of the people in the room. Somehow, Ivy had found them enough seats, and those who couldn't sit on the fold out chairs provided gathered at the back of the room. The hall, with its tall roof and single glazed windows, decorated for Christmas. On the stage stood the set of the nativity play that the local school kids would put on for the community, something they did every year, and something Quinn avoided when the time came. A Christmas tree stood at the back of the room near a serving hatch where there was a kitchen. From the bathrooms to the storage cupboards, tinsel and Christmas lights were strung from the ceiling, hovering above the heads of the town's locals.

'Ahem, hem, hem,' Ivy trilled from the stage over a PA system that whined and wailed.

Where the hell had she got that?

The warm, welcoming hush of voices, that lovely hum, faltered, fading away, and all eyes were on Ivy. She had tinsel in her hair, and she was wearing a Christmas jumper with a waving Santa.

'Thank you all so much for being here with us tonight,' Ivy said as yet more people arrived. 'Yes, there is room at the inn. Come in, come in, get yourself settled. Now, we're here to discuss Kings & Queens, Hay's only LGBTQ+ bookshop. Over the years, Kings & Queens has been a welcoming, safe space, and one that has helped bring Hay into the modern era. Now, it is being threatened with closure. You all already know this from the radio interviews, the magazines, newspapers, and online reports. We've gone viral!'

At that, the room erupted into cheers and applause, and Quinn couldn't help but smile. But as he did so, his eyes kept darting to the back of the room, and then around it. Hoping – hell, praying – Noah might arrive.

'We're here to discuss what we can do to clarify that we will not stand for it, and that yes, Kings & Queens will still be here ten, twenty, thirty years from now,' Ivy said to the gaggle of Hay's locals. Quinn even wondered if there were more than just locals in attendance. 'Any suggestions?'

'Show people how good the shop can be!' a woman Quinn recognised from the town's council said.

'How can we do that?' Quinn asked.

'You're the owner. You should know,' Ivy jested, and the room laughed again.

'Well, my friend here should consider a comedy career after this,' Quinn said, and he walked to the stage and sat on the end. Sitting on the stage felt a lot less daunting than standing on it. Plus, he didn't much fancy glimpsing the nativity's baby Jesus that was at least fifteen years old and was missing an eye. 'But the whole point is to ask you. What do you think shows how important we are?'

'Author signings,' a young woman said from somewhere in the room.

'We actually have one author lined up. Keep an eye out for details on that,' Ivy said.

'Who?'

'Me!'

Blair Beckett raised his hand, and a few people in the audience let out half-hearted cheers.

'And any other author signings?' someone asked. Blair dropped his hand.

'Not right now,' Quinn said. 'But we'll keep you posted on Blair's signing.'

'What about Noah?'

'Yeah, Noah Sage.'

'We can talk to him, but I'm not sure we can guarantee that.' Quinn said, wishing more than ever that he could guarantee that.

'Is he coming tonight?'

'I wish,' Quinn said, then he realised what he'd said. 'I wish everyone could come tonight.'

Swallow me up, baby Jesus.

'Other events,' Ivy said. 'What else can we do?'

'How about a Christmas party?'

'Oh, I love a party!' Ivy exclaimed. 'Quinn! A party!'

'When?'

'Christmas eve,' someone suggested.

'Um…' Quinn panicked, wondering how he could get enough alcohol, party stuff, and fun events in time for Christmas eve. 'That's like at the end of this week.'

'Exactly!' Ivy exclaimed. 'Plenty of time. We can have drag queens.'

'I don't know if we'll get any in time.'

'I'm a drag queen.'

'Me too.'

'Me too!'

'Three drag queens!' Ivy said. 'And the theme will be ghosts of Christmas past.'

'Sleigh,' Quinn said.

A hum of activity spread around the room like news spread of the birth of Jesus himself. 'And what else can we do?'

'A protest,' Daniel Craig said.

'Yes, a protest!'

'Starting where they host the festival and ending outside the shop and the castle.'

Protests?

The idea of a protest scared him. The last thing he wanted was aggravation. He pictured books flying in anger, maybe burning and Santa falling off his sleigh, while the star on top of the Hay Christmas tree fell to the ground and landed on Blair Beckett's head.

'A peaceful protest,' Ivy said.

'Yes!'

'When?'

'The same day as the Christmas party?' Quinn heard himself suggesting.

'Why that day?'

'Gives people an excuse to come to the shop,' Quinn said. 'Protest and champagne.'

'Obsessed with that,' Ivy said. 'Are there any other suggestions?'

'Are you still looking for another author to sign some books?'

His Welsh-accented voice, angelic, majestic, deep and soulful, rang through the room, bringing the spirit of Christmas with it. And that harmonious feeling shattered when Deb and June screamed like someone had stabbed them in Hay's murder and mystery bookshop.

'Is it him?'

'It *is* him!'

'Respectfully lust, ladies,' Ivy said. 'Thank you for joining us, Noah.'

Quinn sought him out. Standing near the back of the room, just a few feet away from the Christmas tree. His blonde, messy hair had one loose, curled strand at his forehead. His glasses were back, giving him that studious look, and he wore a black parka coat with grey trousers, which Quinn noticed were slim fit and clung to him with shapes in *all* the right places. The image of him, topless, displaying his V-cut body, flashed in Quinn's mind. Fighting to keep his eyes at eye level, Quinn smiled at Noah, trying to feel nonchalant, even though every fibre in his being was vibrating, crying out from the hunger and the desire that ripped through his body.

'Yes, we can make room for you to sign some books,' Quinn said. 'I'd be honoured.'

Their eyes met again, and Quinn took a breath, like he'd been plunged into the depths of icy water.

Then Matty No-Face came floating into the ether, and Quinn forced himself to look away from Noah, even though he wanted to study him like he was Michelangelo's David.

Great, now I'm thinking of Noah naked.

That V-line!

'In the meantime, spread the word about what we are facing,' Ivy said. 'Let your customers, your friends, your family know that we could lose this shop. We should remind each other of love, acceptance, and pride. Let's make sure that capitalism will not prevail!'

She said these last words like a king leading his army to battle. The people applauded and cheered, getting to their feet, ready to fight.

'Isn't anyone going to listen to my story?'

Boo. Hiss. Bah humbug.

Harold's voice boomed across the room, and people stopped in their tracks, turning to the Henry VIII figure in the doorway.

Harold found Quinn and walked towards him. Quinn, torn between running away and wanting to stand his ground, felt

Harold's hand on his shoulder, gripping tight. Quinn wondered if Harold was trying to hurt him.

'We're family,' Harold said.

'You're my stepdad,' Quinn clarified.

'Family,' Harold barked. 'And family can be … complicated. Can it not?'

If Harold expected applause at this, he didn't get any. Flustered, he cleared his throat and relinquished his grip on Quinn's shoulder.

'I offered Quinn a room in the castle. A simple moving of premises. Quinn decided he did not want this room that was offered.'

'Show them the floor plans,' Quinn said. 'They'll see how small that offer was.'

'And businesses these days are online,' Harold said, as if he hadn't heard a word Quinn had said.

'Most of my custom comes from physical customers,' a bookseller at Clocktower Books said.

'And our bookshop does better here than it does online,' another added.

'Mine too,' Quinn said.

Harold turned a horrible red. Quinn almost felt sorry for him.

'The point is, Hay changes. Business is business. We need a place to display history, and we need an information centre. Quinn's shop is part of the deal.'

'A deal I haven't signed or agreed to.'

'You don't have to when the castle wants their chapel back,' Harold fumed, turning wide eyes on Quinn.

'But I don't understand why they want it back now.'

'I convinced them it was a good idea,' Harold said to the room. 'You lot have to agree with me. Why refurb and open the castle and not get back its full heritage with the chapel?'

Quinn, shaking, though determined to stand his ground, got to his feet. He looked down at Harold and his thinning hair. 'When you got the contract, Harold, I asked you if my shop would be safe. What did you say?'

'That doesn't matter.'

'What he said was the shop would still continue to run, untouched, and I had nothing to worry about,' Quinn said to the room. Everyone was glaring at Harold, some people even shaking their heads, and Deb had to hold June back. 'Harold has owned my shop for years. He helped turn it around into something habitable again. Now, he wants to give it back to the castle and chuck me out on the street.'

'Business is business.'

'Yes, it is,' Quinn said. 'And we're all businessowners here. And we're fighting the man.'

The room applauded, and Quinn was pleased to see Harold speechless. Noah reached the front of the stage, and this time two people had to hold back Deb *and* June.

'I think you'll find you're not welcome here, sir,' Noah said to Harold, with an ease that made Harold gasp.

'An eviction notice is an eviction notice, Quinn,' Harold said. 'I think you forget that shop is mine.'

'Can't you sell it to Quinn instead?' Daniel asked.

'I'm leasing it to the castle, not selling,' Harold said. 'And there is no way Quinn could raise enough money to buy me out.'

Quinn pinched between his nose as a headache took hold.

'Please, sir, if you would leave, we would appreciate that,' Noah said, and Harold, realising he didn't have the support of the room, stomped out in a rage.

Chapter Twenty-Four

The crowd poured out of the room, and Quinn and Ivy tidied up after them, throwing away finished drinks, food wrappers, and even a wet tissue. Quinn, holding it with the tip of his fingers, and wondering why anyone might have used a tissue, dropped it into the bin in the kitchen. He tidied away the jars of coffee that someone had found and put a box of Tetley tea bags back in the cupboard.

He turned to leave the kitchen and screamed, seeing a figure cast in shadows in the doorway.

'Woah, woah.'

A light came on, that horrible offensive fluorescent lighting, the type that made your skin look like melting wax, and Noah was no longer a demon coming to suck him into the underworld, but a demon who came to suck...

Stop it.

'I preferred you with the lights off.'

'I've been told that before,' Noah said, then he cleared his throat. 'Tonight went well.'

'Blew me away,' Quinn said. 'So many people turned up. And

they all care. They all want to help. Now we just have to make sure they turn up.'

'Why wouldn't they when I'm involved?' Noah grinned.

'I'll throw a wet tissue at you.'

'A wet tissue?'

'Don't ask,' Quinn said. 'So, you really want to do a book signing?'

'If you'll have me.'

Gladly.

'Yeah, that would be good.'

Better than good.

'What day will you have me?'

Any day of the week.

Stop it.

'How about midweek?'

'I can do midweek.'

'Me too.'

'Good.'

'Cool.'

A silence spread between them until Ivy sang a rendition of 'Merry Christmas Everyone' in the main hall, the acoustics of the building doing her voice dirty.

They both laughed, but it wasn't cruel. It was a shared appreciation of the moment. Then Noah stepped into the room, and it was like that pesky demon had sucked out the air.

'Mum is looking forward to talking with you,' Noah said. 'I wanted her to come tonight, but she couldn't.'

'It would have been nice,' Quinn said. 'I haven't had a contract from her yet.'

'She's still getting it finalised,' Noah said. 'Hope you're good with selling your soul?'

'Aw, already sold.'

'Same.'

A smile; a bond.

'I imagine you'll be at the house pretty soon. Although now you're going to have a busy week—'

'I can still write the book.' Quinn stumbled over his words, fearing his opportunity to get to write Hermione's story was slipping away.

But it wasn't just to write her story. And it wasn't to have a back-up in case his shop disappeared. A small part of him hoped for an excuse to get closer to Noah, to learn about him from a trusted source. He hadn't paid it much thought when he first submitted those chapters, but he knew now, with Noah standing before him, that it'd played a factor in Quinn's decision.

Gosh. Maybe I am that stalker.

'Of course,' Noah said. 'Thing is, I was thinking, you know, it might be a week or so before you come back to the house. But why don't you join us this week for dinner? It's a good way to get to know her off the record.'

Did he just ask me to dinner? Off the record?

'Not a date.' Noah smashed Quinn's dreams.

'I didn't think...'

'Oh, right, yes, good.' Noah baulked.

'Matty.'

'Matty, yeah.'

'Yeah.' Quinn faltered.

'I mean, not that I... You know, it's just... No, research purposes.'

'Research purposes,' Quinn agreed. Definitely research purposes. 'I can do that.'

'Good. Cool.' Noah smiled. 'Can you do tomorrow evening?'

Quinn wanted to give a definitive answer, but then he thought, no, why should he? Why should he be at Noah's beck and call? Play it cool, right? Isn't that what everyone does? Aloof. Casual.

'Yes, I can't wait,' Quinn said.

Noah smiled, and then Ivy appeared at the door.

'I wondered where you got to,' she said, looking from Noah to

Quinn. She reached a hand to Noah's cheek, and Quinn had never been more jealous of a hand, or Ivy. Noah didn't flinch from her touch. She pulled a strand of fluff from his cheek. 'This was stuck to you.'

'Ah.' Noah looked at the grey fur in Ivy's hands. 'That's a bit of Mr Lavender. His fur gets everywhere.'

'Mr Lavender?'

'Hermione's cat,' Ivy said. 'I'm always hoovering up his fur.'

The three of them bade each other goodnight, and Quinn headed home, lost in thought.

An evening of research. Research purposes. A talk off the record. How wonderful this week was turning out to be, and it was only Monday. Christmas was fast approaching. Normally, he would go to his mother's. But now, with everything going on, he thought he would need to spend it alone. He wasn't excited about Christmas. Not anymore.

Instead, the protest filled him with excitement. The two author signings. The party.

Oh, one-eyed Jesus, the party!

In all the commotion, he'd forgotten he needed to plan a party. The drag queens were no doubt planning their outfits and makeup, the locals writing their protest signs and then picking out their evening outfits. And him? He was thinking of Hermione, Noah, and the girl band Girls Aloud's television series, *Off the Record*, which Noah put into his head by the power of association.

As he got to his apartment, recalling a quote from Nadine Coyle and trying to voice his own Irish accent in his head, he allowed his eyes to drift towards the castle that he could see from his living room window. Lights were glowing inside, no doubt the last preparations being made for a public opening.

And then he realised.

His planned protest was on the day of the castle's opening.

Oh, what a bad idea that might be. Would the curiosity of a

refurbed heritage site and a much-loved staple piece of Hay distract those willing to protest for his shop's sake?

His phone buzzed. Quinn looked at the screen.

> People will protest inside the castle. Two birds with one stone. Save your shop. Appreciate history.

Ivy, her ever more convincing psychic abilities striking again.

Chapter Twenty-Five

Quinn had almost finished perfecting his invites for the party when the door to the shop opened and Gordon strolled in. He closed the invite design so quickly that scientists would need to study him. Some people were not invited, and his cousin Gordon was one of them.

'Quinn,' Gordon said, as if they were about to enter a very formal meeting indeed.

'Gordon.' Quinn matched the tone. 'Can I help?'

'To be honest, I needed a break.'

The incense on Quinn's desk floated between them, a lavender scent in the air. The Lo-Fi music playing on the shop speakers at a discreet volume clashed with Gordon's plastered stained high-vis jacket, his work slacks, and his black boots covered in dust.

'A break from what?'

'Harold!' Gordon said, his hand darting out and gesturing at the castle on the hill. 'He is on one, and has been on one, for three days now.'

Quinn dusted off his clean clothes. 'I don't know what you mean.'

'Yes, you do,' Gordon said. 'He's pissed.'

'Shame. Daniel, do you mind if I just…?'

Daniel, stocking the shelves, nodded. 'Go for it.'

'Hiya, mate,' Gordon said.

'Yeah. Hi. Hiya, bro … ski.' Daniel blushed at his own words.

Gordon moved aside as Quinn came from behind the table and walked to the back of the shop towards the kitchen. 'Tea? Coffee?'

'Mate, I'd love one.'

Quinn paused. 'Tea? Or coffee?'

'I'm a builder,' Gordon said, as if that meant something.

Quinn, juggling a 50/50 crisis of making the right drink, left Gordon standing in the back of the shop at the altar, like he was waiting to get married on his lunch break. Here in the kitchen, where two monstera plants caught the weak winter sunlight from two small windows, he exhaled. He could stay here, listening to the kettle's water boiling, and hope that Gordon would leave.

'He's ranting about last night.' Gordon's voice echoed from the shop. 'Said he's never felt so humiliated in his life.'

'He didn't have to come.' Quinn added one tea bag to a Roald Dahl-inspired mug, and then coffee to his own Penguin Classics mug. 'He could have saved himself the embarrassment.'

Emerging into the shop again, Quinn was on one hand relieved to see no customers, but annoyed to still see Gordon, even though he'd offered hospitality.

'Lush colour, mate.' Gordon sipped his tea. 'Got any bickies?'

Quinn found the biscuit tin in the kitchen. 'You want to talk.'

'Aye, well, I want a break,' Gordon said.

'Confessional?' Quinn gestured to his booth, and Gordon, after pausing for just a little too long, shrugged and got in.

'So, what am I meant to do here?' Gordon asked.

'Rant away.'

Gordon sipped his tea, a loud sucking sound. 'Ahhh. Well, you know what Harold can be like. Got a temper on him, that man has. Keeps the boys in order with his jibes and his outbursts. Only

I've never seen him like this before. Fuming. Absolutely tamping. Says he won't let this slide.'

Quinn tugged at his jumper, hoping to cool his rising temperature. The last thing he wanted to do was to make any family member an enemy. He knew it would cause aggravation, maybe even come between him and his mother, but would it get so bad? It seemed almost as if Harold couldn't see any solution other than to burn bridges.

He glanced at the grate between him and Gordon, relieved that his cousin couldn't see him biting his lip.

'He thought that by going on the radio he could get the narrative straight,' Gordon said. 'Get the press back on the castle. But now he thinks the restoration is being overshadowed and tainted. He's worried people won't want the castle open again.'

'Well, that's not true,' Quinn said. 'People love the castle.'

'That's what I said,' Gordon said through a mouthful of biscuits. 'Only Harold won't listen. He reckons now that they're going to come for him.'

'Who?'

'The locals.'

'Well, they will,' Quinn said. 'Gordon, look, I know you work for him, but come on. You've got to see my point of view here.'

Quinn waited for Gordon's response. He was quiet, and Quinn hoped he was self-reflecting, thinking about his own role in threatening Quinn's future, his shop, and his dreams.

An almighty belch came out from the other side of the partition, and Quinn rolled his eyes.

'Pardon me,' Gordon said. 'Too many biscuits. Nah, Quinn mate, I hear you. You think I'm evil, don't you?'

'Not at all,' Quinn said. 'I just wish people on the inside would stick up for me.'

'Hard to do when he's paying my bills.'

'You're his immediate family. You have influence.'

'So are you, and so do you.'

Quinn laughed. Influence over Harold? Yeah, right. Harold came into the family and accepted Quinn, sure, but they hadn't bonded. Quinn didn't need to bond with him. Quinn was already in his twenties, and both men knew Harold could never replace Quinn's father. An unspoken truth linked them together, and they always remained friendly. Harold was a new partner for his mother. They would share family events together, and that would be that. Some people got to know and develop a bond with their stepparents, but Quinn hadn't, and that was okay.

It wasn't like Harold was the wicked stepfather, if that was even a thing. Until now, Harold had been nothing but supportive. Casual questions about the shop, a feigned interest in the life of a gay bookseller. Harold was cut from a different cloth, and so the pair sometimes talked business, with Harold trying to relate it back to his own.

Not once had Harold ever given Quinn the idea that he would lose his shop.

'I have mouths to feed. That's why I haven't left,' Gordon said from the other side of the wall. 'Six of them.'

Six? Gordon had been busy! Quinn cleared his throat, imagining the horrors of a house full of six kids. 'I didn't know you had six kids.'

'No, well, we don't do the family thing, do we?'

'You're barely my cousin,' Quinn said. 'Like, stepcousin.'

'That doesn't mean that we can't meet up for Christmas.'

'Six kids? That's crazy.'

'My missus always wanted a big family.'

'I didn't even know you were married.'

'We're not.'

And it reminded Quinn of how Welsh people seemed to call their female partners their missus with affection. Quinn realised Gordon hadn't attended family gatherings – not that there had been many of them.

'He wants me to work Christmas day. Did you know that?'

'Harold does?'

'That's right,' Gordon said. 'Says we have to get the finishing touches in.'

'But it's already opening to the public before Christmas?'

'Aye, well, to the public eye it will look perfect,' Gordon said. 'Bit of leccy left to do in the offices.'

Quinn finished his coffee and stretched out his legs, his feet dipping underneath the curtain that acted as the door. He had never spoken to Gordon like this. Barely three words ever passed between them. He realised now that maybe he'd judged Gordon too harshly. The man he stereotyped to be brash and loud was someone who seemed to work for others, working hard to get by, and doing what he had to do to survive. As he listened to Gordon recount tales of his so-called missus and his kids, it struck him how much affection and love Gordon had for his life and his family.

'You love her, don't you?'

'Her and the kids,' Gordon said. 'We don't have much money, but I wouldn't change a thing.'

'That's nice, Gord.'

'You know Harold doesn't want to turn this into a ticket booth, don't you?'

Quinn's gratitude for the partition increased. 'How do you know that?'

'He told me,' Gordon said. 'Said that he's been sitting on a gold mine for years, and now with this castle opportunity, he's seen another way to make even more money. You remember Harold was broke before this, don't you?'

'Yes, I do,' Quinn said.

'He would often say he regretted ever letting the shop out. Said he should have sold it the moment he bought it.'

So that was why Harold tore away the safety of his shop: money. When his mother met Harold, he'd been doing the odd job here and there. He wasn't raking it in. 'Maybe he held on to it because the value would keep going up?'

'More than likely,' Gordon said. 'Desirable area and all that.'

Quinn didn't know how much Harold earned from the castle, but since getting the contract, he'd employed more people. Oh, and bought a new Mercedes. And went to the Maldives with his mum. He certainly didn't earn enough from Quinn's rent for all of that. Somewhere along the line, when doing the castle, Harold must have realised the opportunity he had to sell up. And if he sold up, he'd net quite a large profit.

They clambered out of the confessional booth when Gordon realised he'd run over his lunch break. He seemed to avert Quinn's eye, as if seeing him made him realise he'd said too much. Oh, the power of a confessional booth.

As they approached the door, Quinn had one more question for his stepcousin.

'Are you going to work on Christmas day?'

'I don't have a choice,' Gordon said. 'I'll have to miss the kids opening their presents, and the Christmas dinner, but there's always next year, isn't there?'

Quinn let Gordon go, watching him disappear through the archway and into the castle grounds. He had a newfound respect for the stepcousin who was also under Harold's thumb. Heading back to the computer, he pulled up the invite list and added Gordon's name.

Chapter Twenty-Six

Hay went a full day with no snowfall, and the locals took advantage of the weather by clearing the roads leading in and out. As Quinn drove gingerly to Cusop Dingle, he passed others who were braving the weather. He approached Hermione's home, driving through the gates and onto her gravel driveway, hearing the stones ping against the metal body of his car. Anyone else may have winced, but Quinn was in a Land Rover from the 80s that once belonged to the local vet. Quinn swore it still had the smell of a sheep that apparently gave birth on the back seat in 2002.

As Quinn got out of the car, the chill creeping through his layers of clothing, he shivered. But not from the cold. He tugged his jacket closer to him and took two deep breaths like he was in a meditation class. The nerves in his stomach lessened, but he still felt tense as he knocked on the door.

Relax, Quinn. Relax.

It's just Noah.

Off the record.

Just Noah.

The nerves that twisted in his stomach were now beginning to flutter with excitement. He felt like electricity, and he was sure that if he touched the door handle, sparks would fly. A cosy night in Hermione's huge home with gorgeous food and a gorgeous author in front of him would be amazing. A dream almost.

He had to admit, if someone had asked him who his dream dinner guests would be, Hermione Sage wouldn't have made the list. Instead, he would have said what every literature lover would say: Hemingway. Austen. Kylie and Kendall Jenner.

Kylie and Kendall Jenner? Someone would ask, to which he would reply, *Yeah, don't you remember the books that were written by a ghost writer for them?*

And that would be that.

Noah Sage would be his dinner date rather than a guest.

The door opened, and the nerves came rushing back. Only now he couldn't wait for it to open, because the night was cold and *the press.*

But Hermione didn't peer around the door.

And it wasn't Noah.

A chisel-jawed Calvin Klein model stood before him, wearing a cashmere turtleneck and black jeans. He smiled at Quinn, and instead of being attracted, Quinn was angry.

Some people were just too attractive.

'Hey there.' The man held out a hand, which was large, and Quinn had no choice but to shake it, noticing that there was no wedding ring. Oh, how he hoped this immaculate man was the gardener. Or the butler. 'You must be Quinn? I'm Matty.'

Of course he was.

Matty no face actually had a face. And it was just as handsome as he thought it would be. How could he forget Matty was in town? What a fool he was to forget that this man existed in the same world as Noah and Hermione.

Matty made room for Quinn, and he stepped into the hallway, noticing how neatly parted Matty's black hair was. It was shiny and bouncy, like it was prepped for a man's hair commercial.

Matty looked like everything Quinn thought he should be. His cashmere jumper, while baggy, still alluded to his biceps. He was fashionable, intellectual-looking, neat and preened.

He wasn't Quinn.

Matty lifted his model arms to Quinn and relieved him of his jacket that looked old and tired compared to Matty's catalogue fashion. He hung it up on a nearby coat rack and, with that same happy-go-lucky smile, led Quinn towards the kitchen.

Quinn could smell the food before he entered. It smelled like Christmas dinner, with cauliflower and broccoli boiling on the stove, and roasting turkey in the oven. As Quinn entered the clinically clean kitchen, he was surprised to see it looking lived in. On the steel counters, there were four bottles of wine, and another one was on the kitchen table decorated with a Christmas tablecloth and pillar candles, flickering a warm glow. 'Driving home for Christmas' was playing on an Alexa speaker.

'Quinn!' Noah was the one cooking. He turned from the oven, wearing an apron that made him look like he was a ripped man in a tight speedo, and Quinn wished the ground would swallow him up. 'You made it.'

He crossed the kitchen and engulfed Quinn in a hug, right in front of camera-ready Matty. When Noah moved away, he kept one hand on Quinn's neck, and the other grasped his shoulder, a smile on his face.

'Nice apron,' Quinn said, looking Noah up and down, remembering that Instagram photo once again. 'Do you always tan like that?'

'No, he burns,' Matty said, coming up to Noah's side. He placed a hand on Noah's back, and Noah let Quinn go, his smile fading ever so slightly.

'He's right, I do.'

'We always have some after-sun lotion, just in case.' Matty smiled.

Quinn managed a smile too, but now he was thinking of Noah with lotion on his skin.

'Quinn!'

'Hermione!' Quinn said, rather too loud, and turned away from the handsome author and his Calvin Klein model with a hot face boyfriend. 'You went all out. You didn't have to.'

'Well, when Noah said you were coming over for food, I thought we should have an early Christmas meal!' Hermione wore a glittering dress, which shimmered as it caught the light from the candles. The room was dim, with the candles providing most of the light, but Quinn noticed the spotlights in each corner of the room glowing a warm amber. He realised that this room could transform into one of warmth with the right setting and the right guests.

Quinn's eyes glanced at Noah, and with a jolt, he saw Noah watching him. Reading him, maybe. Was this some twisted game of his? Get him jealous?

No. It couldn't be. Quinn needed to get real here. Noah was not single. Their romance only existed inside his head. Noah was off limits. Out of bounds. Very much in love with Matty, who had a face.

'Champagne?'

He was in front of Quinn now, close enough that Quinn could see the freckles on his flushed skin. He wore a T-shirt, showing off his book tattoo, and Quinn fought the urge to reach out and trace his fingers over the bookmark that came trawling out of the inked pages on his skin.

'Champagne would be perfect.'

'The chicken is going to burn!' Matty said to Noah, and Noah went back to the oven, leaving Quinn standing with no purpose in Hermione's warm kitchen.

'I hope this doesn't turn into a business meeting tonight, you two,' Matty said to Quinn and Hermione. 'I hear you're writing her autobiography.'

'Yeah, that's the plan.' Quinn eyed Noah again, wishing he had his champagne just so he had something to hold, something to put his attention into.

'I was going to write it, but I'm far too busy.' Matty wrapped his arms around Hermione, bringing her close. She giggled. 'I'm sure you'll do just as well, Quinn.'

Not only did Matty have a face. He had the personality of a dick.

'I can only try.'

'Noah says you're a bookseller,' Matty said, still holding on to Hermione like she was his and only his. 'That must be nice.'

'Yeah, that's right.' Quinn had no intention of bringing up the rocky future he had as a bookseller. 'And what do you do?'

Noah handed Quinn a flute of champagne, and he took a hearty sip.

'I'm a model,' Matty said.

Sure, why not?

'A poet.'

That too.

'A writer.'

Mhmm.

'Got an acting gig coming up in the New Year, too.' Matty smiled.

'Who are you playing?' Quinn asked.

'I can't share too many details right now. Contractual obligations.'

'Food is almost ready,' Noah interjected, and Quinn was relieved from hearing about the rest of Matty's successes, and how much better he was at life.

He chose a seat at the other side of the table from Matty, keeping as much distance from him as possible. He shook the feeling of discontent for Matty's chiselled face because Matty hadn't done a thing to him.

Other than calling Noah his partner, of course.

Quinn drank a little too much of his champagne as Noah served dinner and, as a guest, was the first to receive a plate full of tantalising food. Four slices of turkey lay to one side of the plate, dressed in gravy. Cauliflower, broccoli, carrots, and peas created a burst of colour next to the meat, and potatoes of the boiled and roasted kind let off steam, which floated in front of Quinn's face. His stomach rumbled when he eyed the fluffy Yorkshire pudding.

'We have cranberry sauce.' Hermione gestured to the condiments on the table.

'I know this might be weird, but I'd prefer mint sauce.' Quinn reached for the mint sauce, dropping some over his vegetables. 'Maybe a dash of cranberry, too.'

Matty's food came next, sparing of the food. Quinn noticed he didn't have meat. 'I'm a vegan.'

Why wouldn't he be? His environment-saving diet had one-upped Quinn once again.

Noah served the rest of the food, then added gravy boats to the table. He returned, shedding his apron and sitting next to Quinn with his own plate, which was not sparing of the food and meat. Underneath the table, their knees brushed. Quinn's eyebrow raised as he glanced at Noah, but Noah remained unreadable.

'Cheers.' Matty held out his own glass of champagne, and they all clinked their glasses together.

Chapter Twenty-Seven

Quinn wiped the sweat from his forehead and let out a pant as he leaned backwards. He wished this satisfied feeling in his body was from a sexual activity with the man next to him. Only it wasn't: it was from sheer greed and gluttony. His plate sitting empty before him, his champagne full once more, and the announcement of dessert all made him consider his life choices.

Matty had baked vegan cakes, because of course he did, and he was now at the kitchen counter prepping the final touches, and if Quinn was not mistaken, rehearsing his lines under his breath.

'That food was good,' Quinn said to Noah and Hermione. His eyes found Noah's. 'You should be a chef.'

'I enjoy cooking, but not enough to make it a career.' Noah grinned, making Quinn want to melt. 'Maybe if the books stop selling.'

'They'll never stop selling,' a now-tipsy Hermione said.

'Food always sells.'

'It does.' Noah nodded. 'But I like having something with no pressure, no expectation. Capitalism these days makes you feel like everything has to be a commodity. The things you love to do need to be wrapped up and monetised. I don't want food to become like that for me.'

'That got deep fast,' Quinn said.

'I like going deep.'

Oh, good god.

Quinn was thankful Ivy wasn't here to read his dirty thoughts, and he stifled his wicked grin by drinking from his champagne flute. Matty returned to the table with the cakes, which looked wonderful and not at all hideous like Quinn had secretly hoped. When he bit into them, praying they would be dry, soft flavourful crumbs greeted him with hints of ginger and lemon, but not enough sweetness to make it sour or overpowering.

'I used to have a bakery down in London,' Matty said once they had greedily consumed the dessert and everyone complimented him. 'It's how we met, isn't it?'

'It is,' Noah said. 'Me and my sweet tooth.'

Curse that sweet tooth leading you to him! Quinn thought, though he smiled and laughed all the same.

'But enough about me.' Matty waved his hand, as if they had bombarded him with questions about his bakery, why he might have given it up, and his muse for his acting. 'We're here tonight to talk about all things Hermione.'

'Unofficially.' Hermione smiled. 'I loved Noah's idea of you getting to know me, Quinn.'

'And us getting to know you,' Noah said to Quinn, and Quinn, feeling warm and light, caught the glance that flickered in his direction from Matty.

'Is this an interview?' Quinn asked.

'Not at all,' Hermione said. 'And we can go over these things again when the official writing takes place. But it's only fair that you know why I want to tell my story. And why now.'

'I'm all ears,' Quinn said.

'I know what they say about me out there,' Hermione said.

'The witch of Cusop Dingle, the recluse, the spinster ... and I've heard worse. And it all stems from the fact that I had sex.'

Matty let out a feigned gasp, which was more annoying than funny, but Quinn joined in with the laughter.

'I was shamed and humiliated,' Hermione said. 'Because of course, it got filmed, and it got released, and this was in the eighties. My career was flourishing in America, but they marketed me as the girl next door – the innocent, wholesome woman. I thought I had it all.'

Hermione sighed, looking wistful at nothing in particular, no doubt her mind wandering to a time that she missed.

'Then I met him. His name was Roger. Never trust a Roger. He was a movie producer, so he said. Said he loved my work and thought we could work together. Our relationship blossomed, but he never told me where he worked. Maybe I was naïve, trusting, but I assumed he was a producer for the big studios, you know? Everyone around me was a somebody.' Hermione shook her head. 'He took me to his studio once. It was less than glamorous, but I'd been on a few sets in my career and they often weren't glamorous. Again, I didn't think much of it. Infatuated, I suppose, by this man. He took me onto a set and the moment took us and we ... well...'

'Don't say it,' Noah said. 'I don't need to hear it.'

'Fornicated,' Hermione said, and Noah pulled a face. 'Your mother had sex, Noah. It's how you got here!'

'I prefer the baby with a stork theory.'

Hermione laughed. 'Not the case. Older people have sex, you know. After that night, he didn't see me again. Next thing I knew, I was being told about a sex tape that had me in it which had found its way out into the public domain. We didn't have the internet back then, so it was good old-fashioned video tapes, and it was in all the seedy shops on Hollywood boulevard. Turns out, Roger *was* a movie producer. A pornographic one.'

Quinn gasped, one that was genuine.

'He led me there and filmed me without my knowledge, without my consent, and starring in one of his own movies,' Hermione said. 'Got off on it, apparently. He'd left a camera on and the USP was the voyeuristic home footage aspect of it. Turns out, his studio was going bankrupt, and when he saw me, he spotted an opportunity. An entrepreneurial spirit, some people said. With that one video, with my image and name attached to it, he saved his business from bankruptcy and had a lavish career in Hollywood's porn industry. And me? Well, you know what happened.'

Quinn gripped his champagne flute as if it was the neck of the man that had set Hermione up. He tried to erase the images in his mind of the aftermath of such an event, and he could only imagine how she must have felt. Noah was biting his lip, a disappointed expression on his face.

'You were assaulted, Hermione,' Quinn said.

'I was.'

'That needs to be investigated. The man needs to be arrested.'

'He's dead.'

'Oh.'

Hermione laughed, though it wasn't warm. It was hollow, resigned to the lost justice she could have had, and the peace she might have got from such an event. 'Yeah. About ten years ago. Drugs, apparently.'

'The life of a film producer.' Matty shrugged. 'It's not a glamorous industry.'

'How would you know?' Noah asked him.

'I'm in it.'

Noah scoffed.

Quinn cleared his throat, feeling a little shocked at the exchange between the hottest men in Cusop Dingle. 'Hermione, I'm sorry that happened to you.'

'Don't be,' she said. 'The video tapes kept selling until I used all my money up on lawyers and got them taken down. Only by the time we did, those copies had been bought and distributed. Now I hear there are digital versions floating around the internet. Back then, people could do that. They didn't care. Like I say, he got heaps of praise and I lost all my work, my agent, and most of my money. The only reason I'm able to live like this is because I still get royalties from some of my films.'

'I'm sorry.'

'What I want to see is a clearing of my name, but I want to raise awareness too,' Hermione said. 'Sex isn't shameful. Sex work isn't shameful. I shouldn't be ashamed of what happened. I was embarrassed, and I still am, but I've been learning to deal with that.'

Realisation hit Quinn hard. This wasn't just a regular semi-celebrity autobiography. It was much bigger than that. This wasn't just an opportunity for him and for Hermione, but for victims too. Hermione's story had been crying out for years, ignored because it had become so normalised to just laugh at her expense. If she wasn't the washed-up actress, she was the spinster in the village, or the old porn star.

'Did you consent to sleeping with him?'

'Oh, yes,' Hermione said. 'Oh, it wasn't anything sinister. The only consent that wasn't given was the taping and the distribution. I loved him. And I still do in some silly way. He was kind. He looked at me differently. He wasn't like the other men I met.' Hermione seemed oblivious to the consensus at the table that Roger was not, in fact, kind. 'But he hurt me, ruined me, and broke me. For a little while, I understood why he did it. How silly is that? I justified it by saying I helped him get his life back on track.'

'Bull,' Noah said.

'I know that now,' Hermione said. 'I was hurting, and I tried to heal in any way I could.'

'How did he distribute it without your consent?'

'It happens a lot more than you might think,' Hermione said.

'I've joined a couple of online chat rooms over the years. Revenge porn, I hear, is a big thing. It's now a criminal offence, but it still happens. People have their images, their videos, distributed without their consent all the time. I found out, through my lawyers, that he forged my signature in case anyone asked. Nobody did. They saw who was on the tape and knew there was money involved. It didn't matter whether I consented.'

'But of course, it did.'

'It should have,' Hermione said. 'To them, though, it was just business.'

Just business. The words Quinn kept hearing. Horrible, dirty words that hurt those involved. How many people suffered at the hands of 'just business'?

'A similar thing happened to Marilyn Monroe, you know,' Matty said. 'Playboy. She didn't consent to that cover.'

'Yes. A decision she made early in her career, and then the photographer had the say over who bought the photos, rather than her,' Hermione said. 'I remember reading up on that and feeling like I had something in common with her.'

'And Pamela Anderson,' Matty said. 'Home sex tape stolen and distributed.'

Quinn had heard stories often about the horrible industry in Hollywood. Paris Hilton and Kim Kardashian. Now, it felt very close to home.

'I fled back home, and not too long after, I had Noah.'

Quinn turned to Noah, realising what was about to come.

'Roger is my dad,' Noah said.

Quinn realised then that the things he heard about Hermione were only half true. There was more to the story, hidden truths and concealed hurt.

'Hermione, you've got the opportunity with this book to get control of the narrative,' Quinn said. 'And with that, you regain your power.'

'And you'll help me get it back.'

Noah placed a hand on Quinn's knee, which felt sturdy, warm, and welcoming. It fit so perfectly over his muscle, Noah's fingers sprawling over the sides. Quinn cursed the cold weather, wishing it was the middle of summer, so that he could wear shorts and feel that skin-on-skin contact.

Matty also noticed. That familiar, fleeting warning expression was back on his face, only this time it lingered.

'You *will* do this, won't you?' Noah asked.

Quinn's eyes trailed down to Noah's hand, then back to his face, hovering ever so slightly on his lips. 'Absolutely.'

Chapter Twenty-Eight

Matty and Hermione agreed to wash up the dishes, leaving Noah and Quinn free from any chores.

'Come with me.' Noah guided Quinn into the hallway. The large hall felt cold compared to the kitchen, where conversation had turned to Hermione's career highs, her escapades on set, and a story involving George Clooney and Tom Hanks.

'Shouldn't I be listening to that?'

'It's nothing I couldn't tell you,' Noah said. 'Besides, she will tell you all of that again. Any excuse she can get to reminisce.'

He loved Hermione for wanting to recount her blessings with no shred of shame, knowing he would do the same if he experienced a life like hers.

The house was impeccably clean. Quinn made a mental note to compliment Ivy when he saw her next. A Christmas tree flashed in the hall's corner with wrapped presents underneath the boughs. Quinn noticed that she drew red velvet curtains over windows, no doubt to stop the prying eyes of the non-existent press.

'Upstairs.' Noah climbed the sweeping staircase, his hand trailing along the polished oak banister. Quinn followed him, curious, wondering what Noah wanted to show him.

They emerged onto a landing that was bigger than Quinn's apartment bedroom – he was sure of it. On the wall, a painted portrait of a man with a crown beamed down at them, and Quinn stopped to admire it.

'Richard Booth was a character, wasn't he?'

'Shame the Booth monarchy didn't last. I would have married into it.'

'Me too.'

'Ah, but there would have only been one prince,' Noah said. 'Then who would have got him?'

'A love triangle, like one of your romance novels!' As Quinn said it, he realised maybe he was in a love triangle himself. He knew Noah was well and truly off limits. He rationalised that any attraction, any flirtation, had been in his head. Yes, Noah was attractive, but that was it.

Just attractive.

He fancied him, sure.

Completely normal.

Off limits.

'You alright? You look like you've entered a daydream.' Noah brought Quinn back to the hall.

'Yeah, just thinking about the prince that could have been,' Quinn said, and *no*, he had *not* been thinking about him being a king with Noah as king consort by his side. No way.

Noah smirked, then showed an antique cabinet at the end of the hall. Quinn hadn't noticed it, such was the imposing artwork of Richard Booth, but he saw behind the glass of the cabinet were trophies that made his mouth drop open.

Golden statues winked at him, catching the light from the hallway's chandelier. As Quinn approached, he saw the bright face of a BAFTA and two flaxen statues of knights.

'Hermione won two *Oscars?*'

'She did indeed.' Noah failed to hide his pride. 'And the

BAFTA. She had something from an indie film fest, too, but I don't know where she put that.'

'Noah, this is incredible!'

'Isn't it just?' Noah said. 'Since being here, I've caught her a few times standing here and staring. She won two Oscars in a row, both for Christmas films she was in. The BAFTA was for a drama portrayal she did for TV.'

'I think I underestimated her acting talent.'

'Hey, that's not a bad thing,' Noah said. 'She went into hiding by the time you and I were born.'

'Went into hiding?' Quinn asked. 'You think she's hiding?'

'Don't you?'

There was a meow and then a thud followed by the fluffiest cat Quinn had ever seen. Orange eyes contrasted with tortoiseshell fur, and its tail looked more like a fluffy brush. Without thinking, Quinn fell to his knees, like an olden day peasant seeing their king for the first time.

Mr Lavender the cat trotted straight past Quinn, because of course he did, and rubbed himself instead around Noah's legs.

Never had Quinn been so jealous of a cat.

Quinn cleared his throat, getting to his feet. Noah was laughing.

'I've never seen someone fall to the floor when they see a cat.' Noah laughed. 'What were you in a past life? An ancient Egyptian?'

'Funny,' Quinn said. 'I'm always on my knees.'

Did he just say that?

Noah raised an eyebrow. 'Are you?'

'For cats,' Quinn spluttered. That still didn't sound good.

'Of course.'

Mr Lavender left Noah and came to Quinn, a purr emanating from deep within. Quinn got to his knees again and scratched behind Mr Lavender's ears.

'Wow, he never does that to strangers,' Noah said. 'He won't go anywhere near Matty.'

'Oh, no way.' Quinn tried to hide his pleasure that he was better at something than Matty.

Mr Lavender decided he'd had enough of saying hello to the humans, and trotted down the stairs, running to the kitchen.

'I'm surprised he didn't come for food.'

'He's only now realising there was any,' Noah said. 'By the way, I heard what Matty said to you about writing Hermione's book – that's bull. She didn't ask him and he didn't submit a thing.'

Matty lied? And if he lied, Noah was telling him this because...?

Quinn observed Noah's crossed arms, the way his eyebrows knitted together. 'Are you okay?'

'Matty can be ... difficult.'

Quinn clasped his hands together, the rush of adrenaline sending quivers through him. This seemed like dangerous territory. Him and Noah, alone, talking about Matty.

'How so?'

He needed to play it casual, but he wanted to find out how Noah felt. Quinn thought back to Noah's interview in his bookshop and how he'd mentioned heartbreak. Quinn assumed he'd been heartbroken, but if he was still with Matty, that wouldn't make sense.

Unless something was happening underneath the surface.

And if it was, what did that mean for Quinn? Did it mean he stood a chance?

He pushed these thoughts away before they could fully form. Here he was at Noah's side, and all he could think about was how he benefitted from it? No, that was bad.

'We're having a few problems at the moment.'

But those words couldn't help but alight the hope within him. Problems? If there were problems, then there could be a potential breakup. And if there was a breakup, well … maybe that would mean he had a chance.

Again, Quinn hated himself for even going there.

'What problems?'

'Matty has an ego,' Noah said, not meeting Quinn's eye. 'I don't know why he told you he was going to write Hermione's book, because that wasn't the case at all. Hermione wanted you because she knew your father. End of. She didn't even consider anyone else.'

'Lucky I applied, then.'

'Yeah.'

Quinn nudged Noah. 'I didn't mind him saying that, you know.'

'I worried he'd offended you.'

They turned from the cabinet that held the awards, and Noah walked away from the stairs. Quinn followed, not sure where they were going, but hoping and praying that this moment with him would last forever.

'Not offended. Just…'

'Made you realise what I have to deal with?'

Matty lied. Noah noticed. And now Noah was sharing his grievances with Quinn like they were friends? Like he could trust him? He admitted to himself that he'd been relieved to hear Matty wasn't a choice at all. At least he could whole-heartedly remind himself that Hermione wanted him, and only him.

'Noah. Is everything alright with you and Matty?'

Noah shrugged. 'Does it matter?'

'Yes, it matters.'

'Why, Quinn?'

They hovered in the hallway, lost in the shadows of Hermione's home. Noah, close to him. His eyes were so beautiful. They held him pinned to the wall.

'Why does it matter if everything is okay with me and Matty?'

Even now, in this moment, Matty's nickname sounded playful.

'I want to know that you're okay,' Quinn whispered. 'And I want you to know that you can trust me.'

Noah's hand found Quinn's, sending shockwaves to his heart.

'Matty cares about how he can get ahead in this life,' Noah said. 'He cares more about his career than anything else. I support that, but...'

Noah let go of Quinn's hand and leaned against the wall. Noah's arm, so close to his face. Noah, so close to him.

'Are you happy, Noah?'

'That's a loaded question,' Noah breathed, his eyes darting over Quinn's face.

'Are you happy with Matty?'

'I don't know.'

Quinn closed his eyes, wishing he could say everything he wanted to say. He'd got better at finding his voice. Speaking his mind. He'd felt proud of himself for finding the fight within, something that had faded when his father died. Right now, he sensed he should fight. He could load the gun and shoot the bullet and kill whatever relationship Noah had with him, or with Matty. Because all Quinn wanted to do was kiss the man before him. He wanted to offer his support however he could. Selfishly, almost like Matty, he wanted to do something for him for once. Not care about who he hurt, or the consequences of what he did. But he couldn't go there. He couldn't influence Noah, change his mind. This was something he needed to figure out for himself.

'Do what is right for you,' Quinn said.

Noah dropped his arm, the moment between them broken.

He walked, and Quinn followed. Quinn couldn't talk about Matty. His mind whirled with possibilities of what Noah was thinking, what he was feeling. Not only was he in Hay, a place he didn't want to be, but he was with his mother, being reminded of her health and the troubles she'd faced. Dealing with a man who might not be good for him. That comment on heartbreak had never felt clearer.

'You asked me if I think she's hiding.' Quinn kept his voice low, despite the vastness of the house. 'I've thought of that before.'

'From the outside, what were your thoughts?' Noah asked, and he reached for a door handle. 'And what are they now that you know her?'

Noah led them into a bedroom. He was aware of that familiar, comforting smell of books, one that was earthy and yet clean. A salt lamp cast an orange glow around the room, accentuating the impressive size. Two large windows gave a glimpse of the outside snowy world. The carpet was worn, clean. An oak table at the back of the wall was framed by the many well-read paperback books stacked in neat piles, their creased spines facing outwards. Quinn passed the fresh double bed and looked at the collection, noticing the alphabetised author names.

His eyes drifted to the table, the messiest part of the room, only because two empty mugs sat next to a laptop that had been left open next to handwritten frantic notes.

'Is this your bedroom?'

'It is,' Noah said. He watched him carefully, his deep green eyes taking in his expression, his reaction.

Oh, my god. He was in Noah's bedroom!

His room, where his personality shone through. Noah kept this neat. His wardrobe, which Quinn thought might lead to Narnia, such was its familiar appearance, didn't even have any loose clothes sticking out of the door, like Quinn's own wardrobe.

And now he noticed it. Beneath that paperback smell, there was something else. Something more human. A living smell. A boy smell, but not a teenager – it was a man who took care of himself, maybe even pampered himself. He tried to place the smell, which was like citrus. Quinn wished he could bottle it up and use it as his own perfume.

He spotted an oak door in one corner of the room. 'What's in there?'

'Ensuite,' Noah said.

Of course there's an ensuite.

'Your room is beautiful.' Quinn went back to the paperbacks, his head tilting, reading the spines.

A soft rustle came from behind, and Noah joined him, his shoulder inches away from Quinn. Quinn stepped slowly towards Noah, as if caught by the Oscar Wilde edition on the shelf. Noah didn't move, instead letting Quinn into his space.

'How long have you had these?' Quinn asked, his voice wavering ever so slightly.

'Years.'

Noah caught Quinn's eye, holding him down, trapped between author and bookshelves. 'Eyelash.'

Noah reached out, his fingers grazing the side of Quinn's nose. Quinn didn't move, fearful that if he did, Noah would fracture into pieces.

Words evaded him. They'd escaped and found refuge in the stacks of old books in front of them.

Noah gestured to the bed as he went to sit at his desk. Quinn perched at the end of the mattress, his heart beating hard. He drew in, crossing his arms, feeling like he had infringed on something so private, like this was a moment he shouldn't be a part of. A bedroom was a sanctuary, a place one retreated to when they needed their own time, their own space.

'We're staying here while we're with Mum,' Noah said.

'Childhood bedroom?'

'Yes,' Noah said. 'Never used to be this clean, I'll have you know. I went through a lot in this room.'

Quinn was once again reminded of Noah's childhood, which sounded difficult.

'When did you hear the stories of your mum?'

'Ever since my first day in school,' Noah said. 'I knew something was different. Teachers would force a smile, ask how Hermione was in a sweet voice, but then I'd see them whisper to the other teachers, point me out. The parents would whisper when they picked their kids up from school, crane their necks to see who was in our car. It was Mum at first, and then it wasn't, because she realised people were staring at her.'

'How did you get home if she didn't pick you up?'

'She had a cleaner pick me up,' Noah said. 'Not Ivy of course. Then, when I was old enough, I'd walk home or get the bus. As I got older, and the kids got older, they started making fun of me for being the son of a ... well, their words weren't kind. That's why I drew away and started finding escape in books. They were all I needed.'

'That must have been tough.'

Noah ran a hand through his blond hair, looking down at the threadbare carpet. Quinn wished he could move closer to him, but Matty swam into his thoughts, and he knew he couldn't do it, knew he never would be able to.

'I resented her because of it,' Noah said. 'I couldn't look at her the same way. When I found stories of her on the internet, it made me feel so ashamed, so embarrassed. I wanted to run as soon as I could.'

'Which is why you left?'

'That's right.' Noah sighed. 'Mum wanted me to finish my education, and by that point, I could see her for what she was. She was paranoid, upset, and broken. Then she went on medication for depression. I think she's still on that, you know. But it was heavy, and I was going through my own stuff. You know, discovering that I liked men, feeling ashamed of that, but also her. I hated myself, hated this place. By that point, I was being made fun of for everything. I was too smart. A nerd. I was called posh boy, gay boy. The list went on. At one point, the tape made its way around the school. Can you believe that?'

Quinn had suffered at the hands of bullies during his own time at school, but never like that. Never like Noah. They'd gone to different schools, yet lived in the same town. Quinn wished he had known Noah then, wished he could have been his solace, his peace. Quinn had needed someone while growing up, but this made Quinn realise he hadn't needed someone as much as Noah. It was then that he was on his feet, sitting on the edge of the table, just a few inches away from Noah, who turned towards him. Their knees almost touching. Inches away from one another, that scented perfume reaching Quinn.

'Is this okay?' Quinn whispered.

Noah nodded, biting his lip. Without realising what he was doing, Quinn brushed Noah's fringe away from his face, seeing him in ways he'd never seen him before. Open; vulnerable.

'I needed out of here, so I left,' Noah said. He leaned into Quinn's touch, closing his eyes as Quinn's hand ran through his hair, resting at the back of his head. 'I left her to deal with it. Abandoned her. I was young and selfish, and didn't comprehend what she was going through. We didn't speak for a few years.'

'Do you regret it?' Quinn asked. He knew his hand rested too long, had strayed too far. It took all his energy to drop it, to increase the distance between them. 'Moving away to the city? Leaving this behind?'

'No,' Noah said, looking ashamed to say it. 'Not wholly. I went to London and learned to love myself. Met some amazing people, and not so amazing people, but I found my voice. In London, I wasn't Hermione Sage's son. The world moved on in London. In London, I could be anybody.'

Noah leaned against the table, angling his body closer to Quinn's, closing the gap Quinn had created. This time, their legs touched, and Quinn felt hot lava erupt inside him, pulsating through every nerve and fibre of his being. Every sense seemed to heighten. The warmth of Noah's leg against his own, the smell of the paperback books, and the aroma of Noah himself.

'And I wrote the books and then it all came out,' Noah said. 'People started putting two and two together. Hermione was back in the limelight, the past dragged up. People asked me questions about her like she was dead. I realised I missed her, and that the world, the media, treated her unfairly. I realised she was a victim, and she needed me. So I reached out to her and she let me back.'

'She would let you back,' Quinn said. 'You're her son.'

'I was a pretty horrible son.'

'You were frustrated and hurting, too,' Quinn said. 'You had to cope in your own way.'

Noah's hand found his. That same large hand, larger than Quinn's, the golden-brown hair crisscrossing along the back over blue veins and knuckles. His grip set Quinn's heart racing, and he wondered if he was going to have a panic attack. They were close now, too close, and Quinn, aware of everything, was aware of how much higher he was than Noah. His chair was too low. It wasn't level with the table, and Quinn wished he was level, so that he wasn't looking down on him, meeting those green eyes with his own blue eyes.

'You're the first person I've been able to tell this to,' Noah said. Did Quinn imagine the tightness in his voice? The slightly breathless way he uttered those words? 'Properly tell this to. Without feeling like you'd judge me. Matty rolls his eyes at me.'

He was on his feet, still holding Quinn's hand, but he towered above him now, a shift in the balance. His other hand was on Quinn's knee. Quinn looked up into his handsome face. And it felt right, like they were equal, like this was how it was meant to be.

Noah's hand left his knee, now tracing his jawline. A smile was on his face: one that was kind, one that seemed to be tinged with sadness. Quinn couldn't move anymore. This was all in Noah's power. That familiar feeling of time standing still came back, only this time moving slow, so that every movement, every feeling, seemed ten times longer.

'If I had stayed, I would have met you sooner,' Noah breathed.

Quinn could see every crease in Noah's plump red lips. Quinn reached out, about to touch them, about to feel more of Noah than he ever thought possible. This was it. This was everything he'd craved since that winter day when Quinn first set his sights on Noah.

The door handle rattled.

Noah wasn't there anymore. Sitting on the bed, like his last words never happened, like he had been a mirage in front of Quinn just a few moments ago.

Matty appeared at the door. He looked between them, his eyes lingering a little too long on Quinn's flushed face.

'I wondered where you two had got to,' Matty said, though his voice sounded as cold as the snow that now fell outside. 'I came to say the weather's changing. Quinn, you might want to get back home before it's too late.'

Quinn knew those words held a much different meaning.

221

Chapter Twenty-Nine

'Have we emailed the invites for Blair's book signing?' Quinn asked upon returning from his father's grave.

'Uh … don't think so,' Daniel said.

'It's tomorrow!'

'Yeah, I thought maybe word of mouth…'

'All good. I'll get on it.' Quinn turned to the computer. 'Is it worth ordering stock in now? Too late for it to be delivered.'

'You make the call.'

'You seem down today, Daniel. All okay?'

'Hm? Oh, yeah, fine,' Daniel said, his voice low.

Quinn would have tied up any loose ends way before this. The winter Hay festival had already ended, and by this time, Quinn's shop had mounted a healthy amount of profit to see him through the quiet winter months of January and February. This time of year, for Quinn, usually involved selling last minute gifts, and he could handle that.

It gave him time to plan his own Christmas, start unwinding, and enjoy the season like the rest of the townsfolk of Hay.

This year was, of course, very different.

His shop was stumbling on a tightrope. And he'd never hosted a protest, two author signings, and a Christmas party on the week of Christmas before.

Well, maybe only one author signing.

Last night, at Hermione's home, in Noah's childhood bedroom, everything had changed. Now Quinn was certain that Noah had feelings for him.

He couldn't believe it, but unless he'd misread the situation, they almost kissed.

And he felt awful about it.

How could he have let that almost kiss happen, knowing that Noah's boyfriend was in the same house, in the kitchen playing happy families with Noah's mother and Quinn's now-client.

Yes, client. Hermione had sent through the contract and Quinn had signed it and sent it back, promising to get to work as soon as possible. He'd hoped that today he would have been able to start, but he hadn't found the time, because he'd been fretting about the shop, the protest, the party...

And now Noah.

Would Noah still sign books?

Would Noah even want to see him again?

Was Noah feeling that heavy, gut-twisting guilt that Quinn was feeling? The type of guilt that made him not want to eat, go on hunger strike, change his name, and leave the country?

Noah had been worse. Hadn't he?

Noah had the boyfriend. Quinn didn't.

But if Noah had kissed him, Quinn would not have stopped him.

No, he wouldn't, and that made him just as bad.

His thoughts turned to what would have happened if he'd kissed Noah. Would they have kissed again? And then harder, with hunger? Would they have ended up on Noah's bed, stripped down to nothing, kissed and then...?

No, of course not.

But Quinn couldn't be so sure.

Never had he felt so conflicted, so confused, over one man. He had lost the map to navigate Noah, and now he was adrift.

Despite everything, he wanted it to happen once more.

The hope of Matty not being as perfect as he first thought, that maybe there was trouble brewing between them, didn't fill him with pleasure. Not at all. An upset Noah wasn't what he wanted. Quinn worried about him and wanted to help.

He also wanted to know there might be a chance to be Noah's.

Stupid, really. Because even if Noah broke up with Matty, he wouldn't rush into a relationship with Quinn.

And who even said a relationship would work? Noah wanted London. Quinn wanted Hay.

'I'm thinking of printing posters about the protest, too,' Quinn said to Daniel. 'I've made something up to put around town. Mind printing it for me?'

'Oh, yeah, sure.'

Quinn watched him open the file, his shoulders slumped. Right now, he didn't have the time, but he felt as though he needed to speak with Daniel. Maybe he'd upset him. Maybe it was the Christmas blues.

Quinn turned to the email left in his drafts this morning. An email confirming if Noah could sign his books on Wednesday.

Hey Noah,

Great seeing you recently. Just confirming that you are happy to attend and sign some books here on Wednesday. If so, I can send out the invites and start advertising it. I'm sure plenty of people will come by to see you!

Speak soon,

Quinn x

He re-read the email not once, but thrice. He felt like an editor at work, overanalysing everything he typed, wondering if he needed to tweak something here or there. Was it too casual? Too 'I don't care'? Was he breezy like Monica Geller?

'Recently' was fine, wasn't it? How else could he say 'it was great to almost kiss you last night and now I feel awful' without saying that? Yes, 'recently' worked.

The kiss. The X. Too much? Was an X sign-off too soon after what almost transpired between them? The floating X was like a tease, hinting at what could have been. Should he go full *Gossip Girl* and add xoxo?

Deciding that he was no Dan Humphrey, he erased the x, re-reading the email one more time.

Then he sent it, wondering if they could go on and pretend nothing had almost happened between them.

A few seconds later, an email swooped into his inbox, one that he couldn't ignore.

Noah.

Confirming the signing for Wednesday was 'perfect', and that he 'couldn't wait'. And there, at the end of the email, was a kiss.

An X, to be more specific, but a kiss!

The almost kiss, haunting them like the ghost of Christmas past. Only this was a digital kiss, and he'd sent it, and that meant it happened.

They had kissed!

Virtually!

Quinn caught himself smiling, and a customer thought he was smiling at them, so he went with it, taking a sale of one hundred pounds. 'I travelled from north Wales for this when I heard about the shop. You're not closing, are you?'

'We're doing everything we can to save it in such a short amount of time,' Quinn said, using the words he gave to anyone who asked. Which was everyone. Which was exhausting, but fine because they cared. And they knew he cared.

'Ofnadwy!' they said, using the Welsh word for terrible, and Quinn agreed. It was very ofnadwy.

With confirmation of both Blair and Noah, on two consecutive days, Quinn printed posters and plastered them on the window of his shop. Daniel came back from putting up posters about the protest with snow in his hair. Quinn tacked the remaining posters to the bookshelves so that the influx of customers would not miss the date and time, as well as who would sign what. He then turned to the digital world, posting the details on all of his social media pages. And each time, he enjoyed looking at the image of Noah, with that commanding stare of his.

Turns out, both Blair and Noah beat him to the punch, already tweeting that they would sign copies of their books in Kings & Queens. Quinn noticed that there was more excitement for Noah than Blair and his almost ten-year-old book. It was too late to order the children's copies now.

That didn't matter. Both of them had shown up. Both of them were helping in the best possible way.

The door dinged and Ivy came in, wearing a long parka coat.

'I got your invites.' Ivy held up her phone. 'Perfect, wonderful. I've already spoken to some locals and they're happy to hang up some flyers or posters to help spread the word. Not that we need it. The press wants to come to the protest.'

'Ivy, none of this would have happened without you.'

'We're not going down without a fight!'

There'd been no word on whether Harold would still proceed with the eviction of Quinn, and Quinn didn't expect any. It seemed Harold would not bow to the mounting pressure being put upon him. Disappointment flooded through Quinn every time he thought of his stepdad and his decision, and the floodgates burst when he thought of his mother, allowing such a thing to happen.

'You look different.' Ivy observed him like he was something she'd never seen before. 'Your aura has changed.'

Quinn looked around him, as if he could see such a thing. 'Has it? Does it compliment my skin tone?'

'It does,' Ivy said. 'It's a shade of pink. You're giving off a loving vibe, but it's not happy.'

Ivy's accuracy struck him. 'A lot has happened over the weekend.'

'Get the kettle on and tell me everything.' Ivy turned to Daniel. 'And your aura. You seem ... stressed? No, confused.'

'Don't read my aura,' Daniel said, half-joking.

'Sorry,' Ivy said.

'Enjoy your teas.'

'Don't want to join us?'

'I'm good, I think,' Daniel said.

'Well, I'll tell you what. I'm going to close early. Lots happening. Go get some you time, Daniel. I think you need it.'

Daniel sighed. 'Thanks, Quinn. I appreciate it.'

Daniel got his coat and headed to the door, turning the open sign to closed. Quinn followed him. 'Daniel, I mean it. If you need to talk, I'm here for you.'

Daniel sighed. 'Maybe we can talk once all of this has blown over?'

'Whenever you're ready.'

'Cheers, Quinn.'

Quinn locked the doors, made the teas, and filled Ivy in on everything from Gordon to the shop.

'So, Harold is Scrooge,' Ivy said, 'and Gordon is a good guy?'

'I'm not sure if he is a good guy,' Quinn said. 'But he's better than we thought.'

'I think we can work on him.' Ivy tapped her fingers together, like an evil villain hatching up a scheme. 'We can get him on our side.'

Quinn loaded up more posters on his screen and hit print.

'I've never spoken to him like that before. It made a change. He's human.'

'Shocker.'

The final posters were printed, and Quinn handed them to Ivy.

'There's more, though,' Ivy said. 'I did a tarot reading before I came and I drew the eight of cups.'

'Meaning?'

'Meaning that you're feeling lost and confused,' Ivy said. 'There seems to be a lot of illusions, maybe even options for you, and you're not sure what is best for you.'

Quinn, thinking of Noah, of Hermione, of his future and the shop, dismissed this with a wave of his hand.

'I'm not sure about that.'

'My point exactly.' Ivy smiled. 'What's troubling you?'

Quinn sighed, falling into the armchair behind his desk, his safe place.

He recounted everything. From the meal, to Matty being a thing, to Noah being in front of him and disappearing like a mirage.

Ivy, with every detail, gasped and shook her head. She was a good person to tell a story to.

'Well, what happened when Matty entered the room?'

'He told me I had to leave,' Quinn said, recalling that look on Matty's face, one of frozen shock. 'But not in a Peggy Mitchell get out of my pub way – in a passive aggressive way. Something I think he's rather good at.'

Ivy reached into her handbag, a Louis Vuitton, which looked immaculate. She took out a pack of cards, which Quinn thought were regular playing cards until she shuffled them.

'We need clarity.'

She drew out three cards, each one looking well used and ever so slightly crumpled. One card was called the two of cups, another ominously called the devil, and a third called, even more dangerously, the lovers.

'You set this up,' Quinn said.

'Not at all!' Ivy looked shocked. 'The cards never lie, Quinn, and these make *so* much sense with what you've told me.'

'What do they say, then?'

Ivy paused, looking at the cards, lost in thought. Quinn, with every second of spreading silence, got nervous. He looked at the stack of cards still in Ivy's hand, wondering what else might come out of them. Destruction? A broken heart? Death itself?

'We're looking at a partnership here.' Ivy pointed at the card with two cups, and the two androgynous people standing close to one another, both holding a goblet. They looked like they had been caught mid-moment, like the one that Noah and Quinn had last night. 'This card talks of harmony, a developing bond and relationship. It's one that is meant to happen, unfolding naturally. But then this…'

She pointed at the devil card, one that depicted two people standing before an imposing figure. It filled Quinn with dread looking at it, and the irony wasn't lost on him that the devil card appeared in the shop that used to be a church.

'There's a shadow. Something that is being ignored. A problem.' Ivy's brow furrowed. 'There is something in the way, something that needs working through. You see these two people in front of the devil? They're being kept apart.'

Matty with his handsome face seemed to float between them like a ghostly apparition. No doubt Ivy saw and felt it, too.

'And then this.' Ivy smiled at the lover's card. Two people, male and female, naked, stood together. The devil was absent, and in his dark place grew trees and flowers. 'The lovers. Tells us everything we need to know. Remove the obstacle, the block…' She slid the devil card away and drew the two remaining cards together. 'And these two people survive together.'

Quinn looked at the cards and was reminded of Adam and Eve, thinking that maybe he would be Adam and Noah could be Eve. Or Steve.

'Could it also mean the relationship I have with Hermione?'

Ivy shook her head. 'No. Not at all. I think this is very clear about what it's about. Don't you?'

'They're just cards,' Quinn said. 'They can't tell me what's going on.'

Ivy didn't look offended. Instead, as she packed away her cards, dropping the deck into a silk pouch, she looked amused. 'I can read you, Quinn. You don't have to pretend with me.'

Quinn smiled, but he knew Ivy was right. It scared him how accurate the reading was. How could three cards confuse him yet offer him a glimmer of hope? Because as Ivy had read the lovers to him, it had given him an expectation. The flame inside him, stamped out by Matty, began to blaze again. All because Noah sent that X in his email. Now they burned together as two lovers.

The devil, on the other hand? Well, the sooner he was removed, the better.

Chapter Thirty

Who knew tarot could shake him up so much? After Ivy left, and closing the shop, Quinn tucked himself into bed, with only a lamp and his laptop for light. His curtains were drawn, though he noticed snow falling again from the shadows cast on the fabric. He was pleased to be in the comfort of his own apartment, in privacy, having time to unwind, something he felt like he hadn't been able to do for a little while.

Only he couldn't relax. Such is the way. He tried to sleep, but kept thinking about those three bloody cards. It prompted him to open his laptop and read up on the tarot, and the three cards in particular, trying to think of every situation possible.

His mind, however rational, couldn't help but go back to what Ivy had said. That he was meant to be with Noah, or that a bond should form between them. Matty, the devil, was in the way. But what could Quinn do about that?

Kill him and bury him in the castle.

Those intrusive thoughts did not help.

But what better way to save your shop than to have a murder scandal to distract Harold?

Stop it.

He was more confused than ever. He opened a new tab open to IMDB and found the profile of Matty.

Turns out, Matty hadn't been in much of anything.

In 2018, he starred in an independent, straight to DVD horror film, which, after further inspection, Quinn saw still hadn't been distributed or released. Then, most recently, he starred as a minor character in BBC's *Casualty*. And that was it.

No writing credits.

No directing or producing credits.

Going back to the results page, Quinn came across an article about the closing of his bakery in London, open for a year and a half in Camden. Photos showed a café that was exposed brick and recycled wood. It struck Quinn as one of these hipster places that appeared all over the place in 2012. The shop closed because of rising inflation, according to an old social media post.

It offered a new insight into Matty, an entrepreneur, opening a business in London of all places, and making a good go of it while he could. Quinn admired that, but the words that came from Matty's lips left a lot to be desired. If Matty was honest and down to earth about his struggles, maybe Quinn would have liked him more. This side of Matty, the real Matty that may have failed sometimes, would have endeared him to Quinn.

As Quinn flipped through the photos of the now extinct bakery, he tried to imagine the moment Noah would have walked through those double wooden doors with its peeling rustic paint. He wondered what music might have been playing, what sweet smells had wafted around the room. Did Matty serve him? Or did Matty approach him afterwards, maybe when Noah was eating a rocky road with a mug of coffee next to him? He pictured the day turning to night, the busy shop coming to a close, but Noah and Matty were still in the same spot, getting closer, under the spotlight of the old oil lamps hanging around the shop.

He couldn't think like this anymore. He could be his own worst enemy, and he needed to ignore these thoughts, this imagination of his. Until a few weeks ago, Noah hadn't known he existed. Quinn only had a crush – *still* only had a crush. Soon, Noah would go back to London and life would get back to normal.

Normal.

What would Quinn's normal look like when Noah left, the locals returned to their post-Christmas lives, and his shop closed for good?

Quinn closed his laptop, trying to put any thoughts of tarot out of his mind. He made his way to the kitchen, opting for a decaf tea rather than a coffee at this hour. Underneath him, his shop was prepared for the early afternoon signing of Blair Beckett. Tickets sold well, but as long as people were prepared to wait, they could get a moment with Blair. He agreed to sign as many books as he could. Quinn wondered if that meant until a hair was out of place, his wrist hurt, or he ran out of the limited stock Quinn had of that book.

Quinn knew which books would be the bestsellers in his shop. Anything LGBTQ would sell with speed, along with any queer authors, some of which Quinn advertised under his 'queer spotlight of the month'.

Blair Beckett's book, however, rarely shifted any copies. Probably because of its age, and because it wasn't fiction. So tomorrow would be the first time since ordering the stock that Blair's book would sell out.

When he thought of what might happen after Christmas, it left him with the feeling of swallowing something sour, which then made way for a taste of sweetness, which lingered on his taste buds. He would make enough money this week to afford some time to recoup and decide on what to do next.

As he raised the mug of tea to his lips, he thought about life outside of Hay.

He'd been here all his life, and now, what would be here for him?

He couldn't open another shop. Rent was rising, and so were business rates. He wouldn't work for someone else. He valued his freedom too much. All of his profits let him live how he wanted to live and going to a lower paid job would not be workable.

He looked around his apartment, with the furniture he hand-picked and bought himself, where his plants stood lusciously green, catching the sunlight from the windows. The fear that he might not be able to afford this apartment, or in fact, have to leave it, now became real. It clung to him like a demon, threatening his very identity.

Hermione's book offered him some respite, but the money would run out quickly. With no agreed publisher and no concrete revenue, Quinn knew he couldn't rely on the money from Hermione's book forever.

So, where would he go?

What could he do?

The publisher in London. His connection. A promise that if he ever needed them, he could get in touch. Quinn didn't want to change his small-town life to one of trying to fight for your life in a city, but it might be his only option. Publishing and books: that's what he could do.

That was almost always in London.

Quinn sighed.

He was giving up, and he couldn't afford to give up.

Right now, the shop was still his.

This week could change everything. This week could make sure that he still had a place to call home, and a business that was his pride and joy.

Call it tiredness, call it the decaf tea, but Quinn created a plea on a fundraising website. Ivy's fundraiser had faltered, going out with less of a bang than a wet firework. He needed something more refined that was set up from the heart.

It was late, he knew, but he posted the link on his social media sites, personal and business, explaining the situation. He hated asking for money, but something Ivy said stuck with him, and it wasn't the tarot reading this time.

A page where people could donate to him so he might buy the shop from Harold. Well, that *would* be a Christmas miracle. But that was the only option he had.

He expected nothing; not a bite until morning. He knew there was a lot to raise, and in such a short amount of time. That would be hard to do. Near impossible.

Then there was a ping from his email. He looked confused, only to see a donation.

A donation for £100.

A donation from N. Sage.

Quinn leapt for joy. He wanted to run to the windows and shout into the night that Noah Sage was his first donation, and it was a big one. He was about to refresh his email again, to see if someone else might have donated, when a message came through on his personal Instagram.

Noah.

> What are you doing up at this time?

Quinn replied.

> The witching hour.
>
> I'm a witch

> Figured.

> What do you mean by that?

> I had a feeling you cast a spell on me.

Quinn's eyes widened. He re-read the exchange, waiting for the moment that Noah might unsend the message, but it stayed. A little green ball next to the profile photo of Noah blinked at him, telling him they were both active in the chat and online.

Quinn pictured Noah in that cosy bedroom, maybe alone, but no doubt with Matty. He wondered if Noah was waiting for him to reply. Or maybe he was already offline, and the chat hadn't refreshed.

> Why are you awake?

It was a safe reply, one that wasn't flirty, one that didn't break boundaries.

Though he wanted to break everything. He did.

> I do my best writing at night.

Quinn could picture him now at his oak desk, cast in a low orange glow, maybe topless, his back muscles rippling as he typed.

> Thanks for the donation.

> You're welcome.

Then Quinn thought of something.

> How did you know to message me on this account?

It was his personal account, and as far as he was aware, Noah hadn't followed Quinn back, which was rude but totally okay, of course.

The little three dots came dancing at the bottom of their chat, a chat that flirting had entered and left.

Why was his heart beating so fast?

Why were his palms sweating?

Noah's reply came back, and it made Quinn weak at the knees for all the wrong reasons.

> Might have had something to do with you liking this.

And then that photo, *that photo*, with the topless Noah on the beach, with the sun highlighting every muscle on his toned body, from his pecs to his six-pack, to that V-line, dipping down underneath those red shorts, those thick thighs, toned legs, covered in a dusting of hair.

He sent it in the chat. So now here it was, in a private space, forced to be admired again.

He knew Quinn liked it!

Curse his clumsy fingers!

He hadn't replied quickly enough, and he was making it obvious that he lusted over the photo once again. He needed to say something, anything.

> I hope you know I liked that photo for the beach.

> Oh, I didn't think you liked it for any other reason.

> Good. Because it was just the beach.

> Yeah. Of course.

If Quinn were on a quiz show, and they asked him the colour of the bird in the blue sky, or the shade of the ocean, he would fail every answer. Because he hadn't looked at the beach. Or the bird, if there even was one.

> You should get some rest, Quinn. You've got a
> busy day tomorrow.

Quinn stared out at the dark room, lost in thought. After everything Noah said, their moment together yesterday, it wasn't too late.

> Want to come over?

He knew it was daring. Knew that he was playing with fire. Noah did his best writing at night. Judging by the way he talked about Hay, he did his best exploring at night, too. When the locals couldn't whisper. Because if they knew he was entering Quinn's apartment again, they'd gossip. Not maliciously. But speculatively.

Thudding heart pounding in his ears. No response. He shouldn't have done it. He'd crossed a line, asking Noah over. In all honesty, he wasn't sure where the bravery came from.

But then the dots appeared.

Typing.

> Be there in ten.

And then Quinn *couldn't* sleep because he was as excited as a kid on Christmas eve.

Chapter Thirty-One

'What took you so long?'

Noah buzzed in, because this time Quinn had locked the downstairs door, and he looked amused. His hair was messier than usual, and he was dressed in a thick coat and relaxed jogging bottoms. It was quiet in Hay and late at night, so Quinn was optimistic that he got in without being spotted.

Noah smiled. 'Had to get dressed.'

'You call putting joggers and a hoodie on getting dressed?' Quinn said, taking Noah's coat and hanging it up.

'You're not much better,' Noah said. 'Besides, I wasn't wearing anything.'

Quinn almost dropped the coat. 'You write naked?'

'Sometimes.'

'Oh, Jesus.'

Noah's hands slipped in his jogging pockets. He looked around the apartment, cleaned only five minutes ago by Quinn, who panicked that he'd asked the author over. 'How come you invited me over?'

'I ... don't know,' Quinn said. 'Can't sleep.'

'No, me neither,' Noah said. 'I broke up with Matty.'

Quinn yelped, covering his mouth. 'Sorry?'

'It's okay.'

'No, I mean, did I hear you right?'

'That I broke up with Matty?'

'Exactly that.' Quinn sank onto the sofa, light-headed. Maybe it was the hour of the night. 'What? Why? Oh, god, was it my fault? Did I do something? It wasn't yesterday, was it?'

Noah joined Quinn, but not close enough. Sitting across from Quinn like they were mutual friends at a party.

'Actually, Quinn, yes.'

Quinn shook his head, unable to believe his words. He'd broken up a partnership? How would he be able to live with himself?

'You've gone pale.'

'I'm scared.'

'Why are you scared?'

'Please, Noah, tell me I didn't break you up.'

Noah grimaced. 'Well…'

Quinn let out a groan, hunching over. Noah, next to him now, patted his back.

'It's okay,' Noah soothed. 'Honestly, Quinn, it's not your fault.'

Quinn took a deep breath, feeling hot. He'd never wanted to break them up. Maybe that was why Noah accepted the invite with ease: he wanted revenge.

Sitting up, Quinn braved a glance at Noah.

He didn't look distraught. He looked dashing. Like he had no worries and everything was together for him.

'It was time,' Noah said. 'I think last night reminded me of that and brought it home. Matty and I… We'd been having problems. He flipped when he saw you with me in the room.'

'He knew what happened?' Quinn put his head in his hands.

'Nothing happened,' Noah said.

'But something almost did.'

Noah touched Quinn's hands, removing them from his face

with a gentle ease. They looked at one another, Quinn trying to understand what he was thinking.

'It was the final straw for me,' Noah said. 'The things he said, the way he didn't believe me when I told him nothing happened. There was no trust there. He didn't trust me not to do anything. Assumed the worst of me.'

'Would something have happened, Noah?' Quinn whispered. 'If Matty hadn't walked in?'

Noah bit his lip, almost making any reserve Quinn possessed wither into pieces. 'That was another thing.' Noah moved closer to Quinn. 'I wanted to kiss you last night, Quinn.'

This couldn't be happening. Quinn threw his head back, leaning against the sofa. He glared at the ceiling, aware that Noah stared at him.

'Poor Matty.'

'I'm not saying anything has to happen,' Noah said. 'Especially with what's happened between me and Matty. But we've not been good for the whole year. I'm surprised we've lasted this long. It's not your fault. The relationship was over and it ran its course. It's just… You helped speed up the process.'

If what Noah said was true, Quinn could feel somewhat better about the ordeal. Sure, maybe he'd been the crux, or the straw that broke the camel's back, but that was it. He'd stepped in at the last moment when the foundations were ready to cave in.

'This is … a lot.'

'I appreciate that.'

Quinn fixed Noah with a stare that he hoped told him he was in control of the situation. Even if he felt anything but. 'You mean it when you say it wasn't my fault?'

'Yes. You remember when I spoke about being heartbroken?' Noah asked, and Quinn nodded. 'Well, I've been heartbroken for about six months. Because I haven't had the heart to tell Matty that it's over. And the way he's been towards me, behind closed doors … well, it hasn't been good. We would have broken up after

Christmas, if not now. These things happen. This needed to happen.'

Quinn reached out for Noah, taking his hand in his. Noah breathed, looking down at Quinn's fingers.

'Where is Matty now?'

'Well, that's the thing.' Noah sighed. 'He can't go home. The snow's back. We're snowed in again. So, he's staying in another room. Maybe he'll go before Christmas, I don't know. But it's a little awkward right now.'

'Do you want to stay here tonight?'

Noah looked stunned. 'Please don't think I came here tonight under the pretence of anything.'

'I invited you.'

'I know, but I still came.'

Quinn squeezed Noah's hand. 'I know you didn't come here under any other pretence, Noah. My offer still stands. If you want to stay here tonight, you can.'

'Thanks,' Noah said. 'I'd like that.'

Quinn smiled. Switching on the TV and grabbing a blanket, they settled on the sofa to watch a sitcom. Within half an hour, Noah's snores reached Quinn. He looked uncomfortable, so Quinn tried to tilt his head. Noah groaned, eyes flickering open.

'Sorry,' Quinn whispered.

But Noah smiled, reached for Quinn, and hugged him. Quinn took a breath, unsure what to do.

'Hug me, handsome,' Noah whispered.

Laughing, Quinn wrapped his arms around Noah, as his head rested on Quinn's chest. Quinn watched the sitcom as Noah drifted back to sleep, but he didn't take any of it in.

———————

Without Ivy, the signing the next morning would have been a disaster. Quinn was one hundred per cent sure of that. When he opened the shop, it didn't take long for people to arrive before Blair even appeared. Quinn thought he'd been proactive by prepping the author signing place at the back of the shop last night, but now he realised he didn't know how to make sure people queued adequately.

'Line up, line up,' Ivy ordered as she ushered people into place in the warm shop. Incense burned in each corner. 'Queue in the first aisle. Exit through the second. If you want to buy books, third aisle to the till.'

'Wow, she's got this covered,' Daniel said.

Quinn thought he might have been able to do something similar, but his thoughts were all over the place after last night. Noah was still upstairs.

'Blair isn't going anywhere!' Ivy called to the throng of people, proceeding to explain the queuing situation. 'He will have time for you. We will have tea and coffee available as you wait!'

This seemed to appease the crowd, wrapped up against the elements and now queuing down the street. As Ivy returned to the shop, Quinn beckoned her to the counter.

'We have tea and coffee?'

'I brought urns,' Ivy said. 'Coffee urns. I'll get some made up now.'

There was a commotion at the door, and Ivy turned with searing eyes, no doubt ready to shout at the rowdy customers. Quinn, thinking that these signings were going to be a bad idea, was relieved to see her reach out and hug Noah, who got through the door, looking shocked and relieved to be alive. With a jolt, Quinn recognised the auburn jumper Noah was wearing: it was his own. He still wore the joggers from the night before, but paired with the jumper, they looked less casual. Somehow, Noah made joggers look sophisticated.

'Thank goodness you're here,' Ivy said. 'We need help. Noah, you can direct people at the signing desk down through the aisles. Let me explain to you how the system works.'

Quinn didn't have time to say hello. His mind raced that Noah was wearing his jumper like they did that. Like that was a regular and normal part of their day. He didn't mind one bit, but seeing Noah in the jumper left him dumbfounded.

'Chop, chop, Quinn,' Ivy said. 'Gosh, what's with you today? Hello, you there at the door. Queue like the rest of them, please.'

'This way for Blair's signing,' Noah called, ignoring the shocked stares he got from customers. With the three of them working together, they got the crowd moving with efficiency, and it left Quinn no time to think about anything other than ensuring people had a good time.

Once the teas and coffees were handed out, disgruntled customers thawed, and all was forgotten as soon as they got to meet Blair Beckett, who was as charming and vivacious as ever. Quinn could hear his happy-go-lucky voice from the back of the shop at the counter, so loud it cut through the excited chatter of people here to meet the news reporter.

But he wasn't as loud as Deb and June, who, when they got in the shop, were shocked to see Noah at the signing desk, too. Noah outshone Blair during the signing, but each time, Noah deflected, ensuring that Blair had his moment, and telling them he would sign books at the same time, same place, tomorrow.

There was no appeasing Deb and June, and they got their books signed by both of the men and then promised to come back tomorrow with their other editions from home.

Quinn's eyes filled with tears, but not because of Deb and June. Instead, when there was a moment to breathe, he observed the scene before him. Radiant faces, laughter, excited people craning their necks to get their first glimpse of Blair at his desk. By this point, word spread that Noah was also there, and people couldn't help but whisper about whether he would sign books.

Quinn could see the community coming together, as well as faces he didn't recognise, and he couldn't help but feel overwhelmed. He sank back into his armchair, letting the tears flow, realising how lucky he was to have this, to be part of this, to feel so supported and loved.

Ivy, still at the door, caught him crying. 'Quinn?'

Quinn shook his head, assuring her he was okay. She seemed reluctant to not come to him, but she stayed at the door and greeted those still pouring through.

People seemed to come from all over. To his small shop, his queer shop, the space that meant too much to him. A pang of sadness welled in him, the tears overflowing now; the dam broken.

Noah, who was looking down the second aisle, hurried towards him. His figure blurred from Quinn's tears, but the familiar scent of citrus confirmed it was him. Soft hands were on Quinn's arms again. His breath, minty fresh, brushed across his skin.

'What's wrong? Is everything okay?'

'I'm fine.' Quinn wiped his tears. 'I just...' He gestured to the people in line, a smile breaking through the tears.

Noah wrapped an arm around Quinn, bringing him close. He didn't want to cry on Noah's shoulder, but he leaned against him, feeling exhausted.

'This is all for you,' Noah said. 'Everyone is here for you.'

Fresh tears rolled down Quinn's cheeks. 'I know.'

Noah's finger ran across Quinn's face, brushing away the tears. Their eyes met, stood at the counter of their shop, and Quinn wished he wasn't an ugly crier. Noah smiled, his eyes darting to his hair, to his lips, to his neck. Quinn noticed the inch of space between them and closed the gap, wishing he could be closer, even though he was already against Noah.

'Thank you,' Quinn whispered.

'Anytime.'

Noah moved away first, leaving Quinn standing at his desk, remembering where he was. He looked around, almost expecting the whole shop to be looking at him, but of course, they weren't. Mere seconds had gone by, but it felt like forever for Quinn.

Only Ivy saw the exchange. She raised an eyebrow, a slight smirk on her face, and Quinn shrugged, the image of the lover's tarot card coming back to him.

Noah was back at the signing desk now, helping to guide people out of the shop, and Quinn wished he was still next to him. Daniel waved goodbye, joining the throng of people after completing his shift.

The last customers, being Deb and June, left the shop with reluctance, leaving Quinn with Ivy, Noah and Blair.

Ivy closed the door, a thud that was a bit too loud, and turned the sign to closed. She wiped her brow. 'Phew. What a day.'

Her exhaustion was reflected in Blair's immaculate face, and Noah's casual lean against the nearest bookshelf. Quinn was sure he looked just as tired because he felt like a thirty-year-old Slinky with no slink left.

'I can't thank you all enough.' Quinn fell back into his armchair, feeling like he needed cracking like a brand-new book.

'Thank us? Thank you!' Blair leaned against the bookshelf next to a poster of himself advertising today's event. 'That was the most fun I've had in a long time!'

'More fun than presenting the six o'clock news?'

'So much more fun!'

Ivy made her way to the signing desk, calling as she went. 'I think tomorrow's signing will be just as busy. Quinn, do you have Noah's books?'

'They're in the confessional booth.'

'Blair, would you be so kind as to help me set them up?'

'Of course.' Blair followed Ivy to the back of the shop, looking like a golden retriever who was fetching his ball.

'I can do that later, Ivy,' Quinn called. 'You need to rest.'

'Nonsense,' Ivy dismissed. 'You rest. I've got this covered.'

It left Quinn with Noah at the front of the shop. Noah smiled, walking towards Quinn. He sat on the edge of the counter, a mere few feet from him. The messages from last night, the feeling of him a few hours ago, all came back to him.

Noah looked good today. His hands were in his pockets, and he let his feet dangle off the table, waving them back and forth. How such a simple action could make Quinn want to explode with admiration was beyond Quinn's comprehension.

'My jumper.'

'I hope you don't mind.'

'No, it looks good on you,' Quinn said. 'You should keep it.'

'Oh no, I couldn't...'

'Seriously. Suits you better.'

Noah brushed at the jumper, somewhat self-consciously. Quinn admired him and the way his hair fell over his forehead.

'I'm looking forward to tomorrow,' Noah said.

'I'm glad. Me too.'

'Today was a success.'

'It was.'

Noah's eyes drifted to the window, no doubt taking in the castle above them. Quinn wanted to follow his gaze, but right now he couldn't allow himself to think of the castle, and what the opening meant for his shop.

From the back of the shop came a tumble, and Ivy yelped.

'We're okay!' Blair called, and then there was laughter. 'Ivy dropped some boxes.'

Noah smiled at Quinn.

Quinn sunk back into the armchair. 'What?'

'You're just...'

He said nothing more. Quinn was a fish on a hook, being drawn in, even though he didn't want to be. 'I'm just what?'

'You're fun, Quinn,' Noah said, as Quinn was torn out of the water and into a world where he couldn't breathe.

Fun. Wasn't it time he had a little fun?

Chapter Thirty-Two

'I can't do it.'

It was the evening before Noah's signing, and Quinn was wearing a cherry-scented face mask and a fluffy all in one dressing gown with a cosy hood. And he stood in front of Noah, looking like this, because Noah had turned up unannounced, which seemed to be a common theme now.

'What can't you do?' Quinn asked, glad that his face mask covered his blushing face.

'The book signing.'

'Oh.'

The face mask hid his crestfallen expression, prompting Quinn to think maybe they should use that in their marketing campaigns. Buy this face mask so that hot romantic novelists don't see when you're gutted about what they just said.

'Come in.'

Noah did, shedding his hoodie like he might catch fire. Quinn liked his apartment hot, so of course he turned the heating on full volume.

'Aren't you hot in that?'

Quinn's dressing gown swayed at his shins. 'Not really.'

'Well, you look adorable.'

Noah's hand touched the soft fabric of his dressing gown, and Quinn wished he could shred it and the clothes underneath. Totally appropriate.

'Tea?'

'Please,' Noah said. 'I hope you don't mind me coming over like this. Again.'

'Seems like a regular thing now, doesn't it?'

'The house is awkward.' Noah sighed. 'Matty's not leaving. Says he can't drive back to London because we drove together, and the trains are off because of the snow.'

'Can't he rent a car? The roads are open.' Secretly, Quinn wished he would disappear. Maybe he could go to Cardiff and link up with Dougie.

'I've suggested that.'

'But you've got your room to escape it all?'

'I do. But I know he's in the house. And Mum's been asking me about it and I wanted to get out. And then I started rethinking this book signing, and I got scared.'

'Take a seat.'

Noah settled on the sofa, and Quinn got to the kettle, refilling the water. Making the tea, he fretted about what to say next. It had been a miracle organising the signing to begin with. At such short notice, the haphazard posters and the slapped together newsletter were all Quinn could do to boost the event. Though word spread in Hay, and Quinn was sure they'd get enough custom to make it a success.

Quinn brought the tea to the table and handed Noah his mug. Noah's hand cupped Quinn's before taking it from him, and Quinn sighed.

'I look ridiculous, don't I?'

'No. I love a face mask,' Noah said. 'How else do you think I look this youthful?'

'Botox.'

'Cheeky.' Noah smirked, running a hand through his hair. 'Oh, Quinn. I feel like an arse.'

'That's a way to feel.' Quinn nodded. 'Go on, then. What's up?'

Noah sipped his tea, his eyes widening. He struggled to move the tea to the coffee table without spilling a drop. 'Oh my god, my tongue.'

Great. Now he had a burning hot author with a burning hot tongue in his burning hot apartment.

'I just made it. Have you drunk tea before?'

Noah stuck out his tongue and fanned it with his hand.

Quinn struggled to hide his mirth, but he managed it because the face mask made his skin tight, so it was impossible to crack laughter.

Noah seemed to move past the crisped tongue, and reached for his tea again, blowing on it.

Quinn had never been so jealous of tea.

'I don't think I can do it,' Noah said. 'I thought I could. When I came to the signing today, that was the first proper time I've had to be with people in Hay again. It was a little overwhelming when people tried to talk to me more than they talked to Blair, but there wasn't much I could do about it. It was so busy I couldn't think. But the whole time, Quinn, my heart was beating and my hands were shaking. And tomorrow, it's all me, isn't it? People are coming for me and they'll expect the version of me I can't put on. Not in the town.'

For the first time, Quinn realised how anxious Noah was. The shaking hands, the beating heart, the running thoughts picturing the worst-case scenarios. Quinn put his tea aside and made to touch Noah, but thought better of it. Instead, he hovered, looking at Noah.

Noah held out his hand, and Quinn took it, relieved.

It trembled on its own.

'You're anxious about it?'

'It feels like more than anxiety,' Noah said. 'It feels like a full-blown panic attack.'

'I mean this in the nicest way,' Quinn said, 'but what is it that sets Hay apart from talking on stage at the Hay festival, and doing the signing in their tent?'

Noah let out a small laugh. 'I'm anxious when I'm doing that, too.'

'But you'd never show it.' Though Quinn recalled seeing Noah at his table in the festival bookshop, and how, even though he handled each visitor with ease, there was a moment when Quinn thought he saw the novelist falter.

'No, I wouldn't,' Noah said. 'And you know why? It's because even though I'm back in Hay, I don't *feel* like I'm back. Because I can convince myself that the people coming to see me at Hay are mostly out of towners, because the festival isn't in the town, is it? It's far enough away from the town to make me feel like it's far removed, and that people don't know my history, only my books. They might not have those preconceptions of the kid I was. They see me as someone else, the man I created, and I like that. Here? Not a chance. They're locals. Familiar faces. People in the town who pity me for being the son of Hermione. People who saw me leave at sixteen. They expect something else of me, something that I can't give them.'

'And what is that?'

'I don't know. The guy who ran away when things got tough? The guy who abandoned his mother because he didn't know how to deal with her mental health? A boy who is so self-obsessed, so driven by wanting to carve his own name, that he alienates the people who cared about him?'

Noah lifted his tea and drank, and Quinn steadied his own shaking hands.

Once Noah finished, Quinn peeled off his face mask, aware that he looked ridiculous and too casual for a moment like this.

'Beautiful skin,' Noah mused. 'You're blushing.'

'You know as soon as you tell someone they're blushing, they blush even more?' Quinn asked. 'Never tell someone they're blushing if you want them to stop.'

'I don't want you to stop,' Noah said. His hand extended, brushing his fingers against Quinn's hot cheeks. 'Soft. Beautiful.'

Quinn leaned into his touch, closing his eyes. This had to be a dream. There was no way Noah was doing this to him right now.

'I'll be with you, Noah.'

'What does that mean?'

'I'll be by your side.'

'Promise?'

'Promise.' Quinn wasn't sure what he was promising. To be with Noah forever? Was it to be by his side at the book signing? To be there for him right now?

'I'm terrified of what they will think of me,' Noah said, tracing a finger along Quinn's jaw. 'I'm terrified they will hold grudges against me, or berate me for the life I lived. Scared they'll make jokes to me about Mum. But I'm also scared I'll let them down.'

Noah's fingers hovered over Quinn's lips, and Quinn kissed them ever so gently. This time, his heart beat harder, laced with his own anxious desire to take this to the next level with Noah. Whatever this was, and whatever it meant.

Noah slid his finger across Quinn's lips and down to his chin.

'Look at me, handsome.'

Only now Quinn realised he'd looked anywhere but into Noah's eyes. Looking at him, he felt lost. Like he'd never be able to appease his anxiety, or hold him close, or be the person he could rely on. Maybe *he* would let *him* down.

But it wouldn't be like that. Couldn't be like that. Because underneath it all, Noah was destined to let him down. Listening to him now, his desire to escape the town told Quinn everything he needed to know.

'You don't want to be here, do you?'

'I can't be here.'

'You can't be in Hay, or don't want to be?'

'Both,' Noah said. 'Hay scares me, Quinn. It puts me right back to where I was when I was sixteen. Confused, alone, scared of myself. Of what people thought. It brings back all my insecurities, and it makes me face moments I don't want to face.'

'Like what?'

'Like Mum. I don't know what to do to help her.'

'Be there for her,' Quinn said. He linked his fingers with Noah's, and his hand felt so rough, so gentle, and so strong. The anchor that helped him say what he needed to say. 'Talk to her because she needs someone to talk to. Have you thought that maybe *you* should be the one to hear her story? To write it for her? Have either of you ever spoken about how the other makes you feel?'

Noah shook his head. 'Never.'

'I understand they are hard places to go to. I know it isn't what you want to be doing. But your problems stem from how others treated your mum and how they affected you. It can't have been easy growing up being told your mother was everything she wasn't. And it can't have been the easiest to discover who you were, how that made you feel, and how you were a victim of it all, too.'

'A victim?'

'To learn about what your dad did? To hear what people think about your mum and be okay with that?'

'But what's awful is that for a long time, I believed they were right.'

'And what about now?'

Noah ran a thumb over Quinn's hand, sending shivers down his spine. It took all his willpower not to drag Noah to him and feel his weight upon him.

Stay focussed, Quinn.

'All I can see is how I failed her. I should have been there for her.'

'Be there for her now.' Quinn let go of Noah's hand, almost immediately feeling the chill of where he'd been.

'You intrigue me.'

'I ... what?'

'Intrigue me,' Noah repeated, though they both knew he didn't need to do so.

He intrigued *Noah? How was that even possible?*

'You get me,' Noah said. 'I don't know how, but you do. You understand that side of me I can't show to others. And it confuses me. It intrigues me. It *panics* me. If I'd met you sooner...'

'Stop it.'

'Stop it?'

He looked at Noah now, properly looked at him, and wondered if he'd read him all wrong. A man like him, so put together, so successful, so much more than this small town, could never be his.

The promise he'd made moments ago, already broken. 'Stop talking to me like that.'

'Like what?'

'Like *that*,' Quinn said. 'That I intrigue you? That you wished you met me sooner? I can't do that, Noah.'

Noah moved towards him, and Quinn flinched like he'd been pinched.

'Quinn...'

The way he said his name was perfect. Soft, questioning, curious. Quinn could let this happen, let the feelings unfold, and regret it all later. But now, of all the times in his life, he found his voice.

'No.' Quinn shook his head. 'I might be wrong here, Noah, but I think I've been picking up what you're putting down. It's hurting me. It's keeping me up at night. I can't go there right now. You can't go there right now. You hate this place, and I don't. Speak with Matty, sort that part of your life out. Your mother. You have a whole other life, Noah, that I don't fit into.'

Oh god. It hurt to admit it. Hurt to utter these words that were laced with truth. In an alternative universe peddled by Ivy, Quinn would be with Noah. But this wasn't the other universe. This was real life, and real life was complicated. Since meeting Noah, the days had bordered on fantasy.

Well, now the spell broke.

'Quinn, listen…'

'I can't,' Quinn said. 'Noah. I want to. But I can't. *We* can't.'

Noah moved closer, leaned closer, his eyes level with his own. Quinn felt trapped, but part of him wanted to be trapped. The other part of him wanted to lean forwards so that he could experience that static shock again, that feeling of safety and warmth.

'I'm sorry if I've done something wrong.'

Quinn gripped the arm of the sofa to steady himself. He was a glass and Noah a hammer. His words shattered him right there and then.

'We're wrong,' Quinn interrupted. 'I'm wrong. This is wrong.'

He wished he hadn't ruined whatever might have been forming between the two of them. He wished he could be carefree and go-lucky like Bloody Blair Beckett, but he couldn't.

Sure, Noah excited him. The idea of them being together was one that could develop and it was so easy to get lost in the illusion of something simplistic and fun. But every moment came down to the same thing: Noah didn't want to be in Hay. The only alternative to be with Noah was to leave Hay. What was the point in fighting for his shop if he couldn't be in Hay to enjoy it, to run it, to revel in the success of saving it? Why hadn't Noah realised that? Did he think he could draw Quinn away from what mattered to him on the basis that he was the sweetest man to enter Quinn's life? He couldn't entertain such frivolous moments with Noah. Not when his fear held him back. Not when his life didn't align with Quinn's.

Quinn reached out to Noah and cupped his chin. He felt

stubble that was yet to flourish. Noah looked at Quinn with a pained expression, one so instinctively lustful Quinn was sure it was reflected in his own gaze.

'You said you wished we met sooner,' Quinn whispered. 'I do, too. Maybe our lives would have been different. But whatever might happen here, because I know you've realised something is, just like I have, we can't have it happen. We need to forget it. Come Christmas, you'll be gone, and me? Well, I don't know where I'll be. But it won't be with you. It *can't* be with you.'

Noah, sweet Noah, was broken like a beautiful Christmas ornament before him. The shards cut through Quinn, but he had to ignore the pain and let them slice him.

Noah placed a hand on Quinn's, but he didn't remove Quinn's touch. Instead, his lips found Quinn's hand. Staring at Quinn, he kissed his fingers, his knuckles, the back of his hand. The kiss was light, tender, and it hurt every single fibre of Quinn's being.

He could take his hand away. He could set the boundary right now. But he couldn't. After the third kiss, Noah linked his fingers through Quinn's and let them drop to their knees. Quinn felt his eyes sting, aware now that he was crying, but feeling foolish for doing so.

Noah wiped the tears away once more. 'I'm sorry,' Noah whispered.

'Me too,' Quinn choked. He could still feel the linger of his lips on his skin, wishing to feel them again.

He would not fight. Quinn wanted him to, but he knew Noah had heard him. He must have agreed with his words, because if he saw another option, he'd stay. He'd tell Quinn he was wrong, that there was nothing to worry about, and they could move past this silly moment and everything would be okay.

Then he was gone. The warmth faded from his hand.

Noah pulled on his hoodie. He gave Quinn one last, longing look, and then he left him behind.

Chapter Thirty-Three

Quinn couldn't shake the feeling that something was wrong. First, he almost missed his alarm and tumbled out of bed and stumbled into the kitchen in a way that would make Dolly Parton wince. Next, his coffee was ruined by gone-off milk. He showered, then looked out at the day, expecting a winter wonderland, but instead seeing nothing but black slush, with heavy rain falling down on Hay. Black clouds lingered over Kings & Queens, and Quinn hoped this wasn't an omen for the day ahead.

Today was Noah's book signing day, and Quinn stood in his shop in the early morning, biting his nails as anxiety gripped his stomach, reached tendrils of spiky anger to his heart, and shot pain through his blood, giving him a searing headache.

Noah hadn't replied to Quinn's email confirming if the signing was still going ahead. He sent it early in the morning, brisk and business-like. As he had sat in bed in the early hours, Quinn considered messaging Noah again on Instagram, but each time he saw the green active sign, he closed the app and wished there was a box to lock his phone in.

Why did he say those words? Why then? In that moment, with

Noah so close to him, the clouds in Quinn's life cleared and he could see the obstacles in front of him. He was wasting time by preoccupying himself with feelings for an author that would be gone too soon; on a relationship that would never work because Quinn's life was Hay. He needed to focus on his shop.

What a moment to choose clarity. What a moment to decide, *you know what? I'm looking after me.* Now, Quinn felt worse than ever, hopeless and despondent.

He entered the shop that morning with a determination rooted in distraction. He couldn't bear to stay in the apartment any longer. After two hours of sleep, he woke up feeling wide awake, and like he needed to do *something*. The nerves building inside him forced every part of him to move, like standing still would leave him open to hurt and worry.

With shaking hands, he spent his morning typing out the first few chapters of Hermione Sage's book. He didn't know what she wanted, and now he was unsure if the book would still go ahead, but she was on his side, a relic of what might have been. Mother-in-law, obviously. Before he knew it, 9am arrived, and with it, the time to open the shop.

Customers trickled in, which was always a pleasure, but when Quinn had a quiet moment, he found the old email from the job offer in London. Googling the name of the person who he'd spoken with during his interview, he saw she was still active, still working in the same role, and no doubt would remember him when he got back in touch.

Well, if he needed to get back in touch. The possibility seemed more probable as time went on.

Fearing he'd been sitting for too long, Quinn darted around the shop, making sure all books were in the right places, and that the signing, prepared the evening before, hadn't been destroyed by, say, a tornado or a raccoon. Not that Wales had raccoons, of course, but you never knew what could happen.

'You've been on your phone a lot,' Quinn said after he caught Daniel in one aisle for the fifth time that day.

Daniel jumped, slipping the phone back in his pocket. 'Sorry.'

'Oh, don't apologise,' Quinn said. 'No, I'm not that sort of boss. I don't mind. Who you texting?'

'Um … a friend.'

'Right, none of my business.'

'When is Noah coming in today?'

'You know what? I have no idea if he's even coming at all.'

Daniel's mouth dropped. The signing was ready to go for mid-afternoon, Noah's books were stacked on the table, and when Quinn looked around his shop, all was quiet. With the black clouds swirling above, this was his own calm before the storm.

'So much for a white Christmas,' Daniel said, as if he knew not to pry.

The anxiety within him mingled with dread and fear, like a poisonous cocktail, and he wished Noah would reply, would confirm that despite everything, despite the rejection, he'd still show up.

He refreshed his emails whenever he got a moment. Checked that Instagram message for a green active bubble.

The queue formed outside, most of the people the same from yesterday, this time understanding the queuing process. Faces peered into the window, maybe hoping to see Noah at the counter, but of course, he wasn't here.

Would he be here?

Quinn hadn't thought about the prospect of seeing him. He wouldn't feel excited this time. He would feel embarrassed, scared, even a little awkward. But Quinn could see the bigger picture. Noah's signing was part of the save the shop plan. That was all he ever was and would be. Just part of the plan. He couldn't be anything else.

Customers trickled into the shop, forming the queue from the top of the aisle leading out of the door. They talked amongst themselves, but he felt like he should tell them the truth, letting them down gently, just like he hoped he had let down Noah.

Could you even let down someone romantically if they were only a friend?

Once again, hoping the customers along the window wouldn't see, he checked his emails, then Instagram, flicking between them both like tennis players at Wimbledon, hoping Noah would reply. Noah could be a total dick to him. He didn't even have to be kind. Right now, Quinn just wanted to feel relief that, despite everything, Noah would still be here.

Ivy came through the door, telling customers gathering in a crowd in the shop to form an orderly queue, and that the system was as important as, say, Nicola Roberts winning The Masked Singer. When she saw Quinn's face, she shook her head.

'Oh, no, no, no,' she said. 'Your aura is dark blue today. You don't look good, either.'

'Wow, thanks.'

'Black bags under your eyes.' Ivy peered at him like a doctor. 'You look pale. That blue glow. Something is wrong.'

'Noah hasn't replied to me,' Quinn whispered, aware that customers in the shop might be listening. 'I don't even know if he's still coming.'

'Diva!' Ivy exclaimed. 'No, I will *not* have this.'

She rooted in her handbag and took out her phone.

'What are you doing?'

She held up her hand. 'Hermione, hello! How are you? Oh good, good. Yes, I'm just wondering if we are still on for today? You know … Noah?'

A pause, Ivy nodding, her expression so blank that Quinn wished he could read minds like she seemed to do. That familiar, twisting, horrible feeling inside him made him want to sit down, or drink some water, or get black-out drunk.

Then she said goodbye, turning to Quinn. 'He left.'

'Oh, thank god.'

The anxiety inside him melted like the snow outside. He looked at the shop again, trying to recall that feeling from yesterday, before Noah, of the smiling faces and the experience he provided for his customers.

'No, Quinn,' Ivy said. 'He left for London this morning.'

Chapter Thirty-Four

The customers disappeared, huffing and grumbling that something they'd been looking forward to was cancelled at such short notice. Deb and June fell to the floor with loud sobs, and refused to budge, despite getting their editions signed yesterday. But, of course, they'd shown up as promised with their other editions, forever unsigned. Quinn wondered if he'd been optimistic this whole time.

When Deb and June did move, because June needed to prepare supper, and crying too much was bad for Deb's IBS, they left Quinn with his own thoughts. He sat on the floor in the middle of his shop, almost like he was meditating. The smell of burning incense, intermingled with pages of books, made him feel comfortable. The old pipes, pumping water through to create heat, made it feel like it was mid-spring.

'Do you want to get a drink?'

'No,' Quinn said to Ivy, the last remaining person in the shop.

Ivy crossed her arms. 'I will not have that tone from you, mister.'

'Ivy, please.' Quinn sighed. 'I'm not in the mood.'

'Want to talk about it?'

'Not really.'

She headed to the front door, and Quinn hoped she would leave, as horrible as that might be. Right now, he wanted to understand what he was feeling, or get out of his own head. He didn't need to be reminded of Noah, of the situation.

'What happened?'

'What do you mean?'

'Noah isn't the type of guy to flake like that,' Ivy said. 'He doesn't let *anybody* down.'

'How do you know that?'

'Because I do.'

'Oh, *please* don't give me something about his aura.'

Ivy turned the sign of the door to closed and knelt in front of Quinn. 'If you must know, his aura is yellow. That means he is pleasant, confident, and a wonderful person. He's safety and warmth bundled up in a package. I know from Hermione that he's kind. And there isn't one bad word said about him in the industry.'

'Now, how would you know *that?*'

'Friends of the festival,' Ivy said, and then, with a slight hint of shame. 'And Heat magazine.'

Quinn smiled, a genuine one that made him feel lighter, if only for a moment.

'But I know something is wrong,' Ivy said. 'Do you want to confess your sins to me?'

Quinn shook his head. 'I either misread the situation, or I stood up for myself for the first time and it's fucked everything up.'

'In what way?'

He stared at the wooden floorboards in front of him, wondering how honest he should be with Ivy. Speaking out felt like it would do him good.

'I told Noah that we couldn't do whatever was going on between us,' Quinn said. 'I swear he was flirting with me. We were getting closer, and it felt like we were going to end up doing something we would both regret. And he was scared, and I mistreated him. He kept saying how much he didn't want to be in Hay. It would never have worked between us. But I wanted it to, desperately. And I just cut anything short because I was scared, and I couldn't do that.'

'Oh, Quinn.' Ivy sighed. 'When did this happen?'

'Last night.'

'Oh. And then what happened?'

'He left. Said he was sorry. Then he didn't come to the signing today, and the next thing I know…'

'He's back in London.'

The hurt floated between them, and Ivy placed a hand on Quinn's knee. She said nothing more, but somehow it was enough.

'Don't let this get to you, Quinn,' Ivy said. 'He'll see sense, and then I think you both need to talk about it.'

'He's gone, Ivy. Probably for the best.'

Ivy got to her feet, placing her pink earmuffs atop her head. 'I'll let you be alone. Call me if you need anything.'

'Thanks, Ivy.'

After Ivy left, a part of Quinn wished she'd stayed. Only, if she'd stayed, he would have had to talk, and he couldn't.

It wasn't his intention to sit in the self-help section, gazing at a title about dealing with heartbreak. He scoffed, closing his eyes, and took three deep breaths. As he tried to clear his mind, all he could see was Noah smiling at him. Touching him. Breathing close to him.

He snapped his eyes open, bringing him to the centre in his shop. He would *not* let Noah get to him.

What a dick.

That was the only word for him. What a let-down. What a disaster.

What a fool I have been.

How had he allowed himself to get so carried away with his

infatuation with Noah? The excitement had bundled him up with a bow on top like he was a Christmas gift, making him feel like he could conquer all with Noah by his side.

But Noah had betrayed him. He was embarrassed, but only because he couldn't admit to himself how much he'd relied on Noah's help. All this time, he'd allowed his feelings to explore what could have been, allowing them to guide him, finding any excuse to get Noah involved in the saving of his business. Yet underlying all of that was the feeling that maybe, just maybe, Noah might become something more to Quinn.

Then there was Matty and all the complications that came with a fresh breakup. What if Noah realised the error of his ways and they rekindled their relationship?

Quinn knew he hadn't misread the signs. The feelings Noah gave him, their private moments exchanged, all felt intense, different, brand new.

Noah felt them too. Quinn was sure of that. You didn't get that close to someone and share so much for no reason. No, there'd been mutual feelings. Did that scare him?

The embarrassment, a twisting, horrible feeling, came from the fact that Quinn felt like he'd made it obvious how much he wanted Noah to be involved in his life. Now he could only imagine Noah laughing at his desperation, at the poor shopkeeper losing his bookshop at Christmas, how desperate he'd been to use Noah's name. He imagined the conversations between Noah and Matty, the gloating smile of Matty forgiving Noah for that moment he interrupted between them in his childhood bedroom.

In amongst all the embarrassment, the upset, and the doubt, he thought he might throw up. How *dare* Noah lead him on like that? How could he have failed to hide his feelings, messed with his head, and then done *this*? He left him when he needed him the most, when his future relied on it, and all because ... what? Because Quinn shut down any possibility of romance? Because Quinn took the high ground for once in his life, and realised that

265

when a third person is involved, it doesn't matter if they're the devil, they still need to be respected? Had Noah left because Quinn refused to be his holiday affair?

Or was it because they could never be together, because Noah didn't belong in Hay?

Quinn squeezed his fists together, feeling totally not zen. He needed wine. Or whisky. Or a punching bag. Or a whisky-dispensing punching bag in a winery.

Pacing now, Quinn knew the anger was so much more than Noah. All of his life, he had never stood up for himself. He feared what others might think of him or thought about other people's feelings rather than his own. He watched people flourish, progress, find happiness, and where did appeasing others get him?

Here, on a stormy winter's night, losing everything.

Being made a fool of by hot authors and their model ex-boyfriends.

Being pitied by the locals.

The fight wasn't over yet. Screw Noah Sage. He didn't need him or his perfect body with the V-line. Or his poetic mind. Or his intellect. Or his immense talent, and kind, warm personality.

There were three more days before Christmas. Three more days to save his shop.

The party, the protest: they were the next milestones. Both fell on the same day. Looking up at the castle, as rain fell from the sky and battered its stone exterior, he knew this was his last chance. Either he could build himself back up from disrepair, or he would lose the fight.

Quinn typed out emails, not only hyping people up for the protest and the party, but trying to convince himself that there was something to look forward to. He swallowed his pride as he started the emails with apologies for letting them down that the signing didn't go ahead. He decorated his shop as much as he could for the party, ordering some last minute items. He made a list, and checked it more than twice, of things he would need to buy: party food, alcohol, and mistletoe.

Because everyone needed mistletoe at a Christmas party!

Tomorrow, he could rest. He could open his shop and tell any customers that they were welcome to the party. He'd prepare his own sign that he would parade at the protest.

A small, niggling feeling of excitement came from within, and he nourished it like a caveman to the first flame.

Noah was but a man. A man carved from marble and listed in the dictionary as an example of handsome, sure, but despite that, a mere man. Quinn vowed not to allow himself to waste any more time on him. Guys like Noah were make-believe.

Getting to his feet, ready to leave the shop, Quinn decided he needed a bottle of wine and to watch a good Christmas romcom in his flat. He would witness someone else's Christmas happy ending, and all would be right in the world.

Hell, maybe even a night with a vibrator. Why not? Go wild.

His email pinged. He considered not looking, sure it would just be someone confirming their attendance, but curiosity got the better of him.

His heart plummeted.

Noah.

One simple response.

I'm sorry.

Sorry? Was that it? Seven letters? Two words?

Sorry?

The anger came rushing back to him like an avalanche of killer snow. He could almost feel himself get engulfed in flames, sure that if Noah were here now, his glare would burn him. He typed, slamming his fingers into the keyboard, his eyes not leaving the screen.

Never have I felt so disappointed. Sorry doesn't cut it. You may have let me down, but I don't care. I can move past it. But I can't forgive how you let down a huge amount of people who had been waiting at the shop, in the melting snow and freezing rain, just to get a moment to meet you, get their books signed, and spend some time with you. To meet the boy who grew up in Hay, back at last. To meet you, all of you, but you let them down. You should be ashamed, Noah. I thank you for your help so far and your donation. I hope London is everything it's meant to be.

Send.

No regrets.

No other thoughts.

From this moment on, Quinn's own romantic story ended. Life wasn't a romcom. There were no happy endings here.

Chapter Thirty-Five

'God, you look terrible,' Daniel said as Quinn walked into the bookshop.

'Oh, thanks,' Quinn said. Truth be told, Daniel didn't lie. His hair, sometimes combed, stuck up from a night of sleep. He'd rolled out of bed and walked downstairs. 'I had a restless night.'

'Is it about Noah?'

'What do you mean?'

'Well, word has spread that he left.' Daniel gave Quinn a look of pity. 'And someone else said that they'd seen him go to yours the night before. Did something happen?'

Great. So now Quinn was the gossip of the town because Noah left in a hurry? Knowing that someone had already whispered about them confirmed Noah's feelings. The sense of community in Hay was strong, but it acted like a double-edged sword. Quinn loved the community aspect, but Noah wouldn't, couldn't. In some ways, Quinn almost wanted to tell Noah that he had validation.

'It's not like that.'

'Do you need to go back to sleep?'

'No, I'm here for the day.'

'If you're sure.'

Quinn headed to the counter, checking emails and doing the regular daily admin. Daniel flitted between the shelves, organising for the customers. As Quinn headed towards the kitchen at the back to make them a coffee, he heard Daniel cough.

'So, gay sex.'

Quinn spun around, looking at Daniel. 'Excuse me?'

Daniel, standing at the counter, placed his hands on his hips. 'Uh … yeah. I'm thinking about doing it.'

Quinn blinked, realising he had sleep around his eyes. He rubbed at them, wishing he'd woken up earlier so that he could be more alert.

'You're thinking about having gay sex?'

Daniel cleared his throat. 'That's right, and I'm wondering if you have any tips.'

'I…' Quinn paused, looking at his watch. Ten minutes until opening. 'Daniel, I thought you were straight?'

'I'm … not *not* straight. At least I don't know if I'm straight.'

'Do you want to chat?'

'I thought that's what I was doing.' Daniel rubbed at his neck.

'Normally people don't open with "so, gay sex", but I'll let you off,' Quinn said. He leaned against the nearest bookshelf. 'Tell me what you're thinking.'

'For a little while now, I've wondered if I might be…' Daniel waved his hands, as if unable to find the word.

'Gay?' He shook his head. 'Bi?' Again, a no. 'Pan?'

'Something other than straight, I guess,' Daniel said. 'Um … no offense, but it's why I took the job.'

'Oh?'

'I thought maybe I could start working here and, like, I don't know, get whatever I felt out of my system,' Daniel said. 'Only the more I met people, the more books I put on the shelves, the more I let myself feel what I was feeling. I'm scared.'

'Absolutely normal.'

'It is?'

'Yeah, why wouldn't it be?'

Daniel struggled to find the words. 'You seem so … confident? Especially with this fight to save your shop. The way you're arguing back with people who tell you what to do. I've never seen that side of you before. It makes me realise how … secure you seem in who you are.'

'That's how I appear to you?'

'Yes. Don't you feel that way?'

'Not enough,' Quinn admitted. 'But when I first thought about who I'm attracted to, and started facing my actual feelings, I was terrified.'

'Did you ever feel in denial?'

Quinn laughed. 'Sorry, but yes, I did. There was a time when I hated myself.'

'Wow.' Daniel sighed. 'I can relate to that.'

No matter how many times he heard of similar experiences, hearing that someone hated themselves because of their sexuality always made Quinn disappointed. Society deeming queer people as anomalies because they weren't straight led to people like Daniel, like Quinn, feeling ashamed of themselves.

'Do you hate yourself?'

'Sometimes,' Daniel said. 'I haven't told a soul. Nobody even knows I work here.'

'Oh.' For the first time, Quinn realised how little he'd been paying attention to his own member of staff. 'I'm sorry, Daniel. I've been an awful boss.'

'What? No, you haven't,' Daniel said. 'You've got a bit more to worry about than whether James Bond over here likes men.'

'About that. You asked me about sex? You're seriously considering it?'

'I met this guy,' Daniel said, looking away from Quinn. 'Couple of weeks back.'

271

'Your age?'

'Yes, my age,' Daniel said. 'Kind of in a similar situation to me. Both of us are...'

'Exploring?'

'I guess,' Daniel said, sighing. 'Yeah. I suppose you could say that. It would be the first time for both of us.'

'Is he pressuring you?'

'No.'

'Are you pressuring him?'

'What? God, no.' Daniel looked worried, as if maybe he'd already made mistakes in the world of gay dating and sexuality exploration.

'And you're sure you want to do it?'

'Yes.' Daniel coughed. 'Don't get me wrong. I've had sex before. Girlfriends. Had no complaints.'

'Oh, well, that's good then.' Quinn was unsure of what else he was meant to say.

'Yeah, got a pretty big—'

'I don't need to know,' Quinn interrupted. 'It sounds like you're being safe. Here, I've got some flyers about resources for safe sex. Some details about things like PrEP, too, should you want to consider it. Make sure you're wearing protection, that it's consensual, and that you both want it. Know that by having gay sex, it doesn't mean you're gay. People will tell you it does, but it doesn't have to be. What I'm saying is, you won't have sex with a guy and immediately know your sexuality, and that if you still feel confused, that's okay. You don't need to rush in discovering who you are.'

'But if I like it, and do it, doesn't that mean...?'

'It could mean a lot of things,' Quinn replied. 'The fact you're thinking about the same sex, and you're exploring that, is something to go on. You might not believe it, but some people think they might be one thing and never go back to it. Is that to say they're straight or that they're gay? Sexuality is fluid. Have you read any of the books on it?'

'I'm not ready for those yet,' Daniel admitted, taking flyers from Quinn.

'All in good time,' Quinn said. 'Look, do what you think is right. If you think sex is right, go for it. But maybe consider what you feel when you kiss someone. Or how it feels to be intimate with another man that doesn't involve sex. You don't need to have sex straight away to rule out a feeling.'

'I understand. But I want to. He does, too.'

Quinn nodded, watching Daniel flick through the leaflets on the sexual resources that he'd given him.

'Does it hurt?' Daniel asked, blushing.

'Yes, it can hurt. Go slow, lubricate, and only do what makes you feel comfortable. Don't rush it.'

Daniel inhaled, nodding. 'I wish you could be there to guide me through it.'

'That would be inappropriate, Daniel.' Quinn laughed, heading to the door to welcome in customers.

'And what about poppers?'

'Ah, leaflet in the drawer. I would recommend you don't do those just yet.'

'People always talk about poppers,' Daniel said.

The bell above the door tinged.

'I did poppers once.'

Whipping around, Quinn saw his mother standing behind him, wearing a large white coat and a hood over her head that she fought to peer through. She seemed to blend into the background, her hands in her pockets, trying to shield herself from the cold air.

'You scared me, looking all ghost-like.'

'I'm sorry.'

'Poppers, Mum?'

'I was curious.' Claire shrugged.

'Straight people can take poppers?' Daniel asked.

'I sure did.'

Daniel looked like he wished this conversation wasn't happening and excused himself. Quinn watched him go, wondering how else he might help. The only thing he could do was let him know he was there to talk to him. Knowing his bookshop helped Daniel feel confident enough to talk mattered most.

Claire cleared her throat. 'Listen. Can we go get a drink? I want to talk.'

His mother never did this. She never wanted to 'talk', preferring instead to brush any potential problems under the carpet and pretend they didn't exist. It wasn't like she wasn't there for him. It was that acknowledging problems meant having to deal with them, and they were too British for such a thing.

So that she wanted to talk right now meant it was serious.

'Yes, if you want to.'

'Will Daniel be alright on his own?'

'Yes, he will be,' Daniel called.

Quinn laughed. 'Sorry to keep dipping out on you.'

'You've got lots on,' Daniel said. 'Go talk.'

As they walked down the high street, Quinn felt as though he saw Noah in every face. He double took when he thought he saw him in the crowd, or when he thought he'd heard his voice, even though Quinn knew he wouldn't see him here.

Claire found them a seat in a cosy restaurant playing Christmas jazz music, a genre Quinn didn't know existed until now. They sat in a bay seat window, looking out through frosted glass at people walking in the snow.

The restaurant, an Italian, smelled of garlic and olive oil, making Quinn's stomach rumble. They ordered two coffees.

'Have you been here before?' his mother asked.

'Of course,' Quinn said. 'There's only so much choice.'

'Right you are,' Claire agreed. She whispered, making Quinn

lean towards her to make sure he could hear her over the din of the diners and the sultry music. 'I came here on my first date with your father.'

Quinn realised with shame that he'd never asked how his parents met.

'He knew the owner at the time. Said he had to show me the place.' Claire smiled. 'I found out later that his friend owed him a favour, so the meal was free.'

She laughed, making Quinn smile.

'Did that annoy you?'

'No, it made me laugh,' Claire said. 'And it made sense why he was so insistent on paying the bill. We had *so* much food and drink, I felt like I *had* to pay for something.'

'And nothing to do with hating sexist tropes?'

'Of course not.'

The server came back with their drinks, placing them on the wooden table in front of them. Quinn reached for his.

'You look tired, Quinn.'

'I am.'

'Why?'

'I can't sleep. I've got a lot on my mind right now.'

'Oh, baby.'

His mother looked apologetic, touching his hand. It was a kind gesture, but Quinn couldn't help the annoyance that rose inside him. His mother had let these worries run amok. She hadn't said a word to Harold, and that hurt him. It was like choosing sides, war camps had been set up, and his mother wasn't there fighting for him. She was Switzerland.

'What did you want to talk about, Mum?' Quinn moved his hand away. If the move slighted Claire, she didn't show it.

'What's going on,' Claire said. 'Harold… He's upset.'

'Not this again. I can't have you defending him to me.'

'I know. And I'm not going to,' Claire answered. 'I donated to your fundraiser.'

Quinn swallowed his drink. He placed his mug back on the table with a force he didn't mean, almost spilling some.

'You donated?'

'Yes. I know what this shop means to you.'

'You haven't shown that.'

'No, I know.' Claire took the criticism. 'But Quinn, I am in such a tough place at the moment. Caught between two people I love.'

'Yeah, your son and husband. Hm, must be a hard choice.'

'Don't be like that,' Claire shot back. She regained composure by running a hand over the table, dusting away something that wasn't there. 'Please, Quinn. Listen to me.'

Quinn shrugged, waiting for his mum to talk.

'I know I haven't been the most supportive of you,' Claire began. 'Because I didn't know how much it meant to you.'

'How can you not know how much it means to me?'

'You've never told me how upset you were.'

'I have...' Quinn said, then stalled. When he thought back to his shop, to the threatening of closure, he hadn't told his mum how much it scared him. He'd told nobody. Ignoring every letter, hoping it would go away.

Only it hadn't. It'd weighed down on him and crushed him when it was too late to tell his mother, and even Harold, how he felt. How losing his shop would devastate him and rip everything out of him. His passion, his love, his purpose in life would be gone in one transaction, leaving nothing behind but a shell of himself.

'You never let me in.' Claire's voice betrayed her emotion. 'I know I should have realised what you were feeling. I understand I'm supposed to pick up on those things. But in all honesty, Quinn, I thought you were fine and coping okay. It wasn't until the newspaper, and then hearing you talk, seeing you fight for it, that I realised how much this was affecting you.'

In all this time, Quinn hadn't stopped to consider how he appeared to others. The lack of agency to tell others his thoughts and feelings held him back. He'd never wanted to burden others. Never wanted his hurt, his anxieties, to worry them. But if he'd spoken up after that first letter, perhaps he wouldn't be in this mess. Perhaps Claire would have told Harold straight up that what he was doing was wrong. Maybe then they wouldn't have drifted apart – not only because of Harold, but also because Quinn never told her how he felt after his dad died. Never considered how Claire would be feeling.

'This all happened after Dad,' Quinn said. 'I bottle everything up because I feared being hurt again.'

Claire held Quinn's hand. 'I know. Your silence about the letters, about Harold taking over… I assumed you were accepting it. That you understood. Don't you remember me calling you? Popping in? You mentioned nothing to me. Why?'

'I suppose because I thought I'd be causing problems you didn't need to deal with. I'm a grown man. I should be able to deal with my own issues.'

'I'm your mother. I'm here to deal with your issues.'

The jazz music changed its tune to a slower melody, almost like they were on some bad reality show in real time.

'When he told me his plans, I told him he couldn't do it. I fought with him and it ended with him agreeing not to.' Claire glanced out of the window. 'And then the next thing I knew, he told me he'd sent the eviction notice. I panicked, and when I rang you, I couldn't bear to mention it. And then you never brought anything up. And I think perhaps I took the easy way out and thought you knew what you were doing. That you got the letter, and you weren't worried because you had a back-up plan.'

Quinn recalled the first letter that came through. How later that night his mother called him, not once, but twice. How each time he felt like she wanted to say something, and how he wanted to tell her everything, but fear stopped him. At that point, he thought maybe Harold was bluffing. He hoped maybe he could ignore the letters and no more would come. When they did, he panicked and shut down.

To Quinn, there was no need to get his mum involved. It wasn't until Claire started bringing up the job in London again that he'd suspected that his mother knew what was going on.

'You brought nothing up, either.'

Claire sighed. 'I wasn't sure I could.'

'Me too.'

Claire let go of his hand, instead lifting her coffee mug to her lips.

'This is all because I suffer in silence.'

'Your father was the same.'

Ironic, then, that Quinn's tendencies to shut others out came after his father's death.

'The whole time, I told Harold he needed to give it up. He couldn't do this to you. But you know him. When he has an idea in his mind, there's no changing it.'

Quinn supposed his mother would know that best.

'I donated because I want to help you, but I don't want Harold to become the village villain.'

'He's doing that himself.'

'Please, Quinn.' Claire shook her head, her shoulders slumped. Quinn hadn't seen her look like this since Dad died. 'I don't know what we can do.'

It was Quinn's turn to reach out a hand. She looked close to tears and avoided his gaze, but Quinn spoke to her directly.

'Everything I have done, I have done to protect my shop and the people who need it.' Quinn's voice wavered, but he fought to keep it steady. 'He brought himself into it when he went on the radio. As soon as he did that, he became the enemy.'

'I know,' Claire whispered.

'And that's on him, Mum. Not me. Not you.' Quinn squeezed her hand. 'There's nothing else you can do now. To be honest, I don't know if there is enough I can do, either. But we have to do whatever we can to at least try to keep the shop going.'

Claire moved her hand away.

'Thank you. I needed to hear that.'

'And I needed to hear you tell me you tried,' Quinn said. 'For a while, I didn't think you did.'

'I did.'

'I know. I don't think I'd considered how hard this might be for you. It's not your fault, Mum. It's me, a small business, against a big firm. We all know who wins in these instances.'

Claire shrunk into her chair, crossing her arms. 'Don't give up.'

'I won't.'

They fell quiet, both listening to the jazz music and the happier customers around them. The server appeared, asking if they wanted anything else, though Quinn wondered if she sensed something was wrong at the table.

'All good here.'

'Great,' the server said. 'By the way, my cousin came into your shop. Loved the place.'

'Thank you.'

'I'm very proud of him.' Claire beamed.

'Hope it gets saved,' the server added before heading back to her job.

Quinn traced a finger over the rim of his mug as his mum leaned forwards, resting her elbows on the table.

'Can I come to the protest?'

Quinn's eyes widened. 'You want to?'

'Yes,' Claire said. 'Maybe if Harold sees me there, it will hit home what he's doing.'

'Yes, you can come to the protest.' Quinn tilted his head. 'But is that an excuse to come to the party afterwards?'

'Absolutely. I've got my dress picked out already.'

They laughed, any tension beginning to dissolve between them. It almost felt like an hour of therapy to Quinn. He knew he

279

could go about the rest of this week feeling a little lighter, knowing that whatever the outcome, his relationship with his mother would not suffer.

Claire raised her mug. 'To Kings & Queens.'

Quinn clinked his own mug with hers. 'To Kings & Queens.'

Chapter Thirty-Six

'Let's go Christmas tree shopping.'

'Ivy, Christmas is in two days,' Quinn said. 'You haven't got a Christmas tree?'

'Oh, it's not for me. My house has been decorated since November.'

'Then who is it for?'

'Hermione.'

He felt a kick in his stomach. Last night, a bottle of wine down and on his second Christmas romcom, his vibrator lying just inches away, he'd wondered if he should call off his deal with Hermione, even though the ink on the contract wasn't even dry. If you could call a digital signature ink, that is. The idea of writing for Noah's mum, hearing her story, and hearing stories of *him* made him feel odd, like he was nostalgic for something he never had.

The only thing that had convinced him to stay was watching Hermione's last Christmas film, and seeing how talented, charismatic, and engaging she was on screen. Of course, he watched that when the vibrator was tucked away. Thank you very much.

Feeling nothing but a flame of hope, he watched a version of Hermione that he didn't recognise. She delivered her lines like they were the most important thing on earth. She made Quinn believe that if she lost her tinsel factory, they would cancel Christmas around the world. Drunk, he cried about Hermione's life. But that gave him a new zest; a determination. If he could play a role in getting Hermione back into the public perception, he would do it. That tinsel factory was *not* closing down!

'But she has Christmas trees.' Quinn tried not to recall his time at Hermione's home with Noah.

'She does, but she wants one for the upstairs landing.'

The place where Noah showed him her awards.

'Oh. I see.'

'So, there's a Christmas tree farm nearby. I called ahead and they still have space.'

'But what about the shop?'

'It'll only take an hour,' Ivy said. 'Daniel's got it covered.'

'Ivy...'

'Come on, Quinn,' she pleaded, her gloved hands finding his. 'You need some fun!' Ivy turned wide, pleading eyes on him, blinking theatrically.

He sighed, resigned to the adorable expression on her face. 'Fine.'

'Yay!' Ivy beamed. 'I'll be waiting out front!'

She left him at the shop, where customers were yet to arrive. He wondered if they were boycotting him because of his failed signing. He refreshed his email for what felt like the hundredth time that morning, but still hadn't got a reply from Noah.

Not that he expected one.

His resolve to not think of Noah was not going well.

He found Ivy in her climate-polluting jeep. He hopped into the passenger side and sunk into the worn leather seat. She set off through Hay, a Christmas compilation album playing Ariana Grande's 'Santa Baby' through the speakers.

The Christmas tree farm was in the Brecon Beacons in a farmhouse nestled into the mountain. A hazy fog hung over the crevices of the landscape, like nature had exhaled its chilled breath. As they approached, Quinn was mesmerised by the smoke billowing from the chimney and the snow gathered on the thatched roof.

A man in a plaid coat and with wiry facial hair greeted them, his sleeves rolled up despite the cold to reveal thick hairy arms. He showed them where to park and waited a few feet away as they got out, a smile on his face like a younger Santa.

'Jerry, hi! This is my friend, Quinn. The one I told you about.'

Something registered for Jerry. His quizzical observation of Quinn soon turned to intrigue, and he extended his hand with raised, bushy eyebrows.

'Hey, Quinn.' Jerry shook his hand vigorously. 'Pleasure to meet you.'

Quinn didn't know what to say. Already disconcerted with the events the day had thrown at him, he couldn't help feeling like he wasn't in on a joke.

'Jerry is a client of mine,' Ivy explained. 'And he's Noah's uncle.'

Quinn's hand was still clasped in Jerry's, but now he wanted to break away and run. He threw Ivy a look of horror, which she smiled at. When Jerry let go, Quinn shoved his hands in his pockets and shivered from the cold.

'Pleasure to meet you, too,' Quinn stuttered.

Jerry gestured for them to follow him, and with his back turned, Quinn looked to Ivy, his eyes wide.

'What are you *doing?*' he mouthed.

'I have a plan,' Ivy mimed.

Jerry opened a wooden gate, dusted in snow, and let them walk through. As Quinn spotted Jerry's black boots, he realised his own worn shoes were not snow friendly at all. They rounded the corner of the house, where icicles hung from the thatched roof, and saw that the back garden – if acres of land could be called a back garden – had transformed into a winter wonderland.

The snow here was neat and untouched, despite the signs of life and business activity. Pine trees stood tall and proud, but Quinn could see how many had been sold thanks to the stumps and the spaces between trees.

'Bit late in the year, so we only have these left,' Jerry said, taking them into the land and through the trees. 'Who is it for?'

'Hermione,' Ivy replied.

'Ah.'

'Your sister?' Quinn asked, knowing Jerry couldn't be related to Noah's father.

'That's right. Unfortunately, I didn't inherit the talents for the screen like she did.'

It was hard to tell if they looked alike at all, but as Quinn was trying to work it out, he noticed Jerry had Noah's nose, and the same eyes, and his hair was even...

Stop it.

Why did Ivy bring him here, with Jerry, of all places? Was there not another Christmas tree farm somewhere else? Maybe they should have crossed the border to England instead, where the world expanded and everyone didn't know one another.

They observed the last remaining trees, with Ivy and Jerry commenting on the firmness, the curvature, or the length. As Jerry spoke about the girth, Quinn wondered if they were still talking about trees. When Ivy finally picked one out, he was relieved, hoping they could leave the farm and never see Jerry again.

As he looked around at the other shoppers – couples holding hands, old partners – he experienced a pang in his chest, his stomach heavy as lead. He realised he'd never felt so alone during Christmas. All he wanted was to have someone by his side, especially at this time of year, when so much was changing. This was a time for family and loved ones, happiness and joy. Quinn had none of that.

'Do you like Christmas?' Jerry asked Quinn. He realised, with terror, that Ivy had flitted away to do who knew what, leaving Quinn with Uncle Jerry.

'Yeah, it's my favourite time of the year,' Quinn said honestly.

'Is it?'

'Not yours?'

'I prefer autumn, myself,' Jerry said. 'The transforming of the leaves. We do pumpkin picking here too, and it's very busy.'

Quinn imagined the landscape in bursts of red and orange, and admitted that the view would be spectacular. 'Christmas is surely busier?'

'It has been. Past two years have picked up. I think because people are more environmentally conscious these days and want real trees instead of plastic.'

'So, they cut down actual trees. Makes sense.'

Jerry laughed, and for god's sake, he had Noah's smile. Was he only his uncle? Not, say, his long-lost older brother?

And a hot one at that.

Stop it.

'Whatever action you do has consequences,' Jerry said.

'Deep.'

I like going deep.

Noah.

Stop it.

'I hear your shop is facing closure. Read it in the paper.' Jerry seemed to want to fill the silence. He crossed his arms, looking at Quinn like he could read him.

Quinn thought he needed to match the stance, so he leaned against the tree and almost slipped off and faceplanted in the bark. He righted himself by simply standing with his hands in his pockets. You couldn't go wrong like that. Unless someone ran up behind you and pushed you. Then you'd faceplant into the floor.

'We're trying our best.'

'They tried to take this from me once.' Jerry surveyed his land.

'Developers. A few years ago. Said this was prime land for development.'

Quinn observed the sweeping mountains, the snow hugging boulders, the bare trees dripping crystal droplets. How could anyone think new build houses fit in well with *this* landscape?

'What got you out of it?'

'Because it's the national park,' Jerry said. 'I proved we were in the park, and development would be a lot more complicated than throwing money at me to leave. So, the developers backed off. Your building is listed, is it not? You can go back to them with that?'

'Unfortunately, no.' Quinn sighed. 'I don't own it. Harold does. I rent it from him. Unfortunately, he's given me all the notice he needs for me to vacate. I'm in the wrong for staying as long as I have. I'm lucky he's not trying to take me to court.'

Jerry grimaced. 'I'm sorry.'

'Don't be. It's not over yet.'

'Good attitude,' Jerry said. 'Shame we can't say the same about my nephew.'

It was as if someone had broken off the icicles from Jerry's roof and plunged them into Quinn's heart. He tried to brush it off with a pained smile, hoping no more would be said.

There was only so much two men could say about Christmas trees, especially when it was being bought for someone that wasn't here. Quinn's gaze kept wandering towards the house, praying that Ivy would appear and take him away. Jerry whistled a tuneless melody, occasionally meeting Quinn's eye and offering a brief smile.

It was then that Quinn remembered what Ivy had said.

'Ivy's told you about me?'

Jerry's whistling stopped, and he avoided Quinn's eye. 'That's right.'

'What exactly has she said?'

A funny twisting of his stomach made him wish he was a white hare that could blend in with his surroundings and disappear quietly.

Jerry cleared his throat. 'Well, you know, it's none of my business...'

'I know Ivy and I know when she's up to something,' Quinn said. 'This is about Noah and me, isn't it?'

Jerry finally looked at Quinn again, and if he squinted, it could almost be like looking at Noah, but only if he really focussed on the eyes.

'She told me you might need some advice.'

'And that advice should come from his uncle?'

Jerry laughed, giving Quinn a mutual look of understanding. 'It's probably not my place to say...'

'Go ahead.'

'I don't want to interfere.'

'Interfere.'

Jerry considered this. 'Ivy cares for you, and she told me that Noah had been ... with you, and then...'

'He left.'

A whisper of wind went by, a tune similar to the one Jerry whistled.

'Look, I could play it cool, but what's the point in doing that?' Quinn questioned. 'Your nephew is a mystery to me. A grumpy sod who has snatched my heart, and I can try all I want to act like I don't care, or that him leaving is for the best, but it would be futile. Ivy can see it clearly, and I'm sure you can, too. He's on my mind all day every day and if there's anything, anything at all that you can help me with so that I can make sense of him, of why he's acted the way he has...'

He ran out of steam. There were no other words that could convey the agonising feelings inside him of marred confusion and doubts.

287

'He came here, you know, before he left.'

Quinn tried to imagine Noah here. How the white landscape, with a rugged winter charm, so wild and beautiful, would contrast with his own wild hair, his city boy high-end fashion, and his charming smile. Quinn was like a fan standing on the same spot a celebrity once visited, trying to imagine the person in front of them, feeling like he was a part of something. This was his Strawberry Fields.

'He did?' It was a feeble response, but Quinn couldn't hide it anymore. He cared, and Jerry knew it.

'He did. I hadn't seen him since ... well, a few years now. He never visits. So, when he turned up, I was a little shocked.'

'Why did he visit?' Quinn asked.

Jerry shrugged, sighing, a puff of white breath trailing before him. 'When I opened the front door, it took me a little while to recognise him. I follow him on the socials, of course, but in person he looked different. He looked upset.'

'Upset?'

The icicle in his chest melted, sending freezing water through his veins.

'Said he shouldn't have come back to Hay,' Jerry said. 'I invited him in for tea. He came in, but he didn't want to stay long. He was with someone.'

'Matty.'

So, there it was. Noah went straight back to Matty and left with him. Which implied what? That they were back together?

'Is that his name?' Jerry asked. 'I didn't get the chance to ask.'

'Why not?'

'He wouldn't leave the car.'

Rude.

'I made Noah tea. He said how my house hadn't changed from when he was last here years ago.' Jerry said this with a smile, no doubt remembering a past when Noah was around. Quinn conjured up his own image of what Noah's childhood was like;

how he might have been. 'I asked him why he came by and he said he wanted to say goodbye.'

'Oh gosh. That sounds…'

'Oh, no, not dramatically,' Jerry reassured Quinn. 'Just a melodramatic way. Said he would *never* set foot in Hay again. I laughed at that, which seemed to annoy him. This is Brecon, not Hay. Guess he didn't want to step foot anywhere near it.'

'Why would he come back here? Why would he want to see you?' And why would Ivy bring him here right now, when he was trying so desperately to forget Noah.

Jerry looked back towards the house. 'You see that window up there to the left, with the light on?'

Quinn did. The thatched roof nestled the window, the yellow glow offering a cosy glimpse into a room.

'It was there that Noah came out to me when he was sixteen.'

Quinn gasped. Surely that moment alone qualified this house for one of those commemorative blue plaques.

'Wow.'

'He did that, and two days later, he left for London. That was the last time I saw him. He came out to me long before he came out to his mother, or in fact, anyone. I think he went to London pretending he was still straight.' Jerry laughed at this, but not with cruelty. 'When Noah was growing up, we had a good relationship, and I think he felt like he could trust me because…' Jerry paused. 'Well, because he knew about my own struggles.'

Quinn didn't want to pry, but he wanted to know. He let the silence drift between them, thinking of asking so many things, wanting to know more about the Sage men, about that moment, and about Noah's life in London.

'We were there for each other,' Jerry said. 'I could tell when I saw him all those years ago that he needed someone to listen to him. He told me he couldn't stay in Hay, told me what he knew he was, and then when he left, it left me devastated. I felt like I wasn't enough for him or had let him down. We drifted apart, because I think to him, people like myself, like Hermione, were bad memories.'

It hurt Quinn to hear it. He knew those feelings, the ones that made you feel you didn't belong, or like you were wrong. It was why he had opened his shop: for people feeling the same way.

'When he was here the other night, it was like nothing had changed. He told me he wanted to see me again. Said sorry that it took so long. Gave me his number so we could keep in touch. And then he told me he'd made a mistake. He told me Hay only made him realise how much he couldn't have something. He told me he feared what he was feeling. So, he needed to go, run away from it like he did all those years ago.'

Quinn understood Noah's desire to leave. Something within him, something both childlike and primal, had forced Noah into survival mode. All those years ago, closeted and ashamed of his mother, he ran from it instead of dealing with it. Now, with what happened between them, the feelings that Quinn now knew were unmistaken and undeniable, allowed the fear to creep back in. Quinn almost pitied him, but he couldn't sympathise. Both of them were nearing their thirties. You didn't run away at this age. You dealt with problems.

'He didn't drink his tea,' Jerry said, as if this mattered. 'He told me he was sorry. Then he left. Said he needed to speak to the boy in the car.'

'Matty.'

'Matty. I watched them go. Neither of them looked happy.'

Quinn tried not to feel the flicker of hope that swelled in him at the mention of trouble between Noah and Matty. It didn't matter even if there was. Noah had vowed never to come back to Hay. That meant never coming back to Quinn.

Standing at the tree, which remained tall and proud, realisation dawned on Quinn.

'There's no tree for Hermione, is there?'

Jerry looked like Quinn caught him stealing one of Santa's

cookies. 'I'm afraid not. Ivy just wanted to get you here to talk to me about Noah.'

'How did she know he'd been here?'

'She didn't until I called.'

Quinn laughed. 'Lucky for her. Where is she?'

'Oh, inside cleaning,' Jerry said. 'Two birds and all that.'

Chapter Thirty-Seven

'Are you going to give me the silent treatment this whole time?'

Snow had replaced the rain, and now the appeal of winter, of Christmas, was back again. Ivy drove through the winding country lanes towards Hay, where everything was supposed to be perfect, yet it had all seemed to fall apart for Quinn.

Inside the car, the heaters blasting hot air with a loud whine, Quinn stared ahead, watching the flakes catch in the headlamps and splatter on the glass.

'I don't know what to say.'

It was true. He had learned a lot about Noah and about his decision to leave. Noah, confiding in his uncle, then leaving for London, seemed so raw. He could only wonder how Noah felt, and how Noah needed something new. He'd found it. Found himself.

Was that why Noah always avoided coming back here, because it would make him face a part of himself he thought was long gone?

'What did Jerry say?'

'That Noah went there before he left.'

'And?'

'And told him he wasn't coming back.'

'Balls.' Ivy gripped the steering wheel as they descended into the valley.

'Yes, balls.'

He breathed a sigh of relief when Ivy got back on the even road approaching Hay's village. He watched the snow fall, wondering if it was snowing in London, imagining what mood Noah and Matty were in now. Were they thinking of him, or indeed Hay? Was this all just a faded memory to them?

His thoughts turned to Hermione. It would hurt her that she'd lost a chance to celebrate Christmas with her son again, maybe for the first time in years.

That inkling of sympathy dampened each time Quinn thought of someone Noah had hurt since coming back.

By thinking of that, he could distract himself from his own pain.

They arrived back in town, Quinn seeing a small group of people at his door. He checked the time. Only an hour and a half gone. Hopping out of the jeep, Quinn saw Blair, who handed Ivy a coffee.

'Almond milk?' Ivy asked.

'Of course.'

Quinn wondered how they'd got close enough to know each other's drink orders, then smiled at the customers at his door. He saw Jenny, gathered with the drag performers, each one of them out of drag.

'We're just here to give you this.'

Jenny the influencer handed Quinn a basket with two bottles of wine, a box of candles, some books tied with green and red bows, and biscuits, all sitting on a bed of fake snow. As Quinn took it, he felt tears roll down his face. Wow! He needed to get his emotions in check.

'You didn't have to.'

'We wanted to,' Jenny said. 'A few of us got together and tried to think of what we could do to help.'

'You've done enough,' Quinn said. 'All of you. Honestly, I don't know where I'd be right now without you.'

'We've got our outfits ready,' one queen said, then held out their hand. 'It's Penny Farthing, by the way.'

Quinn shook Penny's hand.

'Oh, we're introducing with our drag names, are we?' Another queen laughed.

'Well, I didn't think George would be as impressive,' Penny said.

'Well, in that case, I'm Ebeneezer Screwed, not John.' Quinn shook the hand of Ebeneezer, who had a bald head and wore a trans flag pin on his denim jacket.

'And I'm Santa Whores,' the third queen said. 'Hay's very own gender bender. A pleasure to meet you.'

'Again, thank you all so much.'

'Will there be alcohol at the party?' Ebeneezer asked.

'Of course.'

'And the protest?' Penny questioned.

'If you want there to be.' Quinn shrugged. 'Show up and fight for this shop. That's all I care about.'

'Oh, don't you worry, we'll all be there,' Jenny said.

'It's going to be jolly and gay!' Ebeneezer said.

With that, the three queens and Jenny headed away, promising to be the life and soul of both the protest and the party. Quinn turned to Ivy and Blair, who were leaning against Ivy's car bonnet, talking. Ivy dusted fresh snow off Blair's Hermes scarf. Too close for people who were just friends.

Quinn left them to … whatever they were doing and entered the shop. He was glad to be back in the warm and headed to the kettle to make himself a coffee.

'Hi, Dan.'

'Yo.'

He unwrapped the hamper, imagining the first sips of wine at the party. The stack of books was perfect: a couple of classics mixed with modern day romances. It surprised him to see they were books he didn't own. It was hard to believe considering he *loved* to add more books to his 'to be read' pile.

At the bottom of the hamper, he found an envelope, sealed with a wax stamped seal. He touched it and…

Was that a penis? Quinn laughed. Snapping the waxed penis, he took out the letter, unfolded it, and felt the thick paper at his fingertips.

He gasped.

It couldn't be.

TEN THOUSAND POUND DONATION it said.

He continued to read the letter, amazed at the fundraising efforts by the three drag queens. In addition to the ten-thousand-pound donation, there was also a separate donation of five thousand, which had been raised by Jenny through her Instagram.

Quinn sank into his armchair, his legs unable to support him. He hadn't kept up to date with his online donations. With shaking hands, he brought up the website on his phone, and saw that there was now a whopping 30,000. Scrolling through the donations, he saw people had donated from as far as Canada. Strangers who'd never been to the shop but wanted to see it survive.

Of course, the money wasn't his. He wasn't even sure he could accept the donations raised by Jenny and the queens. He was nowhere near his target, which he'd set to try to buy the shop himself. Despite the people visiting and donating, it was a big ask to find enough people to reach such a high price.

He slipped the paper back into its envelope, then added it to his drawer, being careful to keep it separate from the other envelopes noting eviction. There was one brief glimmer of happiness in a sea of despair in that drawer. Quinn slid it shut, locking it away, trying to forget about it.

The door pinged as it opened, and Quinn looked in time to see

Ivy waving goodbye to Bloody Blair Beckett. She seemed to float into the shop, and Quinn watched her approach with a knowing smile on his face.

'So … what's going on there, then?'

'I don't know what you mean,' Ivy said.

'You seem happy,' Quinn said. 'Your aura is pink.'

Ivy gasped. 'Is it really?'

She spun around, looking behind her, as if she were trying to spot something on her back.

Quinn laughed. '*So* pink.'

'He makes me smile.' Ivy seemed to choose her words with care. 'He's quite sweet, you know. I was a little worried about the red aura, but soon realised it's more out of passion than malice and anger.'

'Of course.'

'He's ruled by Mars, too.'

'That's right.'

'You don't have to believe me,' Ivy said, her face as flushed as Mars' surface.

'Do you think it's anything serious?'

'We haven't even kissed yet. It may just be a winter fling, but I'm okay with that.'

'Good.'

Ivy's phone pinged. She took it out of her pocket and smiled. Quinn watched her, feeling envious, sure his aura was now a bottle green.

'Is that him?'

'Hm?' Her eyes didn't lift from the screen. 'Oh, yeah. Yes.'

Quinn decided not to push it. As much as he wanted to live a love life through Ivy, it was not his place to enquire about Blair and how he wooed Ivy. But he recognised the beginning seed of love being planted, nurtured during the colder months, ready to bloom in the spring.

Other than Dougie, his love life had always been just so-so.

And Dougie hadn't been impressive. Not too many gay men seemed to live or even stay in Hay. They either went to the cities or settled down with someone they met nearby. It meant that the pool of eligible bachelors was more of a puddle. Besides, Quinn admitted he was a bit of a borderline recluse. He lived above his shop, and he spent most of his days behind the counter or above it. But Noah had been a seed, thirsty for water, stifled and refusing to bloom.

He thought of Dougie, trying his best to think of the positive moments they had shared. The only positive that came to mind was that since blocking his number, he hadn't heard from him. It confirmed to Quinn everything he needed to know. He didn't matter to him. Maybe he never had.

The kettle boiled, bringing Quinn back to Ivy. He made them both a mug of tea, and a third for Daniel. They sat at the altar, a dysfunctional group dealing with their own feelings. Quinn looked around the shop with a wistful air. In just two days' time, this whole thing could be over.

'You can always rely on a cuppa.' Quinn clenched the mug, forever thankful for something so familiar after such a weird day. They could demolish the place, but he'd be alright if he had his tea.

Mostly.

Ivy slurped her tea next to him, looking at him with an intense gaze.

'What are you looking at me like that for?'

'It's not over, Quinn,' she said. 'Far from it.'

'I agree with Ivy,' Daniel said.

'I can only hope you're right.'

'Want another tarot reading?' She was reaching for her bag at her feet.

'No, I'm alright,' Quinn said, afraid of seeing the devil coming back. 'I trust the last one.'

'Hm.' Ivy sniffed. 'Alright then.'

'Can I get a reading?' Daniel asked. 'There's this thing...'

'Yes, let's do one.'

Quinn sipped his own tea, more elegantly than Ivy, his eyes on the shimmering lights of the shop's Christmas tree.

'What are your plans for Christmas?'

Ivy thought for a moment. 'Spending the day with Mum. She lives over in New Radnor.'

Quinn knew the place, a small nestled village in mid-Wales with sprawling luscious green mountains. Only he knew now they would be lethal, covered in white and ice, the perfect postcard Christmas town.

'That will be nice.'

'It will be, but she will insist on going Christmas carolling.'

'On Christmas day?'

'It's a New Radnor tradition,' Ivy said. 'We do it every year. And every year I pretend to hate it.'

'But you love it?'

'You heard me sing,' Ivy said, and Quinn recalled the pitchy tones of Ivy in the town hall. 'You don't hide a voice like mine.'

Quinn smiled just as the front door opened and a customer walked in. They smiled back at him, meandering through the aisles.

'What about you?'

'It will either be spent celebrating or trying not to make it awkward with Mum and Harold.'

'Ah, yes,' Ivy mused. 'Christmas is a time for family, after all.'

'Even when that family tries to screw you over.'

Chapter Thirty-Eight

Early mornings were not Quinn's thing, but he didn't mind when so much relied on the day ahead. Black painted the sky as he showered, and the morning's artist didn't add light until he was wrapped in winter clothing. He peered out of his window at the emerging hazy day, carrying a cardboard placard he'd made the night before that read 'Queer to stay'.

Christmas Eve arrived much quicker than Quinn expected. When he was a kid, he would shake with excitement, and as he entered adulthood, he still trembled with enthusiasm. He would usually spend the day relaxing, the mounting enthusiasm for the next day building with every second that passed.

Only now anxiety had replaced anticipation, knowing that not only were they making a last bid to get their voices heard, but they were about to disturb the opening of the much-loved Hay Castle. He never thought he would disrupt the opening for a heritage site.

Peering out of his window, he could see a crowd already gathered on Castle Street. It warmed his heart to see banners and signs being held in the air, declaring 'slay another day' and 'fuck the patriarchy'. He shivered with excitement, feeling rebellious.

Looking at himself in the mirror, he tried to muster his best attitude face. He settled with something that landed between a pissed off rock star and 'can-I-speak-to-the-manager-Karen', and headed out into the crisp winter morning where the weak sun shimmered on fresh snow.

'There he is!' Ivy said, wearing a long pink coat and a baby pink scarf. The crowd turned and cheered, Ivy leading the pack like a fairy-type Pokémon. Her pink bobble hat wobbled on her head, black hair falling from underneath. Her cheeks were rosy red and there was an air of excitement in her expression. 'Are you ready to stick it to the man?'

'Always ready!'

The three drag queens were what the gays called sickening. Penny wore virgin white robes with a huge white wig. The ghost of Christmas past had never looked so fabulous. Then there was Ebeneezer, floating in green robes and a jolly red beard. Santa Whores came dressed as the ghost of Christmas future in a black PVC boiler suit that would have looked unflattering if it wasn't for the chains that were tied around the waist, making the outfit look more dominatrix than industrial.

'Werk,' Quinn said.

They all held their own signs, their gloveless hands clutching to wooden poles, braving the weather for the cause. He wanted to hug them, but feared he might ruin their drag if he did so.

He took in the rest of the crowd. Jenny the influencer, already livestreaming on her Instagram. Bookshop owners prepared to lose a day's business on Christmas eve to help him out. The butcher, the baker, the café owner and the market organiser, all of them wrapped against the elements, eager to begin. Then there was Emma the reporter, with her camera guy next to her, and Quinn smiled in time for the photo. Sidling up to Ivy, dressed in a gorgeous blue coat, was Blair. His own camerawoman accompanied him, and Quinn realised this was going to make the news again.

Then, running towards him from the butter market, his mother. Quinn laughed at the sight of her. She wore two coats, a bobble hat that almost covered her eyes, gloves, and a scarf. When she approached Quinn and took in his own outfit, she shook her head.

'Are you warm enough?' Claire asked.

'I think my jumper, hoodie and coat will do the trick, Mum.'

She smiled, then looked at the castle. 'So, we're doing this.'

'We are,' Quinn said. 'And how does Harold feel about it?'

'He doesn't know,' Claire admitted. 'He thinks I'm going to arrive before opening.'

'Well, you kind of are.'

He observed the castle, wondering if he imagined the new gleam on the old structure. It would open its doors in an hour, ready to welcome in the locals of Hay who had watched it fall into disrepair over the years. He silently apologised to the castle and the past, then turned to the crowd before him.

'Are we ready?' His voice was like a battle cry, echoing around Hay.

'Yes!'

'I said, are we ready?'

'YES!'

'Long live Kings & Queens!' Claire screamed, surprising everyone.

'Long live Kings & Queens!' the crowd chanted back.

And with that, they turned their back on the castle and made their way down Castle Street, shouting at the tops of their voices. Some people brought whistles, blowing hard into them so that their high-pitched whine disturbed the rural winter setting of peace and serenity. Well, today was about disrupting the status quo. Those who hadn't joined the protest stood at their shop doors or came out onto the street and cheered as they went by, taking photos and videos of the colourful crowd.

Blair handed out books he carried in a red sack to anyone who would take one.

He'd stolen stock?

Quinn peered closer and noticed that each one came with a Kings & Queens bookmark.

I've always loved that Bloody Blair Beckett.

As one book exchanged hands, a flyer tucked into the pages fluttered out, caught in the winter breeze. Quinn saw it land a few feet away, sinking into the snow, and realised it was instructing people where they could donate. Tears welling up, not from the cold, but from the gratitude he felt to the surrounding people, he shouted louder.

It didn't matter that it snowed. Nor did it matter that Quinn's tears threatened to freeze and blind him. It didn't matter that by the time they left Castle Street and walked onto Lion, their feet were wet – except for Claire, of course, who told them off for not wearing thermals and three pairs of socks.

'And a good shoe!' she added.

All that mattered was raising their voices, lifting their signs, and interacting with those who came to see them pass. With rainbow flags flying, the three drag queens both protesting and acting, it was almost like their own Pride parade.

'Keep Hay gay!' Ivy chanted, and people followed her lead.

'Long live Kings & Queens!' they sang. 'Keep Hay gay!'

They descended onto Belmont Road, where some people came out of their homes sporting pride flags and joined their march. Others waved from windows like this was a jubilee celebration, and the fish and chip shop began handing out portions of chips for those walking by. Quinn waved at familiar faces as they wished him good luck, and Blair made his way swanlike to every person, handing them books and flyers, flashing that charming smile. A red robin flitted by, and Quinn swallowed his sadness.

'Where is Noah?' someone shouted from the side-lines.

It was like someone had thrown a snowball filled with bricks at Quinn's face. He recoiled, avoiding anyone's eyes, staring ahead and trying not to let his smile falter. This must be how heckled royalty felt.

Only he knew he wasn't being heckled. It was in his mind. Noah was like a ghost haunting him, and only the two of them knew what his absence meant. They shared it across miles, a missing link. Nobody else needed to know that a small part of Quinn was empty without Noah marching alongside him, showing his support.

Shaking Noah off, Quinn led the chants as they walked up a street known as The Pavement, trying not to slip on the snow, and back onto Castle Street. The castle, now open, shone at them, a Christmas tree visible through the open doors.

As they gathered outside the entrance, Ivy held a megaphone and cleared her throat, which made the people nearby cover their ears.

'We stand outside Hay Castle, the jewel in Hay's crown, the royal palace of the monarchy that never was, celebrating that a historic place is open once more to the public.' Her voice stopped those who were entering the castle. From the castle doors, Quinn saw his stepdad run out. Even from a distance, he could see the anger on his face. His stomach plummeted, but he stood a little taller, refusing to be intimidated.

'Keep Hay gay!' the audience chanted, their eyes on the castle.

'In 1977, Richard Booth declared Hay-on-Wye an independent kingdom, calling himself the king. He was the man responsible for turning this town that we see before us into the town of books. He enjoyed the castle before it fell into disrepair, using it as his royal residence, much to the pleasure of those living here.' Ivy turned away from the crowd and looked up at the castle. 'It's because of Richard, with his insight and flat-out flair, that we could open shops of many shapes and sizes without the need to compete against one another. It gave Gerald Oxford the confidence to open his own bookshop.'

At the mention of his father, Quinn looked to the floor. He hadn't known Ivy was going to make a speech, and now he let those overwhelming tears flow at the thought of his dad. Claire placed an arm around him, and he hugged his mother back.

'Without that confidence, that guidance, that experience, Kings & Queens wouldn't exist today. By opening Kings & Queens, Quinn Oxford brought Hay into the twenty-first century. He spotted a way to not only sell books and nurture a community, but to help a community that is underrepresented. A community that needed a safe place where they could be themselves, find support, and discover who they were. It's telling that Hay's only queer business is facing closure.'

At that, the audience booed toward Harold. A few people heading towards the castle started retreating.

'We're here today to make sure that this isn't the final chapter of Kings & Queens. We want to make it known to developers, to businessmen, to people who don't realise the importance of a bookshop like this, that they can't just toss people aside when they feel like it. If there was a legitimate reason to end Quinn's tenancy, we may begrudge such an act, but we would have no choice. But this is pure greed. This is power at play. This is breaking apart the family.'

Ivy's voice, full of passion and the right amount of anger, stirred the crowd. People who hadn't been on their march joined in the protest, while others shook their heads in a very British manner.

'When Richard Booth transformed this town, he made history. Let's make herstory today!' She said this to the two cameras pointing at her, one for the paper, and one for national news. She performed spectacularly, and Quinn led the round of applause, beaming, his chest raised. Every part of him wanted to reach for Ivy and hug her tight. He looked around at the crowd, his smile getting wider, a rush of adrenaline coursing through his veins.

'Are you ready for this?' Claire asked.

'Ready.'

'To the castle!' Claire called.

'To the castle!' Ivy bellowed over the megaphone.

This battle cry was enough to strike fear into Harold, who ran down the refurbished stone steps, his eyes wide, his face red. But there was no time for him to stop the crowd getting into the grounds, climbing the steps and meeting him halfway. They were an army coming to conquer.

Harold glared at everyone, but then his eyes found Quinn. 'What the bloody hell—'

He stopped. His mouth hung open like he was Jacob Marley.

Claire didn't shy away from her partner. Instead, she walked up to him, apparently used to the anger that he was displaying. 'I had to.'

'You joined the protest?'

'I did.'

'Why?'

'Because you can't do this,' Claire said. A hush fell over the crowd, and Blair made his camerawoman stop filming. 'I've had enough of you not listening to me. I've been telling you for weeks this was wrong. I've made it clear how Quinn has been feeling. You ignored me.'

'It's my place!' Harold boomed, pointing to the snow-capped rooftop of Kings & Queens. 'I am within my right to get my place back.'

'Keep Hay gay!' Penny chanted.

'Keep Hay gay!'

Harold looked at the crowd, blinked, then turned back to Claire.

'I know you're within your rights,' Claire said. 'But that doesn't make you right.'

'Yes, sister.' Ebeneezer clicked her fingers.

'He ignored my notices.'

'And you ignored us,' Claire said. 'Both of us. Quinn doesn't want London or a new job. He wants Kings & Queens. He wants to stay doing what he's doing. Like Gerald used to do.'

Harold pulled at the neck of his fleece jacket, looking from Quinn to the crowd to Claire again.

'He never told us that.'

'No, I didn't,' Quinn said. 'For too long, I've kept quiet. Afraid of what others would think. Afraid that if I spoke up, I would rock the boat and cause unnecessary stress. Well, by being quiet, I've put stress upon myself, and I've had enough of it.'

Harold stared at Quinn as though he were a mirage in a dry desert. 'You can't come in.'

'Yes, we can!' Ivy said, and before Harold could argue, she led the group into the castle.

'Stop!' Harold screamed, the flush of red returning to his skin. 'No!'

He left Claire and Quinn standing on the top step, their back to Hay, their eyes on the protestors now inside the castle hall. That brick snowball came back, hitting him hard this time, making him realise Harold would not change his mind.

Quinn wanted to sink into the ground, give up, and disappear. All of this had been pointless.

Claire was in front of him now, and said nothing, only gave him a brisk, no-nonsense look. Quinn understood what it meant.

Until Harold took the keys, until Harold physically removed him, the shop would belong to Quinn. It didn't matter about deeds or true ownership. What mattered was the community that he'd built, the safety of the shop, and what it represented.

The building might be Harold's, but the shop would never be his.

Quinn and Claire headed into the castle where the protestors were sitting in the great hall. They were ready to protest, but the castle's new lease of life had struck each one of them. They'd repaired the castle roof, in keeping with the era. A wooden staircase had been fitted, leading to floors that once crumbled into nothingness. A glass balcony let Quinn see a hallway leading to the room that had been offered as his replacement shop, just off to the left. The windows were repaired, with the graffiti from teenagers somehow scraped off the stone window sills. A log fire burned at one end of the hall, giving warmth that filled the space, despite the open door. Looking up, Quinn could see the blend of the original stonework complimented with new brick, reinforcing the structure. Christmas music played in the background, and an animated video projected on the wall took people through the castle's 900-year history.

Despite it only opening on Christmas eve, Christmas decorations adorned every space. A Christmas tree twinkled in the centre of the room, with book ornaments on the branches. String lights hung over the banister and balcony, with a sign pointing visitors to Santa's grotto. From upstairs, Santa let out a 'Ho, ho, ho' out of sight, no doubt unaware the place was now full of peaceful protestors.

'This is incredible.' The last time Quinn had been here, it had mostly been a working site, with dust still covering the floor. 'You did an amazing job, Harold.'

Harold crossed his arms, not saying a word. Looking at blotchy red skin, Quinn thought he might explode if he did.

Quinn milled around the hall, passing the sitting protestors. He came to a window overlooking the town. They had printed a quote on the glass.

'"The new book is for the ego",' Quinn read aloud. '"The second-hand book is for the intellect." A Richard Booth quote.'

'That's right.' Gordon, who'd been on the second floor, walked into the main hall. 'We had to honour him here. That was my idea, that was.'

'A good one.'

'And his statue is outside.'

'Wow.'

'This is your protest?'

Gordon looked around the room, his eyes lingering on the drag queens, who were keeping quiet but performing an interpretive dance. Notably, it was a greedy businessman stealing from the locals.

'It is.'

'Nice.' Gordon looked at Harold. 'Think I'll join.'

Quinn gasped, and Harold turned in time to see Gordon sit down next to Ivy, who hugged him.

'What are you doing?' Harold stomped over, causing Emma's cameraman to take a photo, and Blair's camerawoman to direct her filming in their direction.

'I'm joining the cause,' Gordon said.

'You are *not*. Get up.'

Gordon crossed his arms, looking like an overgrown humorous child. 'Shan't.'

'*Shan't?*' Harold said. '*Shan't?* Who do you think you are?'

'You, Harold, are a bully,' Gordon said, and this time, Claire gasped. 'You bully people. This whole time you've bullied us, and you've been bullying Quinn. The rest of the boys agree with me. You're a bully.'

Had the real three ghosts of Christmas visited Gordon? He looked Harold in the eye, his voice stern, not a hint of fear or worry that he was standing up to the man who kept a roof over his head.

'A bully?' Harold spat. 'Say that again.'

'Bully.'

'Don't forget who pays your wages.'

'Oh, right.' Gordon stood, looking crestfallen, and Quinn admired that he'd tried. He'd spoken up, at long last, giving Harold a piece of his mind. Despite everything, men like Harold got their way. Gordon, Quinn and Claire were all pawns in his game.

Harold's angry expression changed to that of a man back in control of at least one half of the situation. Gordon avoided everyone's eyes as he approached Harold, an expression of grief on his face. 'Thing is, I've found work. Good work. For another firm. Take this as my notice.'

The drag queens erupted into cheers, and Gordon started when those nearest him hugged him, patted him on the back, and congratulated him on the new job. His eyes met Quinn's, and he put his thumb up, and Quinn beamed.

Chapter Thirty-Nine

The protest ended, with people beginning to either go home to get changed for the party, or follow Ivy into Kings & Queens, where she had full rein to get the party started.

'You'll regret that,' Quinn said when he heard. 'You *never* give Ivy full control of anything.'

She shouted dance instructions at some local shopkeepers, who looked like they might faint as they tried to keep up with her demonstrated dance moves. When someone stumbled into the wall while trying to attempt a high kick, Ivy seemed to see sense, and realised that having someone with a broken leg wasn't the best idea. Quinn, relieved they didn't need an ambulance, longed to have fun, but he found himself drawn to the castle, not wanting to leave yet.

Today was complicated: he felt like he had ruined a monumental moment for Hay, but they needed to make an impact. Harold had threatened to call the police, but after the sixth time of threatening and then being convinced by Claire that a police presence on opening day wasn't a good thing, he agreed to let the protest fizzle out.

'Humbug,' Harold hissed, missing the irony.

Their mark had been made. Their message had been received. As Quinn climbed the castle stairs, he left his mother talking to Harold in whispers, wondering what they might be discussing. On the second floor, he saw that Harold's idea for a dedicated small box room for his replacement bookshop had changed. Now, books lined the rebuilt stone walls, where people could browse titles and check out downstairs. It felt like a slap in the face that they didn't offer something of this calibre to him.

He supposed having a gay bookshop in the castle itself wasn't the vibe they were going for. That was okay. He didn't want the castle. He wanted his church.

Quinn followed the corridor of books until he came to a room that had been inaccessible all these years, but was now kitted out as Santa's grotto.

It was like someone had thrown up multicoloured fairy lights. They covered every surface so that Quinn couldn't see what refurbishments they had completed. They shimmered red, green, white and blue, then flashed with anger. Christmas music played here, too, and a Christmas elf stood at the door, a smile on her face.

'Have you been a good boy?'

Asking a grown adult if they had been a good boy in this context felt sordid.

'Oh, I'm just having a look around.' Quinn made to back away, thinking the third floor would be very appealing right now, but the elf took his arm and guided him into Santa's grotto.

'He's just in there.'

'Great.'

The elf closed the door, leaving Quinn standing in a twinkling room, facing a black curtain. He'd seen videos like this on not-so-innocent websites.

'Ho! Ho! Ho!'

He looked back to the door, where the elf kept him prisoner, and then to the mysterious curtain. 'Fuck it.'

He pulled back the curtain and saw a very authentic Santa, large, with a beard that didn't appear to be fake, and a red suit that looked like if he were to touch it, he would brush the softest thing in existence. Maybe stroking the suit would teleport him to the North Pole.

Perhaps that would solve his problems.

Santa held out gloved hands, beaming. If this man was creeped out to see an almost thirty-year-old come to sit on his lap, he didn't show it.

Quinn had seen this type of video before.

Wondering if he was being pranked, he was relieved to see a vacant armchair in front of Santa, and he breathed a sigh of relief that the only seating option was not Santa's knee.

'Well, well, well, it has been a long time since I last saw you, my boy!'

The voice had a perfect European slant to it. Not that Quinn would know the regional dialect of the North Pole, but he figured this Santa's voice might be it. It seemed to sing yet talk a melody that made Quinn relax his shoulders.

'Yes. When was the last time? When I was, what, eight?'

He had a horrible realisation that one year he'd sat on Santa's knee for the last time, and never realised it. Now *that* was depressing.

'I believe you were ten.'

'No, that can't be right,' Quinn spluttered. 'I knew you weren't real when I was seven.'

Santa tapped his crooked nose, where half-moon spectacles glimmered in the twinkling lights. 'I beg to differ, my boy.'

'Santa knows best.'

Oh, god, not the flirting. Why was he flirting?

Truthfully, there was something a little sexy about this rugged, authentic Santa Claus.

Oh, God, do I have a Santa fetish?

'What's on your mind, boy?'

One hundred per cent a Santa fetish.

'I have a lot on my mind.' Quinn said, adamant that he would *not* let this man know that he was having a Santa sexual awakening. 'I don't know if you know, but I am going to lose my shop today.'

Santa rubbed his long beard. 'Yes, I know all.'

'Of course,' Quinn said.

'And what is it you want this year, my boy?'

Stop calling me my boy. I can't contain myself.

'Well, the truth is, Santa, I need a Christmas miracle. I hear you're good in that department.'

'That's right!' Santa gave a jolly laugh. 'You are talking to the right being.'

Quinn couldn't help but smile. There was something magical about all of this. He wondered why it was so frowned upon for adults to still visit Santa, to still receive a gift and feel something again.

'My wish this year is that we will save my shop.' Quinn said.

Santa seemed to think about this for a while, and then he reached for a leatherbound book under his chair. Quinn hadn't noticed it, but he watched Santa open the heavy pages and trace a gloved hand down them.

'Ah, here you are,' Santa said. 'Quinn Oxford. Owner of Kings & Queens. You'll be pleased to know that you are on the good list.'

'How the *hell* did you know my name?' Quinn was impressed, wondering if maybe this was some spy operation, and the elf at the door had direct communication to an earpiece hidden under Santa's jolly red hat, as well as being an MI5 secret service agent.

'I'm Santa, of course!'

That warm, wonderful laugh made Quinn laugh too. 'Well, Santa, I hope that means that my wish will be considered.'

'Oh, yes, my boy,' Santa said. 'Everyone on my good list gets their wish granted!'

And as Quinn saw the twinkle in Santa's eye, the warm smile, and heard the joyful laugh, he couldn't help but get lost in the make-believe.

———————

Quinn left the castle, happy that it was open again and safe from any future attack, displaying Hay's history with pride and adding that extra magic to Hay's town. But as he descended the steps and approached his shop, where he saw figures in the window congregating together, he sighed.

It may very well be the last time he enjoyed his shop like this. He knew that this was supposed to be a night of celebration, but he couldn't help but see this as a send-off. Opening the door, he heard Britney Spears' 'My Only Wish This Year' blasting through the speakers that were reserved for meditation music, and saw the drag queens in mid-flow, hyping up the audience. He was so thankful that he'd decorated the night before, and glad to see that Ivy was the perfect host in his absence, offering drinks and nibbles to those in attendance. The party didn't need him, because it wasn't him they were celebrating. They were celebrating the spirit of the shop: a safe place where people could come together to be unapologetically themselves, where drag queens could brush shoulders with burly workers like Gordon. Where people talked about their sexuality, and their gender, and made new friends, without fear of prejudice.

'So, you're a gay man, but you dress up as a woman? But you're not transgender?' Gordon questioned.

'I'm not a man. I'm non-binary,' Santa Whores said. 'Drag is an art form. A staple of queer history…'

Gordon nodded, completely absorbed.

'And I might be gay,' Daniel, sloshed on wine, said.

As Quinn stood at the door, seeing Blair kiss Ivy under the mistletoe, watching Jenny pick up a book on transgender activism, and his mother clapping along to the performance, he felt the tears that had been with him all day unleash.

Without Kings & Queens, he was soulless. He couldn't help people at a corporate job. There would be no educating people on issues that still faced the community. He couldn't be a modern staple piece on historic Hay. He would just blend into a sea of grey, wishing he could afford to rent a shop somewhere else, knowing that this economy made it nearly impossible.

He felt alone. Despite being in this room, full of friends, old and new. He looked back to the castle, where the orange glow of lights acted as a beacon to Hay. It looked so inviting, so safe. Yet it would always be the reason he had to give everything up.

He found himself in his armchair, behind his desk, still crying but trying to smile. Nobody looked at him. They were all too enthralled with the performance and the people around them. Not that they didn't care, it was just the magic of this place rubbing off on them.

He opened the drawer, looking solemnly at his eviction letters, thinking he'd put up a good fight. The protest was perfect. They did everything they could do.

Wiping tears from his eyes, he reached for a champagne bottle and a flute, and poured himself a drink. He sipped from the glass, leaning back, trying to force himself to be happy, to enjoy this night. There was no proof that tonight was his last night. Somewhere, there was still a hope that all would be well, that the lead up to this moment had been for nothing.

Harold couldn't ignore their voices.

He couldn't disregard their donations.

Harold couldn't push this aside.

Taking his phone out, he filmed a video of the crowd, all of them happy, and posted it to his Instagram. He left the caption blank, knowing that he would make a longer statement when the time came. Now, he knew he should be in the moment.

He was about to get up and join the party, fixing a smile to his exhausted face, when the door opened. The room fell silent, and Mariah Carey's opening tones cut short.

Silhouetted by the setting sun, Hermione Sage looked beautiful. Her hair was combed back, sleek and decorated with holly. She wore a red dress with a green shawl. That was not weather appropriate, but in the name of fashion, it worked. Her lips, painted red, were smiling, though she looked uncertain when the silence set in. On her arm was Jerry, her brother.

Quinn couldn't believe that Hermione Sage, the recluse, the so-called scandal, braved the weather to be here. But it was more than that. It was the fact that she'd left the house and faced the town that had turned her into a myth.

Quinn got to his feet, fearful that the people of the town might turn on her like she was a monster. Her eyes found him, just as people cheered.

'Hermione Sage!' Penny Farthing called. 'Welcome home!'

Chapter Forty

Had he owned a red carpet, he would have laid it out. Had the press been notified, they would have shouted Hermione's name. In place of all that, those in the shop fussed over Hermione like she was royalty. Champagne was thrusted her way, and she took a flute handing one to Jerry, who looked like he did when Quinn had met him: rugged and country-like. He contrasted with Hermione's neat image, but it worked. Seeing them standing next to each other, Quinn could see their likeness.

The music filled the speakers again, and conversation erupted, no doubt discussing Hermione's arrival. If she was self-conscious of this, she didn't show it. The smile that had faltered was now back on, and Quinn saw her film-star quality in action as she oozed confidence and spoke to people as they rather tentatively approached her. She fluttered her eyelashes, gave a hearty laugh in the right places, and asked the right questions. The whole time, she held onto Jerry like he was her life raft. Without him, she would drown in the crowd.

This was far removed from the paranoid woman who locked herself away. She even stopped her conversation with an old bookseller to pose for a photograph and answer questions Emma asked. Her fear of the press was no longer apparent.

'Did you know about this?' Quinn asked Ivy.

'Not at all.' She looked rather flushed, no doubt from the wine and her foray into romance with Blair. 'I never thought I'd see the day.'

'Me neither,' one local nearby chimed in. 'I thought she was some hobbit in the hills.'

'I've never seen beauty like it,' Ebeneezer Screwed said. 'She's a hottie.'

'She's more than a hottie,' Ivy said. 'She looks like classic Hollywood.'

Quinn had to admit Ivy was right. Hermione may have not been on a film set for a couple of decades, but she hadn't lost her appeal. She commanded the attention of the room just by standing there. It was quite extraordinary to see.

Hermione found her way to Quinn, who still hadn't left the side of his counter. She turned her back on the audience and looked at him.

'My heart is pounding,' she whispered. 'I can't believe I'm doing this.'

'Breathe,' Jerry said. 'It's okay.'

'Are they talking about me?' She jerked her head back to the crowd, who were in fact looking at her.

'Not at all.' Quinn wondered if that wasn't the answer she wanted to hear. 'Not negatively. They're amazed to see you.'

'Oh.' Hermione adjusted the holly in her hair, a wry smile giving her happiness away. 'Well, I can handle that.'

'Will you have a photo with Quinn, Hermione?' Emma asked, swaying but still working her journalistic job.

'Yes, absolutely.' Hermione turned back to the crowd, faltering when she realised many people were looking at her. She smiled, regaining her composure, and it amazed Quinn how quickly she could hide the anxiety she must be feeling.

'Ivy, Blair,' Quinn said, catching them before they walked away. 'In the photo, please.'

'You too,' Hermione whispered to Jerry, who'd made to step aside.

Emma took a photo of Quinn with those who had helped him the most. He called in Jenny and the drag queens, laughing at the absolute campiness of such a scene. It was the best feeling he'd had all day: love and overwhelming gratitude for these people.

As they dispersed, he wished Noah could have been in the frame with them.

'Thank you so much for coming,' Quinn said to Hermione when Emma and her cameraman slipped back into the crowd. 'I know this must have been hard for you.'

'The press was a bit of a nightmare,' Hermione admitted, though Quinn doubted they had been. 'But I need to realise I can't let them rule my life anymore.'

'That's the spirit,' Jerry said.

'Besides, he brought me here.' Hermione nudged her brother. 'Said he saw you at the farm.'

Quinn cleared his throat. 'That's right.'

'My son is a dick,' Hermione said matter-of-factly. 'There's no two ways about it. But please don't hold him in disregard.'

Quinn sipped his champagne, wanting to choose his words with care. How could he forgive Noah? He didn't want to offend Hermione, or even put her in the middle of the situation like Harold had his mother. As Quinn thought about it, he didn't know if there even was a situation to put Hermione in. Noah was fleeting, like a hot winter's day.

'I would never do that,' Quinn said.

Hermione stared at Quinn but didn't say a word. It made Quinn uncomfortable, and he prayed someone would distract them; take her gaze away from him. It was excruciating seeing those eyes watch him.

'Why haven't you been in touch?' Hermione said. 'I thought you might stop by so we could discuss the book.'

Quinn felt a jolt, wondering what he could say. Was this Hermione's way of letting him go? 'I didn't know if I would be welcome.'

Hermione blinked, a blank expression on her glamorous face. 'Because of Noah's theatrics? Please. That doesn't need to impede us.'

The fear that had been wrapped around Quinn let go, releasing him into the atmosphere. The rush of relief was enough to make him let out a loud sigh. 'You don't know how good that is to hear.'

'Noah will come back,' Hermione said. 'He always does.'

Would he come back? Quinn didn't know what he would do. Forcing himself to believe Noah was gone allowed him to move forwards. That's all he could do. But these comments of fleeting hope kept him tied down. 'Have you heard from him?'

'I have. There's—'

But she didn't get to finish. An old headmaster from Quinn's school approached, holding out his arms to Hermione, who squealed, at last breaking away from Jerry and throwing her arms around him.

'Ronald, it's been *too* long.'

With that, she guided him away from the crowds, lost in discussion with an old friend.

Jerry crossed his arms, looking at his sister with a wistful expression. 'It was hard to get her to come tonight.'

'I appreciate it.'

Jerry scratched at the stubble on his face. 'She is special. She's deprived herself of these moments for too long. I hope tonight, seeing these people accept her, love her, idolise her, will help to restore her confidence.'

Quinn had expected nothing less from the crowd in the shop. Despite the almost legend-like stories of Hermione, it didn't matter. In a very British way, the stories had been part of their childhoods, a fun titbit to tell over a cup of tea. There had never been malice, not really. Hermione was a proud bit of history for Hay, and despite everything, everyone held a soft spot for her.

It made Quinn excited to write her story, to change the narrative, one that he was certain now would have a lot more acceptance than he first thought.

And as he watched the crowd, he thought of Hermione finding her voice to talk about what she'd gone through. How, somehow, he'd helped her find that ability to talk again.

Jerry found his own known faces, getting lost in the crowd, and Quinn wondered what Hermione meant to say about Noah. Her sentence cut off at such a crucial moment. What did Noah say to her? Had he asked about Quinn at all, about his shop?

Part of him hoped that, despite everything, Noah still cared. He checked his phone, almost wishing that a message would come through, a love heart social media like, *something* to confirm that he occupied Noah's thoughts like the author did his.

Alas, nothing.

The party stretched into the early evening until the last drop of wine and champagne had been poured. Somewhere along the line, they agreed to continue the party in the nearby pub and Quinn said goodbye to everyone as they headed out. They wished him luck and he fought back tears as he promised to keep the fight going.

Eventually, only a small crowd remained. Hermione was at the back of the shop, still lost in conversation with Roger and with Jerry at her side. Ivy and Blair leaned against a bookshelf like university lovers. Quinn thanked the drag queens, who were still ready to continue the party, and hugged Jenny, who'd turned out to be vital in getting the crowds.

'This donation... I'm amazed. But if we close, I can't take the money.'

'Oh, no.' Jenny shook her head. 'That money is yours. Use it as

JACK STRANGE

a deposit on somewhere new if you have to. Or just to keep you afloat as you start the next chapter.'

She was drunk. That was clear to see by her wide eyes and her flushed smile, but Quinn could see she meant every word.

She cried, a rather dramatic cry that would look false on anyone else. The drag queens fussed over her and she shook her head. 'It's just so sad.'

'Don't be sad,' Quinn said. 'Look at tonight. Look how amazing this has been. The perfect send-off. If, of course, it is the send-off.'

Jenny took his hands like a woman sending her husband off to war. 'Please, will you join us in the pub?'

'Oh, yes,' Quinn said.

Jenny nodded, wiping tears, and stepped out into the cold. Quinn turned to Penny Farthing, who seemed the most sober of the group.

'Are you sure about this money?'

'Totally. We raised this for you. It's yours, regardless of where it is spent. Take it.'

'I don't think I can ever repay you.'

'That's not the point of a fundraiser.' Penny smiled. 'You deserve it, Quinn. Thank you for this space, and all that you have done.'

Once the queens left, their arms around Jenny, their voices singing a drunken rendition of 'Driving Home for Christmas', Quinn let the tears fall.

'No tears, please,' Ivy said.

'I'm sorry.' Ugly crying. It was definitely ugly crying. And Bloody Blair Beckett looked perfect, even when he had consumed too much wine.

'Don't apologise,' Blair said.

Quinn wiped his tears. 'Look at you two. What's going on then?'

The pair looked at each other, all smiles.

'I saw you kiss.' Quinn pointed to the mistletoe hung above one of the book aisles. 'Don't lie.'

Ivy giggled. 'So, we kissed.'

'So, what does that mean?'

'I think that's a conversation for us to have,' Blair said, as Ivy laughed again. 'See you in the pub?'

'In the pub,' Quinn confirmed.

He watched them go, and then turned back to the shop, expecting to ask Hermione to leave. Instead, he saw Gordon browsing the DIY section. Since the castle, Quinn hadn't had time to speak to him.

'I can't believe you did that earlier.'

'Ah, mate, had to,' Gordon said. 'The missus had my nuts in a vice.'

Quinn tried to push that image out of his mind.

'Thing is, Harold ain't an evil man,' Gordon continued. 'He's just a little inconsiderate of his actions.'

'A little?'

'A lot.' Gordon grinned.

Gordon seemed happier, brighter.

'So, have you got a new job?'

'Aye,' Gordon said. 'A property firm. Ten grand pay rise. Can't go wrong.'

'Happy for you, Gordon.'

Gordon clapped Quinn on the back in that classic masculine way that made Quinn feel out of place in his own bloody shop. 'You're a good man, Quinn.'

He couldn't have a sentimental moment with Gordon. If he did, he would never stop crying.

'They're all going to the pub. You going?'

'Nah, got to get home,' Gordon said. 'I value my nuts.'

When Gordon had gone, Quinn approached the three remaining people in the shop, Hermione, Jerry and Ronald.

'The man of the hour,' Ronald slurred.

'Looks like you've all enjoyed yourself tonight.'

'Of course. I've missed nights like these,' Hermione wistfully said.

Jerry eyed Quinn, and then patted his thigh. 'I think we should leave you alone.'

'Oh, no, you don't have to...'

'No, we know when we've overstayed our welcome.' Jerry got to his feet and signalled for his sister and Ronald to join him. 'Come on, let's leave this man in peace.'

To say my goodbyes, Quinn thought.

At the door, Jerry turned back to Quinn as Hermione and Ronald giggled at something only they knew. 'Don't give up, Quinn.'

Quinn wondered if Jerry meant on the shop, or if his words ran a little deeper. He peered over his shoulder at the empty shop, and then glanced up and down the street.

'Did you see Daniel, by the way?'

Jerry smirked. 'Left with some guy.'

'Ah.'

Well, at least someone was lucky in love.

Chapter Forty-One

This was one hundred per cent a Christmas Eve he would never forget. The emotions he felt today should have been experienced over the course of a year, not a day. Alone, in his bookshop, allowing him time to take it all in. He should be sad, anguished that everything seemed so uncertain. But instead, he allowed himself to focus on the positive: the friends who had gathered, the support for him and his bookshop and a place for the queer community to feel safe.

He deserved to be happy. He deserved this moment of respite, where he'd exercised all he could do to fight for his right to stay open. He should be proud that he finally stood up for himself. At the back of the shop, the last dregs of champagne remained. He could have one alone. A private toast to the shop before joining the party at the pub. Quinn grabbed a clean glass and poured himself the fizz.

One last moment to indulge.

The glass was inches away from his face when the bell above the door dinged.

'Sorry, we're...'

The flute of champagne almost slipped from Quinn's hand. Standing at the display of 'A Christmas Carol' was Noah.

His blond hair was as artfully messy as ever. He wore a black duster jacket coat, a perfect length, and a green jumper, contrasting with his skin. Noah Sage looked at Quinn Oxford, a look that pinned him to the spot, freezing time.

'Oh.'

Was that really all he could say?

'There are some Christmas cracker hats left on this display,' Noah said.

'Oh, yeah,' Quinn said. 'I haven't got round to cleaning up after everyone yet.'

'What was the outcome?' The shop. His future.

'I don't know yet.'

'I see.'

Noah slipped his hands in his coat pockets, looking around at the shop. Quinn crossed his arms, feeling at odds with the situation.

'I suppose I should clean up.'

Any thought of joining the party at the pub slipped his mind. What was he supposed to do? Leave Noah and fear never seeing him again? Just by looking away, he might break the spell.

'Let me help you.'

'It's okay.'

'Please, Quinn.'

Those stern words, spoken with a calmness that made him relax, that familiar Welsh accent that blanketed him in warmth. He shrugged, resigned to the idea, locking the door behind him so that no one could disturb them. Quinn rushed to the kitchen and found a box of black bags. He took one of his own, then handed the rest to Noah.

'Is Matty with you?'

Quinn didn't know why he'd asked. Looking at Noah, he

could see that it threw him. Noah's mouth slightly ajar, as if thinking of what to say. Finally, Noah let his shoulders droop.

'No. We uh …we're definitely done.'

Quinn nodded, lips pressed together, and turned away to survey the remaining mess.

'You know, I'm sorry for what I did.' Noah gathered the empty bottles into the bag. They took an aisle each, losing sight of one another. 'For leaving you in the lurch like that. I wanted to do the signing. I had every intention of doing it. But then…'

The memory of their last night together may as well have been projected onto the wall. Quinn was glad they had a bookcase between them.

'I got scared. I got scared of all of this. Being back here in Hay, with Mum, seeing familiar faces. I realised how much I loved it here. I started questioning why I ever left. Then I saw you.'

Quinn paused, a red cup in his hand. Should he say something?

'I saw you straight away,' Noah said with a smile. 'I looked out the car window when I came to Hay, and I saw you in the crowd, and then at the talk—'

'I did *not* wet myself.'

From the other side of the bookcase came a laugh. 'No, I know. But it was enough to intrigue me. Did you know I was meant to go home after that? But I didn't. I wanted to stay to see you again. The closed roads were a blessing.'

Quinn was on his knees now, like he might pray. Truth was, he couldn't stand. Noah's words made him go weak at the knees. Curse such romantic cliches!

'Even though I wore those hideous trousers?'

'Even more so.'

Quinn shook his head, looking up at the rafters.

'So I went to Mum's, and I forced myself to go into the town, hoping I might see you.' Noah breathed. 'And there you were.

And I wanted to say so much, ask you so much, but I knew I couldn't. There was something I had to deal with first.'

'Matty.'

'Matty,' Noah muttered. 'But here, there was no Matty. And, I don't know, maybe I thought I could pretend here that I was single. I had no intention of cheating on him. I want to make that clear to you. Matty and I had broken up a long time before I came here. At least in my mind we had.'

Quinn closed his eyes, trying not to dwell on Noah's relationship. How long had he been in an unhappy relationship?

'I don't think I would have left him if I hadn't met you,' Noah continued. 'I guess I was waiting for him to get bored and leave me. That's what he would have done. But I saw you, spoke to you, and imagined what life would be like if there was an us. You were the one that brought home what I needed to do.'

Bloody hell.

He could hear Noah moving, and fearing he might come around the corner, Quinn clambered to his feet and tidied again, though he couldn't focus on such a mundane task.

'And all of that scared me.' Noah laughed. 'Ironic, isn't it? I'm a romance writer and I fear falling in love.'

'Love?'

Silence.

The apparition of Noah had gone. The spell broke.

All imagination.

'I think so.'

Not imagination.

Quinn stepped out from behind his bookshelf; at the same time, so did Noah. Now only inches away from one another. He read Noah's green eyes, saw the softness of his skin. Reaching out, he brushed away a strand of Noah's hair, feeling himself smile.

'I left Hay to find myself,' Noah said. 'This whole time, all I needed was you.'

Noah pushed Quinn against the bookcase. His hands found

Quinn's hips, pulling him towards him, before wrapping his arms around his waist. Quinn looked up, taking him all in. He expected to smell the citrus scent, but Noah was wearing something different, something akin to cedar, and he felt safe again, like it didn't matter what happened.

Quinn slid one hand underneath Noah's jumper, feeling warm bare skin on his fingertips. He traced the ridges of muscle, that V-line, as Noah's fingers slipped under Quinn's own T-shirt.

Reaching up, he placed a hand on Noah's chin. 'Look up, handsome.'

Quinn's breath hitched.

Above them hung mistletoe, with full red berries. Noah looked back at Quinn, a smile on his face.

Then everything changed. Quinn's lips were on Noah's, or maybe Noah's were on his, but it didn't matter who did what first. If his aura was dark before, it shone a bright yellow now. A warmth spread over him like it was a hot summer's day. With the smell of Noah's aftershave so close, Quinn almost thought they'd been transported to the depths of a forest, with bluebells at their feet and doves flying above. Quinn tightened his grip as he held Noah's face in one hand, and his back with the other. Noah's soft lips departed, only for a moment, and then they were upon him again, stronger this time.

Noah pulled him closer, and he felt everything. His erection pushing against his trousers, his muscle covered by fabric, the softness of his jumper. They seemed to float off the moss bed at their feet, floating in the realms of reality and magic. Quinn let Noah feel every part of him, from his own erection to his skin.

He wanted to reach every inch of him, to satisfy the aching hunger within, to feel every part. He wanted to taste him and experience him and be part of him all at the same time.

When Noah broke away – or was it him that broke away first – he realised he was, of course, still in the bookshop, not in the ethereal woods. Yet the smell of cedar remained, and the familiar smell of books made him feel secure.

Both smiled, then laughed.

'I have to go,' Noah said, still pressed against him, not making any attempt to move. His forehead was against Quinn's now. 'I have to go back home.'

'To London?'

'To Mum's.'

Relief swept through Quinn like the imaginary brook. 'Your mum is out of the house.'

'She ... what?'

'Didn't you go home first?'

'No, I got here and then walked around Hay like a lunatic psyching myself up to tell you all of this.'

Quinn laughed. 'Come on. I've got something to show you.'

Taking Noah by the hand felt exhilarating. As they ran out of the shop, through the snow, Quinn felt reckless. He brought Noah closer to him, kissing him under the falling snow, illuminated now only by Hay's Christmas lights.

They arrived at the pub, where the crowd from earlier was still in full flow. When they saw Quinn enter, his hand in Noah's, the place erupted. Deb and June, standing at the bar, looked from Noah to each other, threw back their cocktails, and ordered another.

'You're back!' Ivy said. 'And holding hands!' If Ivy could burst into a firework and whizz around the pub, she would have. Quinn was sure of it.

'What colour is my aura?' Quinn asked her.

'Oh, the sweetest pink!'

Everything was perfect. Deb and June engaged Noah in conversation at long last, and they even congratulated Quinn on winning over such a 'dashing young man'. It seemed their rush to get another drink had been to get some liquid courage to speak to their favourite author.

When Noah got away from Deb and June, somehow alive, Hermione came to join them.

'Noah.'

'Mum, meet Quinn,' Noah said.

'Did you fall and bump your head? We've already met.'

'Yes, but that was before he was my boyfriend.'

Boyfriend?

BOYFRIEND.

A choir of angels sang, a halo illuminated his skin, world peace had been achieved.

'Boyfriend?'

Noah looked worried, like maybe he misread their kiss earlier.

'Boyfriend.' Quinn smiled, and he held out his hand to Hermione.

She played along, looking at Noah. 'You know, I prefer him to the last one.'

There would be a time to find out what Matty had been like to Noah, but now was *not* that time.

The drag queens took over the pub, much to the chagrin of the local men that had never seen a drag queen in their life, yet softened when they found their humour to be the same. More drinks flowed, food was served, and everything would be okay. The joy, the pure elation, was enough to keep Quinn going. He stayed at Noah's side, feeling like leaving him would mean losing him again. As the evening went by, everything seemed to be how it should be: perfect and harmonious.

That was until the door opened, letting in a draft of billowing cold air.

Harold stood at the door, his small eyes finding Quinn's. 'I've come to collect the keys.'

Chapter Forty-Two

'You can't take the keys.'

'Yes, I can.'

'Really, Harold, after all of this?'

'Definitely.'

Harold may as well have taken a book and ripped it to pieces. The crowd fell silent, their eyes on him.

'Shame on you.'

'Boo!'

The people heckled, and Quinn could have let it happen, could have watched Harold suffer.

Instead, he raised his hands, silencing the crowd. 'You're not letting me keep it?'

'No, absolutely not,' Harold said. 'I think the eviction notices should have made that very clear, Quinn. It's just…'

He couldn't hear it. Not again.

'Just business, yeah.' Quinn took the keys out of his pocket. Worn with chipped black paint and well used. It was a heavy key, one that took a bit of a push to lock into place and twist. It had a green bow attached to it, to help him differentiate it from the others, not that it needed help to stand out.

He didn't realise how sentimental he got over something so small. The first time holding the key had been a life-changing moment for him. His own shop. His future. His happy place.

Now, with one motion, it was in the hand of another, and it would never be his again.

'You won, Harold.'

Harold put the key into his pocket, clearing his throat. 'Yes, well. I hope this doesn't have to come between us.'

He held out a hand, and Quinn, dumbfounded, shook it. He didn't know why. In moments like that, he couldn't think straight. It was a cold, tense shake, and then Harold left to boos from those behind Quinn.

Quinn didn't move, but he heard the hush fall over the crowd.

'Are you okay, Quinn?'

'Not really.'

All he could be was honest. He couldn't stand here and put a smile on his face and say that everything would be okay, because it wouldn't. His shoulders slumped; his head dropped. He ran a hand over his face, closing his eyes as the warm tears fell down his cheeks.

He looked at Noah, the tears making him appear as a blur. Just a few moments ago, he had felt so carefree. Now the world had crushed him, so coldly and effortlessly.

With a sinking feeling of despair, Quinn knew they had never stood a chance.

He walked to the bar and didn't have to say anything. A shot of whisky waited for him.

'I'm sorry, Quinn,' Daniel said, leaning against the bar.

Quinn looked at the liquid like it was foreign to him.

He raised it, feeling numb. 'To Kings & Queens.'

'Kings & Queens,' the crowd mumbled.

He didn't even get to look at the shop one last time. When he returned, silhouetted by the castle, the door was locked and the lights off. Frost on the window permitted him to look through. Harold's footprints had left indents in the snow.

'What's going to happen with all that stock?' Noah asked, his arm linked in Quinn's.

'I haven't even thought about that.'

There was so much in there he might never see again. The books, but also the opened incense packs, the half-finished jar of coffee, the kettle and the tea, the confessional booth. These things that had become a part of his life, and now they may be taken away or re-homed and he couldn't do anything about it.

'I guess you were my Christmas miracle.'

'Sorry, what?'

'Santa,' Quinn said, as if it were obvious. 'I spoke with him in his grotto.'

'Sexy.'

'Yes,' Quinn said. 'I asked for a miracle. No offence, but I thought that miracle would be saving my shop.'

'No offence taken,' Noah said. 'I'd choose the shop, too.'

Quinn rested his head on Noah's shoulder. His shop was so dark now; the colour gone. With horror, he noticed that the pride flag outside his shop had been torn away.

'I can't believe this is happening. What am I going to do, Noah?'

He was crying again, thankful that it was dark so that the shadows hid his ugly crying face. Noah didn't seem to find it ugly, though. He looked at him, wiping the tears away, and in that moment, everything felt like it might be okay.

Or not completely shit.

'You're going to be alright,' Noah said. 'What do you want to do?'

'I want my shop back.'

'And if that doesn't happen?'

'I don't want to go to that job in London. I don't want to go into some corporate role. I want to help people.'

'Then we'll find you somewhere else.'

'Have you seen the rent around here?' Quinn asked. 'Impossible.'

'You know I'm in London, don't you? We could have a life there. Together.'

London. The scary city. A life so different from the one he currently lived. Could he leave this behind? Except … what would he be leaving behind? An apartment? His mother. Hay, of course, but Hay would always be here. Without his shop, there was no solid anchor or purpose.

And Noah. Sweet Noah. He'd come back, but for how long? Quinn didn't think he could face losing him again.

'But the job…' Quinn said.

'Mum's book,' Noah said. 'I've already spoken to my publisher. They want to publish it.'

Quinn's eyes widened. A publisher? Already? 'Are you joking?'

How could this be possible? He had spoken to Hermione earlier. She hadn't mentioned a thing about a publisher, only that they should meet.

'No,' Noah said. 'Turns out they think her subject is very topical at the moment, and they want to help give her a platform to return to the spotlight, should she choose to. Helps that I make them lots of money, too.'

He made the last words a joke, but they both knew it to be true.

'London's expensive, Noah,' Quinn said. 'I've had some money donated to me, but other than that…'

'They'll give you an advance.'

'An advance? Why don't I know anything about this?'

'They're kind of doing me a favour,' Noah admitted. 'And it's

Christmas. They won't be sending contracts until after Christmas. But my point is, it's happening. Security. Safety.'

'Oh, gosh.'

'And a job that doesn't require you to go into an office and pretend to be everyone's friend. I own my little flat. We'll be okay.'

Quinn held Noah's hand, reading his handsome expression, trying to see if he was lying. 'You're asking me to move in with you already?'

Noah laughed. 'I suppose it is quite soon.'

Very soon. Quinn didn't just move in with someone straight away, no matter how attractive and talented they were.

'What if we did long distance for a little while?' Quinn asked. 'You know, in case you turn out to be a serial killer.'

'Fair,' Noah said. 'That would work. Gives me time to prep my dungeon.'

Quinn smirked. Maybe things would be okay. The universe had ways of putting you on a new track. This was his.

'You know, it's weird, but it feels like someone died.'

'I understand that.' Noah wrapped an arm around Quinn's shoulder, kissing his forehead. 'A part of you died. You mourn how you see fit.'

'Where have you been since, like, forever?'

'In London.'

Chapter Forty-Three

The morning sun sprawled through the loft room where exposed brick walls met buffed-up wooden beams. A year ago, this was dusty attic space, where gigantic spiders laid their babies and did evil spider things. Now it was Quinn's bedroom when he stayed at his mother's home. Her house balanced the border, so that Quinn could sleep in the middle of the bed and half of him would be in Wales and the other side in England. He slept to the left, so that he would be in Wales.

Christmas morning. The heating on, and his room uncomfortably warm. He wore nothing except the blanket, and turning to the skylights, he blinked through the morning haze. He could already hear the noise downstairs; the smell floating up from the kitchen. His stomach rumbled as he thought of a delicious Christmas dinner.

Today should be the most magical of days, where he could celebrate with family and relax. But the memory of yesterday, foggy after one too many champagne flutes, came back to him. The first official day without his shop.

The prospect of having to play happy families opposite Harold made him want to jump from the loft window. Maybe Harold woke up ill and would be bed-bound all day. Or, maybe, he would see sense and give him his shop back.

Then there was Noah.

Oh, sweet Noah.

Their anniversary would be Christmas Eve! Boyfriends! They were Christmas Eve boyfriends! When everything else changed, Noah was there when he needed him most. He ruined a book signing, but that didn't matter anymore. Though maybe he would punish him.

Must find out if Noah likes S&M.

Quinn got out of bed and dressed in shorts and a T-shirt. It might be zero degrees outside, but Claire's house was like Hawaii in the peak of summer. The old house pipes groaned day in, day out as they pumped warmth throughout the rooms.

His mum's house had always been nice and his father's touches were still visible, even after all these years. This loft was Harold's brainchild, another reason he woke up in a bad mood, and it felt too modern for the Georgian home. As soon as he was downstairs, back on the second floor, everything felt right again.

The home had a rustic charm mixed with academia. If that was even a thing. On the landing was an antique table with a chair that had books stacked on it. The bedrooms, with their large ceilings, had a musty feel to them, with netted curtains and lots of natural light, sometimes obscured by ... more books!

The stairs creaked underneath Quinn's Pokémon socks. They were uneven, too, so Quinn held the railing, just in case.

They led to an open plan living room, an oasis of house plants and, yes, more books. Two double doors opened up to a garden full of more plants, which of course were dead now, their corpses mummified by snow. He walked into the beige kitchen with more plants and many more books, and granite tabletops. Harold was already at the dining table, decorated with candles, a wreath, and cutlery, the Christmas crackers placed in front of the plates.

When Quinn entered, his mother, red-faced, smiled. 'Merry Christmas!'

Harold looked up from the newspaper, and Quinn avoided his eye. He could get through today without saying a word to him.

He could.

'Merry Christmas, Mum!' He hugged her, observing the vegetables boiling on the stove. 'Dinner looks good.'

'Yes, it should be. I cooked it.' She winked, then took his hand. 'Are you ready for your Christmas present?'

He credited his mum for keeping the Christmas spirit alive. Every year she made sure that she planned his Christmas gifts out to a tee, making sure they were wrapped and waiting for him when he awoke in the morning. It made him smile.

'Only if you're ready for yours!'

Last night, like Santa himself, Quinn sneaked into the conservatory, where they always left their presents, and placed his mother's gifts next to his own. He had even bought something for Harold, despite everything.

'Come on, then.'

They went into the conservatory together where a small pile of presents waited. Quinn unwrapped his, opening books, some clothes, and then a brand-new plant for his apartment. As his mum talked him through how to care for the lava rock plant, which was the cutest thing ever, he felt a pang of guilt that she had yet to know about Noah, and the possibility of a new life in London.

Finally, there was a rectangular-shaped present left to open.

'Open this before I open mine.'

Quinn picked it up, underestimating its weight, and almost dropped it. His mum gasped, but breathed a sigh of relief when he secured it. He unwrapped the candy cane printed paper and saw that it was a framed photograph.

Upon seeing the photo, he cried.

It was a photo of his shop, only it wasn't his then. He was

younger in the photo, stood to the side, with his dad next to him, his arm around his son. His lost shop, Kings & Queens, centred right in the middle, almost predicting the future.

'I didn't know this photo existed.' Quinn sobbed.

His dad. Him. In front of what would become his own bookshop. He couldn't believe it.

'Neither did I,' Claire said. 'But when we were renovating the attic, I found a box of photos. Gerald had them developed and put them all away. And this was in there. I wanted to show it to you straight away, but then I thought it would make a pleasant surprise.'

'It's a beautiful surprise.' Quinn got to his feet and hugged his mum. He could feel her shake in his arms, and knew she was crying, too. 'Thank you. So much.'

'I miss him.'

'So do I.' Quinn looked at her. 'But he's still with us. He'll always be with us.'

Claire wiped Quinn's tears before she wiped her own.

'Now, open yours.'

He had only bought her one thing, small compared to all his stuff. But she didn't seem to mind. She picked it up, underestimating the weight just like him, and opened a box.

Confused, she opened the box, then pulled out a statue.

This time, it was her go to burst into tears. They had shed so much water between them that if they went outside, they would freeze.

'It's perfect.'

Quinn had spent his money on a marble carving statue of his mother and his father. With perfect precision and detail, etched into marble forever, eternalised. Claire looked at the marble face of Gerald with a smile.

'I'll put this front and centre.'

'Do you really like it?'

'Come here.'

She kissed him on the cheek.

That was enough.

After dinner, where Claire made most of the conversation, they retreated to the cwtch, as Claire liked to call it, and put on a Christmas film. Quinn had a glass of wine, and for the first time in a long time, he relaxed. Now and then his phone would buzz, Noah texting him about Christmas with Hermione and his cat, Mr Lavender, and Quinn would smile.

He spent most of the day not meeting Harold's eye, let alone engaging him in conversation. But as the credits rolled on *Elf*, Harold made the first move.

'What do you want me to do with the stock?'

Quinn watched the credits like they were the most riveting thing on earth. 'I suppose it's best to donate them to the rest of the bookshops.'

Short and to the point.

Maybe he would leave it at that.

But...

'And the furniture?'

Quinn shrugged. 'Some of the stuff is original, so you might want to keep that.'

'Yeah, right.' Harold laughed.

Quinn remained silent. What was the point? It was Harold's space. He could do what he liked.

Claire sipped her drink, sat between them, ready to defuse the situation if need be.

'You know, a couple of the other boys left after Gordon.'

'Did they?'

'Not happy with my attitude, they said.'

Quinn could only wonder why.

'Means I don't have many people working for me at the moment,' Harold said. 'If you wanted a job.'

For the first time that day, Quinn turned to Harold, incredulous.

'Wow. Thanks.' Quinn pretended to consider the offer. 'I think I'll pass.'

'Figured.' Harold reached for a chocolate in a tin of Quality Street, his fingers roving for something in particular. 'I'm probably going to sell it.'

'You *what?*' Claire spoke before Quinn. It seemed she hadn't been as shellshocked as he'd been. Sell it? After everything that happened?

'Sell it,' Harold said, only this time slower, like he was uncertain.

'You said you wanted it as a ticket office.'

'Yeah,' Harold said. 'About that. I saw people coming into the castle and thought, you know what, we can just sell tickets at the front.'

Quinn looked at his mother, and even now he feared the look on her face. It was the 'don't you dare talk to me right now because I'm processing something that has made me furious' sort of look. The type of look that every mother seemed to acquire as soon as their child was born.

'So, you don't want it?'

'Well, I realised I could get more out of it by selling it.' Harold found the chocolate he was looking for – a green triangle. 'It's a much bigger cost if it's a ticket office, isn't it? When I could sell it and get close to half a mil.'

'I am … so disappointed.' Claire said.

'Me too.'

Harold shrugged, mid-chew. 'Just business.'

What was the true meaning of Christmas? Spending a wonderful time with family, relaxing and laughing, playing games? Whatever it was, it wasn't this moment.

Claire was on her feet as the opening bars of Eastenders played, and Quinn hoped, prayed, wished that she would do a Kat Slater and throw some wine over Harold. But she turned her back on him and left the room.

'Where are you going? Phil's facing life or death!'

'I don't care about Phil Mitchell!'

It would have been comical if it wasn't so gut-wrenchingly atrocious. It felt like one big trick, like a dirty secret had been exposed. Their very own Eastenders moment.

'I didn't think you would be so low.'

Harold looked confused. 'I'm not following.'

'You don't think it's an issue that you're selling?'

'Not at all. It's my place. I can do what I want.'

Quinn stood, unable to be in the same room a moment longer. As he was about to leave, Harold called after him.

'I wouldn't have had to sell if you hadn't made my boys get all righteous!'

'They didn't need me to realise what a horrible man you are,' Quinn retorted.

He expected a shout, maybe something thrown, but nothing came. Either he'd shocked Harold into silence, or he didn't care enough to make sense of the situation. Quinn expected the latter.

He found his mum in the kitchen, crying over a strawberry trifle. 'I didn't know.'

'I know you didn't.'

'What am I going to do?'

He realised what she meant. What Harold did hurt her on a much deeper level. Quinn sighed, fearing the outcome.

'That's up to you to decide, Mum,' he said. 'For now, let's have the trifle together and not leave him any.'

Claire managed a giggle and let Quinn dish up the dessert.

Chapter Forty-Four

Quinn normally spent Christmas night with his mum, no doubt because they would fall asleep watching a film and then wake up too late for him to go back home. But this Christmas was no normal Christmas, and after dessert, Quinn knew he needed to go home. Harold had morphed into the Grinch and stole Christmas from them, and as Quinn left for his own apartment, he wondered if he might hear news that Harold was now living on a mountain for the rest of his life.

On his way home, he texted Noah, explaining the situation.

> Harold might get dumped.

> I'm coming over.

It surprised him, but made him smile. The support was going to take some getting used to.

In his apartment, he made sure everything was tidy, and made sure there were no embarrassing things lying around, like stray jockstraps, though he did consider 'accidentally' leaving one on the floor. Wine was chilling in the fridge, a Welsh Pinot made in Abergavenny, and a chocolate log was ready to be served. It didn't matter that he'd consumed half a tonne of trifle. It was Christmas!

The doorbell rang, and Quinn's phone lit up with the notification. He loved his fancy little video doorbell gifted to him by Ivy for Christmas, and as he opened the app, he saw Noah framed like he was about to go on a film set. Snow fell behind him, landing in his hair.

'Come on in!'

Quinn approved the door to unlock and heard Noah climbing the stairs, knocking on his apartment door.

Oh, how he was nervous. This felt different. Intimate. Romantic.

He rushed to light some candles and then opened the door, leaning against it like he was nonchalant.

Only the door kept moving, and Quinn fell to the floor.

'I really knock you off your feet.'

Noah held him up, and Quinn shook his head. 'That's how we open the doors here in Hay.'

'Funny how I don't remember that.'

'Yule log?'

'Stupid question.' Noah smiled.

He took a seat on the sofa, near the Christmas tree, the candlelight flickering over him as he took off his coat and then his hoodie. Quinn handed him an empty wineglass, placed the bottle on the table, and then headed back to the kitchen to get the dessert. And maybe a box of chocolates, for luck.

'So, what happened?'

He wore a tight white T-shirt, showing off the muscle in his arms, one of which was cocked, resting his head against his fist. Quinn wanted to rip everything off him.

But he was civilised. So, he didn't.

Yet.

Coming back with the yule log and even more chocolate, Quinn tried to take his eyes off the perfect vein that went from shoulder to elbow in Noah's arms and focus on what he'd asked instead.

'Harold is selling the shop.'

Noah, drinking his wine, almost spat it out again. 'Sorry?'

'Selling it.'

'After evicting you because he wanted it to be part of the castle?'

'That's right.'

Noah shook his head. 'Fuck. I'm sorry.'

'He's within his right to do it,' Quinn said. 'But it's the principle of it. Not only do I feel betrayed, but I feel lied to.'

'You *were* lied to. He wanted it to be a ticket office, didn't he?'

'Yeah.' Quinn sipped his own wine. 'Said he realised it would cost him more money, and it made more sense to sell it. Also blamed it on the fact his staff has been leaving him.'

Noah ate the chocolate log, closing his eyes as he enjoyed the taste. At that moment, he was the cutest. 'They're leaving him?'

'I got the impression from Gordon that he was a bit of a nightmare to work for during the castle renovation.'

'Harold? A nightmare? Never.' Noah laughed.

A new feeling struck Quinn as Noah recounted his own Christmas, which ranged from Hermione opening the curtains and an elaborate meal for two. It was light, relaxed; the tension released from his back. He was smiling, laughing along at the anecdotes, feeling like time didn't exist. Curled up on the sofa, his hand in Noah's, sat across from him yet close enough to smell an unfamiliar scent on him this time – a spicy one – this felt like happiness.

For a long time, Quinn thought Dougie would be it. Despite his tendency to bring Quinn down, to disparage and manipulate his feelings, Dougie seemed like the choice for Quinn. He realised now that was because Quinn hadn't been able to find his voice. He didn't know himself back then, and thinking now about the man he used to be, when Dougie only talked of himself, only planned for his own life, he couldn't recognise himself. It was always easier for someone to tell Quinn what to do, rather than for Quinn to think or speak for himself.

With Noah, it was different. Like this was how it was always meant to be. Secure, like he could accomplish anything. Of course, it mattered that he'd lost his shop, and that his future now looked like it was on a different, unplanned path, but in some ways, maybe that was what he needed. Maybe Hay had offered him all that it could.

Despite the tense Christmas day, this was what mattered. The snow falling outside, casting shadows in the cosy apartment where the candles burned bright and the tree glimmered. Fruity and refreshing wine with sweet dessert. The warmth from the heating, from the sofa, from Noah's hand.

He could get used to Christmases just like this.

'Why are you looking at me like that?' Noah asked.

'Like what?'

'Like … I'm a marshmallow covered in chocolate.'

'Just wondering how you taste.'

Stop it!

Except don't.

Because despite that line, it worked. A muscle feathered in Noah's jaw, and then Noah was on him, kissing him, touching him, and it was like the apartment roof was ripped off and the light of the angels shone upon them. Quinn swore he could hear the choir singing heavenly melodies as he pulled Noah's T-shirt off him.

He used his fingers to trace a light dusting of the same blond hair on his pecs; the hair continued under his arms. Quinn ran his hands over his freckles, kissing his chest, his stomach. There was a trail of hair from his belly button disappearing under his jeans.

'That wasn't there in the Instagram photo.'

'I'm a big boy now.'

'How big?'

Bloody hell, who am *I?*

'Are you sure?'

Quinn bit his lip before speaking. 'I'm sure.'

His lips were back, frantic, perfect. His hands pulled Quinn's T-shirt over his head, and the warmth of Noah's skin pressed against him. Noah slid between his legs, unhooking the button on his jeans, and Quinn pulled them down.

The singing angels seemed to know it was time to leave as Noah's hands explored Quinn, his touch like a feather playing across his every nerve. Quinn arched his back, feeling Noah against him, closing his eyes as Noah's lips went from his own, to his neck, to his chest.

'Do you have protection?'

'The bedroom.'

Noah brought him to his feet, holding his hand. He was naked, sculpted, the light hair from his stomach congregating at his pelvis. Quinn bulged against his own underwear, smiling as he allowed Noah to guide him to the bedroom.

'This is the bathroom,' Noah said as he opened the door.

'Bedroom is to the left.' Quinn giggled.

'Why didn't you say anything?'

'Your bum distracted me.'

Noah grinned and took him into the bedroom, pushing him onto the bed, climbing atop of him. Now Quinn was naked, and every part of them met, solid yet supple. Quinn reached for his bedside cabinet and slipped out a Durex packet, which Noah opened. Quinn helped him slide it on, feeling the tension under his fingers.

'Lube?'

Quinn nodded to the same cabinet, and Noah reached over this time, dropping the water-based lubricant onto his hands. With a gentle touch, he massaged Quinn, slipping one finger inside him, which Quinn greeted with an audible gasp. Noah's dick, with its blue crisscrossing veins and curved shaft, responded to the noise with a jerk. Quinn added the lube to his own hand and ran it over Noah's shaft, letting his fingers run over the trimmed hair on his balls. Noah groaned, his breath dancing across Quinn's face.

Slowly, his lips on Quinn's, he pushed in.

Chapter Forty-Five

Two Months Later

The for-sale sign above Kings & Queens was pasted over with a red 'sold' sticker. Quinn, standing outside the shop on a frosty February morning, watched his breath catching in front of him. The New Year had been a turning point for Quinn. After Christmas, he had spent every day with Hermione, hearing her tell her story and writing out the recordings he took on his phone. He'd written most of the book, but he knew he needed to go back and tweak it here and there. Noah had been right. His publishers pulled through.

Hermione's life was colourful, but what struck Quinn was her honesty. She shared details of her life that Quinn hadn't asked for, but it made the book all the juicier. Because despite everything, the publisher, a very well-known tuxedoed animal, thank you very much, wanted all the titbits. Hermione was already raising her profile in time for a summer release, the publisher hoping it would make a good holiday read.

Now she genuinely had to avoid the press, hiring security to guard her gate and keep them off the property. Quinn didn't have the heart to tell her that the press until that point hadn't been all that interested in her life. He knew there would be a flurry of activity. Interviews, television appearances, author signings.

It didn't matter that all that glory would be for Hermione and not him. His name wouldn't even be on the book. He was the ghostwriter, and that suited him. Hermione promised him a thanks in the credits, especially because Quinn flat out refused to have his name on the cover.

He didn't want the attention. He wrote Hermione's story for her own liberation. As the excitement built from the publisher, Hermione, the press and Noah, he thought he brought her some form of justice.

His mother left Harold. Turns out him selling the place after saying he wanted it as part of the castle was the final straw. She later told Quinn that she had considered breaking up with him before Christmas, when he ignored her pleas to stop him from evicting her only son. Quinn hadn't seen Harold since Christmas day, but he'd heard that he'd moved to Cardiff, where maybe he'd find Dougie and they would live a wonderful city life together.

Quinn walked to the window of his shop over the wet pavements, clutching his coffee cup to his chest. It hurt him to see the shop so bare. His mahogany table was there, lying empty, the eviction letters long gone and burned in a ritual Ivy had asked him to be part of.

'Cleansing the stagnant energy,' she'd told him, as she threw the red stamped eviction letters one by one into the flames.

Quinn had to admit that watching them curl up into nothingness was rather cathartic.

The books in the shop had all found their ways into the other shops, and others entered the honesty library in the castle grounds. It was a full circle moment, his books entering the castle. Almost as if that was always their destiny.

Daniel still kept in touch. Quinn planned to meet with him soon and discover how his life was going.

At the back of the shop, the confessional booth remained. It made Quinn happy to know that the original features would stay there. Maybe the church would function again, though he thought it was more probable that it would turn into some hip restaurant.

On the second of January, Noah had left Hay. It was hard watching him go, and as Quinn waved goodbye, he felt like an abandoned animal. Noah needed to go to London to 'sort things out'. Quinn later found out that it was to help Matty move his things from his apartment.

Matty. Beautiful Matty.

Quinn had discovered Matty was not as successful as he'd first thought but came from rich parents. Like, uber rich parents who could speak multiple languages. No, seriously. His father held a stake in Uber and his mother in Duolingo. They had set Matty up for life. That was until his father had told him he had to go work for a living, and that had sent Matty crashing to the ground.

So, with twenty-thousand pounds to see him on his way, Matty had opened his bakery. But Matty didn't know how to run a bakery and was more concerned with getting acting and modelling gigs. So, the bakery soon crashed into the ground, but not before he met Noah and realised quite how successful of an author he was.

Noah equalled money and acted as an escape for Matty. Noah had fallen for it.

To be honest, Quinn would have, too. Matty was gorgeous.

So, while Noah did the work, Matty enjoyed living the life he thought he was meant to live –which was to piss about and try to get some acting and modelling work on the side. Those acting gigs meant background artist work. Of course, there was nothing wrong with that, but it wasn't quite the heights that Matty had implied.

Living that life was expensive, though, and Noah soon realised that he was funding Matty's lifestyle. Matty had used Noah's credit card to rack up a bill in Mayfair, Chelsea, and even a trip to Bora Bora with his thespian friends.

As Noah told Quinn everything one snowy December evening, he realised how much Matty had put Noah through.

'You should get legal action.'

'The man is a dick, not a criminal,' Noah had said. 'His heart is in the right place.'

Whilst Quinn didn't agree, he admired that despite everything, Noah still wouldn't hurt him.

Just as long as he kept his devilishly handsome looks away from him, all would be fine.

But any moment now, Noah would be back in town, this long-distance thing mainly only being from one end of the sofa to the other, because Noah had moved into Quinn's apartment. It was why Quinn stood here, reminiscing, but also waiting to see Noah's Bentley come down Castle Street.

'End of an era.' Ivy's voice brought Quinn back to earth. Somehow, she always had that knack of appearing out of nowhere. He wondered if she was a spirit.

It was nice to see her. She hadn't been in Hay since Christmas. Blair had whisked her away to Brisbane, where he had family, and she'd updated her Instagram with wonderful photos of beaches, summer, and a toned topless Blair. They hadn't stayed long, but packed a lot in, Ivy wanting to return home to Hay for New Year. Something about the energy of it all and her astrological cartography.

Turns out, he'd been pretty serious about wanting to get to know her. They were already Facebook official, and with his minor celebrity status, Ivy made *Heat* magazine's worst dressed list, much to her enjoyment. She'd found Quinn one day, tanned after her not at all jealousy-inducing holiday, and showed him the spread, a beaming smile on her face.

Now, wrapped in a blue coat, she joined Quinn in looking at the sold sign on the shop.

'It is.' He spoke. 'Who do you think bought it?'

'I heard an out of towner,' Ivy said this with disdain, like it was illegal to live anywhere but Hay.

'Well, I hope they look after it,' Quinn said. 'It's a special place.'

Even if it is devoid of soul.

He'd made peace with it when the clock struck midnight on New Year's Eve. He would leave it behind, cut it off with a cleaver. 'New year, new me,' he had declared to Noah, Hermione, Jerry and Claire. He didn't tell them he said that every year.

'Are you going to move to London?' Ivy asked him.

The thought grew every day. With Hermione's book being published, and the publisher being in London, it made sense to be nearby. But Noah, who had the same publisher, proved writing could work anywhere.

'I don't think so,' Quinn said. 'Not yet, at least.'

'I'd hate to see you go,' Ivy said.

'And I'd hate to see you go.'

After all, with Blair fronting national news in London, she had her own dilemma to deal with.

'Maybe we're both destined for London.'

A car approached them from Castle Street, and seeing that it was black, Quinn thought it might be Noah. He felt the excitement swell inside him, but deflated when he noticed it was a Chrysler rather than a Bentley.

It pulled up outside of his shop, and Gordon got out of the car, a smile on his face.

'When did you get this?' Quinn asked him, admiring the spotless bodywork of the car.

'With new jobs come new perks,' Gordon said. 'They've made me a partner.'

'Bloody hell, of the property firm?'

'That's right!' Gordon cheered. 'You are looking at the man responsible for acquisitions.'

He was dressed in a suit. Gordon. In a suit! He reminded Quinn of one of those people who went on *The Apprentice*, with their shiny shoes and their pinstripe trousers.

'Well, I'm happy for you.'

'Thanks. Missus is chuffed,' Gordon said, 'but she's not the only one.'

'What do you mean?'

Another car came down the street, this time putting the Chrysler to shame. Gordon whistled as the black Bentley parked next to his car, the window rolled down, The Spice Girls playing from the speakers.

'Girl power,' Noah said as he cut the engine. 'What's going on here, then?'

'Just in time, just in time,' Gordon smiled, tearing his eyes away from the Bentley. 'You are now looking at the owner of Kings & Queens.'

Quinn was drowning. He couldn't seem to breathe as he looked from Gordon to the shop, and back again.

Walloped with the betrayal baton again.

'You bought this place?'

'Our firm did, yeah,' Gordon said. 'First thing I did when I got the job, you see. Paid way over the asking price, but the boss doesn't need to know that.'

Ivy managed a small laugh, but she stifled it.

Quinn felt at a loss for words. He thought he would have been able to trust Gordon.

He had been wrong.

His eyes met Noah's, falling into the green oasis, and he saw his own sadness reflected back at him.

Gordon took out the keys in all its familiar glory.

'Got these today,' Gordon said. Then he did something that made Ivy gasp. 'I think it belongs to you.'

Gordon held the keys out, with its chipped paint work and its familiar bow. Quinn looked at Gordon, feeling nothing, still in that cold pool that numbed all his senses. He reached out a hand that trembled, felt the rough and cold key under his fingertips, and then felt everything all at once.

It was like the key was a thorn. It brought tears to his eyes as he touched it, but he hung on to it, never wanting to let it go.

'I don't understand.' Quinn said.

'Quinn, when I saw the job opening at the property company, I saw an opportunity. They were looking for someone that could help them invest and develop property. I told them about this place, told them the story, and they agreed to help me save it. So, I bought it.'

He was about to say more, but he couldn't. Quinn threw his arms around him and hugged him tight, the closest they'd ever been. He smelled different from Noah. More tobacco than earthy, and he was stiff, because he hadn't been expecting this physical contact, but it didn't matter to Quinn.

He let Gordon go, seeing him breathe a sigh of relief that whatever had happened was over.

'You are the best person in the entire world,' Quinn said. 'I never thought I'd say it, Gordon, but I am so glad you're in my life.'

'Mate, I know how much this place means to you.' Gordon tapped the wooden window panes. 'She's a beauty and only you can look after her. I'll keep the rent as low as possible, and you'll never have to worry about being evicted again. My missus would have my nuts for garters.'

'Thank you so much, Gordon. Words will never express how I'm feeling right now.'

'Welcome back, mate.'

Chapter Forty-Six

Four Months Later

Quinn wiped sweat off his forehead as the sun beat down on him. It was going to be a hot day, judging by this weather. It was only 8am and the curtains were drawn over his shop windows. He slipped through the door, making sure nobody was behind him, and surveyed the scene.

Relaunching a shop was harder than he'd thought. Hermione's book took precedence, consuming every part of his psyche. Also, Hermione had become a total authorzilla, and he'd been a little afraid to do anything but write.

But now it was publication day, which also fell on reopening day. Incense burned in each corner, a sandalwood smell, which was now his favourite. It reminded him of the scent Noah wore when they first kissed. The smoke rose from metal censers, and flames burned in large white pillar candles. He'd set a chair up at the altar, more of a throne, with a red carpet leading from door to throne for added Hollywood effect. The bookshelves were back where they were meant to be, crammed full of titles old and new.

A table in front of the throne, stacked full of Hermione's books, with a photo of her on the cover, captured all of her Hollywood essence. The posters for the signing had been tacked up for two months. Excitement in Hay had started to build when they'd realised that Kings & Queens was coming back.

It didn't matter that Hermione's book wasn't a gay title. They'd made an exception.

A knock at the door. Taking a deep breath, he peered through the curtains, seeing Noah.

He let him in, making him squeeze through the gap.

'This is top secret,' Noah said when he was in.

He looked fantastic. He had dressed for the hot weather, wearing shorts that showed off toned legs, and a red T-shirt. Quinn kissed him, then showed him the display.

'What do you think?'

'She's going to love it. I haven't seen her this happy in forever.'

'She deserves every part of it.'

Getting her to help launch Kings & Queens with her signing had been a straightforward decision. They'd worked on the book in partnership, so this felt like a fair trade-off. With Hermione marketing the book, the publisher marketing the signing, and Quinn marketing the shop, he was expecting a very busy, albeit hot, day.

'*You* deserve it.' Noah placed his hands on Quinn's face, scanning him with his eyes. It always made Quinn giddy when he looked at him like that. 'Do we have time for a quickie?'

Their eyes drifted to the confessional booth.

Whatever desire they had fled when another knock on the door came. Quinn peered outside and saw…

'Bloody Blair Beckett,' Quinn whispered to Noah, before opening the door and letting Blair and Ivy in.

Blair came prepared with a camera crew. 'Lunch time news.'

'Of course.'

As the cameraman set up, Ivy fussed over Blair's suit, dusting his shoulder and adjusting his tie.

'Things going well between you two?'

'Oh, the best.' Ivy smiled.

In no time at all, the queue would be outside the door, and Hermione would be the major attraction. It filled Quinn with nerves as he wondered if his shop was good enough, if people wanted it back. Today would be busy, but would tomorrow?

He hadn't realised he'd been biting his nails, a habit he'd picked back up while getting the shop ready, until Noah slipped his hand away.

'You're going to be alright. This is perfect. All of it is.'

'You think so?'

'Look at it, Quinn. We're all where we're meant to be.'

He could see the shadows at the windows, hear the voices muffled behind the glass, and something changed within him.

Because it didn't matter if every day didn't look like this one. It didn't matter if only one customer came in tomorrow. What mattered was having this space open, where he could help others who needed it most, champion LGBTQ writers, and keep Hay gay.

Kings & Queens was more than just a bookshop. It was a sanctuary, a respite, and a friend.

Another knock at the door as people cheered.

'That must be Mum,' Noah said.

He went to get the door, but then Quinn heard the voices of Deb and June.

'We love you!'

'Is Noah there?'

'We love him!'

'Probably best they don't see you yet,' Quinn told him, a smile on his face. 'They'll rip your clothes off you before I can.'

Noah moved closer. 'But I want June to touch me.'

'Hey, I want June.'

They laughed, Quinn ushering Noah away from the door, and then he opened it in time for Hermione and Jerry to slip through.

'You okay?' Jerry asked his sister.

Hermione wore a dress that reminded Quinn of Diana's revenge dress. She was dressed more for a book signing in Piccadilly than in Hay, and Quinn loved her for it.

But if she felt overwhelmed, scared, or nervous, like Jerry expected her to be, then she shook it off.

'Therapy is helping. I just can't believe all those people have come to see me.'

'How big is the queue?' Noah asked.

'It looks like it goes to Lion Street,' Jerry said.

'I can't believe they're here for us,' Hermione said.

'They're here for you, Hermione,' Quinn said. 'Now get settled at that table and I'll start letting them in!'

'Can I get you anything?' Ivy asked Hermione. 'A tea? Coffee?'

'Latte?'

Ivy looked at Quinn.

'We only have a kettle, milk, and coffee.'

'I'll have a regular coffee,' Hermione said.

As Hermione settled at the table, holding her pen and practising her signature, Quinn took a moment to take it all in. He never thought he would stand in his shop again, with that familiar smell of earthy notes, leather, and books. With the creaky floorboard near the door, or the confessional booth that bore witness to so many stories. The pride flags, from transgender to non-binary, fluttered above their heads, across the counter, and outside the shop. It was like he'd never left, like it hadn't been empty.

And what made it all the more perfect was Noah.

The door creaked open, and two men slipped in.

'Daniel. You came.'

'Wouldn't miss it for the world,' Daniel said, holding hands with the person next to him. 'Quinn. This is my boyfriend, James.'

'Nice to meet you, James,' Quinn said, shaking the hand of the young man. 'Not James Bond, is it?'

He meant it as a joke. Daniel Craig dating James Bond.
Only…

'Actually, yes.'

'Well, blow me.'

'Places, people,' Ivy called. 'It's opening time.'

A thrill rushed through Quinn as he squeezed Noah's hand.
Daniel and James made themselves look important. Hermione sat
a little taller. The room went deathly quiet.

Then Quinn opened the door.

'Welcome back!'

Deb and June entered first. He fought back tears, thinking that
having a breakdown in front of paying customers again was not
the best idea.

'I always loved your work,' Deb said to Hermione.

'And your son is sexy,' June said.

'Thank you,' Hermione said.

'Will you sign my tea cosy, too?'

Noah giggled, and Quinn wrapped his arms around him,
squeezing him.

'Thank you for being here.'

Noah kissed him on the head and slipped a hand to his back.
He did tower above Quinn.

'Look up, handsome.'

Acknowledgments

First, to the people of Hay. This book is a love letter to my favourite place on earth. From the many booksellers, to the creative markets, I will always have a soft spot for Hay-On-Wye. The castle may have a foreboding presence in this story, but in real life it's a glorious refurbishment that everyone is happy to have back open, me included. I promise I didn't write this book just to try and achieve a lifelong dream of appearing at the Hay Festival, though if you're reading this and can make that happen, you know where to find me.

Thanks to Tom at Gay On Wye, Hay's first and only LGBTQ+ bookshop. When I started writing this book in November 2021, there was no gay bookshop in Hay, but I always wanted there to be. When I moved back to the UK from Vancouver, I looked at the premises that would turn into Gay On Wye, toying with the idea of opening Kings & Queens in real life. Obviously, that didn't happen, but I'm so glad that someone else wanted to bring queer literature to the town of books. Tom, you've been so supportive since I introduced myself to you, and I'm so thankful for all that you've done not only to support *Look Up, Handsome*, but also to support queer literature and the LGBTQ+ community. You're a real life Quinn Oxford!

The bookshop love doesn't stop there. To Emma and the team at Book-ish – Meg, Loren, Owen, Hannah, Echo, Lyndsey – you've all been great. You welcomed me as a bookseller, and you've supported my novels ever since. We can agree this book has nothing on *The Woman in Me* by Britney Spears. Special mention to Megan at Firefly, once at Book-ish, for giving me the Book-ish job.

To every indie bookshop I've contacted and spoken to, and to every indie bookseller I've met, thank you for stocking my book, selling my book, and championing my work. Booksellers deserve all the love and independent bookshops deserve all the custom.

To the team at One More Chapter, THANK YOU SO MUCH FOR MAKING MY DREAM COME TRUE. Your enthusiasm, passion, and hard work has paid off, and I thank you all for making me feel like a special author. Honestly, I don't think you understand how grateful I am, and how much it means to me. I first tried getting a bookdeal when I was 18. At 28, you gave me a two book deal, and I will forever be thankful for that. When that offer came through, I sobbed. Thanks to powerhouse editors Ajebowale Roberts and Jennie Rothwell for making my book so much better. You helped draw out the gold amongst the rough and made it the best it could be. I'm so lucky to have worked with you on this. Thank you Hana Rowlands and Federica Leonardis for your meticulous line edits, and for pointing me in the right direction to make my writing stronger. Thank you Charlotte Ledger for welcoming me to One More Chapter and supporting my work. To Arsalan for believing in my writing. Thank you Emma Petfield for all your marketing work, and for the patience you had for me when I trod on toes in my excitement to market the book in ways you already thought of, and could do so much better than I could.

Chloe Cummings, did you think I forgot you? Of course not. It's because of you that One More Chapter signed me. It's because of you I get to write gay rom-coms, and it's because of you this book is in the hands of readers. You, and our manifestations, obviously. Your passion for this book of mine shone through from the moment I first spoke to you, and when I met you and we were both wearing the same necklace, I knew I needed to be your bestie. Keep manifesting for your dream home.

Riccardo Bessa, thank you for your GORGEOUS artwork for the cover of *Look Up, Handsome.* Again, I cried when I first saw it because I couldn't believe this was happening. You brought Quinn and Noah to life, and you captured the Christmas setting of Hay perfectly. You're a natural talent and I hope to work with you again!

To my agent, Stacey Kondla – I'm sorry you missed out on working with me on this book, but this was the book that got me signed with you. Your support hasn't been missing through this process, and you gave me the confidence to continue working on future novels. I can't wait to see what we achieve together.

Mum, dad – thank you for always believing in me. Mum, thank you for giving me the pep talks when I felt like giving up, when I thought writing would never happen for me, and for the life advice you have given me. Thanks for shouting about this book from the rooftops, and thanks for your continued love and support.

Becky, I often credit you for getting me into reading. I'd read the books you read when I was a kid, and then I'd read the books you read when I was an adult. I credit you for introducing me to romance novels, and now look at me. I'm a romance writer! Not you being the first person to ever read romance novels.

Emma, thank you for reading my work early, and for your support of books that should never have been published, and should have remained on the hard drive. Thank you for your encouragement along the way. I feel like I should thank Seb and Sammy, even though Seb called me weird uncle Jack.

James, you've been with me since I was twenty. Which means you've been at my side every time I write a novel, every time I go through the submission process, and every time I've failed. You've been there to hear me vent about setbacks, and you've listened and I've shared my hopes and dreams. You were the first person I told when I knew this was getting published, and I'm so glad you've been by my side during all of this.

Thanks to James's extended family.

To the friends along the way who have listened to me talk about my dreams of being an author. It finally happened! Now, have you bought the book!?

Thank you to the 2024 debut group that I joined. I'm honoured to be publishing in the same year as you, and I thank you for all your support in the run up to publication.

Most importantly, thanks to you, the reader. If you're reading this now, that means you've finished the book and you're not looking ahead to the acknowledgement pages, because that's the only way to read a book! It must mean you loved this book and you're giving it five gold stars and that's that. No, but seriously, thank you for picking up this book, giving me a chance, and I truly hope you come back for me. I hope you fell in love with Quinn and Noah like I have, and I hope you fall in love with Hay. If you want to help me campaign to be at the Hay Festival, dear readers, I won't be mad about that.

Without readers, I don't get to write my gay romance novels. Thank you for supporting LGBTQ+ reads.

ONE MORE CHAPTER

The author and One More Chapter would like to thank everyone
who contributed to the publication of this story...

Analytics
James Brackin
Abigail Fryer
Maria Osa

Audio
Fionnuala Barrett
Ciara Briggs

Contracts
Sasha Duszynska
Lewis

Design
Lucy Bennett
Fiona Greenway
Liane Payne
Dean Russell

Digital Sales
Lydia Grainge
Hannah Lismore
Emily Scorer

Editorial
Laura Burge
Arsalan Isa
Charlotte Ledger
Federica Leonardis
Bonnie Macleod
Jennie Rothwell

Harper360
Emily Gerbner
Jean Marie Kelly
emma sullivan
Sophia Wilhelm

International Sales
Peter Borcsok
Bethan Moore

Marketing & Publicity
Chloe Cummings
Emma Petfield

Operations
Melissa Okusanya
Hannah Stamp

Production
Denis Manson
Simon Moore
Francesca Tuzzeo

Rights
Vasiliki Machaira
Rachel McCarron
Hany Sheikh
Mohamed
Zoe Shine

**The HarperCollins
Distribution Team**

**The HarperCollins
Finance & Royalties
Team**

**The HarperCollins
Legal Team**

**The HarperCollins
Technology Team**

Trade Marketing
Ben Hurd

UK Sales
Laura Carpenter
Isabel Coburn
Jay Cochrane
Sabina Lewis
Holly Martin
Erin White
Harriet Williams
Leah Woods

**And every other
essential link in the
chain from delivery
drivers to booksellers
to librarians and
beyond!**